M.E. Hirsh

Dreaming Back

WORLDWIDE®

TORONTO • NEW YORK • LONDON
AMSTERDAM • PARIS • SYDNEY • HAMBURG
STOCKHOLM • ATHENS • TOKYO • MILAN
MADRID • WARSAW • BUDAPEST • AUCKLAND

Author's note: The title is from W. B. Yeats's *A VISION: BOOK III, The Soul in Judgment*. In Dreaming Back, the spirit is compelled to live over again the events that had most moved it.

Portions of "The Truth Is" and "The Pond" from *Seeing Through the Sun*, by Linda Hogan, copyright © 1985 by Linda Hogan (Amherst: University of Massachusetts Press, 1985), reprinted by permission.

Portions of "The Waking," copyright © 1953 by Theodore Roethke. From *The Collected Poems of Theodore Roethke*. Used by permission of Doubleday, a division of Bantam, Doubleday Dell Publishing Group, Inc.

"Do-Re-Mi," by Richard Rodgers, Oscar Hammerstein II. Copyright © 1959 by Richard Rodgers and Oscar Hammerstein II, copyright renewed, Williamson Music Co., owner of publication and allied rights throughout the world. International copyright secured. Used by permission. All rights reserved.

DREAMING BACK

A Worldwide Mystery/March 1996

First published by St. Martin's Press, Incorporated.

ISBN 0-373-26195-0

Copyright © 1993 by M. E. Hirsh.
All rights reserved. No part of this book may be reproduced or transmitted in any form or by any means, electronic or mechanical, including photocopying, recording or by any information storage and retrieval system, without permission in writing from the publisher. For information, contact: St. Martin's Press, Incorporated, 175 Fifth Avenue, New York, NY 10010-7848 U.S.A.

Printed in U.S.A.

To David and to Nora and Robert for
suffering many pages

Note: Although a number of Strategic Materials exist in
reservation lands, the Addison Crust is fictional, as are
all the characters in this book.

Out of denied selfs,
and denied realities
the mind creates an enemy.
—Susan Griffin

The trouble with this building
is that it's really built
on an old Indian burial ground.
—David Letterman

Behold, I have given you
every herb bearing seed
which is upon the face of the earth.
—Genesis 1:29

What kind of motel is this anyway?
—Linda Hogan

ACKNOWLEDGMENTS

To the Hopi people who gave me instruction and documents from which part of this story is drawn,

A'skwali.

I am also indebted to the insight and archives of Rosemary Blanchard, Judith Gaines, Gloria Keliiaa, John McLean and Anna Wexler; and to the work of Walter Houston Clark, Vine Deloria, Jr., Marlene Dobkin De Rios, Alvaro Estrada, Jack Herer, Wendy Rose, Martin A. Lee and Bruce Shlain.

My thanks for the generous assistance of: T. E. Maez, Chief of the Chama, New Mexico, Police Department; Dr. Patricia McFeeley, Chief Medical Investigator for New Mexico; Doug Couleur, Assistant District Attorney for Rio Arriba County, New Mexico; and, in Boston, Kate Hines and her Modern jewelry studio. Also John DeLancey and Janet Langsam, then of the Boston Center for the Arts, for inventing a space where this could be written.

I'm grateful for the varied contributions of Ellen Bartlett, Ernest Bristow, Carla Brown, Carole Chanler, Dore Gardner, Mariana Gosnell, John C. Hirsh, Jonathan Kelly, W. David Laird, Ray and Caroline LeDuc, Stephen McCauley, Andy and Lori Merliss, Barbara Neely, Garrett Rosenblatt, Baryalai Shalizi, the late Michael Siff, Patty Stone, Josef Wexler and Louisa Williams. Salutations to my editor, Ruth Cavin, my agent, Upton Brady, and my sister-in-law, Rachael Montenegro, for drawing me to Chama; and to Margaret Kelly Hirsh, Margo Hirsh Kelly and Stewart Wooster for many fêtes.

To David Montenegro, Nora Charney Rosenbaum and Robert Rosenbaum, more is owed than can ever be repaid.

I

CHAMA, NEW MEXICO
Chapter 1

REDBIRD CALLED IT his hare net, a lacing of thread in the scrub around the house low enough to give warning if anything bigger than a rabbit came through. So far it was raccoons that broke the string at night, rattling the brass wind chime against her window. Even after Leni took the covered cans of trash inside, the web had to be repaired most evenings.

It would help only when she was home, she had pointed out. And then what, since it was hard to imagine using the pistol he'd given her. Though their last target practice had been fun. Tin cans on a fence, like in the movies.

The hare net came from a movie too, coached by a genuine Viet Nam vet. And Redbird's name, which had been bestowed by a Hollywood agent's secretary to make him more saleably Indian. A name he then used with white women he met, giving it back, he said. By the time he told her his real name it was hard to call him Ben, if a relief to try. Ben seemed more accessible, at least on days that needed the comfort of wishful thinking.

Catching the string on a twig of juniper, she let a length fall, then hooked another branch and stepped around the corner of the house.

The sky was purple and a V of storm clouds raced along the mountains. 'Taking aim at Chama,' the weatherman said—an example of making nature seem malevolent that she used in class. No sound of Ben's pick-up yet and rain would come like hail soon, rutting the dirt road, seeping through the ceiling.

Adobe at this altitude was not a great idea. But the soft brown walls were irresistible after three years in the old tin can Airstream trailer. Driving up from Albuquerque to take the job at Cather College, she had found the house the first day. Not the good omen it seemed then. Whoever built it was bright enough to sell before the flat roof started crumbling.

It was also hard to hide anything in two adobe rooms. No niches carved for santos. Which left the beehive fireplace. Under its slate floor was just enough room to dig a space for the laptop computer. So no more incense of piñon smoke, and if they really were being watched, even that might have been noticed.

Burying the laptop made more sense than taking it everywhere. At least until she had been fired. Now she was home quite a lot with the web and the Colt .22 automatic and questions about their mutual sanity.

"Ay, vienen los Apaches," she said, "par el chapparal!" Here come the Apaches through the underbrush. The Mexican who made up that song must have been nervous too, but here it was cowboys, not Indians, who came creeping along the ravine.

Below, a flash of white through the pines, and the cough of Ben's engine shifting as a few drops fell.

"GOD, SOMETIMES I WISH I was still drinking."

She smiled. "Right now, you couldn't hold a glass."

He was wearing rubber gloves to clean the green chilis, slimy, flecked with blackened pepper skin, and in the pulsing of the quartz heater he looked like a demented dissectionist in a '50's horror movie.

He nodded toward the blue down vest hanging on the chair. "I picked up a joint at the gallery. Want some?"

It would have been tempting another night. "No, thanks. I'm already paranoid. That's why I'm smoking your stupid cigarettes again." She gave the stew a stir. Corn and beans and potatoes, and chicken instead of lamb as a concession to her.

"Have a drink, then. I won't run amok." He nudged her with his shoulder. "There's some Bushmills left under the sink, if you don't hate it too much."

At Thanksgiving, he'd brought it with a joke about doping the pilgrims, to have the vicarious pleasure of watching her drink it. His favorite drink in the old days before the movie money was gone. Pouring a shot over ice, he had watched it go down and been disappointed by her faint enthusiasm.

"All right, maybe I will have one. That's about all there is, so I won't run amok either. Which is actually an academic term. Running-amok behavior. When the Kuma Indians in New Guinea eat nonda mushrooms they get to do all the things that are taboo the rest of the time. The women put on their best feathers and run off and have sexcapades, and the men zoom around with spears terrorizing their relatives.''

He lifted an eyebrow. ''Not all the men. Or who'd take care of the ladies?''

''Want to volunteer?''

''That could be fun. If I didn't get eaten too.'' He scraped the diced chilis into the pot. ''The only thing we've got like that is Mastop kachina, faking sex with married women. For fertility. And the clowns can be pretty lewd. Mastop's scary, though. All black, with white handprints all over, wearing animal skins. My mother used to have a carving of him. I wonder what happened to it.''

Crouching, she took a minute finding the Bushmills. We, the collective pronoun, meaning Hopi. The first time he'd said it that way. Before, 'my people' meant the Indians he drank with in alleys in L.A. It was only for a few months that he'd been going out to the Hopi mesas, trying to know the side of his family he'd left so long ago. Except for summer visits, Ben hadn't lived there since he was five.

When he first went back, he joked that he was doing field work for her thesis. Maybe the old chiefs chewed datura root to get their prophecies? Instead, he found they were getting ready to take back their old power, thanks to his father's efforts. A revolt, in reverse, to how things used to be. And he stayed there more and more now.

She watched him run water over the gloves, scooping up seeds so they wouldn't clog the drain. A steady drip of rain fell into the bucket next to the stove and the wind chime rang hard enough to shatter the glass. If a spook was out there tonight, the web would be useless.

Pouring the last of the whiskey, she sat down at the table. ''That Kuma tribe's about the only one to use drugs without any religious ritual. They're strictly hedonists, into controlling their women and accumulating pig wealth.''

''That doesn't sound bad either.''

Stripping off the gloves, he went to the row of drawings propped on the bookcase shelf. ''Nonda mushrooms? Which is that?''

''Boletus. Second from the left. And right now, if I had a specimen, I think I'd try it myself.'' They were ink drawings for her thesis, and finally they looked all right. The Boletus' round cup and fat pear-shaped stem, vaguely obscene. Next to that her favorite, because it was hardest to draw: Datura Stromonium, jimson weed, native to the Americas. The long stem foreshortened between its fluted white blossoms and the pale roots used to get visions.

"So you're finished." A relief for him too.

"I hope so. Mostly. I'll have to defend it at some point, but I'm bringing the last part to my advisor on the way to the airport."

"That's great, Len. I guess I'll have to call you Dr. Haring now." She knew that smile, and what would follow.

"Maybe. I might like that. Can we eat? I'm hungry."

"Me too." He ran a fingertip down her cheek. "It's our last chance for a month. For the ceremony, I've got to practice being pure. No fooling around with you pahanas."

"I know. We whiteys are no good at all. Maybe you better stop now."

He dropped his hand. "What's wrong."

She felt his touch fade. "What do you think? I'm nervous about going home. While you're out on the mesa bringing life back to the world, I'll be sitting in Brookline trying to sell this to my father. And if he doesn't think I'm crazy, my sister will talk him into it."

She could see Leigh's carefully penciled mouth. The chaste glass of mineral water.

"Look, it's not so easy with my old man, either," Ben said. "He practically sniffs me every time I come back. Then we have to sit for half an hour so he can decide if my spirit feels right. Nobody trusts me. They just believe in using anything that shows up."

"Well, that's something you can relate to."

He stood still. "Wait a minute. Going home was your idea."

"Right. When you turned up at the college that was what you had in mind."

The thermostat on the heater clicked and his face glowed red. "I told you. The first time, I came because Vera said your class on ads reminded her of my pictures. When I found out about your father, all right, by then I had another reason. But in between, we had something too. We still do. Or don't you think so?"

"Till I found out your vision of me, I did."

Putting away another photo. Opening that drawer. An 11 × 14 print of her, sleeping, bare from the waist up, with a cowboy hat tipped at an angle next to her head on his sheepskins. "I couldn't help it," he'd said. "It was so perfect."

For his American Customs series. She was out the door and in the car and he was after her on his Harley all the way back to school. Waiting by the gate every day with his reason for being so determined to get her back. Infrared pictures this time, from a satellite camera her father had developed. Pictures that could prove what his father said was happening out in the desert. If she could get them. Which would test a number of other things as well.

"Forget going home, then." He pressed a hand along the edge of the table. "If you're still mad at me, forget about this. But go somewhere, all right? I can't come back till after the Soyál ceremony, and I'm sure they've figured that out. They cut the brakes on my truck, remember?"

He wouldn't look at her when he was angry.

"Don't worry, Ben. I'm out of here. At three o'clock tomorrow." She tapped a Camel from his pack and lit it.

"What about that." He jabbed a thumb at the old computer setup on the corner table. "You can see it from my window."

"So?" A plume of smoke floated toward the ceiling. "If they steal that while I'm gone, whoever they are, they'll get the pleasure of reading my thesis. I put our notes on the laptop, and I erased them last night. I don't need them anymore. Do you?"

Tonight she couldn't seem to stop hitting at him.

Taking her glass, he got down bowls and silverware, and stood with his back to her while he sampled the stew. "I told you I'd never show that picture," he said. "You're just mad about the hat. If I hadn't put that hat in, you wouldn't be so mad."

He was smiling, she could tell, in spite of his tight voice. Dishing out the stew. The first man who had cooked for her. The first anyone, since she was nine, who had done it on a regular basis. The way he fussed over his mother in their trailer in L.A., rinsing out her vodka glass and waiting for her eyes to close so he could move the smouldering ashtray. A blond woman, still pretty when she died at forty-eight, and the reason why he had mixed feelings about going back to the mesas. If he were the child of a Hopi woman, he'd belong to her clan whether his father wanted him or not. Being born to a pahana adulteress meant he had nothing to reclaim there, except what he called the memory of an absence.

She got up to slide her arms around his waist from behind. "That smells incredible."

"It is. So we'll eat. Then I'll show you the map."

"Ben, I'm sorry. I told you I'm hyper. I wish I could spend the solstice in a kiva."

She felt a grudging ease against her chest. His twitchy warmth, so familiar now that a week apart was hard and the looming distance of the next month frightened her.

The muscles in his back shifted. "Drinking champagne in Boston doesn't sound too tough to me. Anyhow, it's the Soyál priests who get the sun to turn around. The rest of us just have to keep our thoughts right. If I'm worrying about you, we could be in for a long winter."

She reached around him for the loaf of bread. "So, I'm going. And I'll try like hell. But my father signed petitions against Star Wars, and he's retired now. For all I know, he's lost his security clearance." He was cranky since his stroke, too. Potentially a loose cannon despite his former fame at MIT.

"If what we want's classified, that's worth knowing by itself."

Bringing the bowls to the table, he turned down the overhead lamp and lit four candles. Four, the Hopi number. Four worlds, four directions. He made a point of doing things in fours now, she noticed, as if using the form would somehow lead to the substance.

He crushed out her cigarette. "How much did you tell him?"

"About this? Nothing." A tang of chilis came up in the steam. "Just that my contract wasn't renewed and I'd be home for Christmas. Out of a job, as usual."

"But you finished your paper. Wasn't that the problem last time?"

"I'm the problem. For Leigh, at least. If I get up early enough, I think I'll stop in Santa Fe to buy her a present."

A silver buckle. Or Acoma pottery. Offerings to the gods. To the silent, relentless disapproval she had felt from Leigh since they were children.

"Presents from Santa Fe! Thanks for reminding me!" He reached back into his vest. "Tomorrow I won't be able to smoke this thing." Unwrapping the sliver of tinfoil, he lit the joint from a candle. "Phew. It tastes like fertilizer."

She smiled. "You can't be pure tomorrow if you smoke that tonight. It stays in your system for at least four days."

The number stopped him. He looked from the curl of smoke to the ashtray. "Then I better not."

"Ben, I'm kidding!"

"No." He put it out. "My grandfather can smell it. Not the weed. The sin. He keeps saying I have to change. 'The seed must give up its life as a seed for the plant to be born,' and all that. The only way I can stand them all checking me out is if I don't feel even a little bit guilty."

Smoke hazed the candlelight. She pushed the ashtray away. "Who gave you that stuff, anyway? It stinks."

He was catching the last piece of chili left in his bowl. "You know that blond guy with the ponytail who has a rock shop off Palace?"

"Ed Harris? Sure."

"He hangs out at the gallery, when he gets sick of the tourists. He gave me this, too." Fishing in the vest again, he brought up a polished brown stone striped with yellow. "He says tiger eye helps stop bad habits. Like smoking."

"Cute. A drug and its antidote."

"Yeah. Because being in balance is the Hopi way. He's always trying to prove how much he knows, like it's more than I do. Hell, maybe it is."

"I doubt it. He probably read the same books I did."

On Hopi religion. The cycle of mystery plays. Casually consuming all the secrets that had been betrayed. Not for the thesis, since there was no communal drug use. But it led the farthest into the past, enacting knowledge that had been lost, and to the future along a thread of prophecy. When she visited the mesas the first time, at fifteen, the painted dancers had astounded her, stone villages teetering high above a blasted, brilliant desert. The books came later, some when a Hopi woman joined the faculty at UNM four years ago. Vera Naya. Tough and vibrant as their patchy corn and full of surprises. One of which had turned out to be Ben, although Vera wasn't glad when he turned up.

He held the stone to the candle. "I guess maybe this worked. Score one for the ponytail. Did you go out with him or something?"

"With Ed? You're kidding. Why?"

"I don't know. The way he asked about you. He said to wish you bon voyage."

"That's just schmooze. It's you he's curious about. Now that the gallery's got your pictures in the window all the time."

She stood up to clear the table and he stretched back in the chair. "Yah, I forgot to tell you. They jacked up the price on my stuff. By doing less work, I'm making more money." The chair creaked behind her. "It's late. I've got to go soon. Even if I floor it, I'll be on the road all night."

Turning she saw he was holding a folded paper that he opened on the table. Black irregular concentric circles ran across it, with coordinates down the margin.

"Here's what you bring Dad. It's a standard topographical map that will work with any other one. I marked the part we're interested in."

A red box framed the stretch of desert south of Second Mesa where an old Snake priest had been stalking a specially rigged Huey helicopter that came down only at night. Prospecting, he thought, when there was supposed to be a ban on mineral development. And looking in an area with sacred, hidden shrines.

That was in the laptop in more than one place, and she wondered if she'd gotten them all. Buried, using the command for Cut/Hold, always after the word 'remember' for a cue. It had taken a while to go through the whole mess.

"Okay." She folded the map. "Now let's hope I can talk him into it."

"Oh, you have excellent powers of persuasion. I know that better than anyone." He ran his hands under her sweater. They were rough from chopping wood and his eyes narrowed with delight that she was ticklish. It always went like this. Uneasy distance. Then a look or touch, some crosscurrent of feeling, and they were inside each other's skins. Before, she thought it would have to be self-conscious, the body not so good now, a greater need to please. But that first time at his cabin when she turned up without warning they were in bed five minutes after she knocked on the door. Pushing her coat back, he started to kiss her, unbuttoning her blouse, and it was this same giving up of protection like a sudden telling of secrets they had kept even from themselves.

Shameless. The bed banging into the wall in her own house on the side of the mountain without any neighbors to hear. Keeping on, with an urgency coming from all the loss in his life. Making her love him, because he needed it then. Not so long ago as it seemed.

Pulling the quilt around her, he reached for his jeans. "Let's have a smoke. Then I've got to hit the road."

"At least it's stopped raining."

The candles had burned down. He picked up the ashtray, then started toward the window. "Great. It stopped raining, all right. It's snowing."

"Rats. That wasn't the forecast."

He buttoned his shirt, and came and lit a cigarette. "Is somebody meeting you at the airport?"

"No. It's easier to get a cab."

"Any chance you'll decide to stay out there?"

"Nope. How about you?"

He shook his head, and ran a scratchy hand under the hair at the back of her neck. "You know I'm still going to love you if you can't get the damn pictures."

His cheek, and breath, against hers. The improbable shelter they had made, for however long it lasted. "That's nice."

"I'm a nice guy." Passing her the cigarette, he put on his vest. "Now go to sleep. And we'll bring the sun back for you."

"Don't forget to check the brakes."

He blew the candles out.

When he opened the door, she saw him outlined against a field of white. Then he closed it and a minute later came the start of the engine.

Settling back against the pillow, she took a drag of the Camel. No smoking in Brookline. Tomorrow night Ben might be smoking over some prayer sticks. Or was it only the Soyál priests who did that? It wasn't a public ceremony, open to visitors. Soyál meant prayer and silence at the dawn of life, an invocation of the coming of warmth, and plants, and birds.

She had gone back to the books when Vera asked her to visit in December two years ago. First, Soyál Kachina in his white robe, stumbling like a baby to show new life is being born. Then black Mastop, hurtling through interstellar space, his handprinting the human touch on all creation. After that, days of preparation for the solstice, underground in the kivas. It was probably no accident that she'd been there to see the kachinas announce its coming. Clever Vera, using a privileged glimpse to persuade her to take a cut in pay and move up to cowboy country.

Being let go by a mining college was hardly a feather in the cap. Paranoid to wonder if it had something to do with Ben. But having the degree should at least make it easier to get hired now. Tomorrow night, a shot of Dad's Glenmorangie and drink to the end of it.

Then a string of other nights before it would be possible to come back here and live this way again.

Putting out the cigarette, she felt Ben's unsmoked joint. The one remaining vice that he said kept the others at bay. In L.A., the pockets of his vest had overflowed with coke, sinsemilla, and crystal meth, his passport to parties with the stars. Pockets that could be filled again even in Santa Fe, so he lived nearly twenty miles out of town.

Styles of intoxication. By race and tribe. Most of which opted for some ecstatic form of liberation. The necessary lapse: chaos as the source of order, not to be resisted but kept in proper balance. Horror of the friars in Mexico that the Indians drank to get drunk, freeing emotion that had no place in their hard work in the fields.

Or in Brookline, either. The requirement there being not to get drunk. Order firmly in the driver's seat. Just a steady infusion that let them smile over supper as if all arguments were forgotten. Except for Leigh, ever-vigilant behind the mineral water, adding new notes to her mental ledger.

Might as well smoke the joint as throw it out. A private celebration.

Flare of Ben's lighter, a sputtering glow, the smell of peat and an undertaste that could be DDT or worse. Probably it was from Mexico, which would make a fitting circuit.

Five years on the thesis, but more than twenty since it had been born. Climbing up a mountainside in Oaxaca, at nineteen, with the ragged *Life* magazine article she had kept since fifth grade. Asking in high school Spanish for the man who could take her to the old Indian woman in the photograph. Maria Sabina. It showed her passing a mushroom through the smoke of incense in an adobe house not much different from this.

In Oaxaca, there was a bandstand. The cathedral gaudy with blood and gold. A sudden procession of children in yellowed Sunday shirts and bad shoes. The altitude had made her breathless. Squinting in the summer sun, "Por favor, dónde es el síndico Cayetano?" Bright enough not to show the article with Cayetano's name by a New York banker who had written about the ritual.

But the official, Cayetano, no longer lived there, and she had gone alone up Fortress Mountain to the thatch-roofed village of Huatla. Frightened, dressing carefully, she sat day after day in the back of the small church. The woman tending the altar finally took pity when she said she had come not to see God through the mushrooms but in hope of a healing from La Señora, for a sickness of the heart that began with the death of her mother—a woman who also saw visions.

At nine, she had written down the words, misunderstood, misspelled, trying to make sense of what the doctor called psychosis as he sat tensely in the living room with papers that had to be signed. Her mother, upstairs, whispering, 'Leni, all the glory! If I could only make you see.... How can I take his silly tests when that's happening? One picture comes, then another, then something else, like the movies, you can't touch them, but it's true. There isn't any separation, you and me, you and that tree over there. It's hidden, but if you could see it you'd know there's nothing to be afraid of.' Then, with a shaky grin as the car pulled away, 'Remember, when the fireflies come, look for the falling stars!'

She could see herself the next year, turning the pages of that *Life* magazine, riveted, somehow knowing immediately it held a clue.

In the thatched house in Huatla, the old woman deeply wrinkled, touched the center of her chest. 'The spirit is what gets sick. The spirit travels and the person dreams it.'

All through that night the woman from the church, Aurora, murmured Spanish translations of the Mazatec and the litany of their voices closed the circle, touching springs of memory the white cubes of acid never had found.

Ben's grass, acrid as the mushrooms she had chewed one by one from the tin cup on a moonlit mat in front of the simple altar. Candles burning by a wooden crucifix and picture of the infant Jesus, and a pitcher of white lilies adding perfume to the incense.

A taste of roots and earth. The old woman sitting with her legs folded under her dress like roots under leaves. Then a wave of nausea swelled, and she felt it now in memory or else from what she was smoking.

It wasn't necessary to close her eyes, Aurora said. When the saint-children began to work, the darkness would be a background for what came.

She watched Maria Sabina break a flower from the bouquet and use it to put out the only candle still burning. It flared and disappeared like a bird rising into the dark, the beautiful red bird embroidered on the front of her white dress. Her sing-song chant, 'I come with language only. God is a book that is born from the earth, a sacred book, whose birth makes the world shake. I see the words fall, they come from up above, as if they were little luminous objects falling from the sky. Then, with my hands, I catch word after word, and I sing: I am a woman standing in sand, because wisdom comes from the place where sand is born. I am a woman torn up out of the ground...'

She went on naming her many forms, and the vibration made a pathway that could be followed into the dark. Getting up to dance, her arms moved with the sound of rustling leaves and then a cascade of colors opened the room to the starry sky. Clapping, whistling, she turned it like a wheel in the unfolding landscape, mountains flowing into deserts, into oceans, gardens, fields of grass, the same atoms visibly re-forming in a continuous labyrinth.

Lying motionless, Leni had felt the old woman touch her chest again. The hardness there dissolved as a red jet of blood shot up to the sky, but her horror turned to joy when she saw it was a red bird, flapping its wings lazily as it veered away toward the light.

Now it was only cold and dark. A shudder in her stomach. She tried to reach for a cover but her arms lay like wood on the quilt. With effort, she opened her eyes. Her hand was resting in the ashtray. A small red ember glowed between her fingers.

Something in the grass. The room began to spin and she tried to let herself go with the dizzying spiral. Something very wrong. She was struggling up on her elbows when the door banged like a drum, the room filling suddenly with rushing wind, an eddy of snowflakes blowing in like a constellation of stars. Lifting her head, she saw a dark figure bent in a halting dance, not the woman whirling but the shuffling step of a kachina, the black mask of Mastop showing in the pale light from the window. She could make out the white rings drawn on the black paint, and at his back stars glittering in the sky.

He moved closer, stretching out his hands. Ben's idea of a joke? But the breath caught in her throat as he leapt and the force of his body drove her deep into the bed. Smell of wet wool. Not black paint, a ski mask ringing shadowed eyes and lips that drew back from white even teeth.

Struggling against his weight, she thought, I can fight. I'm strong, but knew she was losing, and it was so surprising, so queer, such a stunning revelation that she wanted to laugh. To have thought it always would be possible to win, the great scientist's daughter, protected, inviolate…not an assumption Ben would ever have made.

Wrenching a hand free, she pried at the grip on her throat. Choking. Black dark pounding in her head.

A red field, shattering.

Falling stars.

II

THE SOUTH END OF BOSTON

Chapter 2

LEIGH PUSHED UP the window to watch the sunset flooding down Tremont Street. December, and already the glass was filmed with road salt, even on the fourth floor. But with the window open, light spilled into the cluttered studio. Turquoise, deepening as the band of magenta rose up, then last a roiling 24-carat gold.

The old studio had looked east, so the sunset came as a reflection framed by the windows of skyscrapers downtown. Here, on clear nights it still seemed that reaching out she could touch the colors, mix them with her fingers and apply the iridescence to the mountings of her jewelry. A perfect patina for the Spring II collection.

On the new workbench stretching the length of the room, designs for Spring I were lined up next to the stones she had chosen for them. Leopard jasper, riverstone, jade, adventurine and pearl. The metal would be finished with matte silver, a light feel with just a frosty memory of winter.

Spring II needed drama, peach and mauve and hyacinth, and so far the color washes she had tried weren't coming out right. In spite of which the staff wanted Christmas shopping time off—except for the Hmong women who assembled the jewelry down in the old studio, whispering to each other as if she could understand the language.

At least they were here. It was a good decision to get rid of the art students, who always seemed to have a late class, or PMS, or a hangover. The Hmong women came on time and were happy with what she could pay them, and now that the company was marketing coast to coast there was no room for excuses. Orders had to be shipped on time and production costs kept even.

Moving the studio upstairs had been enough of a disruption, and now Dad was calling every hour because Leni had missed her plane. Leni, whose sense of time had always been vague, to put it mildly.

Going around the partition to the office, she turned off the fluorescent lights. Soot from the window left a streak of black on the switchplate. Powdery, slightly oily, distilled essence of diesel fuel. Not a bad patina, if you didn't have to breathe it.

The outer door clicked open, and she called, "Hello?"

"It's only me, dear. Santa Claus. What do *you* want for Christmas, little girl?"

Setting a brown paper bag on the bench, Alan unzipped his leather jacket. "It's so damp out there my hair's congealing."

"Poor you." She held up her grimy fingertip. "Look at this. How about black pearl, for the Fall I collection. We could collect it ourselves, up on the roof."

"Hmmm. I think it might be a little too fragile. We'd get too many returns."

It was Alan, she thought, who looked fragile lately, his skin paler in contrast with his wiry auburn hair. Last year he had tested negative, but the virus moved so unpredictably she couldn't pretend not to worry. From the first day, when, for simple survival, she began to talk about giving up the one-of-a-kind pieces she had been making since art school, Alan had encouraged her. After ten years of 2 a.m. with the blowtorch, coaxing stubborn metal into the form she saw it could take. The way she had played with clay in her room at home when Dad was gone, leaving them with whatever grad student came to babysit for the week. Her hands were scarred by molten silver and she still missed that risk of forcing elements together, fire and water turning ingots into sinuous bracelets and earrings.

For a while, it was a kick living illegally in the studio. Futon hidden during the day. The jewelry sold and won prizes. But in the real estate boom, just to pay the rent her prices had to be exorbitant. She began to resent always scraping by, the isolation of work consumed by what Leni called the Junior League Outing Club. Then, at a trade show in New York, she found herself attracted to eclectic pieces, not forged but made up of stones and beads from all over the world. Guiding Alan around the booth she said, "Look, I like the feel of this. I'm tired of being austere. And it's costume jewelry. Even we could afford it."

She could see him making calculations, then came a slow smile, "But your designs would be better. Mass market art. No one else is doing that. Not yet, anyway. If you mean it, let's get going."

Given the crash that followed the boom, switching to costume might have been seen as prescient, had she not at the same time invested in a tiny overpriced rooftop condo.

It was Alan who made the business work. Her best friend. Maybe the only real one now. After her third *Vogue* cover, other designers in the building started treating her differently. It was subtle, but she could almost hear what they said at the lunches she was no longer asked to join. How would Leni view the new setup, she wondered. Call it a sweatshop, probably.

Alan took off the black jacket, her present to him last year. "One, UPS will pick up the rush orders tomorrow. They should get there with a few shopping days left to spare. Two, I passed out your case of wine to everyone within earshot. That was smart of you. Roderigo, you know, Rod, the new guy downstairs, said we're making too much noise for his artistic temperament. I told him it's the Christmas crush, nearly over now, so there's really no need to call the cops."

Reaching into the bag, he held up a split of Mumms. "Three, I have some treats for us. This is for a toast, to our third and best year. Though I must say, you don't seem to be in a champagne state of mind."

"Sorry. It's Leni. She missed her plane. My father's going bonkers. He called the frigging Chama police. Ever since his stroke, every little thing has to be a major disaster."

"You should be grateful he's getting around again. He's feeling shaky, that's all. So everyone else seems that way too. I'll bet you didn't have lunch today."

"I had a pear."

"Very virtuous. Now have one of these." He took out a small white bag. "They're swiss cheese croissants. A little bizarre with champagne but it's the best I could do. And darling, there really is such a thing as too thin after all."

"That's just what I was thinking about you."

Crumpling up the brown bag, he shot it into the waste basket. "All I need is a few more stops at the Yum Yum Tree. Then I'll be nice and fat again."

The new bakery was their standing joke, run by druggies who started the day with cocaine, then segued into grass that billowed out with the clouds of chocolate, and finished up with smack. At closing time they could be seen behind the steamy windows eating whatever pastries were left over. Alan said it gave a new meaning to the term junk food.

"Come on, eat that. It's hot off the microwave. I know you're down on dairy, but you need the calcium."

She smiled. He was full of nutritional warnings, gathered from his friends. The effects of alcohol, precise calibrations of this or that vitamin, a plant toxin in broccoli that meant it should always be cooked uncovered. All of which seemed to add up to whistling in the dark.

Carefully untwisting the cork, he poured the champagne into glasses from the bag. "So, here's to Leigh Haring Designs, Inc. May it never see red."

"Thanks to you, I'm not so worried about that anymore."

"Cheers."

She took a sip. Tiny bubbles. "Maybe this is a good idea. The mess here's driving me nuts." Waving at the crates stacked along the partition, she turned back to the window. The bow-front row houses had darkened as the sun withdrew, leaving a glowing red that backlit the chimney pots and church spires leading down the street to Roxbury.

Alan set his elbows next to hers on the bench. "We'll have it all sorted out by New Year's. I promise."

"Deo gratias. And speaking of God, you missed one helluva sunset. I was wondering. If we could figure out the exact chemical composition of that light and smog, or whatever, couldn't we make it into a color wash? I mean, wouldn't that theoretically be possible?"

He laughed. "Like alchemy in reverse? I guess so. Theoretically. But it would take more of a scientist than I am. Ask your father."

"I was thinking maybe copper nitrate with a dash of Mumms champagne."

"Ah. Okay. We'll give it a try." He tipped some more of it into her glass. "Now tell me about Leni. She was due in last night?"

"Yup. Coming through Chicago. The plane got in at ten, so Dad figured she'd be at the house by eleven."

"And she didn't call? Did you leave your machine on?"

"Yes. And he's been home the whole time. Limping up and down. Goddamn it. I mean, this is not exactly without precedent. Last time it turned out she was visiting a student on the Navajo reservation, and there was trouble with her car and no phone for fifty miles."

"Definitely a hanging offense. I wonder why it is I like your sister more than you do."

She let the champagne percolate. "Because you don't have to deal with my father. Who went out and bought smoked salmon yesterday, so it would be perfectly fresh. They had some major fight on Christmas a few years ago, and he's still trying to smooth it over."

"Yes, you mentioned that before. What was it about?"

She shook her head. "They wouldn't tell me. But he's never run out to buy smoked salmon for me."

He rubbed her arm with the back of his hand. "I know. We stay-at-homes get taken for granted. But, look, you aren't responsible for what she does. You're powerless over Leni, to use the twelve-step lingo, so why not try to relax."

"Great. Except I have to drive to Brookline. We're supposed to decorate the frigging tree tonight." She could picture Dad dragging it into the house, pine needles all over the hall rug. Why couldn't he have waited for her?

"All right." He straightened up. "I'm off, then."

"Got a date?"

"Not exactly. Let's say, a party with potential."

"Wouldn't you rather come to Brookline?" It was only half a joke.

"Well, if you really want me to…" He reached to muss her hair, cut very short now under his supervision to show off the jewelry better. "God, you look about ten years old. Are you going to be okay?"

"Sure. Go. Have fun."

As he was zipping his jacket, the phone rang behind the partition. He took a step toward it, then turned with an uncertain smile. "Maybe you want to get it."

"It's probably Atlanta, changing their order again."

"Right."

He disappeared around the wall, and she heard him say, "Yes, Doctor Haring, she's right here, just one minute." A click, as the receiver hit the desk.

She put the glass down. Alan's face was white. He said, "I think he's crying."

Whatever the news was, it wouldn't be good. The bench at her back seemed to hold her and she closed her hands around it.

"Leigh? He's waiting."

Making her fingers let go, she walked toward Alan and past him, into the office. The row of computer screens distorted her reflection across the middle.

The receiver was cold and clattered against her earring. "Dad?"

"Leigh. Come home please. Come right now." The slur in his speech was worse than it had been in months.

"Dad? What's wrong?"

"Please. Come home. Quickly."

She heard another voice in the background. Not Leni. A man.

"Dad? What's happening? Are you all right?"

"No. He says...your sister.... Please, you talk to her."

There was an interchange she couldn't make out. Alan came to stand behind her.

"Miss Haring? This is Sergeant Robbins of the Brookline police." His voice was low and tight. "Is there someone there with you?"

"Yes. Why? What's the matter?"

"Sit down, if you can. I'm afraid I've got some bad news. It's about your sister Elinor."

A car crash, like Mom, she thought. Leni always drove too fast.

"Miss Haring, I'm sorry to tell you this. Your sister's been killed. We got word from the Chama police a little while ago."

She wrapped her hand around the twisted cord. "Leni? Are you sure?"

"I'm afraid so. Your father called the Chama P.D. and an officer drove out to her house. He found her body there. They've got a positive I.D. A woman who worked with her came by a few minutes later. Your father had called the college too. So there doesn't seem to be any mistake."

She felt Alan guiding her down into the chair and didn't resist the pressure of his hands. "But.... How? Did they say what happened?"

"They're investigating that now."

"But they must have told you something. Was it an accident?"

"No. It's being treated as a homicide. I'm sorry."

"You mean she was murdered?"

"Yes."

"How?"

"Apparently she was strangled. I'm afraid I can't tell you more than that without compromising the investigation."

She could feel the weight of other words behind what he was saying. "That means there is more. What?"

He was silent.

"Look, you're saying my sister's been killed and I want to know what happened. We're her family. Don't we have a right to know?"

She heard him exhale. "Yes, I think you do."

"Then tell me."

He muttered something under his breath.

"Please."

"All right. I'd want it all, in your place. They won't thank me, but I doubt we'll be needing help from the Chama P.D. any time soon. This isn't official, understand. They've got two agents flying up by helicopter from the state crime lab in Santa Fe. But the officer said from the contusions . . . I'm sorry, but it looks like she was sexually assaulted too. They'll know more about that after the tests."

Closing her eyes, she pressed the receiver against her clammy forehead. Impossible to picture. She had never even seen Leni's house, in Chama, wherever that was.

"Miss Haring?"

The voice was a squeak and she brought the receiver back to her ear. "I'm here. I'm trying to get this straight. They found her at her house. In bed?"

"That's right."

"And she was raped. Someone came in and raped her and then strangled her?"

"That's what it looked like to the officer at the scene."

"Do they know who could have done it?"

"Not at this stage. I'm sorry. That's all I've got. Technically, I shouldn't tell you, but you're likely to get stonewalled out there till the investigation's over. I hate to see families go through that. Not knowing can make it harder to accept."

Accept? She thought. How about, believe? Leni always seemed to be moving farther away, receding into the distance. Now to that place, and house, and bed. . . . The bed at least must be the same. Bent willow. The one good piece of furniture she had in the trailer at Albuquerque. Blue sheets with a beige comforter. Her brown hair fanning out on the pillow when she turned over, smiling, to take the cup of tea on their last visit there two years ago.

Strangled. Bruises on her throat. Probably undressed. Maybe she still was lying like that, with strangers looking down at her. Leni, who was so private, almost secretive. Cover her up, she thought. Please.

"Miss Haring, can the person with you drive you over here? You shouldn't drive right now."

"Yes."

"I'll stay with your father till you come then. He's naturally pretty upset."

"I'll be right there."

She hung up.

I didn't say thank you, she remembered. And I should have told him Dad isn't drunk. It's just the stroke that makes him sound that way.

III

NEW MEXICO

Chapter 3

KICKING DOWN the accelerator, Leigh swung the rented Toyota out to pass the blue van that said in red: Sanitary Tortilla Factory. As compared to the other kind, she thought, like that take-out place Leni used in Albuquerque. Tin trays of enchiladas smothered with green chilis they had eaten under a cottonwood tree at a bend of the Rio Grande.

Night was coming quickly. Stupid to have taken the back road up to Santa Fe so late. Maybe a way of trying to make this real. The scenic route, Leni called it. Old mining towns they had visited named Golden, Madrid, and Cerrillos, repopulated by artists who put up teepees and sold batik shirts and pottery. Dirt roads snaking off to variously titled ranchitos hidden in the brown foothills linking the Sandia and Sangre de Cristo mountains.

Sandia meant watermelon, Leni said, and the difference between that and Blood of Christ could measure the psychic distance between the sprawl of Albuquerque and the old Spanish villages to the north. And all around, the peculiar mix of government and Indian land, Los Alamos a shot away from San Ildefonso pueblo, where they had chosen the gleaming black bowl that stood on the mantelpiece in Brookline.

Three mostly good visits here, thanks to Leni's planning that had kept them in constant motion. Soon it's got to hit me, she thought. Being here again alone.

Ahead, the junction with the interstate. Just a few more miles to go.

So far she felt numb disbelief. That and anger at Leni. As if she had purposely been murdered to spoil Christmas, Leni, the tragedy queen. It must be shock, she told herself, but it was shocking to feel this way. Last night, in a theatrical moment, she had put on the grey cashmere robe that was Leni's present and still couldn't cry.

Now it was lost with the suitcase, somewhere in the Dallas airport.

The Cerrillos Road exit. That was right. Then around the shopping mall to the plaza.

Weaving into the Christmas traffic. A season well under way. The old adobe buildings around the plaza were crowned with brown paperbag lanterns that gave an orange glow in the dusk. One year Leni made some for the windows at home, using aquarium gravel instead of sand to anchor the candles. Farolitos, lighting the way for the Christ child and numerous party goers.

A whiff of piñon smoke and cinnamon came through the open window. Under the wooden portál along the Palace of the Governors, Indian women sold jewelry from rugs spread out in front of them, barely glancing up at the crush of customers—a lot of Texans, judging by the amount of turquoise on wrists and belt buckles.

She aimed for the rambling adobe inn at the corner of the plaza. La Fonda, where they had drunk margaritas in the dark bar to celebrate Leni's masters degree. Eight years ago. It was Dad's treat that time, though he couldn't come and Leni said getting an M.A. was a dubious achievement anyway at thirty-three.

Leni was thirty before she finished her B.A. Dropping out of Brandeis to wander around South America, sampling the local hallucinogens. Then four years as a VISTA volunteer, making bricks in Arizona. All the tutoring jobs that never lasted. The American Studies department at the University of New Mexico was probably the only place that could make sense out of those credentials.

Even UNM's patience must have a limit, though, if little Cather College had fired her for not finishing the thesis that was supposed to be 'almost' done when they hired her last year.

Still, being here with Leni that day was one of their best times together. The light alone had felt like grace, radiant, almost incongruous with the scene on the plaza. 'Share the fantasy,' Leni murmured as a woman in mauve suede hurried by, the fringed hem of her skirt grazing purple cowboy boots.

They both had been wearing sunglasses, but walking along the arcade Leni seemed to know what she was drawn to in the windows, pointing out which pots were plaster casts instead of clay ones built by hand. Zuni fetishes and cheaper copies—the stone and shell animals less distinctly carved. In a display of kachina carvings, the tall central figure spreading feathered wings showed materials no good Hopi artist would use, but this little brown one with the black kirtle was real and probably much more expensive, authentic spirit being the highest currency.

On the white park benches and under the trees, clusters of kids with bandanas and backpacks radiated disdain for the commercial traffic.

As the sun climbed the ridge behind the Romanesque towers of the cathedral, the crowd had thinned and shops began to close, gathering in the painted furniture, cow skulls, and kiva ladders set out during the day. In the twilight, Indians came with pick-up trucks to collect their wives, and the lines of the older city began to show. Brown shoulders of adobe shadowed by jutting viga beams and hanging ristras of red chilis, the dark faces and snatches of languages she couldn't identify, except for occasional phrases called in Spanish.

Maybe it was the tequila, but when they took off their shades, she thought they both had the same look in their eyes. 'I know,' Leni smiled. 'When you think about it, it's been going downhill here since about 1650.'

'So let's go stuff our faces like the rest of the honkies.'

'Anglos, you mean. And I have to admit, the critical mass of green chili has only improved.'

That's one thing I won't try, she thought, turning into La Fonda's parking garage. Eating green chili by myself.

An old man in a blue jacket stuck his head out of the booth. She said, "I have a reservation for tonight." One they had made clear she was lucky to get at this time of year.

"I'll call someone down for your luggage."

"Don't bother. It got lost. Are any clothing stores still open?"

"Most everything is, for Christmas. You ask at the desk."

Inside, a maze of shops and galleries ringed the courtyard restaurant, with its small brightly painted panels of glass.

The desk stood across the crowded lobby, under a shelf of earthen pots gleaming in the light from iron lanterns. It shone on the pink and red ribbons decorating the turquoise shirts the clerks wore, a Spanish or Indian style, or combination of the two, like everything else here after four hundred years. Woody Allen's joke, 'The lion may lie down with the lamb. But the lamb won't get much sleep.'

She took out her credit card. "I have a reservation. For a single. Leigh Haring."

The woman looked down. "Yes, Ms. Haring. Would you sign here, please?"

Taking the card, she turned back to the office.

"Leigh?" A blond man came around the desk, putting out a hand to her. "Leigh. Ed Harris. I was a friend of your sister's."

"Oh." She shook the hand awkwardly and got a gentle squeeze in return.

"Please accept my sympathy. We're all shattered about this."

"Thank you." She hadn't thought about Leni's friends here. People who knew her well. This one looked like Alan's fatal type, when Alan was feeling masochistic. Late thirties, with a silver bolo tie centering his white shirt and tan jacket, straight tawny hair tied at the back of his neck—only a man with those shoulders could get away with that hair.

"Lourdes told me you'd made a reservation. I wanted to see if you needed anything."

"It's funny. Stupid, really. I didn't think anyone would know yet."

"It was in the paper today," he said quietly. "We had state police all over town. Look, you must be tired. Would you like a cup of coffee?"

Taking her card and key, she moved out of the way. "What I really need is to get to a store. My suitcase didn't make it here."

He glanced at his watch. "For basic stuff? I know a place. But we better hurry. You can get a toothbrush at the newsstand, and there's shampoo and all that up in the rooms."

"Great. Just tell me where, though. You seem pretty busy now."

One side of his mouth curved up. "I'm sorry. I haven't introduced myself properly. I don't work here. I just hang around a lot." From an inside jacket pocket, he took out a brown wallet and handed her a card. Oyster white, with russet engraving. RARE EARTH. Edward Harris. Minerals, Crystals, Geodes. Then addresses for Santa Fe and Sedona, Arizona.

"We're sort of in the same line. You're a jeweler, right?"

She nodded.

"Leni told me. I've wanted to meet you. Not like this, though. Keep that in case you need directions or something. Now let's see if we can beat the clock."

Tucking it in her purse, she followed him out.

Her quilted jacket was too warm. "It must be sixty degrees."

"Yah, we've been lucky. The tourists like to have snow, though."

"Send them to Boston."

"Gladly, after Christmas. I'm hoping to make up for a slow year."

Along the portál, pine boughs were wrapped around the columns and their scent recalled the bare tree she had dragged back out to the yard last night.

Turning down an alley, he opened the door to a small courtyard. "On the left here. Black Mesa Dry Goods."

A shade was pulled down over the door window, but the lights were on. He rang the bell. "Someone's here."

The door opened a crack. "Hi, Ed. We were just closing."

"I've got a friend here from Boston who's lost her suitcase."

"Oh." It swung back slowly. "Come in."

"Leigh, this is Rose."

"Hi, Leigh. From Boston, huh?" She was young, with curly black hair and lines of tension around her eyes.

"Leni's her sister. She needs a couple of things. I'm sorry," he said, "I told you the police have been around."

"It's on the radio." Rose locked the door. "I'm sorry too. About your sister. I didn't know her. Just Bird. It doesn't say if they caught him yet."

Leigh looked from her to Ed. "Who's Bird?"

"Redbird. Ben Naya. Leni must have told you about him."

"No. I don't know."

"They've been seeing each other for months."

"I haven't talked to her much in months." Walking to the counter, she put down her purse. Naya. It rang a faint bell. And something in one phone call. A part Indian guy. Leni didn't think it would work out. "And that's who they think killed her? This Redbird?"

"It said there's a 'Be on the lookout' for him." Rose held out a hand. "Want to take off your jacket?"

The room shimmered. She braced an elbow on the counter. "Maybe I can't do this after all."

"I'll do it for you. Just sit right in this chair. How long will you be here?"

"I'm not sure. A day or two, I guess."

"You'll need something to sleep in. A nightgown, or pajamas?"

Nothing, was the answer. "It doesn't matter."

"What else? Like, jeans and a sweater?"

"Not jeans." She looked down at her black jumpsuit. "I have to talk to some people."

"You could wear that too. It's pretty casual here. But let's see what I can find." She turned towards the rack of clothing.

"You look a little rocky. How about a glass of water?"

She looked up. "No. I'm all right. It's just hard to take this in. On the phone, they didn't know who did it."

"Well, they don't. But he's got a record. He could have been with her that night and now he's not around. Probably, he's gone back to the rez."

"Oh? Which rez would that be?"

"Hopi. In Arizona."

Part Hopi. That's what Leni said. "And he's got a record? For what?"

"Bird?" He gave a short laugh. "Being a wild man. Till recently, anyway. He used to be a bar fighter when he first came out here. From L.A. He made a pile in the movies and it all went up his nose. Then he was on bug juice for a while. I don't know how he got together with your sister, but she was good for him. It may have helped that she was older."

"Really?" Leni always made sure there was no hope for her relationships. "How much older?"

"I think Bird's thirty-four."

He smiled, as if remembering something.

"What?"

"It's just . . . Hopi means peaceful. Bird? I don't think so."

"Do you think he killed her?"

He folded his arms. "That's what I've been wondering. Six months ago, maybe he could have killed someone. In a fight. Now, and your sister, I'd say no. Unless she tried to break up when he was drunk, and he flipped out or something. But a friend of mine owns the gallery that sells his photographs, and when I've seen him there lately, he's been steady-on sober."

Six months wasn't exactly a lifetime conversion, though.

Rose brought up a flannel nightgown and blue jersey pajamas. "These are a small."

She pointed to the pajamas, embarrassed suddenly. "Great. So he's a photographer?"

Ed nodded. "Kind of interesting stuff. He had a one-man show at the museum. Pictures of tourists in Winnebagos, with the kids wearing war paint. And these businessmen in Arizona who call themselves Smokis, and do a rip-off of the Hopi snake dance. After some of the junk Bird was in, I think it's a role reversal. The Pueblos have a myth about a lost white brother who'd come back someday to help them. The Hopis called him Pahana. Only, when the pahanas showed up, it didn't work out that way. Now it's like this is all one big open-air diorama set up by the Park Service. So he makes exhibits of his own. I can show you if you want. The gallery's closed now, but there's usually something of his in the window."

Terrific, she thought. "If he hates white people so much, how come he was going out with Leni?"

"Well," he shrugged, "he's white too, on his mother's side. Too much of either one to be the other. Maybe native women make him feel how white. And vice-versa."

"Here." Rose had an armful of clothes that she held up one by one. Black slacks, pleated at the waist. A dark red sweater with a black geometric band across the chest. A soft grey shirt.

"You're a genius."

"Want to try them on? I know they'll fit, though. Except maybe the pants. They're an eight?"

"Perfect." She took out her credit card. "No, just put them in a bag, please."

Outdoors, it was colder. He took the bag so she could button her jacket. "If you feel like a walk, we could try the gallery."

"A walk would be good. I'm not so sure about the other."

"Then let's go this way. There's something I better show you." Taking her elbow, he steered her left down a side street, then right onto Palace Avenue.

She watched his reflection in the windows. A high forehead, bent forward as if he were working out a puzzle. Cool, but with something going on not too far below the surface.

Not an old boyfriend, though, apparently. Unless from a long time ago. "How well did you know Leni?"

He slowed his pace. "I guess you could say I liked her more than I knew her. If that doesn't sound too strange. I saw her here with Bird mostly, and we hung out a few times when she was waiting for him. She's intense. I think she brought out my protective instincts. And she was interested in my rocks, and what's in the ground out here. So I got to show off. I guess I liked that too."

Down the alley, she saw the cinnamon lacquer sign.

"Rare Earth. That's your shop?"

In the window, a spotlight shone on a perfect obelisk of moss agate resting on pale grey velvet.

"That's wonderful."

"Thanks. The good stuff's in the safe. My insurance company insists." Unlocking the door, he switched on the lights.

The display case was nearly empty, but the shelves held a rainbow of minerals, only a few of which she recognized. Chunks of green malachite with one surface polished. Brown discs of agate cut like cross-sections of a tree, and some kind of matrix rock imbedded with spikes of colored tourmaline crystal.

He went behind the counter. "It's mostly jewelry that's in the safe. There are two Navajo brothers who make incredible settings for me. Do you use raw stone or buy it finished?"

She picked up a small glowing sphere of carnelian. "I buy everything finished. Then I finish it again."

"Really? I thought you're a metalsmith."

"Used to be."

His blue eyes held hers for a moment. "You know, you surprise me."

"Why is that?"

"I don't know. For one thing, you're so little. When Leni told me Bloomingdale's and Neiman's carried your stuff, I pictured someone tall and hard and intimidating."

"Well," she smiled, "I try to be. Size isn't everything."

"She never mentioned me to you? I think my feelings are hurt."

"Not that I recall. But she doesn't know my friends, either."

"I guess I was hoping sometime we could collaborate on a line."

Bending, he took a section of newspaper from a lower shelf and handed it to her. "You might want to see this. It's at the top left corner." Under the column WRAPUP: NEW MEXICO:

MURDER IN CHAMA

Police report Chama resident Elinor Haring was found dead at her home yesterday, the victim of an apparent homicide. Haring, 41, a native of Boston, was an instructor at Cather College in Chama, and had lived in the area for over a year. Anyone with information that might aid the investigation is requested to call Chief Antonio Arias of the Chama police department, or James Welch of the state police criminal bureau.

So there it was. In black and white. Official. A thud in her chest, like being kicked from inside. Leni in the past tense. A victim, to be investigated. As though her life belonged to the police now.

She could feel Ed watching her, and didn't look up. "Chief Arias. That's who I've got to see."

"Tomorrow? You're driving up there?"

"Yup. Me and my rent-a-car."

"Then let me give you something to take with you."

He pulled open a drawer, and his fingers hesitated over a pad with an array of colored stones. A long hand, tan and well kept, except for faint white scars that looked like her silver burns. But his must have come from prying rocks up with a geologist's pick.

Newsprint had streaked her own hands and she put the paper down.

"This one." He held out a curved stone. Midnight blue, with a faint coppery vein.

"That isn't lapis lazuli?"

"Hardly. I'm not that generous. It's sodalite. To give you courage and endurance. I hope it does."

"Thanks." She turned it slowly. "You don't really believe in that? The mystical power of stones?"

He shrugged. "Would you be a jeweler if you didn't? That they've got power in themselves, at least. As far as healing anything, it's probably belief that does that. Anyway, they can't hurt. Oh. No. Wait a minute." The scarred hand wavered and he brought it to his forehead. "Oh, Jesus. That's not true."

"What?"

Someone was looking in the window. He switched off the overhead lamp and the spotlight threw jagged shadows on the wall.

"I just remembered something. Damn. I told you the state cops were here? At the gallery. All over. They asked me if Bird ever bought any rocks from me. The day before yesterday. I gave him a good-sized piece of tiger eye. So I said that. You have to tell them something when they're staring you into the ground. But if they found it at Leni's house, it would prove he was there that night."

"So? If he was, they ought to know it."

"Yeah." He pushed the drawer shut. "But any Skin with a record of punching people's lights out can't afford to have much circumstantial evidence lying around."

Her hand closed around the stone. "Excuse me. I know this guy's your friend, but you said he could have lost it if he got drunk. Maybe he raped her and then strangled her in a panic. Unless some lunatic just wandered by. You seem to care more about him than what happened to Leni.''

"Jesus, Leigh. She was raped? They didn't tell me that.''

"I'm not supposed to know either. The police at home said 'from the contusions' it looked that way.''

He came around the counter. "Let's get out of this fishbowl.''

Going back was a silent walk along the high adobe wall. His boot heels made a hollow sound on the pavement. At the corner of the plaza, he said, "Maybe we're missing something.''

"What?''

"The other things the cops kept asking me about was drugs. Did he use drugs, did she use drugs. Maybe there was some kind of deal going down.''

"Oh. Great. He's a dealer?''

"I'm not saying that. He likes reefer. So does half the town. But he hasn't sold many pictures lately. He might have needed money. I don't know if Leni used. Like I said, I didn't know her that well.''

"That's funny.''

"Why?''

"You've never been to her house?''

"No.''

"Drugs are her specialty. She's got about eighty books on them. The title of her doctoral dissertation is 'Chemical Ecstasy.' It's sort of a history of visionary drug use. Last time I was here she had a shoebox full of specimens. Maybe they found those.''

"Huh. And the state cops don't make fine distinctions when it comes to controlled substances.''

"A few old dried up mushrooms? That's hardly an ounce of coke.''

"I don't know. It wouldn't look good for a teacher at Cather. People are touchy about drugs up north. 'Just say no,' when half the parents are in the Native American Church and take peyote. If you want to see Bird's pictures, it's up there.''

He pointed to a sign that said Severo Gallery.

"All right. Why not.''

Coming closer, she saw there was only one shot in the window, sitting on a low wooden easel.

A black-and-white photo. Two women, looking at each other through a windowpane set in rough plank boards. The distortion of the glass made it hard to tell if one was superimposed or a reflection. Leni, and he had caught the wry look her eyes sometimes held. The other was an Indian woman with short razor-cut hair and

a blank expression, defying the gaze of the camera. The label read
DOUBLE EXPOSURE. NOT FOR SALE.   "That wasn't here this
morning, Leigh. I would have told you. Sorry."

"You mean it's like a memorial? When he probably killed her?"

In the picture, the two faces blurred the boundary of the window. One came forward. Then the other.

"I guess. I've never seen this one before. He must have taken it out at his cabin."

"Who's the other woman?"

"I don't know."

Another girlfriend, probably. The one who made him feel white. Unlike Leni, who made him feel like a hero, at least when he was sober.

"How about that coffee now? We could go to the bar at La Fonda."

"No, thanks." She turned back toward the hotel. "I'm really tired, and I have to get up early."

"I could go up with you tomorrow, if you'd like some company."

For a moment, she considered it. But didn't want to have to talk. "No. Thanks for the offer, though. What's it like there?"

"Chama? Kind of spooky. Mountains and pine trees, and a strange mix of people. It used to be all lumber, but that's winding down now. So there are the old Spanish families, and the Jicarilla Apaches, and some hunting lodges and dude ranches for the Anglos. Wild West stuff. A little train that used to go up to the mines is the big tourist trip, but it won't be running this time of year."

He held the heavy wooden door for her. "Call me if you need anything. Or if you find out anything? It's not out of the question I'll hear from Bird so maybe I'll have news for you."

TAKING THE ELEVATOR to the third floor, she opened the door to a cheerful room—yellow bureau painted with red birds and flowers, a high four-poster bed. A flashing red light on the telephone.

She picked it up. A message to please call your father.

To tell him what? she wondered. That Leni fell for some semi-drunken, semi-Indian with a history of violence, a lot younger than her and maybe a dope dealer on the side? That was Leni. Find a victim. The worse off, the better she'd feel.

She called the number and he answered on the second ring.

"Hi, Dad. How are you doing?"

"I'm all right. Harriet's with me."

She sent a silent thank-you to her aunt, who was not his favorite person. "Is she staying over?"

"If I'll let her. How was your flight?"

"Okay. Everything's fine."

"Leigh, they called me back today, and it seems they've taken Leni . . . her body down to Albuquerque. To the state Medical Investigator's office, they call it. They're going to do an autopsy tomorrow. They didn't ask me this, they 'notified' me. So I guess you'll have to go there. Have you got a pen?"

She rummaged in her purse. "Yup."

"The name's Dr. Alex Ford. At UNM Medical School. Back to her alma mater. How's that for irony. It's at Yale and Lomas. I'm sorry you have to cope with this. I should have gone with you."

"Come on. We went all through it."

"I know. But I feel useless."

"You wouldn't feel any better here. Anyway, one of us has to be stationary to get these calls."

"I suppose so. I just hate to think of you handling that alone."

Her purse had spilled on the bedspread and the RARE EARTH card was facing up. Not completely alone. She had forgotten to take Ed's newspaper article. But why tell Dad about that, either.

"I'll be fine, Dad. Get some sleep. I'll call you tomorrow."

"All right. Good night."

"Bye. Love to Harriet."

She hung up the receiver.

An autopsy tomorrow. And what would she do then? Sit in the hall and wait to ask how the operation went?

She pushed off her boots.

Opening the map of New Mexico, she added up the numbers. A hundred miles north to Chama. And not even an address there. Leni, care of P.O. Box 33.

The house she had never seen.

No toothpaste. Forgotten also. Not one more thing no v. Sleep.

The pajamas. Rose had known what she was doing.

Putting them on, she turned off the light and let the starched sheets engulf her, but in the dark she began to feel a creeping nervousness. There was a slice of light on the far wall, from a gap in the curtains, and the shadow of a tree cast over it, huge leaves waving unevenly as if someone were climbing the branch. Down the street a dog barked, and then came a low whistle. What had Leni heard or seen while there was still a chance to do something about it?

All night she kept waking up to the flickering shadow. Better to keep moving than to stop.

HE RAN. Blindly across the highway from the pay phone at the Hopi Cultural Center, through the bare orchard and down over the rim of the mesa to crouch, shaking, out of sight.

Vera said that she saw Leni's body. It must be true. But first she had to ask, Were you with Leni last night, Ben?

The catch in her voice describing the wreck of the house, the smashed whiskey bottle and the roach in the ashtray.

His ears filled with the sound of things being tipped over and smashed.

String in the bushes. That was going to be enough? She wouldn't keep the gun out where it could do any good.

Last night. Leaving her. Not saying it was hard to go. Not saying he could go because of her.

Broken sandstone grated underfoot and he tried to ease against the mesa wall, looking out over ragged terraces of rock falling to purple desert. In the distance, the San Francisco peaks jutting white against the sky. Snow there. Where the kachinas lived. And spirits of the dead.

Leaving. Someone coming. Breaking in. Or with a key.

That Jeep, with the big locked tool box on the back. The one that had been at the village the day his brakes were cut. Tan and fading into the scenery. Then yesterday, parked on Route 87 south of the Mesa where the Huey came down.

Here. Not in Chama.

Vera, on the phone, 'How could anyone know? Did you tell anyone, Ben?'

Asking Leni to get the satellite pictures had been his idea.

So he could bring the answer here. To his non-relatives, the way they counted it, or else Vera would be his sister. Wanting to show them his pahana side had something to offer. An explanation. Not a mystery.

Using Leni, even after the brakes were cut, to get technical books from the library.

Not telling Vera about that either. But anyone could find out if they wanted to.

All his fault.

The cops would think so too, with his fingerprints everywhere. On the bottle of Bushmills and the gun. Traces of him in her bed. Her body.

If Vera had any doubt, nobody else would believe him. Not once the DWI and disorderlies from Gallup popped up on the computer.

At least it would be a cleaner cell than the last one. Not so much puke on the floor.

Handcuffs.

Questions he wouldn't be able to answer.

If they showed him photos of Leni, it would be easy to confess.

Guilty, of pushing it too hard because finally all the pieces were starting to come together. Here. The trailer park in L.A. The darkroom. Leni's house. Getting the pieces back to see a pattern.

After living like a ghost for so long it cut him open to think he could be of some use to his shadow of a father. Taking night pictures in the desert when the Huey came down. At the heart of the snake nesting ground.

That was supposed to be a secret. But someone had found out.

'The home of our snake-brothers,' non-brother Randall called it. Scattering the snakes would mean the end of the snake dance. The sacred cycle. Maybe, of the world.

Of his own world now, anyway.

It might take the cops a day to trace him here—at which point the jurisdiction would switch to Arizona. Then they'd have to go through the tribal court to come onto the rez. At Soyál, Vera thought, that could stall things for another day or two. Cops all over the mesas would wreck the ceremony.

And wreck what his father and Randall were trying to do. Which was what the Huey really wanted. The strategy they were building with the religious leaders to challenge the tribal council would collapse.

Killing someone like Randall would have brought the chiefs together just on principle. But for this mostly pahana murderer to bring sacrilege at Soyál... pahana cops, unwelcome attention.... They'd go back to their villages disgusted and it could take a year before they'd be ready to make a move again.

That was a reason to kill Leni even if no one knew about the satellite pictures.

Taking out a Camel, he fumbled for a match. Lit it, cupped against the wind.

If the leaders didn't get their act together, a mining lease could be signed and drills and backhoes would make a sandpit of the snake nesting ground.

Finding out which enemy to plan for was the first thing or had been up to now. The U.S. Office of Mining or Peabody Coal—not that there was a dime's worth of difference between them. Or maybe the tribal council sent the Huey.

Proof. It was good to know the sorcery of cameras, his non-grandfather had said, and that was all he needed to hear.

But a story went along with it, in Kayaamuya, the month for telling stories: When he was very small, living with his mother in Keams Canyon, he got sick for a long time. She sent a message to the village and his father had taken him to a snake priest for prayers. So there was a connection, even after all these years. Once, a young Hopi named Tiyo had gone far away, like him, a long time ago when there was an awful drought. In the underworld, Tiyo found the snake people who knew the charms to bring rain. Accepting his prayer offerings, they initiated him into their priesthood and taught him their songs and rituals. So he married a snake girl and brought her back to the people. And their children were snakes who could carry prayers for rain. If the ceremony was done exactly right, rain would always come as it had in the mist house of the snake girl.

Soft soap. A fairy tale it was too late to hear now. The old guy knew just how to jig him along, with his grey bangs and bandana like a sepia postcard from the rack at the Cultural Center. And like a tourist he'd bought the whole picture.

Once on summer vacation he had seen the snake dance, though. The only open part of the ceremony. A kid, lost in a crush of bodies on one of the flat roofs—until a pair of strong hands lifted him from behind, high enough to see the feathers on the heads of the dancers coming into the plaza.

Silently, they circled it, bodies painted black and white, with zigzags of snake-lightning on their kilts. Antelope priests called to the clouds and a rattle of shells asked mother water to bring rain to the fields. Two by two the dancers came, one holding a wriggling rattler in his mouth while the other charmed it with a feather. He could see its forked and darting tongue. And then a snake escaped from where they were kept, aiming straight for a row of women, and he still remembered their startled cries, the flash of white leg-wrappings as they scrambled up onto their chairs.

Gathering the snakes, the dancers ran down to the valley, setting them free to carry their messages.

If it always was done this way, the spirits would understand the signs and rain would always come. The only magic he had ever believed in because that day it poured.

Leni was the one to figure out it was that same August she came to the dance with her father, who was testing an aerial camera in New Mexico. A primitive one compared to what was up there now from programs he had worked on since, with pretty names like HALO and Teal Ruby.

If there was any chance to get the satellite pictures, she said it was worth a try.

Something cold touched his hand. A snowflake. He looked up into a funnel of them spinning gently down.

Spirits of dead people were supposed to come back as rain to say goodbye.

Shivering, he closed his arms around his knees. Even if he ran, Vera said, the cops would be coming here. And the Soyál chief was going into the kiva tonight. Bringing this back to the village could spoil that. No one there could help him now.

On the other hand, if the sun didn't come back, he'd be a lot harder to find.

There was nothing left to run to in L.A. and that would be the second place they'd look.

A roll of bills filled one vest pocket, from the gallery. But the truck was useless. They'd have the license number by now.

If cutting the brakes on the truck had worked, he'd be dead instead of Leni.

So all of this was really borrowed time.

That cave, he remembered. Up the canyon on the spur of mesa, where Vera left him when he was so strung out one more bottle would have been the last. Ugly red spots all over his face from what was happening to his kidneys. You're dying, she said, packing up the groceries. And left him out there to sink or swim.

You had to know how to get to it. There was even a trickle of water. And a good view of the desert where the Huey landed. It ought to be coming back. Soyál was a perfect time to go hunting at midnight.

Kwikwilyaqa, the old man called him. The name of the kachina who wore pahana shoes and copied people, like an actor. Kwikwilyaqa followed watchers at the dances, shadowing every move until it drove them nuts.

A better nickname than he'd thought.

Standing up, he climbed the slope and went back through the orchard. Taylor, the kid who brought Vera's message, was still in the pick-up in the lot at the Cultural Center. And Taylor's brother Keith had spent a year at the Sherman Indian School in California.

He crossed the road, to the passenger window. Taylor had his phones on. Metallica, from the box on the dash.

Popping out one earplug, he said, "I'm a fugitive from justice. Want to help me out?"

Taylor grinned. "Do I get to drive?"

"Move over."

It took a while to collect the groceries, given the distance between stores. He didn't want Taylor to buy much at any one place.

Keith was happy to switch clothes. He got the down vest. And the truck, to take to Gallup, where he'd leave it and buy an Amtrak ticket to Los Angeles.

Chapter 4

TESUQUE PUEBLO. BINGO. Friday and Saturday night.

The ristras hanging at roadside stands were twisting in the wind, but even though it was raining the pale earth looked dry, Leigh thought. Against the grey knife of mountains, pastel-colored mobile homes seemed huddled for protection in parks named optimistically: Sunshine, and Butterfly Springs.

At Española the trailers multiplied, with junked cars in the yards like a cash crop raised to feed the auto salvage places.

Earth-moving equipment. Radio Shack. Jehovah's Witnesses. Shutting off the blare of the radio, she turned left onto Route 85.

Ahead were churning hills and fields marked out in grey and brown. Santa Clara Pueblo. Cows and neat adobe houses under the cottonwood trees Leni loved, their soft branches fanned by the wind into dramatic or comic gestures. A sign for Rio Chama, and the first streaks of pink showing through the rocky crust.

The road followed the curve of the river straight out of the rain, a veil opening onto the chalky headlands at Abiquiu. Above on the left, the old Georgia O'Keeffe house where they had tried to see over the wall, the KEEP OUT sign making them giggle when Leni's hair caught on some thorns just as a black Lincoln pulled into the driveway.

Then the shock she remembered, the sudden, incredible distance, weird Mars-red buttes and salmon cliffs carved by the wind and persistent thread of the river.

Ghost Ranch. The farthest north she had come with Leni. Undulating bluffs of rust and cream held barely in balance by the radiant sky. O'Keeffe had had some nerve to set up an easel here. Antlike, against the sweep and scale of it.

She had taken only snapshots home, to stick on the studio wall. Colors for last year's Fall I collection. With all the lifelines that fed her immediately on tap—telephone, take-out, extra hands and feet—like a larger body built around her own. Here, the nearest grocery store must be thirty miles away. She had never changed a flat. Hadn't thought to take water along.

On impulse, she turned in at the brown sign with the cow skull, to the ranch now owned by the Presbyterian church.

An enclave dwarfed by the gigantic mesas and dark Pedernal ridge. The true face of the planet, Leni claimed, totally indifferent to the creatures moving across it or anything but the force of wind and water. She'd made fun of the irrigated lawn that ran down to the scattered buildings. Transplanted, cozy scenery as a defense against this power. What the hell were Presbyterians doing on Spanish and Indian land? The ghosts of the artists who painted here must be howling up in the cliffs.

The moral superiority of bone-gazing. Maddening. Till then that visit had been going well. But in Leni's view, nothing was supposed to change. Everyone should just stay where they were and keep piling up on each other.

Send the Spanish back to Spain and clean out South America. What was Leni doing here any more than the Presbyterians?

Now she thought she had felt defensive then, having just given up the metal work. The hiss of ice on hot silver for safer, manufactured elements. She had wanted to talk about that and then couldn't. It made her mad. At herself as much as Leni.

At Christmas she was going to tell her how well it had worked out. Only the risks were different, not the challenge of the work.

Rounding the loop, she came back to the highway.

A few miles further on, a sign for the Ghost Ranch Living Museum. She had passed the lot and pulled over onto the shoulder. Walking back she remembered how deceptive distance was here. A much longer walk than it looked.

Outside stood a column of rock slabs cut from the striped layers of the cliff beyond. A vertical spectrum, dark red at the base, pale as sand on top. She had to squint to read the descriptions. The upper crust was merely 100 million years old. The silt of an ancient swamp.

The Age of Reptiles. In a book on O'Keeffe, there was an old myth about the ranch. The locals called it the Ranch of Witches. A huge evil serpent named Vivarón, who had a taste for human infants. A joke, until the skeletons turned up fifty years ago. Phytosaur, the giant lizard. Maybe there were still a few creeping around up in the caves.

A surge of wind rattled the dried heads of chamisa, cutting through her sweater. She pushed her hands up into her sleeves. Next the Morrison Formation, purple shale from when New Mexico was underneath the sea. Ocean creatures. Her eyes moved down the column. Fossils of the first animals with backbones. Sponges. Worm burrows. Last, the oldest known rocks, called metamorphic, or 'changed.' From what? she wondered. Two-hundred-million years ago.

A man in a Forest Service uniform was standing at the desk inside but she couldn't bring herself to ask the question. Stupid, anyway. An explosion of gases and a slow cooling. Meteors crashing. Asteroids. A lungfish gasping out of the swamp. Then the patter of little feet. No wonder the Presbyterians wanted some grass to look at. Something human. On the column the top layer for the Age of Man was thin as a piece of paper.

Behind the wheel, she couldn't put her hand to the ignition. A weight that might be from the altitude but there seemed no point in going on. Too much history, the message of which seemed to be that nothing really mattered.

Why not go straight to Albuquerque, and take Leni home, and make this as painless as possible. Sifting through the things at her house would be only slightly different. If they mattered once, they didn't now.

A drop of rain streaked down the window. Another. Then it came in a wall, blurring the shades and edges of the landscape.

It was farther to Santa Fe now than it would be to Chama.

At least the country ahead was new. As fast as the cliffs had appeared, they were gone. Piney hills with a purple mountain range looming in the distance. Snow on the summit. And finally some signs of civilization. Patched-up adobe stores with people running in from the rain.

Flat-bed trucks rolled by carrying piles of lumber, stripped logs that looked thirty feet long. For ten miles she followed a pick-up with a semiautomatic rifle strung inside its rear window. The rain stopped, and she could see the houses, little clusters of stucco and wood with round tanks of gas in the yards. The mailbox names were Spanish—Martinez, Chavez, Vigil. What did people live on here, she wondered. Not much, by the look of things.

Then, before she was ready for it, the sign for Chama. POP. 1000. ALT. 7860. A low white sky. The old train Ed had mentioned resting at an orange depot down by the river.

The brown stucco buildings across from it had sharply slanting roofs. Hard winters here, in the shadow of the mountains. The village seemed turned in on itself, with more dogs than people in the street. Spooky, Ed said, and there was a sense of conflicting realities. A short tourist season, maybe resented because so obviously needed. Then, behind the western facade, a life led by stricter rules. There wouldn't be many single women living alone out in the woods.

THE POLICE STATION was at 4th and Pine, the voice on the phone had said. A left turn after Fosters Hotel, Saloon, and Restaurant. SINCE 1881. GOD AND COUNTRY.

The small cream-colored building was marked CITY HALL AND LIBRARY. There was no sign for Police, but a radio antenna shot up from the tin roof.

Inside, children's laughter came from one end of the hall. The library. At the other, a sign, REGISTRY OF MOTOR VEHICLES.

Across from the registry desk, a padlocked wooden door had chief Arias' name and a post-it note: At riflery range. Back at 1:30.

In the restroom there were fixtures made for children, set two feet off the floor. Bending to the mirror, she combed her hair.

Then she stood with her back against the wall in the hall, looking down at the pebbly linoleum. There was no reason why Leni should be a priority here. And this guy Arias was heading the investigation.

A burden on the taxpayers. Bad for the tourist trade. Putting on pressure from Boston would probably do more harm than good.

Then he stood filling the shadowed archway by the registry door, massive in a heavy black jumpsuit, black boots, belt, and bandolier. Impenetrable smoked aviator glasses, and the curled cord of a walkie-talkie over his silver badge.

She could feel him taking her in too and wished she'd worn her own jumpsuit. In case he had a sense of humor.

They moved at the same time. "Chief Arias?"

"Yes." He had the padlock off and motioned her into the cluttered office. A police radio was sputtering in the corner, "...Diaz, of Lumberton. Open container. Expired registration..."

Pointing to a low brown chair, he walked around the desk. Even sitting, he seemed out of scale with the place. Maybe the mismatched chairs had been chosen for that effect.

"I'm Leigh Haring, Elinor's sister."

"Yes." His smooth face was impassive. "I'd like to see some identification, please."

He studied her driver's license, recording, she felt sure, her age, height, weight, and social security number. Straight, thick dark hair, brushed back from his forehead with a little grey at the temples. Not quite fifty, she guessed. Some Indian mixed with the Spanish? Handsome, in a way she wasn't used to. Like the rest of the scenery.

Putting down the license, he said without looking up, "You know your sister's body is with the pathologist now. In Albuquerque."

She nodded. "I'd like to see her house. Is that possible?"

"Yes. We finished there this morning." He folded his hands on the desk. "I wish there were something I could say that would be of comfort to you. This is a terrible thing to have happened."

His tone said he had seen how terrible and a hazy picture came again. She kept her eyes on his folded hands. A gold wedding band. The fingernails cut short and straight across.

He said, "Are both your parents living?"

"Just my father."

"Well, please know, and please tell your father, we'll do everything possible to bring the person who killed your sister to justice. I didn't know her well. I met her once out there," his chin moved toward the registry, "and we spoke a time or two after that. She had a nice face, and a nice manner about her. Whenever we passed on the road, she always..." He lifted a hand.

Her throat was tight and she had to open her mouth to get a breath. It shouldn't be surprising he knew Leni. In such a small town. Leni was still attractive.

She said, "Did you find her boyfriend yet?"

He pressed the tips of his fingers together. "Miss Haring, I can't comment on anything concerning the investigation."

Looking straight at the dark glasses, she nodded, "The police at home said you'd say that. But in Santa Fe, it's on the radio. That he's wanted for questioning."

"Picked up from a police band. All I can tell you is, no arrest warrant has been issued. That may change. A fair amount of physical evidence was taken to the crime lab, and the medical investigator will be running tests. When all that's been analyzed, we should know more. But I still won't be able to talk about it. You could speak to the district attorney, but he'll tell you the same thing."

Over her shoulder, the police radio hummed, a woman's voice this time. "On Diaz, four prior DWI convictions..."

She said, "I thought you already have proof he was at her house that night."

"Who told you that?"

"Someone in Santa Fe. Who said this Redbird's out on the Hopi reservation."

"I see." He handed back her license. "You'll probably be hearing other things. I expect this case will get some attention. But generally speaking, the fact that an individual may have been present at the scene isn't sufficient evidence for an arrest warrant."

"Then what would be?"

"We'll have to see. Did Elinor talk to you about anyone she felt afraid of?"

She shook her head.

"Or anything she was worried about?"

Her thesis, Leigh thought. Cracking up, like Mom. Whoever Mom had been. A face in some old snapshots, most of which Leni had stolen from the album.

"Not the way you mean."

"If you should remember anything, let me know."

Unsnapping the pocket under his badge, he took out a small key. "We had to force the front door. Bring that back to me when you leave."

She took it. "How do I get there?"

Standing, he went to a map on the wall, surrounded by fliers for substance abuse counseling, office memos, and tot-finder decals. His forefinger traced a route back out of town, and a left turn toward Brazos Peak. "It's about five miles from there, half on dirt. Just follow the stream. You'll cross two little bridges, then the road forks," he held up three fingers. "Keep bearing left. You can't miss it. There are only two adobes out there. Hers had a little garden on the side."

"Okay. Thanks."

He put out a hand and she shook it. A big hand, slightly calloused.

THE SKY HAD CLEARED in patches and light caught the last gold leaves on the aspens along the river. The mountain ridge was a black wall, bare rock with streaks of snow. To the south, a smaller village came into view as the car climbed steadily. A sign for Los Brazos. The turn.

For a few miles, the road was bordered with tall pines but when it turned to dirt the foliage changed too. Scrubby green cedar and hedges of chamisa growing up around the thinning tree trunks. The ground was strewn with dry branches left behind by some old storm.

With the window open, she could hear the rush of the stream even when it curved out of sight. The air was so pure Alan would joke about it damaging their city lungs.

As she came to the first bridge, a metal grate over a narrow neck of water, a squirrel scampered out of the way. Something odd about it. Then she saw another, sunbathing on a log. Its reddish fur ended in long soft ears that could have belonged to a small rabbit.

The next crossing was a real bridge, and she felt confused. Maybe the grate didn't count and there was another bridge further on.

The road didn't fork, it spread like fingers. A straight shot ahead, but bearing left would mean driving through rutted mud. Recent traffic there, which made sense. Probably from a four-wheel drive. The Toyota might not be up to it, and there was no pay phone to call Triple A.

Pulling up on drier ground to the right, she got out and peered through the trees. Some structure was just visible, though it looked more like wood than adobe.

Whenever anyone said you can't miss it, she knew she would get lost.

The sun was warm enough to leave the jacket. Taking her purse, she started down the trail.

First came a log house, closed for the season. But beyond the stand of aspens more light showed, as if the road opened up.

Her eye caught a dart of movement in the scrub. Then came a crackling, and she stood still. A young deer moving on delicate legs walked out a few yards ahead and stopped with its ears up and black nose quivering. Leni had said deer came up to the house, hoping to find food. And that hunters came after them, even out of season.

The doe turned, switching its tail, and started down toward the stream.

Leigh followed the glistening water over the rise.

The chief had failed to mention the most obvious feature of the house, sitting like a crumbling loaf of brown bread up on the rocky ledge. Yellow CRIME SCENE DO NOT CROSS tapes ran around it like ribbon.

Her boots sank into mud on the winding driveway. Half way up, she saw a red Jeep parked at the end behind Leni's old white Blazer.

Not an official vehicle. And the front door of the house still wore a padlock.

What murderer would drive back to the scene of the crime in a bright red Jeep? Still, it was unnerving.

Pulling the strap of her bag across her chest to leave her hands free, she stepped over the tape and walked up to a side window.

After the glittering water, it was hard to see into the room. A jumble of furniture, pulled out from the walls. Leni's rattan armchairs, and through the doorway to another room, the arc of the willow bed.

In the far corner, someone was crouching in front of the beehive fireplace. A woman with a wedge of dark hair, in jeans and a blue sweater. Her right hand held a chunk of knotty wood and there were others on the floor beside her.

Adding it to the pile, she reached in for one of the bricks it rested on. Then her hand stopped and traveled sideways for the hearth brush.

Leigh saw her own shadow move on the wall by the fireplace as the woman rocked back on her heels, turned toward the window and pointed to the rear of the house.

The back door. When she got to it, the woman was wiping her hands on a towel.

"Hello, Leigh. I'm Leni's friend, Vera. I wanted to clean up before you came. They left things in a mess here. When I talked to your father he said you'd be in Albuquerque today."

"I decided to skip the autopsy."

"Oh. I know. I've been trying not to think about that."

She looked about Leni's age, and as if she might actually run in those Reeboks. Looked ready to now, for that matter.

"I guess we scared each other. Sorry. How did you get in?"

"I have a key. I worked with Leni. We're always needing to borrow things." She stepped back, "As you can see, I didn't get very far with the house."

Something was familiar about her, and then it came across. Her hair was longer, but her face had that same look of not giving anything away. The woman in the photograph at the gallery. Vera. The one friend Leni had mentioned. The reason she left UNM to take the job here.

She put her purse down on the kitchen table. Vera had gone back to pushing furniture around. There wasn't much. The armchairs and their footstools. A long bookcase, with volumes tipping at angles as if several had been removed. A grey-and-white Indian rug on the wall, and a darker one on the floor. Neutral colors, after the crowded trailer in Albuquerque.

"I saw a picture of you in Santa Fe," she said. "One her boyfriend took. So you must know him too."

Vera stopped with her arms around the brown chair cushion. "He didn't kill her, Leigh. He told me so, and I believe him."

"When did he tell you?"

"Yesterday. On the phone."

"From where?"

"That I couldn't say."

Her eyes were as evasive as her answer. "How long have you known this guy?"

"About two years. There's a picture of him over there. Of you, too."

Turning, she saw the bulletin board on the back of the kitchen door.

Another black-and-white shot. He wasn't quite what she had expected. Smaller, for one thing, given the size of the Harley he was pushing. He was wearing old aviator goggles under the hedge of dark hair, and his T-shirt said Buffalo Bill's Wild West Show in letters that looked like rope.

Whoever took the picture had set the speed so low that the bike and his forearms were blurred in motion, giving the feeling he was about to take off at a run.

"There were more," Vera said. "The police must have them."

Pinholes, in the cork. But here was the color snap Leni took the day of her graduation from the Museum School. She and Dad sitting outdoors at the Cafe Florian with a bottle of wine on the table, grinning up at Leni whose purse sat on the empty chair.

Her chair would always be empty now. What would they talk about without her? The absent one, who had to be kept track of, written to, worried about. Leni had insisted on paying for lunch at the Florian, even though she was almost broke. And brought a present, a necklace of heavy round silver beads. Expensive. Too much generosity. As if she could keep spending herself and important years of her life on other people, like an investment. Implicit that when she had nothing left, it all would be returned. Blackmail almost, Leigh thought. A bill that would have to be paid in the future. But she had been wrong about that.

The few other pictures on the board were of some young women in UNM athletic costumes.

"They took her computer, too," Vera said. "And some books. You should get a list of what they took. I don't see her dissertation either."

Leigh followed her glance to the corner table. The printer was still there, and a heap of diskette boxes and manuals. "Well, she won't be finishing it now."

"But she did. Her advisor has a copy of it, except the last chapter and that must be in her computer. UNM should award the degree. Wouldn't that mean something to your father?"

"Yes. I guess it would. We can put it on her headstone. Elinor Haring, Ph.D. Tell me this. If your friend here didn't do it, who did? Could it be a student?"

"No." There was just a touch of a smile. "I'm sure not. The police were over at the college, but . . . Leni was only there a year. The kids liked her." She was doing something with her hands, knotting the fingers together as if they were asking each other questions. "I've been thinking a lot about this, Leigh. I saw her," she tipped her head, "in there. And the way the house looked. It was different. The police have taken so much away. I think whoever did it killed her in that bed and then tried to make it look as if there'd been a fight. Smashed things up. That's why I'd like to know about her computer. The table was knocked over and it's not exactly in the way."

"Maybe he was drunk," she said. "I'm sorry, but from what I've heard that doesn't seem out of the question." In fact, it fit with her sense of the place. The rifle in the pick-up truck. Sudden eruptions to break the monotony. "Maybe he doesn't remember it, but he was here. The police already know that."

"Yes, and the district attorney will be glad to hear he has a record. That makes it all very convenient."

"Do you have any other candidates?"

It took one second too long for her to shake her head. "No. I don't know who did it. I think it's going to be very hard to find out. Listen, I know you want some time alone here, but before I go, why don't you take a look in the bedroom and get it over with. I cleaned up in there first. I hope you don't mind. It was something I wanted to do for Leni."

Reluctantly, she looked past Vera to the bedroom door. And found she had to tell her feet to go there.

A black-and-white woven blanket covered the willow bed. Spread over it was a kind of wild bouquet—tall reedy grass, stalks with dried pods, some rusty flowers and a branch with small orange berries. Bittersweet, she remembered. It grew in the yard at their old house in Newton.

When she went in, there was a smell of incense. Cedar, and something else, In a bowl by the phone on the bedside table, a half burned knot of twigs tied with colored thread.

Over the bed hung a row of straw plaques that hadn't been in the Airstream. A red bar of late afternoon sun came through the open window.

She sat down at the foot of the bed. No pillow. Taken for evidence. But even knowing what happened, it was impossible to picture it now. There was nothing but peace in the room.

Vera came to the door and said quietly, "Is there anything you'd like to ask me?"

She ran her palm over the nubby weave of the blanket. "You're the one who identified her body?"

"That's right."

"Did she look . . . horrible?"

"If you mean her expression, no. Of course she suffered. But I don't think there was much of a fight. There weren't any bruises on her face, which struck me as peculiar. Like whoever killed her knew what he was doing."

Meaning that it wasn't Redbird. But if Leni hadn't fought, it could be because she trusted the person too.

"I keep seeing her lying here . . . with ten cops looking down."

"It wasn't like that. There was a quilt over her. The officer who looked in the window thought she was sleeping at first. And they said they had to take pictures before anything could be touched. I felt respect from them."

She stood up. "I guess that's a relief. Even though it doesn't feel that way right now."

"In case you want to talk more later . . ." She held out a folded slip of paper. "That's my phone number. I'd be glad to hear from you. I'm going to miss your sister very much."

Following Vera outside, she saw the view from the front of the house. A confluence of snow and sky boiling along the ridge, as if the elements couldn't decide what form to take.

Vera said, "If you stay long and get cold, use the quartz heater, not the fireplace. The flue doesn't work. You'd smoke yourself out."

"All right." She felt clumsy. "And thank you. I wouldn't have known where to put things."

Climbing into the red Jeep Cherokee, Vera backed it down the driveway.

Leni's friend. But also Redbird's friend. Maybe more than that.

Friendship only went so far. Maybe he wanted them both, and they'd fought about Vera and Leni told him to shove it. The picture at the gallery showed their faces in intimate opposition.

A long-eared squirrel ran across the path, disappearing into the shrubbery at the side of the house. The garden, or what was left of one.

Walking over to look at it, she caught her foot on a line of string and jumped at a jangle of metal striking glass. She pressed the cord deliberately, and saw the wind chime ring again. Clever. A home-made alarm to scare rabbits out of the vegetables. Tomato and squash vines still clung to the runners nailed to the windowsill.

More string was trampled and there were heel marks where the police had come up looking through the window. From here only the lower half of the bed was visible.

Drawn back into the bedroom, she sat down beside the bouquet. A matchbook lay next to the bowl of twigs and she picked it up and lit them. The silvery leaves were sage, but there was still one other herb she couldn't identify.

Stretching out on her back, she closed her eyes.

A steady breeze from the window kept the scent of the herbs in motion, passing in and out of her consciousness. Leni had died here, made love here. There ought to be some breath of her left, a charge to the bed or turbulence in the air.

Nothing came, though. Vera had exorcised the room.

Vera acted so sure about Redbird. But given the timing, he had to be in it somehow.

After years of Leni's letters from odd corners of the world, there seemed almost an inevitability to this. With all her conspiracy theories, she'd trust any Indian or campesino on the basis of ten minutes' conversation. Sooner or later, she was bound to wind up in bed with the wrong man.

Not that either of them had ever found a right one. The nearly middle-aged Haring girls, who spent so much time alone growing up they weren't able to make the normal accommodations. A vague equation between marriage, loss of control, and Mom. Once the business was on its feet, someone who could take the pressure was supposed to turn up, of course. He was always just a few months down the road. Meantime, there was post-verbal Sven, in his studio on the third floor. The smell of paint and turpentine wafting up when they made very safe sex in his lift bed. The one thing Alan didn't have to offer.

A breeze came across her forehead. Smell of pine and melting snow. A crow cawed. Then it was quiet. A dim thought of the car that turned to smoke and drifted away.

SHE OPENED HER EYES in darkness and twisted up, beating off the claws pulling at her hair.

The dry reeds and the branches. But she couldn't swallow the panic, even as she began to see the pale light at the window. Icy air came through it, and a rustling of dead leaves. Her skin felt clammy under the new clothes.

She fumbled for the lamp on the bedside table. Light flooded the parchment shade.

Her watch said nine o'clock. She got up to close the window. The tangle of vines looked grotesque in the moonlight, snakes with dry wings climbing toward the sill. It was odd Leni hadn't cut them down.

Taking a long breath, she let it out slowly. Spooked, in spooky Chama. No one was out there but the wind and whatever animals came out at night.

In the other room, she found a green lantern lamp hanging over the kitchen table, and a pottery one with a pleated shade between the rattan chairs. Throwing the switch in the bathroom, she blinked at the shiny cubicle of white tile.

The medicine chest. Advil, etc. A small amount of make-up and the face cream Leni used. A bottle of shampoo stood in the shower.

For some reason it seemed menacing, and she backed out of the room. Low blood sugar, Alan would say. First eat something and then decide what to do. In Boston, it was eleven o'clock, and on Tuesday nights he volunteered at the hospice till after midnight.

Dad would tell from her voice that she was spooked and have a fit.

The car was a twenty-minute walk downhill. There could be bears here. Or mountain lions. Leni must have a flashlight somewhere.

Opening the kitchen cupboard, she smiled. A few cans of Pepperidge Farm soup were mixed in with the rice and pasta. Those must have been bought in a fit of homesickness. A rare departure from green chili.

Thirteen hours since breakfast at La Fonda.

Taking a can of BLT, she lit one of the burners and poured the soup into a small red saucepan.

Only the front windows of the house had curtains. She went to pull them shut.

The room looked softer at night, a tinge of peach coming out in the whitewash, but she could see the steam of her breath. The quartz heater sat by the fireplace. When she plugged it in, the rods rattled and started pulsing with light. It had taken Vera so little time to put the room back together. The fireplace looked like a picture from *Santa Fe* magazine.

Leni's spartan house. She would set them each a place, and light the candles, so why not do it. A first and last visit here.

Getting the matches from the bedroom, she caught a glimpse of herself in the mirror on the closet door. The cuffs of her slacks were crusted with dried mud. She put a hand to the doorknob and turned it. A thin ribbon ran to the lightbulb. When she pulled it, she almost stumbled, so much of Leni poured out.

Her sandlewood smell. Her flannel nightgown on the hook inside the door. Familiar clothing pressed together in the narrow space—Mexican sweaters folded over hangers, the Guatemalan shawl, a long grey cowl-necked wool dress and one of Dad's old jacquard bathrobes faded to dull amethyst. A homey warmth seemed to come from them, as if from her living body. A wardrobe hardly different now than it had been in high school. Turtleneck jerseys and black Levis pushed into leather boots. Even in the '60's, straight-leg jeans. No love beads. No embarrassing pictures. Rugged things, softened by her hair, a strand of which gleamed on the bathrobe.

Opening this closet anywhere, she would have identified it as Leni's.

The soup began to hiss on the stove. Taking down the old robe, she went to turn off the gas.

On the kitchen counter sat a boom-box with stacks of tapes. Lou Reed, Ferron, Robbie Robertson, some Spanish and tribal music. The Zuni flute at least shouldn't mask any sound from outside. Wrapping up in the robe, she carried over the bowl and lit the four stubs of candles.

Bacon, lettuce and tomato soup. The single woman's BLT. The clear notes of the flute were lonely too, like the call of a bird wanting an answer. But the house felt warmer now, and she could picture Leni sitting across from her. Or in this chair, facing the room while she ate, a blaze of piñon in the fireplace. The flue must have

broken recently or she would have fixed it. Having no fireplace was
what she'd minded most about the Airstream.

Lifting the spoon almost to her lips, she stopped. If the flue was
broken, there wouldn't have been any fire. No ashes. Nothing for
Vera to clean up.

Vera had knelt there with a piece of wood in her hand. Not burnt
wood. None of it was. Then she reached for the brush. But there
hadn't been any ashes even then.

She went for the brush because a shadow from the window
moved on the wall in front of her.

Pushing the bowl of soup away, she went to try the iron flue
switch. It creaked, but moved easily and stayed open. Crouching,
she pulled back the screen and felt up along the flue. No wobble.
And no sign of ashes. In the few minutes she'd been in the bedroom alone, Vera couldn't have washed the flagstone.

In the bedroom, where Vera had sent her while she put the wood
back in place. 'Your father said you'd be in Albuquerque today.'

She was looking for something.

The flue again. Nothing was caught above it. One by one, she
lifted out the chunks of wood. Nothing. Maybe Vera found what
she wanted.

But she had gone for the bricks too.

Taking them out, she pried at the flagstone and felt it give a little. Leni had always been stronger. By pushing it back, she found
she could get her thumbs in at the edges, and with effort pulled it
up and over the lip. The sudden weight was unbalancing. It started
to slide and she grazed a finger guiding it to the floor.

She looked down at a piece of green plastic. A folded garbage
bag.

Underneath was a small typewriter. And next to that, a red and
gold tin box with monkeys embossed on the lid. A box she hadn't
seen for twenty years.

Leni's old jewelry box, that at some point had become her
treasure box, filled with shells and odd things she found, and slides
of bugs and plankton for her microscope. Daubing on balsam to
seal the panes covering the specimens—a scientific pursuit that had
looked hopelessly beyond her own reach.

And then, exactly when she couldn't recall, it changed to what
she thought of as the Box of Ruth, where Leni kept her souvenirs
of Mom.

Leni had been ten when Ruth died. Herself not quite three. So Leni owned the Mommy franchise. Whatever memories there were from before the crash.

After it, only a name carved in granite at the Newton Center cemetery. Ruth Fromme Haring, May 15, 1926-November 12, 1957.

Two days before her own third birthday.

She could see herself sitting on the kitchen floor, covering her ears and screaming when Leni talked about Mom in that chummy way, as if they were still in touch by telephone. Keeping her in front of Dad like a ghost, when it upset him too. Finally, the stories stopped, but the next phase was just as bad. A hurt silence, the snapshots disappearing from the album into the monkey box that Leni kept well-hidden in her room.

And still kept hidden, apparently. What a joke, she thought. In the last house at the end of the world, here are these monkeys grinning at me again.

By junior high, when she had wanted to know more, Leni was living at Brandeis and would only say: Ask Dad. What he told her wasn't comforting. The accident had involved only one car, and a woman on foot who had just walked out of Mass. Mental when no one was paying attention. The amount of Thorazine in her system probably explained why she hadn't been able to make it across the Fenway.

Her diagnosis was schizo-affective, borderline to manic depression. It wasn't hereditary, he assured her, and might not have been serious if only Ruth had taken that time to rest. She was under a terrific strain, pushing to finish a doctorate in philosophy at Harvard, with two young children and a husband constantly away because Sputnik had scared the daylights out of the Senate Armed Services Committee. He blamed himself, and knew Leni blamed him, but it was the height of the cold war then. For the Russians to have launched the first object into space, polished and tuned so it could be seen and heard all over the planet . . . it was impossible to overstate the impact. Smiling grimly, he quoted a poem written by some politician,

Oh little Sputnik flying high
With made-in-Moscow beep,
You tell the world it's a Commie sky
And Uncle Sam's asleep.

She could understand that. But he was wrong, she thought, about it not being inherited. Maybe the illness wasn't, though he'd been anxious for Leni to finish her degree. It was more Leni's attraction to smash-ups of every kind—injured animals, friends with problems, tribes in the Amazon jungle. An unconscious way, perhaps, of punishing him.

The box was pinned in by the case of what she now saw was a laptop computer, no bigger than a hardcover book. Vera wouldn't have been after the mememtos. It must be the laptop she wanted.

If it belonged to her, she could have proven it easily enough. Unless there was something in it no one else was supposed to see.

Lifting it, the weight surprised her. No heavier than a book, either. The monkey box slid down next to a cord that matched the computer's buff color. Taking it, she opened the machine on the table and pushed the power button.

An aqua cursor sprang up on a chocolate brown field. Batteries, still charged. Instinctively, she typed the command for the program they used at the studio. The letters appeared, but nothing followed when she pressed Execute. On the corner table, there was no manual that matched the brand name.

Sitting down in front of the soup again, she turned the laptop to face her. A manual at the college, maybe. Or in the morning some genius at 47th St. Photo in New York could help with the commands.

Chief Arias would want it. No doubt about it. But then it would go into the black hole of things he wouldn't discuss with her, and if those were his terms, he could wait. He hadn't forbidden her to take anything from the house.

Beyond the glowing cursor, the fireplace gaped. Vera might decide to come back, thinking the house would be empty now. And might not come alone.

The lights on in both rooms had to be visible from some distance. For better or worse, it was obvious someone was here.

Closing the computer, she set it on the floor.

There were bags in the bedroom closet. Some camouflage might be useful to get past any further encounters. A few of Leni's things, taken away for sentimental reasons.

Passing over a duffel bag near the front, she felt behind the clothes and came up with a green day pack. Less awkward for navigating downhill. Even with the striped shawl wrapped around it and a sweater over that, the computer fit with room to spare.

A small relief. She went back to the fireplace. The monkeys continued to scratch their heads and pose, long tails curling up over their heads. Now or later, it would have to be opened. Now she would be the keeper of old snapshots with Leni buried next to Ruth. Who had been ten years younger than Leni when she died. Haring women were an endangered species.

The box was heavier than she remembered. Setting it by the basket of kindling, she reassembled the flagstone, the bricks and knots of piñon.

Now to light a fire. Then if anyone turned up, they could roast their fingernails.

Staying here had more appeal than bolting for the car. Left unlocked. A bogey man in the back seat, if not right outside or somewhere on the road winding through the mountains.

Fraidy. Scared of the dark.

But even if Fosters Hotel and Saloon were open in December, it might not be a safer place.

Scraps of bark, for under the piñon. And crumpled newspaper. As soon as the match hit, it flared up, throwing off red curls of ash. Quickly, she put back the screen. The bark was catching. Not bad for a city girl.

Pulling an armchair close to the fire, she picked up the box again. It must have traveled in the bottom of a backpack for some of those years. The paint was scratched in places and one side was dented in.

She put a thumb to the hinged lid and pushed it open. On top, nesting in the folded papers, a small chrome pistol glinted in the firelight.

Flat, with cross-hatching on the grip. Leni's detective-kit craze. But even as that memory floated up, she knew it came from being braced for old ghosts. From the weight, it wasn't a toy. With a finger, she lifted the grip end. Loaded.

Going to the tape player, she shut it off. Then the overhead lamp. It wasn't the computer Vera wanted after all.

Pulling the sash off the robe, she used it like a pot holder to take the gun and rest it on her knees.

Leni wouldn't have a gun. It must be his. For the dope deal. Or one he'd used somewhere else and needed to hide. Leni might not have known about that.

Vera knew, though. For sure. With that sad little sympathetic smile on her face. She was probably rerunning the scene now too, wondering how it had gone over.

Poor planning. It was stupid to come here without thinking where to stay. Leaving the car down there. Falling asleep.

Underestimating the situation, the same way Leni did.

It was better to find the gun than not to know. To be the one who held it. But the feel of it in her hands was sickening.

Carrying it into the bedroom, she sat down next to the phone. Eleven tones for Alan's number. He answered before the first ring ended, "Hello?"

"It's me."

"God, I thought you'd never call. Where are you?"

"At Leni's. Are you ready for this? I'm sitting here with a loaded gun I found buried in her fireplace."

"What?"

"And that's not all. There was an Indian woman here when I came. I think she was looking for it. And my car's about a half mile away." She smiled. "Got any advice?" Just putting it into words took off the curse a bit. Their jokey way of communicating disasters.

"How about, Call the police?"

"Hmmm." She pictured Chief Arias taking the gun, asking where she'd found it. Lying about that wouldn't work. He'd gone over the place himself and missed it, which he wouldn't like. Behind the granite exterior, a kind of coiled energy said he was good at his job. He'd want to know why she lit a fire on top of possible evidence. So she'd have to tell him some of it. And he wouldn't stop until he'd got it all away from her.

She described their meeting to Alan, grinning by the end. "I'll tell you, any rocker at Avalon would kill for his uniform."

"Hot stuff. Maybe he killed Leni."

A joke. But she thought of how his head had moved toward the registry where he met Leni. From his desk he would have seen her from behind. The wedding band on his folded hands, boredom of the winter... driving up to 'check on her,' after nights of thinking about it. A fumbled pass that he could be too macho to walk away from.

He had a gun. Leni might have got one to protect herself from him. Which didn't explain why Vera would try to steal it.

Alan wanted details, from Santa Fe to the bare windows looking out on a slope in back of the house. From his monosyllables, it sounded as if he were writing it all down.

"I knew I should have gone with you," he said. "I'm coming tomorrow. I already decided that. Now let's take your worst case scenario. Probably this Vera and her gang aren't out there. But if that's wrong, and they saw you find the gun, they'll know you could blow their brains out. On the other hand, you're a sitting duck. So the safest thing to do is call the big Chief."

Putting the gun down on the blanket, she moved a branch of bittersweet to cover it. "But what if I don't. If I don't tell him. Would that make me an accessory after the fact, or something?"

He exhaled slowly. "I'm not sure. If I remember my Perry Mason right, that means concealing something you know is evidence in a crime. Since Leni wasn't shot, this might not be related. Why do you ask? You aren't planning to keep it?"

"No. I don't know. I might be planning to leave it. And then call him from Santa Fe once I get the other things out of here. Why should I just hand them over, when he won't tell me anything?"

"Hon, I doubt the police will want your old family pictures. And if you haven't looked through the rest . . . Do you really think it's worth the risk?"

"See, that's what I'm thinking. Tomorrow I can get the computer commands, and I'll know."

"It's tonight I'm worried about." He was tapping a pencil. "Wait a minute. You know how you griped when we had to change our software at the studio? Didn't your father give you two the same IBM clone? Is that what Leni's been using?"

"As far as I know. But the disc slot on this one is tiny."

"Radio Shack, my darling. There's a little machine. Stick in a big disc, and transfer to a small one. That's what my brother did. She could be using exactly the same program on both computers."

If Leni knew about that, probably she would have done it. Neither of them were agile with computers. "Great," she said. "I'll give it a try."

"Okay. You try. I'll call you back in five minutes. That way, if anything happens, I can hang up and call the cops. The way it is, my line would be tied up. And I'm going to make a plane reservation. Bye."

The broken connection left her feeling pinned to the bed. One of the few spots that couldn't be seen from the back. Even here, someone could come right up and look in the window.

If. A word for imaginary things. It might be nerves, adrenaline, but now she felt sure the house was being watched.

The windows could be covered. But instinct said to leave them alone. While she could see out too, whoever it was might keep a distance. And not see a movement as small as her hand slipping the gun into the right pocket of the robe.

Or anything much below the level of the window. A figure on a lighted stage, cut off at the waist.

She walked out to the other room and swallowed some cold soup. Then kicked the day pack gently across the floor to the bathroom. The only real blind spot in the house.

Unwrapping the laptop, she opened it on the floor and typed in the old command. Familiar lines naming the software came up. A shift to the logo, and then the folder menu. There was only one document, begun last year, and it was labeled Chama.

From the first sentences, it was Leni's writing.

    < September 1.

    < Little beauty. My reward. I thought you'd never get here.

    < Today I cursed for half an hour following the UPS truck, and it turned out to be bringing this and a box of Adelina's chili noodles, both of which are now in use. But the old computer is giving me a dirty look—the faithful consort forced to watch the new love interest being caressed >

Leni's journal. Queasy, suddenly, she put a hand out to the wall. Another monkey box, with its own secrets.

She scrolled down:

    < When I told Vera how handy this would be to use in class, so portable, perfect for students to try out drafts of things, she gave her winning smile and nodded. Knowing, I guess, that I needed a symbolic break with UNM. Some transitional object. Because, of course, Cather has computers. Banks of them. Brand new.

    < No library to speak of. But 'a heck of a database,' as one of the board members put it. The junior college of the '90's should not be burdened with musty volumes from the past. A lucky few will get converted. The agreed-upon set of sources. As for the rest, why clutter up the picture?

    < Especially here. Mining is where it's at. Natural Resource Management and Pre-Engineering. 'The conservation of community resources for the benefit of future generations,' according to the catalogue.

< Sure. So what's Vera doing here? Learning from the enemy, she says. An old Hopi tradition. And balancing their geology and hydrology with courses on native history and land law. She wants me to teach my media class, disguised as composition. But only a toned-down version of the dirty-ads part. I can't ask native students to go picking out cocks in the cocktails, and that's 80 percent of the enrollment.

< It turns out the campus belongs to that little troll who comes around. Michael Zinn. He lives up in the bell tower and plays Corelli on his synthesizer while the sun is going down.

< The board wasn't thrilled about my dissertation, but allowed it may be just as well as I know about peyote. Such a problem. A drug that's actually legal for the Native American Church. Never mind how well it's worked at getting people off booze. It isn't possible to distinguish between use and abuse—as if the two words are unrelated.

< No one asked if I knock back a couple of whiskies at night. And there were plenty of cigarettes gassing up the room.

< That's what I'm most worried about here. The couple, which is more like three lately, turning into four. Lashings of it, because while I'm teaching I feel responsible not to break 'the law' with grass—even though it's healthier and the only way to tap some productive areas of my brain. So really I'm being irresponsible and a hypocrite.

< Maybe I should take some peyote again myself.

< Well, this is what I claimed to want. An adobe, away from the city. Now to finish unpacking so I can get a look at the view. >

Peyote. Leni and her plant alkaloids. Still at it, while the rest of the world sped by. That might be why she had been fired. Or something about the gun.

The document menu listed 78 pages. The final entry could have something. She switched to it, but as the page appeared, the phone rang in the bedroom.

"All quiet on the western front?"

"Yup. You're brilliant. It's her journal."

"Oh." He was quiet for a moment. "I guess that means you won't be calling in the cavalry yet. And I'm not sure you're right. Leni got murdered, remember? You don't know what you're getting into."

She felt the weight of the gun in her pocket. "I didn't say I'd never give it to him. Maybe I can finish it tonight."

"That isn't where your attention ought to be right now."

And if anyone came, there might not be time to hide the laptop. Already, the fact of it sitting there made her nervous. "Screw it. I'm going to put this stuff away. Hold on."

She went out and bent toward the fire, letting the robe fall open over the monkey box. Getting a grip on the papers in it, she pushed them down into her sleeve. Tomorrow, the gun could stay here. A present for the Chief. In the box under the flagstone, almost the way it had been before. By the time the fire was cold it should be light enough to leave.

The last entry was short.

< December 14.

< 4 a.m. and I can't sleep. I guess it's hitting me, finally, that I won't be here next year.

< Not a great tragedy, except that I like this house. The necessary level of illusion about what good I'm doing just isn't there anymore.

< What I'm doing for Ben could pay off, though. If I can pull it off.

< Home for Christmas. Last year I was too afraid I'd break my promise and tell Leigh. And knew Dad would be waiting for it. Spontaneous combustion. But he's probably right she wouldn't want to know.

< So we'll all pretend to talk. Plan some outings. Steer around the icebergs. I've given up hoping it will change. Her judgment really gets to me, and the good moments only make me nervous about what's coming next.

< A self-fulfilling prophecy, no doubt.

< Tomorrow, my last night with Ben for a month. I wish I could take him with me. >

The entry was a perfect miniature of a visit. Even dead, Leni managed to be irritating. She, if anyone, was the critical one. Of the whole eastern seaboard.

Something Leni had promised not to talk about. At Christmas. That fight she'd had with Dad three years ago.

And the last bit. Doing what for Ben?

Alan had a point about giving this to Arias.

Not yet, though. Until it was finished, no one was going to take it away.

Bundling the computer and papers, she felt at a distance from herself. Whatever it took to keep them would be all right to do. It was as if the gun was there to guard the rest, like the soldiers buried in ancient tombs.

Spending the night in the bedroom would be too creepy though. And might not be the best place. Find the spot a cat would choose. She looked around the room. The corner next to the fireplace gave reasonable protection and a good view all around.

Nudging out the day pack, she moved the kindling basket and turned the armchair to face the room. With the footstool drawn up, the pack was hidden.

She picked up the phone, "Wait one minute. I'm making a little camp here." The cord reached far enough to rest the receiver on the chair. She opened the refrigerator. Bottles of soy sauce and chutney. Three green apples in a bowl and a third of a quart of milk. No other perishables. Leni thought she was going home.

Putting the apples by the fireplace, Leigh found a blanket in the closet and sat down with the phone.

"All right. I'm here. Will you sing me to sleep?"

"At these prices, why not? Leigh, the flight you took is booked, but I have to get to a bank machine anyway. Assuming you're still alive tomorrow, could you pick me up at the airport? At 4:45? It's rush hour, but that's the best I could do."

"This is New Mexico, sweetheart. It's not like getting to Logan. Sure. I have to go to the medical investigator's office, but I can get down there by noon."

"Oh. I'm supposed to tell you that your father will be using Waterson's funeral home. And they gave him the name of a place out there. Stone and Douglas. I've got the address written down. Leni's body has to be embalmed, to be taken across state lines. Sorry to be so gruesome right now."

"No, I'm glad you called him."

It would be like a stranger's funeral, she thought. Most of the mourners Dad's friends, or her own. Except for Leni's old pal Diana Clausen, if she saw the notice. "Was there an obituary in the *Globe?*"

"About three paragraphs. And her high school picture."

"Which doesn't look that different, right?"

"I know. It sort of surprised me. What's her house like?"

"A little crumbly, but nice. It's beautiful up here, in an eerie way. You can see for yourself if you want to come back and help me clear her things out." She pushed the blanket down. It was too warm now.

"I'd be glad to. So where are you sitting?"

"Right by the fireplace. You?"

"In bed. But even if I fall asleep, I'll hear you if you shout. I got the number of the Chama police, and just for fun, I called it. A woman answered. I'm not thrilled about this, Leigh."

"I'll pay you back sometime."

"That's not what I mean and you know it."

The flickering shadows were lower on the wall. She felt a part of the red glow, surrounded by it. "Don't try to make me nervous. I just got comfortable."

"I don't want you to be comfortable."

He sounded sleepy. She fixed the gun so it wouldn't blow her foot off. "If someone comes crashing in, I've got the drop on 'em. Now let me tell you about Santa Fe. The man of our dreams. Like Nick Nolte with long hair."

He liked dishing about Santa Fe with Leni, but in fifteen minutes his end of the conversation stopped. Then came uneven breathing. As if he were having a bad dream, and she wanted to shake him gently. Instead she paced her breath to his, calming it down. A technique he had taught her from the hospice.

Resting her head on the arm of the chair, she wedged the phone in with the blanket. Sleeping with Alan. Another thing she had thought would never happen.

A CRUNCH ON GRAVEL in front of the house woke her with a start. Morning light came through the curtains. Six o'clock. She grabbed the receiver, *"Alan?"*

"I'm here." he said hoarsely.

"There's someone...." Putting it down, she went to look through the side of the curtain and saw the chief, a newspaper clamped under one arm, sorting through a key ring. Out of uniform, in chinos and a grey jacket, but the dark glasses still in place.

She let the robe fall in a heap on the chair and pulled the blanket to cover it. As the key turned in the lock she sat and picked up the receiver, "It's Arias."

The door opened. "Miss Haring. You didn't return my key. I'm surprised you're still here."

"So am I. It got dark so fast.... I didn't want to walk back down." A rush of words, and probably a guilty look on her face. But he had frightened her.

"You're on the phone."

"I'm talking to my business partner. Excuse me just a minute." She lifted the receiver, "Alan, the chief of police is here. If I don't have time to call you back, I'll meet your plane at quarter to five."

"Is he packing a heater?"

"Sadly, no. Bye."

The chief hadn't moved, but she knew his eyes were busy behind the glasses, comparing the state of the room now to how he had left it.

His head turned back to her. "Did someone come up here last night?"

If he asked, there must be a reason. "Why?"

"I was looking at the tracks out there."

"Yes. An Indian woman. In a Jeep."

"After you were here?"

"No. She was here already. She has a key to the back door."

"Uh huh. Did you get her name?"

"Vera...something." She hadn't given a last name. "It was the person who identified Leni's body."

"Vera Naya."

"Naya? As in, Ben, Redbird, Naya?"

"That's right. She's his half-sister."

"She told me she'd only known him for two years."

He shrugged, "It's possible. Late yesterday we got his record from NCIC. He was living out in Los Angeles for some time."

He went to push back the curtain of the window looking out on the driveway. "Did she tell you what she wanted?"

"Just to clean things up, she said." She felt with her heel for the day pack. "I think she might have done some kind of ritual before I came. Look what's on the bed."

When he crossed the threshold, she pulled out the pack and put her purse in on top of the other things. Then let him see her take out a comb and run it through her hair.

"And she came back later."

"No. I don't think so."

He sat down in the opposite chair. "There's one set of tracks that come up to the door and cross yours going back down. And another, from the same type of vehicle, that stop at your car and reverse. Someone got out and walked at least as far as the ledge in back. I didn't drive up to the house because I wasn't sure what I'd find here.''

With a chill, she knew why he didn't want to spoil the tracks. The comb slipped and she bent to pick it up. ''I had a feeing about that.''

''You should have called me.''

''That's what my business partner said.''

''Well, I'm glad you're all right.'' He shifted his weight and rapped the folded newspaper on the arm of the chair. ''Miss Haring, I have to show you something I'm not happy about. Usually we have a good relationship with the media, for the simple reason it's to our mutual benefit. If they want information from us, they have to use some discretion, particularly about quoting unnamed sources in an active investigation. After you left yesterday, I got a call from the *Boston Globe,* and I'm sure I'm not the only one who did. That puts our local press under pressure not to be out-gunned. Which I don't offer as an excuse.''

Her eyes moved to the paper. ''What is it? Show me.''

The *New Mexican.* The paper Ed had in Santa Fe. An article at the bottom of page three said NO ARREST IN CHAMA HOMICIDE.

Santa Fe District Attorney Wyatt Matthews had no comment today on the homicide of Elinor Haring, 41, of Chama.

Haring, an instructor of basic studies at Cather College in Chama, was found dead at her home on December 16. A source close to the investigation reports Haring was strangled and may have been a victim of sexual assault. According to the source, police removed a quantity of unidentified drugs from the scene, now being analyzed at the state crime laboratory in Santa Fe.

''Goddamn it.'' She stopped reading, ''That's just her box of specimens, right? Leni was doing legitimate research. This makes her sound like a dealer. And it's going to wind up in the *Boston Globe?*''

''Very likely. And only because this happened, I'll tell you, un-officially, we found what appeared to be some marijuana here too.''

A tremor started in her right hand, rattling the paper. Why couldn't Leni ever think.... This was like being found guilty without a trial, though. Just in time for the funeral. All the discreet little whispers in the parking lot. 'Her poor father.'

"Who's this so-called source?"

"I don't know yet. I called the D.A. before I came out and he doesn't know either. One guess is when the state police called for a team from the crime lab drugs were mentioned and someone was listening on their frequency. Another possibility...this might sound strange to you. But the kind of plants your sister kept are used around here in some of the villages and pueblos for what you might call witchcraft."

"Great. Now she's a witch?"

"I'm only saying, one of the officers at the scene may have ... misinterpreted what he saw. I'll be talking to them today. Have you finished with that?"

The article went on:

The office of the state medical investigator has yet to issue a death certificate, pending results of an autopsy.

Wanted for questioning in connection with the slaying is Ben Naya, 34, of Cerrillos, described as a close friend of the deceased.

Haring was the daughter of Richard Haring, professor emeritus at the Massachusetts Institute of Technology. Dr. Haring is known to New Mexico's scientific community for his pioneering work in the field of infrared communications. Several of his early tests were conducted in Otero County. He also led primary research for the $10 million large-format camera for the space shuttle, credited with starting a world-wide mapmaking revolution, and has developed imaging sensors and high-acuity reconnaissance systems for Skylab, optics for the Viking lander on Mars, and photographic mapping cameras for land-based telescopes.

It read like his obituary.

The chief cleared his throat. "I'm sorry this happened."

"But it did."

"Yes. Unfortunately, we can't issue a denial. Miss Haring, if you're about finished here, I need to lock the house."

He wanted his key back. And that was all he'd get now.

"If you don't mind, I'd like a minute here alone."

"All right." He stood up. "I'll wait for you outside."

When the door had shut, she tried to get a focus back. The gun. Maybe that should be disappeared too, or it would wind up in tomorrow's edition.

But if he searched the pack and found it, he'd take the computer as well.

The monkey box. Back where it started. She lifted the flagstone quietly. It was easier this time. Just a scrape when the box went in. A puff on the ashes to cover the line where they had been disturbed.

If Vera wanted the gun, she could have it. The chief would be visiting her too.

At the sink, she rinsed the soup bowl along with her sooty hands. Just take the pack and brazen it out like a piece of personal luggage.

Leaving the outside flap untied, she slung it over her shoulder.

At the car, he said, "I'll be in touch with you, Miss Haring."

His black-and-white Bronco was pulled off sharply across the trail. He stood beside it while she made a turn and started down. The last glimpse, in the rearview mirror, was of him looking down at the key and then, slowly, back up toward the house.

Chapter 5

IN THE RESTROOM by Leni's old office at UNM, she changed from the muddy trousers back into her jumpsuit, wishing for Chief Arias' badge and bandolier to go with it for her meeting with the medical investigator. The idea of seeing Leni's body and shaking hands with the man who cut it up had left her unable to eat breakfast. Even with make-up, her skin looked grey under the fluorescent light. Somewhere in the lost luggage was the dark green dress chosen to bring some dignity to this.

Probably he'd think she was a cracked-out punk. Which would fit with the article about Leni.

The students bending to the mirror looked younger than ever, but some of them could have taken Leni's course two years ago. If only Leni had stayed here. If not for Vera . . . who had lied to both of them. Maybe Vera gave the newspaper her eyewitness account, to make it sound like a drug deal instead of her little brother flipping out again.

In the hallway, people seemed to stare as if they knew she was part of the story on page 3.

Asking for directions would be like announcing it.

Driving down Lomas to Yale, she got lost in a maze of parking lots around the medical school. The tan and grey stucco buildings went on in rows, and whenever she tried to stop the car someone honked at her from behind.

By the time she saw the bronze lettering for the Medical Investigator's Laboratories, she felt nearly out of control. It wasn't only Leni who had been raped. From now on there would be this angry defensiveness and the need to hide it, knowing what would be said before or after any meeting. How she would be identified even in Boston. Not as the designer who won the Milan prize, but as the sister of that woman who . . .

The *Globe* article should certainly boost attendance at the funeral.

She looked up at an expanse of stucco columns and smoked glass. No grubby city morgue for Leni. The building was new and somehow intimidating.

Taking the Mexican sweater from the pack, she got out and put it on over the jumpsuit. It had a little more authority than the jacket. Wearing Leni's sweater could be armor too.

Inside, the reception area had cream walls and brown furnishings. Muted colors, for grieving or frantic relatives. On the wall hung a blackboard with movable white lettering, like the one listing daily specials at the deli on Berkeley Street. The first name was Alex Ford, M.D. The boss.

A Hispanic woman was selling burritos from a blue-and-white Playmate cooler to someone behind the counter.

The smell of warm meat made her stomach turn and she waited until the transaction was finished to go up and give her name.

"Oh, Miss Haring. We expected you yesterday. I'm Jeanette Avila, Dr. Ford's assistant." Coral lipstick framed perfect teeth, and the jacket she was wearing looked like English tweed. "Come in, please." She gestured around the counter, then through the door behind it to a small room on the left marked LIBRARY. DO NOT DISTURB.

"This is all we have for a family room now. Please..." She opened her hand toward the striped chairs at the conference table. "Ordinarily, we'd have you meet with the lay investigator who viewed the scene. But in this case, Dr. Ford will speak with you."

Just to make sure I don't actually find out anything, she thought, setting down the pack.

"Let me see if the doctor's free now. Could I get you a glass of water?"

She shook her head and watched the door swing shut.

The family room. The air was stuffy, as if all the oxygen had gone into the heavy breathing of other relatives who had sat here recently. At one end stood a blackboard with a blur of chalk erasure. She wondered what facts or diagrams had last been written there. A little floating voice started whispering warnings that always kicked into overdrive before an important meeting: strategize, deal with it, don't let them see you're ready to bolt. A legacy of too many years alone with the blowtorch. But according to Alan, no one ever did see.

By her watch, ten minutes passed before the door opened again.

"Dr. Ford can see you now."

She took her time, to turn the voice down. A fiddle with the pack and the sweater. Her guide was several steps ahead, by the doorway to a large office where a slender blonde was leaning over a table in front of the desk.

A secretary, she assumed, until the introduction was made. Before she could take in the doctor's face, she saw the hand extended, a tidy hand with unpainted nails, firm and cool to the touch. She looked up into shrewd blue eyes and a measured smile.

Four chairs ringed the small table. A semi-formal setting. Part of the conveyor belt to process the mourners who came after the corpses. The walls were lined with bookcases and soft Indian rugs. A careful balance, businesslike, but easy on the nerves.

Alex Ford had the same effect. A woman where a man had been expected. She looked about forty and crisp in her white blouse and teal skirt. From a cabinet behind the desk, a computer screen and a photograph of two young children faced the room.

The doctor sat down, crossing her legs. "You've come a long way for a sad reason. I'm sorry."

Deciding to mirror her body language, Leigh crossed her own legs. "Thank you. Did you find out what happened to my sister?"

"I signed the certificate last night. The cause of death was strangulation."

"And what about the rape?"

The blue eyes glinted. "We're looking into that."

"Don't tell me. You can't comment on an ongoing investigation."

She gave a wry smile. "That's correct. Miss Haring, Chief Arias called me this morning. Believe me, I understand your concerns. But you have to understand the legal constraints we're working under. For instance, even when seminal fluid is present, rape can't always be distinguished from consensual sex. It isn't helpful to jump to that conclusion."

She remembered what Vera said about there being no bruises on Leni's face. So the ones the cop in Brookline mentioned must be on her body. Or arms and legs, where good sex sometimes left them. As any defense attorney would remind a jury.

Sex under the influence of drugs.

"Not even if he was known to be violent? Wouldn't that count at all?"

"That would be the district attorney's decision." Fine lines deepened at the outer corners of her eyelids. A woman who knew how to use her face. Lines that came from smiling, and squinting into microscopes, emphasized to give weight to her words. Her testimony in court. No woman her age could be in this job without good political instincts.

Still, an element of pride could often be counted on. The gratification of describing one's particular passion to someone who showed a fascination for it. Once at a trade show in L.A., she had nearly talked away her patina process to a jeweler who gave the right nod at crucial moments.

She said, "But you can match sperm, can't you? The DNA? Look, Chief Arias talked to me hypothetically. That's all I'm asking for. I need to get a sense of the momentum to this, so I can tell my father what's going on."

"I can explain our testing procedure. But not the results. I won't have them myself for a day or two." She folded her arms. A sapphire-and-diamond ring glittered next to her wedding band. "We've taken samples for three tests. First, for prostatic acid phosphatase. That would indicate the presence of seminal fluid. If it's positive, we'll do a secreter typing. Many people, not all, secrete their blood type in other bodily fluids. And we've frozen a sample for a DNA profile. The odds of two different genetic samples looking the same run from one in one thousand to one in one billion. Depending on how many probes of the chromosome chain are performed. The FBI lab in Washington handles that."

"In Massachusetts, you can't use DNA in court anymore."

"Here you can. Unless the testing procedure's challenged. Once in a while it's been ruled out as evidence because of sloppy lab work. But the technology's getting better all the time."

She sat back. So there would be proof. Not just the piece of tiger eye and fingerprints in the house. To match the sample, though, they'd have to get one from him. And there was no arrest warrant yet.

When she asked about that, the lines came out around the doctor's eyes again.

"If the district attorney determines the evidence is sufficient, he could issue a search warrant for blood and hair samples. But as I said before, that's his decision." A glance at her watch. The allotted time must be coming to an end.

"Did you see the paper today?" Leigh glanced down at the *New Mexican* sticking out of the pack. "They seem to have an inside track on this."

"I did. And that information did not come from this office."

"But you tested for drugs."

"Yes. And the crime lab's running a series. We don't have the results yet." Her toe tapped. "If you'll give me the name of the funeral home you'll be using, I'll arrange for the remains to be transferred."

The remains. What was left when they got through cutting and sampling. This meeting must be some kind of apex of civilization, she thought. To sit here counting the carats in her ring, pretending not to see the hand covered in blood, cradling Leni's liver.

"Miss Haring?"

"I was just wondering which would have worn out first. Her liver or her lungs. Last time she was home she was smoking and drinking scotch and I told her I'd outlive her. Could I see her now? I'd like to get that over with." The same words Vera had used.

"I'm sorry. We don't have facilities for that here." She reached for the Filofax sitting on the table.

A dismissal. "What? That's what I came here for."

"No. The viewing's held at the funeral home." She gave a straight-on look for emphasis. "Do you know which one you'll be using?"

"I think—Stone and Douglas. But I don't have the address."

"I do. They're very good. They'll handle the transit forms for you." She was back on safe ground and the clipped recital was suddenly infuriating. Load up the meat wagon and send the emotional baggage on to the next functionary.

"Wait a minute, Doctor. I've been psyching myself up for this all day. I feel marginally ready now. And you want to ship her somewhere else and I'm supposed to run along behind? I'm her next of kin. I think that means I have the right to see her."

"Because you've seen it happen that way on television. But not here. All we can do, if you're concerned there's been a misidentification, is show you a Polaroid photograph of her face. Would that be helpful?"

She looked down at her folded hands. The knuckles were banded with white. There was a dot of ink on the left cuff of Leni's sweater, probably from the old Pelikan fountain pen she carried in her purse. Down the hall, or downstairs, she was lying in a drawer while another version of her was taking shape—subtle distortions of attitude and fact that got worse at every turn. It seemed important, now, to take some measure of control.

"No," she said. "I've been getting the runaround the whole time I've been out here. The Chama police talk to our cops at home, but

Chief Arias won't tell me anything. That paper makes Leni sound
like a criminal, but no one knows who the source of their information could be. Now you're telling me the same thing. It's like
you're all being careful to protect each other's turf, and I'm an in-
convenience. Sorry. But I want to see her. Not tomorrow. Now."

"Miss Haring . . ." Her voice was lower. "Leigh, I want you to
listen to me. Your sister's body has been violated twice. First by
whoever killed her, then by us. She's been dead for four days. She
doesn't look the same now. You'll have to live all your life with the
memory of how you see her next. Believe me, it will be less upsetting if that happens in a place prepared for both of you. We could
arrange the transfer by this evening."

She pictured going with Alan. The dimly lit parlor. Men in black
suits hovering with stock condolences. Artificial satin bunting.
More decorum and disguise than she would be able to stand by
then.

She shook her head. "That's your opinion. I don't want it to be
dressed up. I want to see what happened to her. Just the way it is."

"Why?"

"Because it did happen. And that ought to be witnessed. I feel
like I need to comfort her."

Uncrossing her legs, the doctor stood up and walked around to
the desk. "This is against our policy. If I allow it, you'll have to
keep it to yourself. In a local case, I wouldn't, but I know you have
arrangements to make." She pressed a button on the phone. "Wes?
Would you prepare the remains of Elinor Haring to be viewed,
please? That's right. And be sure the doors to the autopsy suites are
closed."

She hung up. "You'll have to see her in the crypt area. It's close
quarters. We don't have viewings here because, without the right
facilities, it can be extremely upsetting to see a body like this. In a
murder case, people sometimes decide to go off and settle things
on their own. Are you very sure you want to do this?"

"Yes. Thank you." Her voice sounded tinny. But it would be
over soon.

"Then excuse me for a moment." The doctor went out down the
hall.

Getting a Kleenex from her purse, she blotted it along her forehead. In fact, she wasn't sure at all and it could be a bad idea. Some
wrinkle in her brain had started spitting out unwelcome information from a book or TV show. The elongated Y incision in the

torso. The hanging scale. The scalp peeled forward like a bathing cap.

She got up to look through the vertical window blinds. Another parking lot, but no people in sight. When she turned, the doctor was standing at the door. "We're ready now."

In the hall, a lingering hint of spiced meat passed into the sweetish smell of disinfectant. A left turn, and the carpeting changed to beige linoleum. A second windowless hall, leading into what must be the heart of the building. The doctor glided on, her hair a neat curve over the collar of her shirt. A sign said NO ONE BEYOND THIS POINT WITHOUT A VISITOR'S BADGE.

At what age, she wondered, had Alex Ford discovered her talent for dissection? In medical school, probably, after the first few bodies. Organs and orifices giving up their secrets more completely than living tissue could. Or younger, the one girl in class who didn't squirm over the frog in formaldehyde. A similar odor now, as the door opened to a room that was all shiny surfaces.

Beside the stacked metal drawers hung a blackboard with a chalked tic-tac-toe grid. Leni's name in the upper middle box. But instead of going there, the doctor turned toward a white-draped table a few steps around to the right. "I'll have to ask you not to touch."

A biting whiz, like a dentist's drill, started up somewhere behind them. Stopped and started again.

At the head, behind Leni's head, a window looked out on a dark loading dock where some kind of iron cage was visible. The white sheet came up to her chin, and it was hard to see her face at first because someone had rolled up another sheet and put it around her head in a crude turban.

She took a step and stopped with the buzz of the saw starting. That was what it was. Another step. No one was going to peel back the sheet. Leni's face but not her face. A color it was impossible to name, no color, but a kind of iridescence. Her cheeks sagged, distending the line of her mouth. Her lips were erased. Muddy crescents of grey showed at the rims of her eyelids. In the blackened scroll under her jaw, the bruise of a thumb angled toward her earlobe.

The remains. What was left. There was nothing left of Leni to comfort in her body. Leni had been evicted, she thought, and felt a tremble of laughter. A moment when the consciousness flew out and could look down. At its own corpse. Being strangled.

Beyond the table, the empty loading dock waited patiently. A refrigerator she hadn't noticed to the right of the window was marked NOT EXPLOSION PROOF. What was the need for that, she wondered. A warning. Not explosion proof. The scene she had always pictured of some time in the future when they would have finished bickering and could sit on a veranda at the Cape and talk like friends. The assumption being, she realized, that Dad would be dead by then. A spring giving way. Surprising. They hadn't competed much for his attention. Leni was usually off the screen somewhere. Would always be, now, had taken herself away completely.

No. It only felt deliberate.

She turned her eyes back to Leni's face. The thumbprint. The sludge of her eyes. He had made her helpless. Horrified. Crushing her windpipe and raping her. Or had that come afterward.

"Miss Haring."

The words had a descending pitch. A note of caution from someone who had seen this go on too long before.

The body on the table wasn't going anywhere except the Newton Center cemetery, in one form or another.

The last time. Time to make some vow. So many grade-B movies there was almost no other way to experience this.

Following Dr. Ford back through the maze of narrow hallways, she kept her fists in the pockets of the sweater. Some coarse sand left on one side, scraping her knuckles.

The light in the office was much brighter, and it seemed as if a long time had passed and this was a room left hours or days ago.

The doctor walked around the desk. "That's a hard thing to do. Are you all right?" She took an envelope from the blotter.

"Yes." No other answer was available, having forced this.

"Mrs. Avila's marked Stone and Douglas on the map. You can go any time after 6 p.m."

Putting the envelope in the pack, she folded her arms around it. An odd meeting, through the medium of Leni, biologic versus emotional intimacy. Autopsies meant abnormal deaths, a procession of distraught and hostile mothers of mangled teenagers, husbands of missing wives, sisters from Boston, all carrying personal histories. The same scene, everybody wanting to see the body now. Whenever the doctor relented, she probably regretted it. The boy and girl in the photo behind her must take a lot of energy.

"Miss Haring . . ." She picked up a fountain pen, rolling it between her thumb and forefinger. "I want you to know that everything is proceeding as it should. That's what you should tell your father. Do what you need to do for your sister now. We'll have the test results in a few days, and Chief Arias may decide some can be released to the family.'' She put down the pen and held out her hand, "You have my sympathy."

Outside, she stood on the concrete and scanned the parking lot. The Toyota was grey. She had driven in from the left.

Half the cars in the lot were grey subcompacts.

Flashes of Leni's face came as she walked up the row. That would happen too now. The doctor had a point. The high cost of having needed to prove something.

The funeral home would probably put lipstick on Leni. Her first real cosmetics consultation.

Blue-and-yellow Alamo stickers showed on two grey bumpers. Her jacket was in the first car. She got behind the wheel. Leni would go out on the loading dock now, to be pickled, crated and shipped. Maybe they'd get Redbird and the samples would match, or maybe it was some out-of-season hunter and no one would ever find out who.

Knowing about Redbird should come first, though. By process of elimination.

The laptop could have something to say that would give grounds for the search warrant. But Alan's plane was due in less than an hour.

She opened the computer on the passenger seat. A posthumous ventriloquism, Leni's voice talking while her body stayed quietly in the drawer. The optimism of the first entries was painful to hear—descriptions of her students, dinners with Vera and Michael Zinn. Redbird not in the picture.

She switched to the end again. The next to last date.

<December 12>
<Signs of mental softening. I just spent half an hour watching a huge beetle break into the bag of sugar. A new one, not in the cannister yet. Chewing through the paper was such hard work it must be a pregnant female. If there are any bugs that get pregnant. Even this knowledge eludes me now.
<It glanced up once or twice while masticating to reassess the situation, and was confirmed in its original diagnosis: anarchy reigns, foundations crumble, neurons fire at will. No effort will be made to keep the infrastructure from being dis-

mantled. The bag is out in the trash now, though, where the raccoons will dine on it if they also slip through the perimeter.

< Vera says they fired me because they can't fire her.

< It's black out tonight, raining through the roof again. Like Don Alejandro's shack in Guatemala, before he lit the twenty candles we were told to bring. Incense coming up from an altar with a picture of the virgin, little clay saints and stones and crystals he kept fingering, going from one to another while he hummed and prayed in Ixil. Sprinkling corn liquor all around. He told Viviana her brother would come back safely from the fighting and that time he was right.

< A Maya with the dangerous gift of prophecy. Ten years ago there were more than thirty shamans in those highlands. Now, Viviana says there are only ten left, and each one murdered is like burning a library in terms of the damage to the culture. 100 thousand civilians killed. The sacred caves and holy mountain of Juil bombed to rubble by the army. The shamans are specially targeted, though, in case they really can predict how the troops will move, and warn the guerillas.

< 500 years of it. The Spanish learned the language to find out who had that power and needed to be killed, to prove their magic was stronger than the shamans'.

< I was supposed to be helping there, too, piping water up the mountain, courtesy of the Hermanas stipend and Leigh's soldering lessons.

< Some of the Hopis were smarter. They knew what else the pipes brought and ripped them up and threw them off the mesas.

< 'A sickness of the heart,' I said to Maria Sabina. What fifth-grade textbook coughed that up. What Cortes said to the Moctezuma: a sickness that could only be cured by gold. A month after I left Oaxaca, Maria Sabina was arrested thanks to all the heartsick Anglos coming after the mushrooms. I wasn't the only kid who read that *Life* article. And a year before it was published, the CIA had already found her. Funded the expedition on which the article was based, and gone along in the person of one of their academic minions.

< The touch that withers. Before she died, Maria Sabina said the saint-children had lost their force.

< There has to be something left. Somewhere. It feels awfully close to the end now.

< The snake ground. 12 thousand years of snakes.
< Just to try to save what's left. In this case, a critical area.
< So the photographs. Blackmail may be in order. I'll tell
Dad if he won't do it, I'll spill his beans to Leigh.
< Might as well get some mileage out of that. >

What was left. The remains. Leni's guilt complex. Close to the
end of . . . snakes? And what photographs was she talking about?
Vera would know. Vera knew a lot more than she said.
Closing the computer, she turned the key in the ignition. An in-
heritance of a kind. Keeping the machine did seem to entail some
responsibility. It held all that was left of Leni now.
The doctor's other piece of advice. Do what you need to for your
sister. For Leni, that could mean more than just hauling her back
to Boston.
The funeral wouldn't be for another day at least. Time enough
to drive back to Chama and pay Vera a visit. Alan might not like
taking Leni home on his own, but given his work at the hospice, he
must be used to juggling caskets.
At the entrance to the parking lot, she stopped to let a white van
pass. It was out of sight before the insignia on the license plate
registered and she realized what it must be carrying.

Chapter 6

SEEING ALAN COME THROUGH Gate 5 was such a relief she wanted to crawl inside his leather jacket and stay glued to his warmth. At the airport hotel they got silly on room service tequila and the black humor he always had on tap. When she got up the nerve to tell him her plan though, he cooled off considerably. He said it was just more heroics that should be left to the police.

He kept saying no until the third margarita—more than she'd ever seen him drink. Then he read some of Leni's journal and agreed, with stipulations. From what Leni said about Vera, she didn't sound homicidal. But he also was struck by how quickly Leni's tone changed from her early days in Chama. The edginess that came in, of being on hostile ground.

Words and phrases came back now, as she drove north at dawn through the pueblos. And one passage that she found she knew after a single reading:

< When I came into class today, a man was sitting in back of the room. Native, about thirty-five, with sunglasses he never took off. He asked if he could sit in and I thought I better say yes. Not a board member, but probably sent by them to give me a bad report. We were doing cigarette ads and he had a pack in his pocket. Then he disappeared before I could get his name. >

Redbird. Ben Naya. That was in April.

Scooping ice out of the plastic bucket, Alan had said, 'When did she tell you she was dating this guy?'

It couldn't have been later than May. And her first instinct had been not to trust him.

Tierra Amarilla. Yellow Earth. The last town before Chama, where Chief Arias might be cruising around in his Bronco. Turning right on Route 64, she looked for a place to ask for directions to the college.

But the streets of the village were empty. A clarity of light on the red painted doors of a white garage. A second garage, sprayed with chains of the slogan Viva Tijerina. Ruined stucco buildings, their windows boarded up, but the sun gave a patina to the weathered surfaces it would be impossible to imitate in the studio. Materials that hadn't outlived the people who made use of them. A low abandoned ballroom with faded turquoise trim, then the shock of the Rio Arriba County Courthouse—its row of formal columns and the police cars parked in front. Turning quickly, she pulled up by the slant of Esquibel's cash store and found out it would be easy to avoid going through downtown Chama.

A left turn, by the gas station, and follow the sign for Dulce. The low white clouds were back again, flattening the landscape. She passed the sign and had to double back.

The school stood at the end of a long driveway bordered with aspens. From what Leni said about mining, she had expected tacky new construction, not this rather elegant mission-style building. A square bell tower was set apart up in the pines behind it.

A veranda ran along the front, and from the beam holes in the stucco it had once been shaded, a place to sit looking out across the valley.

A school without any students, it seemed. One other car was parked in the drive, but the door to the administration office was locked and no one came to answer the bell. Damp cold burrowed through her sweater. Snow, maybe, before long. A phone call from Albuquerque might have been a good idea, though it seemed early yet for Christmas break.

The bell tower. Where Michael Zinn lived. The troll with the synthesizer. A strip of driveway led around to a service entrance in back, then, steeply, toward the tower and the gleam of a blue van.

His name was under the doorbell. When finally a voice came through the speaker, the abrupt "Who is it?" was followed by "Haah?" As she started explaining again a buzzer rattled the doorknob.

The staircase curved out of sight. A scrape of a door opening at the top. He was silhouetted against the light and there was something odd in the outline apart from his long hair and thick woolen robe. An Ace bandage wound around one ankle. He stepped back, "Please, come in. I'm sorry I can't shake hands. Leni's sister. This is unbelievable."

Brown hair fell in tangled bangs over his eyebrows, giving the impression of a very intelligent animal peering out through some shrubbery. Across the room, a synthesizer the size of a piano fronted a picture window facing toward the mountains.

He pulled nervously at the robe. "Forgive my appearance. I'm what you might call a bathrobist these days. Sit down. Want some coffee?"

He padded toward the galley kitchen in his green foam slippers. Hospital slippers, she realized. Brown pill bottles were scattered over the counter as if resorted to in a frenzy. "Who'd do such a thing?" he said. "I can't get over it. This is the second one, too. Another teacher here got killed in a car accident last week."

Taking the mug he offered, she followed him to the couch. A slightly distorted body, swellings or bandages under the robe. As if he heard the thought, he said, "I'm the one who's supposed to be dead, you see? Not Leni. Well, I guess now we'll find out. If there's any afterlife, she'll be there too. But I don't think so. Excuse me, what did you come here for? Her office?"

It was like walking in on a nervous breakdown, she thought. "Not exactly. I'm looking for Vera Naya."

"Well, she's gone. Back to the reservation. There's a ceremony now. In a lot of places. That's why..." He brushed a hand toward the window. "Exeunt. What did you want to see her for?"

"Just to ask a couple of questions. Do you know her brother, Ben?"

"Know? Not very well. He used to screech around here on his motorcycle. I didn't think he was right for Leni, but that's my mother hen. Fussing. I don't like noise, you see?" His eyes stayed on her face with shy curiosity. "Vera says he's okay, though. Sometimes I make mistakes. Why am I still here, anyway? A New York Jew. Why don't I just go home."

He reminded her of a tin box full of marbles rolling in different directions. The resident recluse, Leni had called him, before they got to be friends. Alone here now, maybe not by choice. "If you're sick...it does seem kind of isolated."

"I know. Just give it up, hah? I can't even play anymore." He stuck out his right hand to show the swelling between his thumb and forefinger. "That's melanoma. It's terminal. But it's been going on for years. I get these things, sometimes get them cut out, but so far it hasn't hit any vital organ. Some Navajos I know did a ceremony for me. Not to cure it, maybe, but to pray I keep living in harmony, they say. Because once I'm gone, the creeps will take over here completely. Did Leni tell you? God, you don't look like her." His chest rose and he exhaled with a shudder.

"I don't think so. She mentioned you, though. That you own this place?"

He seemed pleased to hear it, but then shook his head. "Owned. Past tense. It used to be a hunting lodge. I invested in it, sight unseen, because my brother wanted to run it. He did. Straight into the ground. By the time I came out it was a relic. That was right after I got diagnosed, and it was so beautiful here I thought I'd camp out for a while." Prying himself up, he went back toward the kitchen. "Did she say anything about the Living Mesa Foundation?"

"No." Through the door opposite, she could see his bed. A knotted jumble of blankets.

"It sounds great, though, doesn't it?" Without asking, he refilled her cup. He wanted company now, it seemed, however embarrassing it might be to have a stranger see him like this.

"Yes. It sounds . . . ecological."

"See? That was my mistake too. I was trying to figure out what would happen to this place when I die, and the Living Mesa Foundation asked me about making it a school. For, like what you said, conservation studies, and all scholarship students. That sounded good to me. I knew some of their funding was from mining companies, but I thought it was conscience money. So I donated it in an irrevocable trust, with three conditions. I got to name the place, live here for the rest of my life, which was supposed to be about a year then, and I got a seat on the Board of Directors. Vera has one too. She clued me in that the Foundation's a straight conduit for the companies. But as long as I'm on the Board, we can keep the terms of her contract in force."

"But you couldn't keep Leni." She put the cup down, annoyed at the edge in her voice. It was pointless to blame Vera.

"No." He looked uncomfortable. "Vera's got the only five-year contract. Leni was sort of a function of her. The science faculty's white as snow, but for the humanities, she got to hire according to racial mix. Leni was for the ten percent white."

The token Anglo. Poor Leni, she thought. And fired anyway.

"See . . ." he said, "it's really about brainwashing these kids. They had a sign up, before Vera threatened to quit: Tradition Is the Enemy of Progress. She said the same one used to be in the Indian mission schools. It's like that friendship college in Moscow for foreign students? They get sent home to open the door when these guys come around. The leases are very long, so they can afford to be patient. If you're trained to be a miner, you're going to want to mine."

A ray of sun was moving toward his face, making his pale skin artificially rosy.

She nodded. "As opposed to not having a job."

"True. But it's like committing suicide. There are three thousand open uranium mines just abandoned around here. People dying of cancer from the tailings. Black lung from the coal mines. You must have read about it. So the companies take kids who already hate themselves from BIA boarding schools and give them a way to get rid of the part that hurts most. The mutilated part, Vera calls it. She explains this better than I can. But if tradition's the enemy, then you can feel good about selling it down the river."

She was starting to feel the resistance Leni usually brought out. An inability to take in one more problem, cause, or bad situation. There were just too many of them, pouring through the mail slot. If you thought about it all, you could go crazy.

He must have seen it in her face. With a small shrug, he got up and went to look out the window. His left hand picked out four notes on the synthesizer, the dirge she always thought of as Pray for the Dead. "You could try calling Vera. But there's no phone in her village. You have to leave a message and she calls you back. Sometimes it takes a day or so." Seven more notes. And the Dead Will Pray for You. "Would you like to see Leni's office?"

"Yes. I would. Can you get in?"

"I can get in anywhere. I used to sleep in a different room every night." He put a hand to the window. "It's cold."

Getting a blanket from the bedroom, he draped it over his shoulders and took a set of keys from the kitchen counter. At the door he said, "Wait a minute. She left something here. Maybe you want it."

"What?"

He went to rummage through the sheet music stacked on the table and came back with two bound reports. "U.S. Government Issue."

One, from the General Accounting Office, was titled SOUTH AFRICA: TRADE, INVESTMENT AND STRATEGIC MINERALS. The other, in a dark blue jacket, STRATEGIC MATERIALS: TECHNOLOGIES TO REDUCE U.S. IMPORT VULNERABILITY.

"How do you mean, she left them? For you to read?"

"No. By mistake. Or else not by mistake, but she didn't say anything. She came to visit me a few days ago and after she left, I found them over there. Do you want them?"

"I guess." They felt warm, from the sun or a radiator. "Unless . . . could they be from the library here?"

He shook his head. "Look in the front. I couldn't imagine where they came from at first. It's all about platinum and chromium and industrial diamonds, and whether we'll be able to get enough when the Soviet Union and South Africa fall apart."

Inside the cover of the GAO report was a pink slip of computer tractor-paper. A copy of Leni's order phoned in on December 1. Maybe for her final semester here she was planning to get revenge by teaching a course on the politics of mining.

Fitting them in the pack, she followed him down and through empty whitewashed halls, stopping to scan the bulletin boards announcing tests and activities. In spite of what he'd said, there was no sinister feel to the place. Not everyone wanted to spend their lives making jewelry, Indian or otherwise.

Michael seemed to be going along in a trance. A small, eccentric figure with bare white shins showing under the folds of the blanket. Having given up his kingdom, he must only come to visit now when the new people were gone. Wandering like a ghost. If Leni's ghost turned up too, they could haunt the place together.

Her office was at the end of the passage, a tiny room taken up by a grey metal desk, file cabinet, and visitor's chair. The single window looked out on a row of trash cans.

Not a high-status view. She walked around the desk. Above it hung a poster, one red geometric circle intersecting another, with the words LOVE CAREFULLY painted in an arc. The desk top held a dictionary and a cup for pens and pencils. No personal things, in the drawers she opened. A stubborn anonymity. In the wastebasket, some loose soil mixed with broken pottery and clumps of dying foliage.

Michael came to look. "Oh, her dish garden! It was really a beauty, too. One of her classes made it because she sponsored some field trips for them." He bent to shake the dirt off a few green leaves. "It was on the windowsill. The damn cops must have broken it. Do you think these are too far gone to save?"

A plaintive question. One he could be asking about himself. "If they've lasted this long, they must be pretty tough."

A cassette player stood on the file cabinet. She went to look at the tapes. Self-improvement programs. Quit smoking. Stop procrastinating, which must have been for the thesis. Subliminals were another of Leni's obsessions. Messages hidden under music and shadow images in ads. At UNM, the walls of her office had been covered with samples cut from magazines.

She held a tape up. "Practicing on herself."

"Yah," he smiled. "They didn't work. She didn't know why, because she thought the ads must or the liquor companies wouldn't keep using them. Then there was some new research that it's only the real creepy Freudian stuff that gets through. The biggest feel-good line was, Mommy and I are one. Do you believe it? On thousands of grown-ups this worked. They listened to Mommy and I are one and all their test scores went up. It makes my skin crawl."

Last night she had skipped the class notes in the journal. Would a Mommy message work if there weren't a mother to remember? Or could it have a negative effect.

"It's funny," he said. "Leni thought since she had proof now, they'd have to let her keep teaching those ads. But I guess it didn't help."

In fact, it probably hurt, she thought. Leni's relish at ferreting out the skulls and breasts drawn into the detail. Once, on the subway, they'd sat across from an ad for an obscure brand of Russian vodka showing the lower half of a young woman's body, in shorts, perched at the top of some stairs. A frosty glass of vodka tonic stood on the step below. Without saying a word, Leni stood up to trace the outline of the ice cubes—the shape of a phallus aimed at the model's crotch. It was so obvious, once seen, that a woman watching her gasped. And Leni smiled, as if she had just been thanked for the performance.

Michael pulled the blanket tighter. "Damn, it's cold in here. Those idiots. The pipes are going to freeze."

His shift in tone made her smile. "So? It sounds like you'd be happy for the place to shut down."

He went to feel the radiator. "This is on. No, it's the window."

It opened vertically, the sash didn't quite meet the frame. She pushed but it wouldn't catch and swung back further.

There was a dent in the metal, and a scrape on its finish. Pried open from outside. Not crudely, either. Forced by some tool that didn't crack the glass.

A streak on the windowsill. Like a heelmark. Where the broken planter had been. The sill was too deep for a passing nudge to have knocked it off.

It was the neatness of the job that was chilling. The careful tidying-up, so a glance into the room would see no damage.

Not a simple burglary, if the cassette player hadn't been taken.

Chief Arias wouldn't have missed the forced lock. Or have left the window open. So whoever did it must have come after the police, looking for something that would be likely to survive their investigation. Like government reports on minerals at a college that taught mining. But who would want those except somebody here who wouldn't have needed to break in.

Michael raised a hand to the lock. "No, there might be fingerprints. Let's go. I'm going to call the police."

The chief. Who might have other questions by now. But taking off with the reports could make him mad enough to have her stopped on the road. Arrested.

As they walked back, she asked if he'd wait to call, so she could look through the reports and leave. It was time to do his meditation, he said—the only thing that kept him sane—but he should have thought to tell the cops about those books before. He wasn't a good liar, and the janitor had probably seen her come in.

Upstairs, he went straight into the bedroom and shut the door. As if she had brought a new curse on him, another threat to his safety, and she wanted to argue the opposite was true, if the reports were the lure.

The thin one first. Strategic Materials 101. For the national defense stockpile, a list of ten groups had been certified by the state department as 'essential to the economy or defense of the United States.' The platinum group included names never mentioned in art school metalwork classes: ruthenium, osmium, palladium. They sounded like planets in a science fiction galaxy. She looked for paper to take notes, then remembered the computer. Keeping the pieces of the puzzle together made sense.

Moving the cursor to Create a Document, she had to give a title and typed: QUERY.

On to the fat blue report. A string of random facts:

<'In the last 25 years, the U.S. has had at least 4 major disruptions in the supply of materials critical to the economy, etc. Cobalt, for jet engine parts—10 million lbs. could be produced in 20 years if 4 sites in the U.S. were mined.... Manganese, as with chromium, virtually no exploitable domestic deposits. Platinum group—the U.S. has one of the world's most promising sites that has yet to be exploited.'>

Then there was criticism of the president for focusing on minerals available in federal lands, instead of on new research and development.

Four hundred pages of it. Too much to take in now. Leni had ordered them by phone, and they came in less than two weeks. GAO report NS IAD-88-228. The one from the Office of Technical Assessment wasn't on the order form. But maybe could be had by calling there.

She switched back to Leni's journal. If they were important, there ought to be some mention of the calls on that date.

< December 1 >
< Today, remember. >

Enigmatic, but promising. She kept her finger on the Page Down key.

< Ben left after breakfast to go back to the mesas. Half here and half somewhere else, like me. The bizarre sense I always have before I go home that I'll run into my double—a me who has a house with all the pictures framed, two sweet kids like Diana's and a husband with a day job. I can never get the face, though. A wad of Silly-Putty. Probably, he's having an affair and complaining to his girlfriend about how badly I entertain.

< Diana has a decent marriage. Why do I get this eraserhead? A failure of imagination. When I tell her I'm leaving here, she'll give me her speech about there being community colleges around Boston that need good teachers. And I will once again fail to explain that those are kids who want into the system, and I seem to want out of it, or something different, so I wouldn't be good for them.

< I think Diana likes having me out on the fringes. A vicarious life, to keep her from feeling too tame. When I hear from her, it's usually about the old days, some bit of flotsam that's resurfaced. Yesterday, a scrap of newspaper flew out of the envelope, almost into the fireplace. An obituary: Susan Martino, 42.

< At first I didn't know who it was. In Newton, we knew her as Susan Leary, daughter of Timothy of the same name. 15, like us, that summer we had the Leary house staked out.

Our old girl scout leader's house, and suddenly there were motorcycles in the driveway, jazz musicians, Allen Ginsberg, and the gossip of an academic neighborhood. Leary fired by Harvard on a technicality, but really for letting undergraduates in on his psilocybin experiments. Synthetic mushroom, of the kind Maria Sabina used.

< Earnest students of the Beats and whatever skinny joints we could get, we started our night patrols. Creeping up to the window as the sitar music went on to watch the ravishing doctor dispensing tablets. Then the show would start unfolding in the candlelight—pantomimes of ecstasy and terror. A woman in a caftan striking weird chords on the piano. Chanting. Hysterical laughter. More than we'd hoped for.

< Susan never appeared in these scenes; was safely up in bed, and when we saw her on the street she looked very uncool. A child. And now, like her mother, a suicide. Found hanging from a shoelace in her cell at a loony bin where she'd been for 17 months, judged mentally unfit to be tried for the attempted murder of her boyfriend. Shot while he was asleep. She leaves two children.

< I never saw her again after that summer. Dad got nervous enough to take me to New Mexico to see his balloon experiment (& the snake dance), and in the fall their house was empty.

< Then in '65, the big newspaper story: Tim and Susan busted for grass at the Mexican border. Glamorous, from a distance—the forces of light and dark squarely arrayed. By then we'd been given acid by an adept from the house and the universe had opened to us.

< Leary got a 30-year sentence, and went on the lam. Susan got 5 years, suspended.

< After that are numerous missing chapters.

< When Leary's autobiography came out in '83, it said Susan was a geriatric nurse, a member of the U.S. Army Reserve, a student of computer science and a true individualist. What would her version of their story be? Unless it's written down somewhere, I'll never find out now.

< Going back to his book tonight, to a photo of Susan at 18, curled barefoot on the floor, looking up in nervous adoration as he talked to their lawyers in Laredo. She had always been an obedient child, wanting approval, he writes, and she was never the same after their arrest. He says he was slow to

understand how deeply she had been hurt by what seemed to her so great a public disgrace.

< Not glamorous. What little morons we were.

< And his description of her at 13, in bed with rollers in her hair, asking what he'd like for Christmas at the precise moment he was seeing their relationship as two trillion-cell brain circuits colliding for an instant of eternal space/time, but forced into playing the father-daughter game.

< At first reading, his book was like a time warp back to the fun house. Now, looking for Susan, there's a striking lack of women throughout who aren't either models or heiresses. Always 29 and beautiful, while the men age gracefully. (29 seemed ancient to us then, of course. As far into the future as we could imagine.)

< Each chapter head is a bio note of some influential source, Socrates to William Burroughs, and of 41, only two are women: Margaret Fuller, 19th-century transcendentalist and revolutionary, who died at 40, shipwrecked off Fire Island; and Mary Pinchot Meyer, a painter who allegedly gave acid to JFK, mysteriously murdered at age 43 on the Georgetown canal towpath. Maria Sabina doesn't rate, but the banker who wrote about her in *Life* does. And Demeter, goddess of grain, is absent, though LSD is synthesized ergot—a grain fungus that was almost certainly the basis of *kykeon,* the visionary drink given to initiates of the Eleusian Mysteries sacred to Demeter. For 2 thousand years, the Mysteries were the heart of Greek religious life; the origin of the riddle of Plato's cave.

< Demeter, mother of Persephone who was raped and kidnapped by Hades, god of the underworld. To avenge her daughter, Demeter refused to let grain grow, until Persephone was returned to her for six months of the year. Then, in celebration of the life she had borne out of death, the gift of the ceremony: torchlight bathing in the September sea, a procession to the shrine, the secret rites. Set and setting, Leary would call it, the prescribed elements for a good trip.

< If there had been grass instead of hard drinking at Berkeley, he writes, his wife might not have killed herself over his affair.

< Car exhaust in the garage. Shoelace on the cell bar. Daughter following mother down, with no ritual to save her. A gun aimed at a man asleep. The pull of darkness.

< Looking back, we must have got the message there was
no growing space in that scene for us, and the sheer imbal-
ance makes me wonder if it could have come out differently.
If there had been some other women. If my mother had lived.
If the research hadn't been discredited. When it was banned,
there were a thousand clinical reports on file proving the value
of those drugs in treating addicts, career criminals, the men-
tally and terminally ill. As in fact they've been used for mil-
lennia.

< Diana says she kept Susan's obituary for three months,
knowing it would upset me. From the timing, I guess she
hopes by Christmas we can joke about it. But she doesn't
know about Ben's gun. The feel of it in my hand going off.
The way that sound divides the past and future. I can see Susan standing over that couch and want to roll the film back.
But to where? for either of us. >

Taking her finger off the Page Down key, Leigh touched Es-
cape. Then sat back, rubbing her eyes. The aqua type, and per-
ambulations . . . was Leni saying she'd shot someone?

Diana didn't know about the gun.

Michael didn't like secrets.

Which, again, left Vera.

No mention of the reports there and no conceivable connection
between them and Susan Leary. Still, a minor mystery was solved.
The reason Dad took Leni to New Mexico that summer. Fear, not
favoritism after all. He must have known she was sneaking around
the Leary house, hoping for free samples.

The rest of it was almost prescient. Leni naming her color-guard
of forty-year-old victims. Another short obituary, with drugs
lurking in the background.

Missing chapters.

That day Leni came to the studio at Christmas. Two years ago.
Her first time home since her blow-up with Dad. The tension ruined everything. In the old studio, the armchair was pushed up
against the window, so light came in around her face but her features were in shadow. The buffing wheel was on, to sand the edges
off some castings, and after a while they had given up trying to talk
over the noise and Leni lit a cigarette. A corkscrew of smoke un-
curling toward the ceiling. The sight of that had triggered some-

thing—contempt, almost, out of all proportion, and Leni must have felt it. After that she was even more guarded. It seemed ridiculous now. The dusty sunlight a wall between them. The scream of metal filing. What order was so urgent the wheel had to be on?

She looked at her watch. Half an hour gone.

Sliding the computer into the pack, she opened her purse to find the slip of paper Vera had given her. It was folded around Ed Harris' business card. He had offered to give directions.

Two phone numbers for Vera, one with a 602 area code, the same as for Ed's other shop in Sedona, Arizona.

Going to the kitchen wall phone, she used her credit card. A woman's voice answered, "Rare Earth."

When she asked for Ed, she heard "He's just left, but . . ." and the receiver hit the counter. A minute later he said, "Hello?"

"It's Leigh Haring. I'm glad I caught you."

"Well, so am I. We wanted to send flowers, but I didn't know where. How are you?"

"All right. I'm still here. Leni had to be embalmed and all. Could I ask you a couple of questions?"

"Shoot."

"How long would it take me to drive out to the Hopi reservation? It's in Arizona, right?"

"Yup. Right in the middle of the Navajo reservation. You aren't going after Bird?"

"No. His sister. It turns out she's the other woman in that photograph. I need to talk to her. I can't explain it all. I just want to know, can I do that and fly back to Boston tomorrow night?"

He gave a short laugh. "That depends on how fast you drive. Are you in Albuquerque?"

"Chama."

"Oh. How did it go up there?"

"All right. I met the police chief. I saw Leni's house. In fact, I stayed there. Now I'm at the college, which turns out to be closed. So I thought of driving out there."

"Well, it would be a push. It's too bad you don't have one more day. I'm going down to Sedona tonight. That's my real base. Let's see. You'll have to go back to Albuquerque and then, say, 200 miles west, on the interstate to Gallup, but then it gets tricky. Buy a map. If you step on it, you ought to be able to get there before the Cultural Center closes. That's the only place to stay right on the mesas. What's so urgent? Couldn't you come back after the funeral?"

A full day of driving. On four hours of sleep. "It's . . . crazy. I just feel like if I don't see her now, she'll disappear or something. She's the only one who really knew Leni here, and I can't call her. She doesn't have a phone."

"A lot of people don't there. But you ought to be able to find her."

"Here's a quiz question. Ever hear of osmium?"

"Boy. That's dim. It's either some kind of drug or some kind of ore?"

"It's a platinum group metal. Pretty rare, I think."

"Well, you ought to know. You're the metal expert."

"Did you know this was a mining school?"

"A sort of junior techie version. I was surprised Leni wanted to teach there."

"It's nicer than I thought it would be." The sound of his voice was steadying, somehow already familiar.

"Why do you ask about osmium?"

"I read something about it here. I never heard of it before."

"Thinking of working it into your line?"

She smiled. But there was too much to explain. "No, just curious."

"It's a different part of the planet here, you know? Like you don't have turquoise in New England."

"And you don't have lobster."

"Yah. I miss the ocean."

"There used to be one here, from what I read at Ghost Ranch."

"Not recently enough to help my backstroke. Here, I've got the number of the Cultural Center. You ought to make a reservation."

She wrote it down. "Thanks."

"No problem. So, good luck out there. If you need anything else, call me in Sedona."

"I will."

It was the number for Vera she tried first. A crackling on the line, like an electrical storm, then after a minute a barely audible ring.

A voice said, "Hello," with a slight break between the syllables. Its sex and age were unidentifiable.

"Hi. Vera Naya said I could leave a message for her there?"

"Uh huh."

She wanted to say, Do you have a pencil? "Okay?"

"Okay." A mimic, she thought. Be patient with these Anglos.

"Will you tell Vera that Leni's sister, Leigh, will be at the Cultural Center tonight? Kind of late. Would you please tell her I'd like to see her?"

"Okay."

"That's all. If she could get in touch with me."

"Okay." There was a click and then the howling static again.

It might have been smart to ask if Vera would get the message today, she thought. Or even to have it read back. The voice hadn't asked her to spell her name.

Glancing at the bedroom door, she picked up the credit card and punched in her code and the number in Brookline.

IV
HOPI LAND, ARIZONA
Chapter 7

FOR A MOMENT he knew he was in the cave. Then he closed his eyes again. He'd been dreaming of his mother and it happened so rarely he wanted to stay in the dream, in the trailer, and look for forgotten things, distortions that could tell the meaning of this or that detail.

But it seemed as plain as a memory. The clean, cracked, red linoleum and bolt of sun on the kitchen table, her hand with the bogus wedding ring taking down the peanut butter. Her voice asking, How was school today? Bright with booze, though she kept that hidden then. Still kept the linoleum clean. Mrs. Naya, green trailer, last row in the corner. When they moved to California, she legally changed their name, taking what his father couldn't give. It had caused a problem with the welfare checks, though. A social worker came, and he heard their voices through the open window. There's no man, she said, and that was true.

Julia Robbins Naya. In the '50's, she was a teacher at the Indian school at Keams Canyon. Then, making Hopis pahana was federal policy, though it didn't allow for agency staff contributing to the gene pool. To save her job, she briefly married a bachelor administrator. But their eyes were blue and nobody was fooled.

A thirty-year-old English teacher who learned enough Hopi to try small talk with the parents of her students, at a boarding school where for years they had been beaten for speaking Hopi. Stolen language, coming from the mouth of their latest savior. She considered herself an old maid then, and he wondered how his conception had occurred, since his father would only say, I didn't know your mother very well.

He already had a wife. Had children. Vera. Randall. Pahana names, for the convenience of pahana officials. In some throwback to his own years at Keams he had wanted that blonde teacher though. Not love. No real affair. And afterward, just one contact. A sick kid, taken to a Snake priest for prayers. Maybe the scandal of that had forced her to leave.

Hopi stories, in the trailer. Summer visits to the dances. It was probably a mistake for her to try to give him that much. Vera had grown up hearing about every time they set foot on the mesas. And Randall, a snake priest now, kept carefully out of reach so as not to be contaminated.

Only their common grandmother said everything must have a use. Taiowa, the Creator, didn't make mistakes. Even the pahanas who ate the earth were part of the pattern set out at the dawn of Tokpela, the First World. They were the test of this Fourth World and would end with it, and then the Hopi people would evolve into their Fifth World, and in time, two higher worlds beyond it.

He wanted to ask what would happen to a half-breed like himself. Maybe his head and shoulders would get wiped out with the pahanas, but there would still be two legs climbing around out here.

Racked again, in the middle of the day. Up here there was nothing to do but sit shivering, wrapped in blankets, or stand flattened against the rock face like a human petroglyph. Below, the ocean of desert rippled in streaks of color under the racing clouds. Looking out, he scanned the horizon for a glint with the buzz of an insect, a police helicopter coming from the south.

Tonight, if the other helicopter came down in the same spot, there ought to be time to get close enough for pictures.

Four o'clock. A wash of floating purple. Vera was late and she wouldn't use the light on her bike.

Zigzagging down from the elbow of highway through dried clumps of chamisa and creosote shrub, with her head bent forward.... No snake would dare take a shot at her. When she made up her mind about something—him, for instance—it became a point of honor. She hadn't wanted him around, but could see his problem and had to admit it wasn't his fault he had been born. There must be a way to put it together somehow. He could tell what she said was tangled with feelings about her own distance from the village, and that she'd never tell him what it cost her to make that trip. She helped him dry out and gave him to Leni. It was as close as she would come.

And no favor to Leni in her eyes.

Talking to Leni had been a way of explaining himself to Vera. A bridge that was gone now. Yesterday when Vera was crying, he'd been afraid to touch her, that she'd pull away and say things only drinking would let him forget. He wanted to put his arms around her, then thought it was Leni he wanted to hold, and either way it wasn't going to happen.

When he tried to think of Leni, a black hole opened up, burning away the image like acid on film.

It was easier to remember the women in L.A., who never asked to be seen as more than beautiful—more beautiful than the competition for the jobs they wanted. All he had to do was play Redbird, and keep the pockets of his vest full, and swallow whatever the evening called for.

Redbird. No last name. By the end, a quart of vodka and ten lines of coke were minimum working rations. It didn't get much in the way until the accident with the horse during the Disney filming at Cerrillos, when one of the extras mentioned the other Hopi she knew. Her old teacher at UNM. Professor Naya.

Vera might forget the Camels, and there was only a butt with an inch of tobacco left in the pack. Saved up, like in the old days in the alleys after the next one went out. Unreliable. No work. No coke, so more juice. Wishing he'd never heard her name. After his mother's funeral, when the trailer went up for sale, he had thrown out everything, even the painted bow the kachinas gave him when he was five. Then, for ten years, Redbird. Generic Indian on the resume. A lot of bad TV jobs, and lots of sex. It was easy for a long time. Sign-language, he called it, running a finger down the curve of an arm. Telling stories worked, too.

Using the old stories the way his mother did to get him into bed. See, the Hopi lived in three other worlds before this one. First, Tokpela. Endless Space, where people and animals could talk to each other like in the garden of Eden. Only this mockingbird, Mochni, and a big-headed snake started spreading lies and gossip around and pretty soon everyone was fighting. So a few good Hopi were sent down underground to live with the ant people, and the world was destroyed by fire. Volcanos going off all over the place.

Hopi songs had hand motions that went along with them and he told the stories with his own, touching, exploring the geography.... So, after a while things cooled off and they came out to the Second World called Topka. Dark Midnight. They couldn't talk to animals anymore, but they got pretty rich. Got greedy. The more they had, the more they wanted. Then the killing started again, so that world had to be destroyed too. By ice. But first, some good Hopis were sent down to the underworld to be safe.

The hand motions got more interesting, because in the Third World it was even worse. They lived in big cities but started having sex with the wrong people. Using their powers in the wrong way. They made flying shields, like planes, so they could go attack each other, and the wars got so bad the only way to save the ones who still sang songs to the Creator was to seal them up in some hollow reeds and destroy the rest by flood.

Here, depending on who he was with, he might say the reeds were maybe rafts from India or China, landing somewhere on the coast of Mexico. Or maybe it was a story about evolution. Or both. When they came out on this Fourth World, its guardian, Massau, told them before they could live together they had to make migrations to the four ends of the earth, to get rid of any evil left over from the Third World. So bands left in different directions, becoming clans when they took the name of a spirit-guide that appeared along the way. Bear, sun, snake, tobacco, corn, coyote, sand . . . the list went on and on. Following their own stars, they reached the Atlantic ocean, the Pacific, the frozen back door to the north and the tip of South America, then spun right or left, leaving spirals carved in stone to show the way they were going. Their trails across the continents and sudden turns made a cross like a swastika that was still painted on children's rattles. Each clan had its own story of the journey, its own secret ritual to add to the religion. Clan was the most important piece of identification, and since it came from the mother and he had no clan he made up answers to that question. I belong to one of the groups that didn't make it back. The weasel clan. We settled Hollywood.

Leni loved his act. She knew all the stories so it didn't work and that was a relief. Earlier things started coming up, like details in a dream, from good times in the trailer before the 'glass of water' started running things after school. He began to think his own drinking had been a way to keep the trailer sealed, intact. It was Leni who pointed out that, like his mother, she was a white teacher. Maybe that was the attraction. Not so good. But it was more just being able to talk again. Freedom, in that same way.

Leni more often than the AA meetings Vera wanted him to go to, where 'I've switched to pot' wasn't seen as a win. It worked though. Three tokes and into the darkroom to find out what was happening with the negatives. No tricks, because no training. It had to be there when he hit the shutter. Except for a few lucky accidents and one roll shot after a peyote night at Shiprock.

Leni and Chama, which he knew better than she did after four movie jobs at Mesa Verde. A cameraman turned him on to the owner of the gallery. Things were going so well that when Vera told him about the Huey, it felt like the last piece falling into place. If he could be useful, getting pictures of it fast, he might feel more welcome in the village.

There were real Hopis who knew more about photography than he did, but during Soyál they wouldn't be doing night shoots.

He didn't ask for permission he knew he wouldn't get. It was a way back to an older dream. Standing in a plaza on a mesa thirty years ago when the kachinas came out and he couldn't breathe or get his mouth shut while they danced by—fantastic spirits, animals, distant stars—feathers and skins and rattles shivering with their painted bodies.

Or sitting on a man's lap at night in front of a pick-up climbing the sheer wall of First Mesa, springs jouncing, a large hand tracing constellations through the windshield, then lifting him down into a room lit by coal fire where an old woman sat rolling strips of clay. He remembered the man's strong smell. It wasn't his father.

That could have been a hundred years ago. A thousand. While the clans were still winding their way back, offering some special power in return for the first real estate titles in North America.

Night pictures needed infrared film. Like satellites used before digital. Leni had gone with him to buy the film.

Four nights of freezing up here and he knew it all was gone. With her. All the day dreams. He left her and someone else came in. A thrashing in the dark that he could feel. Then it was over. Someone getting up and going out the door.

To come back where it started.

Now that he was a murderer, the pictures weren't going to make him any friends on the mesa, but they might show a face or uniform or serial number. Vera wanted to get the bastards too.

The middle of Soyál now. For four more nights it would be safe for the Huey and probably for him. When the ceremony ended, some villages would hold the traditional rabbit hunt, and for the tribal cops, he'd be on the menu.

Which left four days for some hunting of his own.

Crouching, he looked for dust from Vera's bike, then out to the buttes curved like horns in the distance that were supposed to transmit power from the universe. Hopi antenna, plugged into the magnetic navel of the earth. Last night the Huey landed in line with the tip of the one called Montezuma's Chair. Not more than five miles out, he hoped, glancing at Keith's bike pushed against the rock wall.

Reaching for the camera bag, he remembered the clerk's warning that infrared couldn't be processed in metal pans. Wherever the pick-up was, someone must have taken the new plastic ones in the back. They'd make good seed trays. Getting the film developed would be Vera's problem now.

The instructions said 'Load in Total Darkness,' which seemed to fit the circumstances. Pulling the blanket up into a tent, he tore the foil off a new roll of film. Infrared worked by heat, but it was slow and needed filters. There might not be enough IR to get an exposure, and how the Huey's red light would mix in was an even bigger guess. All those library books about optical systems... Load in Total Darkness was the only sense he could make in the charts of IR wavelengths and color sensitivity curves. He could hardly thread the film on the sprockets, his fingers were so cold.

The lens cap slipped off, and feeling for it in the bag he pulled back from a brush of something soft against his hand. Lifting the blanket, he saw what it was. The narrow white silk scarf Leni kept in that pocket for her hair when he'd pick her up on the Harley.

It still smelled of her hair. Her soap. Felt like her, touching his face.

A gust of wind and he almost lost it. He wound it around his hand. Then tied it to the strap of the camera bag to keep him company.

Fitting a red #25 filter on the lens, he looked out through the viewfinder. Dark on dark. The focus and metering were: Infinity, wide open, and see what you get.

He rolled the camera in his sweater to make a backpack.

Up on the rim of mesa, sandstone houses were melting back into the ledge the way they seemed to grow up out of it at dawn. Lights started coming on. Looking over here from the buttes, he thought, you could tell a lot from the different lights that shone in the villages. In Shungopavi, the faint white glow of gas lanterns. At Kykotsmovi, the tribal seat, electricity had won. Before, the People could have split and gone off in different directions, leaving another Anasazi ruin. But apart from a slow leak of talent, no one would be moving on from here. Except Randall's snakes, if a mining lease got signed.

Randall and his snake-brothers. He wrapped them around his body.

Randall, with his Master's degree, who said with a straight face, Money can't give birth to anything. Our religion is to help life. Not just people. Plants and animals, and even insects and minerals. If this land is ruined, the world might end.

The last time the tribal council signed away rights to dig up the snake ground, women sat down in front of the bulldozers until they went away. For someone on the council to call the snake dance devil-worship set off old alarms. Every Hopi knew that when Spider Woman created life, she first made twins and sent them to the poles of the earth, one with the gift of wind to keep the right spin on the gyroscope, the other to echo the Creator's voice in vibration along the axes. The ceremonies here at the center of the cross kept it all in balance, and even some Hopis with two VCRs didn't want to mess with the snake dance. Not when there was already less than ten inches of rain a year. Snakes lived in touch with the vibrations underground. They could help bring lightning, if that was how it worked, but whatever, it had worked pretty well for the last thousand years or two. When the dance was banned by pahanas, the rain stopped until some hidden ceremonies brought it back again. Everyone knew that. So there would have to be quite a reason to risk starting another uproar. Even a fat vein of gold wouldn't be enough. And that would have shown up years ago on pictures taken by Landsat.

Massau, the guardian, who was also the god of death, had given a prophecy: There were riches in the land that could be used 'someday.' The mining companies hadn't waited for a Hopi interpretation of that. A Persian Gulf of coal was being strip-mined out of Black Mesa, slurried away in water lines that were sucking the aquifers dry. Coal dust clouded the view of sun-watchers in the villages as they looked out to the notched buttes to set the right dates for planting and ceremonies.

It was sacrilege, they said. Those leases were signed before they knew the voraciousness of the pahanas; by trickery, when they could barely understand English. It was up to the religious leaders to decide what 'someday' meant, not Mormon lawyers, or Peabody Coal, or the U.S. Office of Surface Mining. Given land and birds, you don't destroy them. The ruined palaces left behind in the south showed what happened when money and so-called progress took over. Here, in the desert, the religion would survive because it was needed to bring life to the corn. All of life could be comprehended through the growth of corn, every act a planting, a growing, or a harvesting. The transformations of the seed were the most profound teachings, and as long as the people preserved the land and kept their knowledge, they would live long after the electric lines and oil pipes of the pahanas became empty and useless.

The old chiefs didn't watch a lot of TV. They'd been known to cut wires and pour cement into transformers. But they couldn't stop the airwaves—satellite dishes pulling in stations from Texas. Car batteries, in the oldest villages, running black-and-white sets. Game shows to grind corn by.

Randall, with his straight face, turned out to be one of the best clowns at the dances, slithering head first back down a ladder and break-dancing across the plaza, and he got the biggest laughs for his TV commercials—squinting over a wild bow-tie, banging old skillets together, 'Ladies and gentlemen, these pots will change the way you eat forever!'

Tonight Randall's mind would be clear as glass, aimed at the arc of Chööchökam. The Pleiades. The Harmonious Ones. Seven stars for seven universes. Eight thousand Hopi, praying on their sacred pile of rocks, surrounded by two hundred thousand Navajos and two hundred and fifty million pahanas. All of whom needed Soyál to be done just right to bring the sun back.

A last streak of red shot out across the valley, burning away on the floor, and a scrape of metal came from down the ledge. Vera, setting her bike brake. With smokes, if she had time to stop. Just getting away this late must be a problem.

Leaning out, he saw her cousin Taylor climbing up the rocks, the sleeves of a grey parka tied around his neck. Taylor, who had been grounded since his brother Keith took off without asking anyone.

He smiled at Taylor's heavy breathing and put out a hand to pull him up. "You'll never make the track team if you can't cut a three-mile bike ride."

"I'm not trying out." Shrugging into the parka, he worked a bottle of Pepsi out of the pocket and emptied half of it. He was wiry, tall for a Hopi, some Pima blood on his father's side. Another Indian boarding school romance.

"Isn't it kind of late for you to be here? I thought this month ghosts can get into your body after dark."

Taylor pulled a hand across his mouth. "Yah. Or ol' Massau, with his bloody rabbitskin face. As long as he doesn't snap my bike chain . . ." His shoulders heaved. "Vera had to go to the Cultural Center. She said to tell you Leni's sister's going to be there tonight. Maybe *she's* out to get *you.*"

Taking the bottle Taylor held out, he lifted it and found he couldn't swallow. Leigh. That was her name. That picture in Vogue, a little black-and-white shot in one corner of a layout on her jewelry. Sharp dark eyes and spiky hair, wearing earrings that looked like manhole covers. Yesterday, when he was wondering what must be going on in Boston, that picture of her came flying out of nowhere.

"Surprise." Taylor smiled.

"Did she say anything else?"

"Just that she'd come when it's light and tell us what's happening."

"You're staying?" He let some Pepsi fizz down his throat. Taylor knew how to keep secrets, but if the Huey came back, that would be one more person involved.

"Yah. I'm scared of ghosts. I brought some nails so we can hang a blanket and use the lantern." He fished for them in his pocket, and picked up a rock for a hammer. "But most people here, if they see a strange light at night, they're going to think it's Massau and not look. A plane used to come down with drugs out there. My grandfather thought it was him. When I told him, he says, 'That's just Massau in disguise. To get you to the underworld. Same thing.'"

Taylor laughed but kept his back turned, wedging nails into cracks in the sandstone. Taking possession before he could be evicted. Trying to get closer, but the person he wanted to know didn't exist anymore, if he ever had. The hip guy from L.A. Who was going in the opposite direction. Away from the candy store, toward what had turned out to be another mirage.

Lighting the rusted Coleman, he opened the bag of groceries on the bedroll. Camping out. With the blanket up, the cave could pass for the treehouse he'd dreamed of having once, when he was paying protection to the older kids to get back to the trailer. Trying not to hear their war-whoops about squaw-with-fire-water. Weeding out the longer words he knew, his mother's words, the ones that made him different. If a treehouse came with this mirage, might as well enjoy it. Maybe Leigh would come up too, and they could have a little party.

She must have found the gun at Leni's. And might have decided to use it. Vera would probably be glad to show her the way here.

In the picture, her arms were folded and against the dark sleeves her hands looked dangerous. A black bird with a sharp beak, wanting a piece of meat. For which she'd have to stand in line.

He took out the loaf of spongy bread. "We've got ham and cheese and peanut butter. And three Cokes. Are you sure your folks won't be worried about you?"

"Nah." Taylor popped a can with his thumb. "I told them my aunt asked me to do some stuff, so I'm staying over. She doesn't have a phone. My sister and her kids are home, so it's stacked-up anyway."

Like going home for Christmas. Soyál wasn't so different. A son redeeming the darkness of the world. All you had to do was change that to sun and forget about buying presents. There must be a crowd at the sandstone house where Vera and Randall grew up, on the tip of Second Mesa. Their mother's house, inherited from her mother, who had to choose which of her daughters would make the best mother for the family. Birthcords of ten generations were planted in a corner of the ceiling, over the spot where they had been born. Cotton strings with little feathers hung down. A white enamel basin sat on the wood table, and he could still feel the slats of the plank bench. When he went there, a cup of coffee was put in his hand so he could be studied carefully.

Next it would be Vera's house, and he teased her that he was going to move in too. But living full-time in the village might even be hard for her now. Being watched to see if she did things right. One day he'd watched her making piki bread in the shed over an open fire. The oiled cooking stone another heirloom. She dipped her hand in the blue batter and without missing a beat, smeared it across the hot stone in a Z. As the wafers came up, she turned them back in spools, and he saw a rhythm kick in. The Vera he knew disappeared. His palm began to burn, but she kept going until the bowl was empty and the tray was covered with blue cornmeal clouds tasting like smoke.

Taylor was whistling to himself, slapping a sandwich together. A yellow ridge of mustard glowed along his finger. Any excuse for sneaking out would make him happy. There wasn't much to do in the village at night—the other problem with the pipe dream. If you weren't fully into either the Hopi way or TV, it could get pretty boring. Still, having all that family around had to be better than this free-fall. Everything before the cabin was gone. Leni's house would belong to Leigh now.

He said, "I hope you're making that for me."

The sandwich stopped half way to Taylor's mouth. Silently, he gave it up and shook two more slices out of the plastic bag. His fingers were knobby at the knuckles, bones and joints growing faster than muscle, but he was good with his hands. His elbows rested on air-pump sneakers bought with money he got carving kachina dolls to sell to tourists outside the Cultural Center—wild ones that he made up, to thumb his nose at everyone. Those sneakers had probably made him some enemies at the high school. When you weren't supposed to want crass material things, seventeen must be a hard age.

"So," Taylor squinted, "do you think some of those big-time city cops will be coming here to get you? Like in *Billy Jack,* when they got him pinned down at the church?"

He was probably looking forward to that. A swat team and a pack of tracking dogs. "Maybe. I don't know if there's a warrant yet." Leigh could be the first to hear that. But wouldn't have come out to tell him.

"The cops here take their time about solving things," Taylor said. "You could still get away. Get the sister to take you. In the trunk of her car."

He'd thought of it, once the first shock was over. A roll of the Huey, then a quick fade to New York or San Francisco. But the Huey hadn't shown up till last night. Maybe it wasn't a bad idea to climb in the trunk of Leigh's car. Except that she'd probably turn him in faster than anyone else.

Taylor touched his pocket. "I've got some bucks for you. Keith sold your truck to some Navajo who's going to paint it and change the plates. I wish I had one. That's what I'm saving for. You can't buy it with corn, you know? And all I ever hear is I'm not a good Hopi cause I don't want to work my mother's fields all the time."

"So what do you want to do. Be a carver?"

"You sound like the guidance counselor." His triangular face was tight with effort not to show what was going on behind it. "I don't know. Maybe a musician. Metal, not that reggae shit they have at the Civic Center." He pulled a set of phones out of the collar of his shirt. "I just got the new Flayer tape."

The cord caught on a silver chain that had a ram's head pendant. It figured the one kid here who'd follow him up the rocks would be hoping to find the devil. He reached over to untangle it. "Is that for real?"

"Sure. Maybe. 666. The goat. Why not?" Dropping it back under his shirt, he smiled angrily. "Even when I was a little kid at the mission school, the teachers said I was bad. What am I supposed to do? Stay in and listen to the same old stories, about how when the ears of corn got passed out, other people took nice fat ones to have an easy life, but the stupid Hopi took the short little blue ear so we could starve all the time? For what? To save the world for the pahanas? Let them take their butts out to the outhouse tonight and see how much they like it. Maybe I'm not a good Hopi, but I'm sure not Christian after what they did to us. They've got the Bible? So this is like the opposite. If they're the sheep then we're the goats."

He sounded about half convinced. But that Taylor and Vera and Randall came from the same clan showed a lot of variety. How did Taylor picture Satan, he wondered. For Vera and Randall, he'd probably look like a pahana bureaucrat.

For himself, maybe four lines of white powder on the glass top of a certain table.

No. After that. The last week in L.A. Filling a syringe with rum and shooting up with three other strung-out alley rats. The scare that gave him had got him on the train, though, as far as Gallup, where it started over.

Taylor stretched his legs out, sneakers pressing the rear tire of the bike. "I wish I was born in the old days, man. Things used to be heavy around here. The Ya-yas could change themselves into animals. They had all kinds of powers. The two-hearts. Maybe there's still a few left. Witches. Did you ever hear about that?"

A quick pass at forbidden material. "Maybe a little something."

"Right. That's why I think Randall's the coolest person out here. He's got some of that old-time power."

"But he's a priest. Isn't that the opposite of a witch? Unless you think the snake dance is devil-worship too." He tried not to smile. In Taylor he had finally found someone more confused than he was.

"Get serious. That's ours. I'm glad the pahanas can't see it anymore." With a start, he pointed. "What's that?"

"What?"

"That white . . . a paho?"

The ends of Leni's scarf were floating in the draft coming under the blanket. They looked a little bit like feathers on a prayer stick.

He pulled the camera bag over. "No paho. Just a ribbon."

Taylor touched the silk with the tip of his finger. "It looked like . . . the one for a person who died. That you plant four days after. You know?"

Vera had said something about the fourth day too. When Leni's spirit would go free into a new life. This was it. So maybe her non-Hopi should have a non-ceremony for her.

"Then maybe I'll plant this. Come on, we should go out anyway." He turned the lantern down to a thread.

Standing up, Taylor folded back the blanket.

Moonlight fell over the rocky ledge in a path down to the valley. The clouds were gone, and the long wheel of the Milky Way ran across the sky. In the thin air, the stars were bright as fireworks. Chööchökam, the Pleiades, climbing in the east, and below it, the tipped line of Orion's belt, whose Hopi name he couldn't remember. When it reached the right position, the Soyál priests could tell the minute of the solstice.

Everything had to be read then. An end and a beginning.

Bending, he untied the scarf. Pahos asked for blessings and the way they were trimmed was another language he couldn't read. Randall said feathers were for the breath of the soul—the spirit living within the prayer.

They were supposed to be planted at a shrine.

The spring was the only feature here. Just one of a hundred trickles seeping down through the sandstone from Black Mesa. But water was always holy. Knotting the scarf around a spool rod from the case, he started down the ledge.

"Wait," Taylor said. "I have to think of something. You aren't supposed to dig in the ground now. But if someone dies . . . I don't know which comes first."

In Kayaamuya, the month of the quiet moon, the whole earth was supposed to be sacred—which was why Vera had chosen this place as a camp for him last year. The spring came out of sheer rock, so there weren't even pocket gardens below that his sick mind could harm. Any killing or destruction or bad thinking could disturb the coming of new life underground.

It was a luxury only Hopis could afford, he thought. That much peace and quiet. A crystal of water, and a seed case cracks, touched by prayers that were more than a wish, Randall said, but a force of collective will. 'Comes true, being hoped for.'

"Go ahead." Taylor showed a flash of white teeth. "Just stick it in the rocks. But remember, your thoughts have to be right."

Then it might not count, he thought, going to the end of the ledge. I'm not sure I want her soul to leave. Whose prayer is this anyway?

He reached to push the stick into a crevice a few inches above the spring. The most he could come up with was that she would like it, however it was done.

It felt as if Randall had somehow tricked him into doing this. Let go, because you have to. As a prayer, for which your thoughts have to be right, because holding hatred or anger will only make you sick again.

But anger had its uses too. Even up here. If the Hopis hadn't always been so evasive, they might be a lot better off.

He stepped down, and could see the white silk fluttering against the rock.

"All the time I was at boarding school I forgot how to do things," Taylor said. "I mean, we'd come home in the summer, but if you didn't know, people make fun. The clowns used to tease me. After a while, I gave up. Randall's the only one of those real traditional guys who doesn't blow me off. Most of them, if you don't go all their way, forget it. They want it to be like it was a hundred years ago."

"Isn't that what he wants too? You could have fooled me." Sitting down, he reached back for a Coke. Taylor stuck out his hand, and he passed it to him.

"Yah, but...he's strict, and all, but he doesn't...blow you off. It's like he's giving you time to come around."

"To wanting things the old way."

"Mmmm." He drummed his fingers on the can. "But, see, a lot of kids my age don't remember that. My village . . . it's still sort of like it used to be. When I went to boarding school, it was like two different things. Home and Phoenix. Now we're all at the school here, and that's supposed to be so great, but it makes it harder, too. The differences. Like, my village won't send anyone to sit on the tribal council, but the council has most of the power now."

"Except for Randall."

"No." Taylor glanced at him. "A lot of the priests do. But they're over here, and the council's over there . . . and it's like you have to choose. Some of the guys on the council are big guys in the religious societies too, but it's still two different sides. That's why I won't give in. To either one.''

Then you'll probably spend your life trying to stick them together, he thought. The Creator and the government. It was a good way to go nuts. With the help of a lot of vodka, it had driven his mother zooey. She wasn't a missionary, but the BIA schools had been started and staffed by them, and she had been part of it, the light that was being brought to savages. Trying to mend it, in the trailer, she read to him from the Bible to show how many parallels there were. 'And the earth was without form, and void . . .' from Genesis. Like Tokpela. Endless Space. The big-headed snake spreading gossip was the serpent in the garden of Eden, and the Third World being destroyed by flood could be the same as Noah's Ark. Massau had been guardian of the Third World, before he lost his humility and Taiowa made him god of the underworld, like Satan being a fallen angel. And while it was true that Spanish priests had enslaved the Hopi, torching with turpentine those found practicing their heathen rituals in secret, the men who did such things couldn't have been real Christians. Never mind that every street, town, and river in the southwest was named after one of them.

The snake dance didn't quite fit that picture, either. In Genesis, the serpent meant the fall of man, a splitting-off from nature that made as much sense to Hopis as the idea that babies were born in sin. For Randall, the snake dance showed the unity of all life. Not magic, black or otherwise, but a working of the web pahanas had forgotten how to see.

Taylor nudged his arm. ''So, do you think the council's sending the Huey? Or the BIA? Or what.''

He shrugged.

''What's it looking for? Uranium?''

''They surveyed for that a long time ago.''

''I read our Chairman said since the Iraq war, there's been all kinds of pressure to find more oil and gas. And where there's coal, there's gas. And we have lots of coal.''

''Mostly up north, though, right? I guess Vera didn't give you any smokes for me.''

''No way. Those things will kill you, man.'' He showed his teeth again. ''I've got weed, though. Want some?''

''I'm supposed to be the bad influence here.'' To keep from being tempted, he took out the folded Camel pack. ''I'm hoping we'll

have work to do. You want to ride in the dark when you're
stoned?''

"It isn't so dark. But an old guy like you, I guess you'd break
your bones.''

"Maybe. But you'll never get that truck if you spend all your
change on dope.'' It was about all he could say without being a liar.

"Just weed, man. To watch the sun go down. I could get coke
if I wanted. I can't buy a CD player, or people will get bent out of
shape, but coke's real easy to hide.''

"Great. Be an addict.'' He looked down at the Camel pack. Not
smoking the butt would mean he'd have it later. Putting it back in
his pocket, he took another look at Taylor. If there was much coke
around now, Randall might as well hang up his snakes. It took a
while for trends to catch up here. Maybe, a five-year lag. That
hadn't been a good time in L.A.

It might sound good to Taylor though. Heavy metal. The reverse of his own fix—that growing up here would have kept him
from spinning out so far. Vera said even Randall had been pretty
wild for a while at the school in Phoenix. A safe distance from the
village. That didn't seem to exist anymore. If there wasn't a place
for the Taylors coming along, someone else would make one.
Somebody always was waiting to pick up the pieces.

"Look.'' Taylor's hand touched his arm. "Over there.'' He
pointed straight out. A pink star drifted in the space between the
horned buttes. "Is that it?''

"Could be.''

"What happens when it lands?''

"That depends on what equipment they've got.'' Rolling the
camera tighter in the sweater, he knotted it around his waist. "The
first time, it was boom antennas on the fuselage and a dish on the
belly. Not state of the art, but I think what they're using now is.
Remember in the Iraq war, in the pictures of the bombing, they
kept talking about infrared damage assessment?''

"From satellites. Yah. It didn't work half the time.''

"That's because the sensors can't see through smoke or fog. But
they can in the dark, and through the ground. So, last night these
guys had a bank of screens on the console, and they were walking
around with a little hand-held job that looks like a TV. I'm pretty
sure it's from what they call an AIS—airborne imaging spectrom-
eter. If you get a picture showing the right kind of radiation, you
can use that to check it out. It takes readings in different wavelengths, and puts them together in a graph. Each wave comes out

a different color, so it makes like a signature of what the deposit is. Then the computer matches that to all the graphs it has stored and you can ID exactly what you're looking at. Like blue and yellow and red all go with gold."

"Huh. Cool."

"Sure." He stood up to wheel out Keith's bike. "Unless you're sitting on something you don't know is there, and someone else finds out about it first. Come on. Let's see how fast you really are."

Taylor kept far ahead of him all the way down the trail, shifting his own bike from one arm to the other, then rode out in the moonlight pumping hard. His route made a map of obstacles to avoid, veering into the shadows when the sound of the rotors came.

A shaft of red light searched the desert, dropped, and disappeared behind a shelf of rock.

Creaking to a stop, Taylor swung off and bent double. "Wait, I've got a cramp."

"If we leave the bikes here..." he gulped the icy air, "can we find them again?"

"I've got a maglight in my pocket." He looked back toward the mesa, sighting along his arm. "I know where we are. Don't worry. But you'll never make the team if you sound like that from one little bike ride."

It felt good to be moving again, though, after sitting so long in the cold. He kept his hands in his pockets as they picked their way across drainage gullies and through the frozen bunch grass. A reddish glow came from beyond the ridge, so dim it could have been a ghost. A spirit. Massau checking up on his buried treasure.

Climbing the loose shale, they had to go in a crouch to keep from making noise. By the time they got to the rim, his hands and knees hurt. He heard Taylor whisper "Cowabunga," and caught up to lie flat beside him.

The red light made the view like a scene on Mars.

The big Huey's bay stood open. Thirty feet to the right, two men were working on a platform with some kind of drill rig.

He'd wondered how they could operate in such bad light. This time they had helmets with heavy goggles attached. More infrared sensing. Military night-sighting gear, diagramed in the same book that described the AIS.

Plain coveralls and no stencils on the Huey. An automatic rifle with a curved clip rested against the side of the platform.

The optics for the goggles might not be classified anymore. But having those and the AIS meant either the feds or serious private money. Not some moonlighting geology professor hired by the next village.

Every time it landed, the technology got better. As the readings got more precise.

The drill on the platform had a thinner bore than any he'd seen on an oil rig. From behind it, a third man came out, aiming the handheld scope. He walked in a straight line out of sight. Then his voice came back. "The ratios are looking good. Let's go."

Recoiling from the sudden high-pitched whine, Taylor sent an avalanche of pebbles scattering down the slope.

No one looked up. They were opening the bore to get the sample out. Not oil. Something solid they could pass from hand to hand.

He remembered he was supposed to be shooting and reached back for the camera. "I'm going to use you for a tripod. Hold still."

Propping it on Taylor's shoulder, he squinted through the viewfinder. The Huey and half of the platform showed. Which proved exactly nothing, he realized. This was when you should stick a newspaper in the picture, for the date. And some familiar landmark. Desert could be desert anywhere.

"I can't get in enough of the butte to show where we are."

The men in goggles were rolling the platform further off into the dark.

"Hotomkam." Taylor snapped his fingers. "That'll be enough for the Soyál priests."

Hotomkam. He smiled. Orion's Belt. With even an edge of the butte for reference, the priests could read the day and time.

The platform kept moving out of the frame. He made three quick shots. Another burst from the drill. Both times it ended in a squeal, as if the bore hit something so hard it made the metal shudder. Given how fast it worked, they could have taken half a dozen samples. Working along whatever profile was showing up on their screens.

Two of the men began shutting the rig down. The third picked up the rifle and went to scuff over the holes.

A job the wind would finish by morning.

When the platform had been loaded into the cargo bay, the ramp slid back and the door closed with a hiss.

A beating of air came with the rotors starting, and the Huey took off. A red light, going south toward Flagstaff.

Taylor was on his feet. "Could you see what they got?"

"I saw a shine of something. It could have been a wristwatch."

His eyes were still adjusting, but Taylor started down. "Come on." He stopped and held out his flashlight. "Use this."

For its size, it had a strong beam, but he could feel Taylor holding back to give him time. Respect for the old guy. At the bottom, Taylor walked straight out for several yards. Then crouched, putting down a hand.

He must have been keeping track of where they'd drilled. The flashlight showed a tire tread there.

"Nice going." The light followed Taylor's hand. His fingers traced a circle, the mark of the bore, gently brushing through the sand and gravel. Kayaamuya. He seemed to be apologizing for the injury, patting away the scars.

"Here." He picked up a shard that looked like bottle glass. One side was curved where the bore had cut. A ridge ran down the other.

Handing it up, he kept feeling along. "Here's another one."

A splinter the same size, across from the first. Both sheared off by something on the drill case.

"Let's try over there," Taylor said. "If there are more holes, I'll find them tomorrow."

He came up with a second pair of shards, about the same width but shorter.

The light shone through them. Clear as glass. But not glass. Maybe silica, from fused sand. You could find it on any beach. Sand was what the bulldozers had wanted here the last time. For road work. It was only snakes who had a better use for the stuff.

He ran his thumb over the stone. The edges were smooth, as if the heat of the bit had melted them.

Taylor held one silvery dart up to the moon. "It might be rock crystal. My grand uncle uses them, and he comes somewhere out here to find them."

"Uses them for what?"

"When people are sick. Sometimes he can see what's wrong with them with these."

"Oh." So maybe some crazed new age doctors were looking for an alternative to X-rays. But it didn't seem likely. He wondered if the priest who healed him thirty years ago came shopping for his instruments here too.

Leni's list of strategic materials. Vanadium. Rutile slag, bearing titanium. There was only one he could picture. "What if it's a diamond vein. Or pipe, or whatever. Even some industrial kinds are worth a bundle.''

"Then I guess the snakes are rich."

"We better get them an agent."

Taylor laughed. "They don't like publicity. Last time, the council said if the Snake priests would show where their holy places are, they wouldn't be disturbed. But that's secret. Randall won't tell anyone. He said if they did, by spring there'd be a Coke machine here for the tourists.''

It was a perfect Hopi catch-22, he thought. If the council didn't know where the shrines were, how could they protect them? But to tell would destroy them too.

Vera called the council a pahana puppet, foisted on the tribes to undercut the old leaders and make it easier for the White Father to work his will. But even she couldn't envy the position the council was in now. The White Father had grown any number of heads that couldn't be ignored. And Hopis ran from Mormon converts who thought mining was the will of God, to Two Horn priests who saw the white invasion as signaling the 'end days' in prophecy. Then true Hopis had to live more carefully than ever, so the Fifth World could come from seeds of the Fourth.

The end would start with a war in one of the countries that first had the light. A spiritual war with material matters. Islamic oil could fit. Or maybe this.

"That was a joke," Taylor said. "The Coke machine. Do you really think it's diamonds?"

"More like quartz, the way they sawed into it. Why don't you ask your uncle?" How else they could find out soon, he wasn't sure.

"Look." Touching his shoulder, Taylor pointed to a star above a streak of grey on the horizon. "I have to get the bike back for Vera."

Taláwsohu. The morning star.

Turning off the flashlight, he followed Taylor back along the wash.

When he left him at the foot of the mesa, it was almost dawn. He fought the bike up the rocky slope, tracking the white scarf with his eyes. His paho. The first one he'd seen had been colored for the lights of dawn. Cotton thread wound around the stick for the mystery of creation. Dusky purple first, when man was just an outline coming into being. Taylor, on his bike, starting to throw a shadow as he pedaled back along the arroyo.

Then yellow. For pollen. The breath of life. Climbing toward the cave, he could see it turning the sandstone a tawny gold.

Gold was the mineral of the First World. Silver of the Second, and copper of the Third. For this World, it was sikyápala, mixed mineral. Whatever that was.

Wrapping up in the blanket, he took out the shards. They didn't look mixed. They didn't look like anything to kill for.

Vera must know what sikyápala was. Taylor too, though he might not volunteer it. He was one of the few kids still fluent in Hopi, so he could get away with his pumps in the village.

Taylor's great-grandfather had been one of the Hopis sent to hard labor at Alcatraz for fighting the pahana schools. He wouldn't have any trouble seeing past Taylor's pumps. It was attitude that counted.

Unfolding the Camel pack, he took out the half cigarette and replaced it with the shards.

Leni's sister being at the Cultural Center might keep Vera from coming. Leigh. Who could have been followed here to the center of the universe.

Taylor was right about his old bones. They felt as tired as the Camel. Why not stay here and dry up like a mummy, and then in a few years someone could scatter broken pottery around and charge admission. Cliff Dweller. Late Migration.

Lighting the butt, he saw the white smoke give shape to the cloud of his breath as Tálawva, the red light of sunrise, angled across the valley.

Chapter 8

AFTER WINDOW ROCK it was dark. The cruise control was broken and Leigh had to keep her foot down on the gas. An overhead light coming every few miles, and suddenly the ghost of a face in the side window disappearing when she turned to look. Like the Twilight Zone with the man in a plane and someone outside trying to get in.

Scared by a shadow. A lizard, then a rabbit darted out of the glare of the headlights. Wildlife no doubt mentioned in the southwest travel guide she had picked up at the gas station in Albuquerque. 'Today's Hopi are the direct descendents of the so-called Anasazi—a Navajo word roughly meaning ancient enemy.'

Snatches read along the way. 'From the southern rim of Black Mesa, the three Hopi mesas reach like fingers into a multicolored desert . . .' Then, she was driving north on Route 66 in Gallup, the old part of town with all the bars. 'Apart from the odd defunct appliance stored outdoors to preserve tight living space, the older Hopi villages seem little changed by time. A few by choice are still without electricity and running water . . .' That was at a stoplight by an enormous plastic bull grazing along some blood-red dunes on the Navajo reservation. She realized how badly she wanted a shower.

Oncoming traffic flashed to low beams with a speed she tried to match. A sign for Keams Canyon. On Hopi land now. The guidebook announced a dramatic shift from red to yellow earth. She could make out a headland. The road began to climb. Twenty miles of nothing and then the first village at the foot of the mesa. Polacca. Scattered cement block houses with TVs on inside. Dinnertime. The restaurant at the Cultural Center closed early.

On the steep curve up Second Mesa, high beams of a Jeep came down, and in the white light before it passed, a rabbit arced from across the road into the path of her car. Seemed frozen in midair so every detail could register. Then the thud, felt more than heard.

A brown rabbit. Small. Confused by the cross-beams. Jumping the wrong way. It must happen a lot here. A glimpse and then a thud. There was no room to maneuver. Swerving would have meant crashing into rock or going off the cliff.

The damn Jeep. But her lights were on high, too. She turned them down. The other driver hadn't signaled. Taken by surprise, both of them. All three. The rabbit had to have been killed. And if it were still alive, what could she do? Except get hit by a car herself.

There might be some kind of law about it. Further on in the travel guide. After no taking pictures and no alcohol. No murdering rabbits.

Leni had sent a recipe once, from a book called Hopi Cookery. The first ingredient was one fresh-killed prairie dog per person.

Maybe rabbit would be on the menu too.

Ahead, a scattering of houses that looked very old. A few signs for galleries. Shungopavi. Described as one of the most traditional villages.

A glow coming up on the right. The Cultural Center parking lot. She pulled in by a smooth white wall. Pueblo-style, the book said. Climbing out, she took a deep breath, turning away from the building, from the tight perimeter caught by the headlights to a universe of stars.

Stars in all directions. The mesa, thrust up in their midst, fell away across the road. Far below it there were stars, and out to the horizon, and overhead they ran in clouds of light. The few she could pick out—the Dippers, Orion—looked smaller among so many others that were invisible in Boston.

Starlight seemed fragile in the city. Driven off by the neon. This was nearly frightening. The rabbit. Fat chance it had, or she would have out here without the rental car, the room held for one night by credit card. Magic numbers on plastic.

Inside, the clerk behind the desk reminded her of the Hmong women who worked at the studio. A precise reticence, taking the credit card impression, then pointing toward the restaurant. "I think you're just in time."

There was no message from Vera.

The booths that lined the dining room were upholstered in blue and purple. About half the tables were full and most of the diners were Indian. Peaceful and industrious ones, according to the guide, but no one looked delighted to see another out-of-season tourist. Calling home from Chama, she had lied, saying there was paperwork that would keep her one more day. It might have been smart to leave a different message on Alan's machine.

One side of the menu offered Hopi specialties. No prairie dog. Hitting the rabbit made hamburger out of the question. The salad bar. But that would mean walking across the room. Making choices. It was too late now to put on sunglasses.

She ordered blue cornmeal pancakes from a young waitress wearing native dress—a black tunic, off one shoulder, with the modern addition of a tailored red shirt underneath.

Taking out Leni's computer didn't seem like a great idea either. She resorted to the guide again. It would show a desire to learn. 'Village names describe their natural settings. Oraibi means place of the oray rock. Shungopavi, water place where reeds grow. When Columbus landed in the new world, Oraibi had been the spiritual center of Hopi land for 500 years...''

There was no reason to feel uncomfortable. Maybe Vera was already here, somewhere, waiting for her.

The pancakes descended. Purple, as big as the plate they sat on, fragrant with maple syrup. She ate quickly, keeping her head down. '...a land known to the Hopi as Tuwanasavi, the center of the universe. Several of the twelve villages still refuse to recognize the tribal council mandated by the U.S. government, and function as ever under the authority of hereditary chiefs, or Kikmongwis.'

Those must be the villages that didn't want phones. One of which would be Vera's.

At the desk, no message had come. She walked along an inner courtyard to number 17.

Its peach furnishings and the shower looked brand new. If Vera didn't show up, it wouldn't be so bad to scrape the mud off and have a good night's sleep.

The cable TV got three channels clearly—an evangelist, a rerun of Barney Miller, and a country and western festival. Turning down the banjo music, she shook Leni's pack out on the bed. After the computer and tangled clothes came the wad of papers that had been in the monkey box under the gun.

The gun under the ashes. Unless Chief Arias had it now.

But here was the old blue paper wallet where Leni kept the album photographs. The three of them, and then the baby with one tuft of black hair. Sort of how it looked now.

Putting that aside, she opened the first brown envelope.

The deed to Leni's house in her monkey safety deposit box. Then her passport, with squinty photograph. An inoculation certificate. Insurance for her car. Most of these would need some attention. It was lucky they had turned up at all.

A strip of film negative in the next envelope. She held it up to the bedside lamp. Leni, in the middle shots, in black and white, so he would have taken it, and given what it showed, she must have taken it back. Cheesecake. But in these she looked the way dead people did in the movies. A peaceful expression, eyelids shut, her bare breasts soft above the crumpled blanket.

What had been expected at the morgue. Not muddy eyes and that sheen of decay. In the negative, her hair and lips were light and her face dark, like a fetish. She was lying on some kind of rug with a stetson hat by her shoulder, and there might be a hint of a smile.

Printed, it would probably be a good picture. Smooth skin and wild hair, with lots of interesting greys. Whoever killed her might have seen her like this in the moonlight just before she opened her eyes.

A picture taken while she was sleeping. If the cops had found it, the *Globe* would have pornography to add to drugs and guns.

She put it in the inside pocket of her purse.

The envelope underneath showed a return address for Diana Clausen, from when Diana lived on Beacon Street before she moved to Belmont. Postmarked December 10, 1987.

A xerox of a *Boston Herald* article, with Diana's scrawl in blue ink around the margin:

Len—

This is a reprint from the *Times*. There was nothing in the *Globe* file—it's from before they went computer. But I'll try the library—and get that book, of course. Meantime, hope this helps. (And I thought Timmy Leary practically invented LSD!) What are you after?

Have a pina colada for me.

Love,
D.

The article was dated August 9, 1977.

HARVARD, MIT STUDENTS IN CIA'S TEST OF LSD

Washington—Students at Harvard, MIT, and Emerson College were among 200 persons who received LSD in experiments secretly financed by the CIA at the Boston Psychopathic Hospital in the early 1950s, researchers who worked on the studies said over the weekend.

The students, both young men and women, were said to have been paid $20 each to drink a tall glass of water with the mind-altering drug added and then to participate in a series of psychological tests for 10 to 12 hours. They had been told that they were getting LSD and that their reactions would vary.

The research was done under a grant from the Society for the Investigation of Human Ecology, a funding mechanism created by the CIA in a 25-year project to develop ways of manipulating human behavior.

The CIA's sponsorship of the work was uncovered by a team of *New York Times* reporters, sifting through more than 2000 agency documents and interviewing dozens of past and present intelligence officers and researchers around the country.

"There exists within the agency," one 1960 document says, "a continuing requirement from the operations division for a substance or substances that will render an individual or animal helpless and immobile, either consciously or unconsciously, until definite control measures can be instituted."

In 1956, other documents indicate, the agency directed that 60 percent of one $40,000 contract be devoted to studying "the feasibility of utilizing aerosols as a delivery system for various psychochemicals" such as LSD. In the end, the CIA decided that spray cans of LSD would not make an effective weapon.

Dr. Max Rinkel, who initiated the LSD research at the Boston Psychopathic Hospital, died five years ago. But others who participated in the work, including Dr. J. Sanbourne Bockoven, now a regional service administrator for the Massachusetts Dept. of Mental Health, say they did not know that the intelligence agency was paying for their research and receiving their reports.

Dr. Bockoven said he and others had studied the psychochemical as a possible tool for treating schizophrenia.

After the LSD study in Boston, which ran from 1952 to early 1957, according to Kyio Morimoto, a sociologist who was part of the research team, "a couple of people" had gone into psychotherapy as a result of having participated in the experiments. But Dr. Bockoven said he did not recall anyone who suffered any untoward consequences from the LSD.

Which to Leni would mean it was safe. Or that the CIA was everywhere. The Society for the Investigation of Human Ecology. Leary could have thought that one up himself.

But this had happened years before he came to Harvard.

The article went on about Senate hearings and experiments with alcohol and curare. At the end, a note that the Boston Psychopathic Hospital was now named the Massachusetts Mental Health Center.

She put the pages down.

Mass. Mental. In the '50's. But it didn't say any patients were experimented on.

The box of Ruth.

Ruth was a grad student then. At Harvard. Till she went around the bend.

The words "*New York Times* News Service" were printed under the byline. August, 1977.

The summer after her own first year out of the Museum School. Living in that dump on Yarmouth Street. The year Leni got her B.A. The August Dad took them to Mexico. To celebrate. In the 120-degree humidity.

She walked over to the sink and turned on the cold water. The pancakes felt like a baseball under her ribs. Diana had written to Leni ten years later, in December. After which Leni came home for Christmas and had that fight with him.

The one they wouldn't talk about. The one he said was private.

The CIA experiments weren't a secret anymore. There had been stories . . . even a play a few years ago about agents using hookers to dose men they picked up, watching from behind a two-way mirror. Operation Midnight Climax. She had sent the review to Leni with some remark about the real national interest.

In the mirror she caught a streak of motion at the window where the curtains didn't quite meet. A hand came up, knuckles rapping on the glass.

The papers were fanned across the bed. She threw the sweater over them, and thought at last minute to put the chain lock on the door.

Vera smiled. "It's only me." Against the orange light in the courtyard, she looked like a shadow, except for her red lipstick.

"Just a second." Taking off the chain, she realized the computer was in plain sight at the foot of the bed. Vera followed her glance. "Ah. You found it."

"Thanks to you."

"You're welcome. Interesting, huh?"

"Especially the gun. It's your brother's?"

"So he tells me. I didn't know about it before."

"I'm sorry, but that's hard to believe."

"I don't tell him everything, either." She unzipped the black parka.

There was something different about her. An easiness. And more distance.

"Anyway, it isn't here. I left it where it was."

"The gun? That was probably wise." Lifting the edge of the curtain, Vera looked out at the courtyard.

"Is your brother here?"

"Is there a warrant for him yet?"

"Not as of yesterday afternoon. They need the test results."

"Then why are you here, Leigh?"

"You said you'd be happy to talk to me."

"So, here I am." She smiled. "You want to know what's going on. But we don't know each other very well."

"I know about Strategic Materials, though."

She let the curtain drop. "From the computer?"

"No. Leni left some books with Michael Zinn."

"Ah. Michael. Would you mind if I got some water?" She went over to the sink. The mirror framed a mask of a face, so serene it was irritating. "I don't think the computer will have much to say. Ben says Leni erased all her notes."

"But you wanted it. And you didn't bother to mention he was your brother."

"We don't...describe that relationship quite the way you would. I met Ben for the first time two years ago, when he came to my office at UNM. Is there anything else I can tell you?"

"What...you know. Why won't you?" It took effort to keep her voice down. "Leni got into this because of you."

"Doesn't that ignore she may have had reasons of her own?"

"So it's her fault? I guess it is, for trusting you. Michael said you were ready to quit over some sign up at the school, but you didn't even try to save her job."

"Oh, I'll go further than that. I got her in trouble in the first place, asking her to teach her liquor ads. I knew it would be a problem, but so's alcoholism, and if people's worst feelings and...taboos can be used against them that way, it should be known. That's why Ben went to her class, in fact."

"How romantic. Leni drank, though. At home those ads are sort of a joke. I sent her one for Absolut vodka with the word subliminal floating in the ice."

"I saw that. Cute. But it isn't a joke. It's millions of dollars every year, to target heavy drinkers. It stands to reason if they use death masks, their market research shows that works."

"I should think you'd call that very Anglo neurotic, and a denial of serious social problems."

"Good." Vera smiled. "I would. Except that we may be better at reading symbolic language than you are. And the damage it plays on is getting passed along with the disease. If you people have a cold, we get pneumonia." Turning, she again looked out through the side of the curtain.

"Expecting someone?"

"I hope not."

"Just trying to scare me. Like when you came back to the house that night. It worked, too. I would have shot you."

She tipped her head. "I don't know what you mean."

"Come on. I knew someone was out there, and the police chief said the tracks were from a Jeep. What I haven't figured out is what you wanted. I just found a picture your brother took of Leni the cops would have some fun with."

"Oh." Vera blinked. "I'd like to see that."

"You mean you haven't?" She picked up her purse. "It's not a print. Just the negative."

Vera took it to the fluorescent light above the sink. "Mmm, I thought it might be this. Leni was mad about it. He didn't tell her, and she found it. But I think if you saw it printed, you wouldn't believe he killed her."

"How about, if I saw him?"

"Ah. Is that what you're here for?"

"Maybe. Now that you mention it."

She rested the small of her back against the sink. "Leigh, I have to tell you this. What's going on . . . isn't over yet. For your own sake, I wish you'd go home before it gets any more complicated. I didn't go back to Leni's after I left you. If someone else did . . . it must have been another Jeep. That's what most people drive in the west. Maybe somebody's following you."

The road had been empty, coming down from the college. And black in the rearview mirror for the last twenty miles or so. "Not out here, if that's what you're worried about. Someone broke into Leni's office, though. Did you know that?"

"No."

From her surprise, that seemed to be true.

"And she got fired for the ads. Not minerals?"

"Actually, it was drugs. The last straw, anyway, and that was my fault. We did a teach-in after the supreme court ruling on peyote in the Native American Church. It's been legal in twenty-three states, and we could lose that now. It's the only ceremony a lot of people have left. So I asked Leni to talk about the history in her thesis."

It wouldn't have taken much to persuade her. "You mean, going back to Siberians eating mushrooms in the ice age?"

"Not quite." Vera smiled. "I think she started with the Maya. A measly two thousand years ago. She went on for three hours, but it was a hit. After which, the board accused her of advocating drug use. They said in her first interview, she promised to keep off the subject here, and if she didn't go quietly they'd give her a bad reference. Like Cather's such a great place to have taught." Reaching into her pocket, she took out a small brown paper bag.

A pack of Camels. A red plastic lighter. She gave it a flick and a jet of yellow shot up. Quickly, she passed the negative through the flame. It caught with a hiss and twisted back, a wisp of smoking plastic. "Now this can't cause trouble for anyone."

Destroying evidence. Again. With the cool assumption that it was her right. "That's pretty funny, coming from you. When you encouraged her."

Vera dropped the melted film into an ashtray. "To what? Tell the facts? You know, if it were only your own history you wanted to bury, we wouldn't care. But as usual, you have to start with ours. And there's just too much at stake, or maybe I should say, too little left, for that to be all right anymore."

"So drugs are okay for some people and you get to decide. You ought to come to my neighborhood. It's right on the edge of crack alley."

"Yes, we're starting to see that too. And twelve year olds huffing gasoline, which is about the worst. If you tell kids it's all terrible, and they've smoked grass, they'll think coke's the same. Any youth worker here will tell you, off the record, they're less worried by pot than glue and alcohol."

That was Leni's mantra. The annual statistics. Fifty times more people killed by booze and nicotine than illegal drugs. Great theory till the bullets started whizzing by at night. "Where I live, you'd have to factor in homicide," she said. "I think it's thirty kids this year, within a mile of my studio."

Vera smiled. "And half of natives die by the age of forty-five. From alcohol, most of the time. I've never taken peyote, but I know it's not addictive. Or unhealthy. The Native American Church is about sobriety and hard work. For the Court not to make a distinction between that and heroin says a lot about the drug problem in your culture. For us, it's like the Spanish Inquisition all over again. Banning our ceremonies. That happened here. Our snake dance. It's the same old story—the one you're never taught in school. Did you ever hear of the Bureau of Indian Affairs Religious Crimes Code? Which was in effect till 1978? This country's supposed to be founded on freedom of religion. It's a legal right the government has to show a 'compelling reason' to abridge. What's so threatening about some red people eating cactus? But, once again, any experience you can't control has to be obliterated."

She had fidgeted her way across the room and stopped near the foot of the bed. Getting ready to disappear. With the laptop, only inches from her hand.

Snakes in the computer. The snake ground. Some link between that and what Leni wanted from Dad. Photographs. Not family pictures.

Find the right place to stick a pin in Vera and it might pop out.

Pointing to the window, she said, "Somebody's watching us."

Vera looked through the side of the curtain again. "I don't see anything."

"Well, I do." She picked up the laptop. "Starting with the satellite maps you wanted from my father." The words fit so neatly she didn't need to see the leap in Vera's eyes for confirmation.

"Is that a guess, or from Leni's notes?"

"What difference does it make? You could kill me too, I guess, but there are people who know where I am. So it wouldn't be a permanent solution." Ed Harris knew. One person. But if she disappeared, he'd probably put it together sooner or later.

"No one here wants to do anything to you, Leigh."

She smiled. "Or for me, apparently. So why don't I just give Chief Arias all these bits and pieces and let him figure it out. The snake ground, where the snake dance is, where the strategic minerals are, right? So that would be a 'compelling reason' to . . . ban the dance? Or what."

In Vera's eyes, she could see a choice being made. However unwillingly.

"Not the dance. It's where the snakes live. Where they're gathered. If you dig up their habitat, they won't come back again."

"And you think the government's going to do that."

"I didn't say that."

"You certainly implied it."

"It might not be that . . . straightforward. We can be our own worst enemy sometimes."

"How about Leni's worst enemy? Who didn't want her. . . to get the photographs?"

"That, and smear Ben, and scare some other people off."

"Then why is it a secret? That doesn't make sense."

"Because we can't prove anything yet. If there's a fuss, it will just go underground. Temporarily. Right now we have a chance to find out what's happening."

"Even if Leni's killer goes free."

"No. To find out who that is. Frankly, I think we're the best hope you've got." Glancing at her wristwatch, she zipped up the parka.

"Then let me see him. I'll make a deal with you. If he tells me he didn't kill her and I believe him, I'll go home and shut up. For a while, at least."

Vera met her gaze. "I can't speak for him." She folded her arms. "I can ask him. All right. Let's try this. At 5:30, go out and get in your car and turn right at the entrance. Across from the Silvercraft Guild you might see somebody hitchhiking. A young guy. Pick him up. If he isn't there, it means Ben said no. But you can get a really good breakfast here."

"Thanks. I already had one."

Opening the door, Vera went out past the window and into the shadows.

5:30.

And no travel clock.

A phone sat on the bedside table, but at this hour it seemed unlikely there would be anyone at the desk to ask for a wake-up call.

5:30. And while she went on this wild goose chase, Vera could come in and clean up the loose ends.

Sitting down at the small table, she opened the computer. Make a record, and then lock all of this in the trunk of the car.

She typed.

< It's 2 a.m. on Dec. 20. At the Hopi Cultural Center. This is the latest installment. >

Her hands felt sticky. Three hours of nerves to go. Leni must have written more about Ben. Clues to his behavior.

Tapping through the journal, there were only shreds. Trying not to want too much from him. Missing him. Finding the picture. After that, a string of entries where the sentences didn't quite mesh, though no cut text came up when she touched the Paste button.

Deleted information. What other subjects had Leni edited getting ready to come home.

On each reading, the story seemed to take a different shape. Things in the background coming forward. In what must be a reference to the mineral reports:

< After I made those calls yesterday, it occurred to me they probably keep a record of people who request this material. >

Getting the termination letter. Then something Vera mentioned that made Alan laugh last night, pointing at the screen. 'The Spanish Inquisition! That's what we need! Torquemada! Bring on the thumbscrews!'

< Characteristics of the Inquisitor: (always with us, inside each of us, according to W. H. Clark) An enthusiastic, hard-working servant of God. Sincere, conscientious, responsible, concerned for the public order. A man of affairs, held in veneration, combining the exercise of absolute power with a zeal for doing good.

< Methods: Entrapment, false accusation, agents provocateurs, mass hysteria, spying, torture, witch hunts, public executions.

< In 1620 the Inquisition in Mexico declared peyote the work of the devil. From questions for Indian penitents:

< 'Art thou a soothsayer? Dost thou foretell events by reading signs, or by interpreting dreams, or by water, making circles and figures on its surface? Dost thou know certain words with which to conjure for success in hunting, or to bring rain?

< 'Hast thou drunk peyote in order to find out secrets? Dost thou know how to speak to vipers in such words as they obey thee?'

< 'Have you killed anyone?'

< 'How many have you murdered?'

< 'Have you eaten peyote?'

< In return for giving up the help of their visions, they got a concept of sin that translated as 'damage,' and the teaching that pleasure was an evil to be avoided at all costs.

< After that, they died out pretty fast.

< Randall can talk to snakes that bring rain, though.

< If we could learn to have sympathy for the Inquisitor, Clark says, we might begin to recognize him in ourselves. But if that means I have to love the board at Cather, forget it. And most of the self-righteous fanatics I respect, like Randall, are too broke to be dangerous. Like me. >

The orange light in the courtyard had been turned off. Through the gap in the curtains, a few stars showed.

Chapter 9

WHEN SHE WENT OUT it was barely light, a grey haze with one spoke of sun that faded when she turned onto the road. The craft guild was set back and she almost missed him in his grey parka. He didn't stick a thumb out, just opened his hand and she hit the brakes, thinking of the rabbit.

Walking around the car, he tapped on the back door window. She only had a glimpse of his face before he slid down on the seat. "Let's go."

"Sure. Hi. My name's Leigh." A nice looking kid, with no name forthcoming, who didn't want to be seen in her car. In the mirror, his big sneakers jutted at an awkward angle. "How far are we going?"

"Just a ways."

In that position, half a mile would seem far.

Fog drifted between the stone houses clinging to the mesa, a cascade of amber and ochre rock banded more subtly than the cliffs at Ghost Ranch, but with the same vertiginous sense of time peeled back. No roadside signs for bingo or Presbyterian grass. As far as could be taken in, emptiness and distance, out to the snow-streaked mountains on the horizon. It was like driving along the high coast of an ancient sea bed, shell and bone ground to dust by the wind, so vast the play of weather ran from bright sun to sand squalls to a blue line of rain in the west.

"There's a tourist lookout a little way up. A stone wall. Pull in there."

It headed a fork of rock between the mesas. She turned the engine off.

His knee hit the back of the passenger seat. "Okay. Go look over the wall, down the wash all the way to the left. You have to see three rocks in a pile, with the biggest on the top. When you find it, come and tell me."

The wind outside was raw and all the rocks looked piled up. Falling away in layers. A pick-up rattled by and she glanced back. He was out of sight in the car.

A shift in focus from panorama to infinite detail. Tracing the line of the gully, she worked along the slope and finally, on an outcrop of rock, saw something like a mushroom.

"Like a hat," he said when she got back. "That's it. So, under the wall is a drain pipe with a bike inside. Bike down the wash to that pile and past it you'll see another one that's out of sight from here. When you get to that one, look straight up. You ought to see a white ribbon. There's a trail up most of the way."

A white ribbon in white fog. But if she couldn't find it, he'd probably say it wasn't meant to happen.

The clear print of a sneaker showed on one side of the wall. She scrambled down around it. Now he could hot wire the car and take off with everything in the trunk.

An old black 3-speed lay on its side in the clay pipe. A heavy bike, minus the wings it would need to get down to the gully. Wrestling with it, the pedal bar kept hitting her leg in the same place. Vera must have planned this.

Ten years since she had ridden a bike. When she got on, the front wheel swung unevenly, but in places she could make out a tire mark to follow. A jolting, and she teetered off and had to start again. The second pile. Looking back, she couldn't see the road anymore. Just cold mist, settling everywhere. Death by stupidity. Another happy tourist, wanting exercise, whose bones turn up a year later.

A white dot, up by a cleft in the mesa. It flickered like a scrap of paper. Now spend an hour climbing up and find a potato chip bag.

The trail was only scuff marks. Shattered rock, and pebbles of it that shifted underfoot. Sliding back for the third time, she lost her breath and realized she had lost sight of the ribbon. A fake trail designed for maximum humiliation, if nothing worse. Fog lapped up, covering her footprints and the others.

"You're almost there." The voice was right overhead. "To your left. Be careful. Here . . ." A hand stretched out, and she took it without thinking. A cold, tight grip that got her over the last boulder and onto the ledge.

He let her hand go. "Welcome to my cave."

She saw blankets, and a lantern. "Thanks. I was starting to think your sister sent me to Siberia."

He looked thinner and older than in the picture at Leni's, when his eyes had been hidden by goggles. Taking her in, they showed a dry amusement that surprised her. She still could feel the tension of his body in her hand.

"Vera said you wanted me to tell you. So, I didn't kill Leni."

"Why are you hiding, then? There isn't a warrant."

"There will be. Once the lab work gets done. Meanwhile, what a view."

He took out a pack of Camels and offered one.

"No, thanks."

His palm cupped the red plastic lighter. "We were together that night. With my record, that should be plenty."

"Because you can't prove about the minerals."

He shrugged. "The whole southwest's full of stories like that. Fantasies and paranoia."

"But that's why you bought her the gun?"

"Someone cut the brakes on my truck. It seemed like a good idea, with her living so far out."

"Just not good enough."

"Yah." Turning, he blew smoke into the fog. "For someone who claimed to be cynical, she believed a lot of slogans. Like, if you have a gun around, it's bound to be used against you. It was about as much help to her as this is to me."

"You mean, as I am."

He smiled. "Vera thought, since you're here, it might be useful later on if you believed me."

"But you don't care."

"I don't think it makes a difference. Unless you want to be the sole contributor to my legal defense fund. I was worried about who else knows you're here, but maybe this is good. It might speed things up a little. That's Leni's sweater, isn't it?"

She looked down at it. "Yes. I took it to wrap her computer in. The one your sister was trying to steal when I got out to the house."

"She didn't have to do that. She thought it might help. Or might hurt, to leave it there. But it's lousy evidence. You could have re-written the whole thing by now. You should have given it to the police." He reached to take the collar of her sweater between this thumb and forefinger. "Now let me ask you a question. What do you want? To make a citizen's arrest? Or just curious."

She moved the hand away. "I want to find out what happened. Since we seem to be involved. She was doing something for you. Getting satellite pictures from my father."

"That's right. But you'll just forget all about that if I'd talk to you. Why? Do you think you can tell by looking?" He flipped the cigarette butt in an arc over the ledge.

"Maybe."

"That could be dangerous. I used to be an actor, ladies and gentlemen of the jury. I'm surprised you'd take the chance when you and Leni weren't that close."

Looking at him, the sign on the refrigerator at the morgue came back. NOT EXPLOSION PROOF. But it shouldn't be over now. Summed-up like that, before they could get any further. Least of all by him. "Did Leni tell you about some secret she was supposed to be keeping from me?"

He cocked his head. "I don't think so."

"About my mother?"

"No."

"You were more interested in my father. I should have brought you the newspaper. Like the one he'll be reading today. It makes her sound like a pusher who probably got what she deserved. That's not even counting the gun yet." A spiral of mist came floating up, like a pinwheel, slowly turning.

"Hey." He gripped her arm. "Are you all right?"

"No. I haven't slept in two nights."

"That's one up on me." Bending, he took a blanket and draped it around her, folding it over the sweater. "Look, go ahead and blame me. I do. Join the club. Especially since we've got one hope in hell of finding out who really did it. I'm all over that house. I'll tell the cops it was my grass, but Vera said there was only a roach left, so Leni's saliva must be on it too." He dropped his hands. "I can't believe I'm saying this."

"You should have seen her body."

"Meaning you think I didn't?"

"Not like I did, anyway."

Turning, he walked to the end of the ledge. She heard the scrape of the lighter. It seemed to be the only weapon around and it sounded pretty feeble. A search warrant for blood and hair. From the way he held his shoulders, he was ready to cut and run. But if he didn't want to make a case, why let her come up here?

She walked over, trailing the blanket. "Can we go back a step? I'm just a middle-class white person, all right? I don't like snakes. But let's pretend I'm not a total cretin for a minute. What's so important about them?"

He exhaled smoke. "I don't know all of it. I'm not sure it's translatable. But the religion's like one ceremonial that goes on all year, with all these different parts. All connected. If you cut one, it breaks the cycle. And then that's it for good. As it is, only one village still has all the rituals. The snake priests say if they lose their dance, the world could come to an end."

She couldn't tell if he was serious. "Well, I wouldn't want that to happen."

"They might be right, too. A lot of their prophecies have come true. But that's not it with me. I just don't want the bastards to get away with it. Not with every last thing. Or anyone they decide is in the way."

Leni. Run over. It was how she looked. "But you don't know who these guys are, or what they want."

"Not yet."

"And the pictures could tell you."

"Maybe. There are three sources for them. The feds, and two commercial companies. Leni thought your father might be able to use his connections to trace a buyer at the companies at least. Maybe the feds too, unless it's something really hot. There was already one stink at the CIA about satellite surveys used illegally in the commodities market. We third-world countries get nervous about hardware in the sky. It's always supposed to be for the military, but that's bull. They've been able to see anything above ground for a long time. It's what's underground now. That's where the money is. One detail we turned up is that camera your father built for the shuttle first got funded because of the Arab oil embargo."

If it had been used out here, Leni would feel responsible. Even if it also found water in Ethiopia. "But they can't just come in and dig a mine without your permission, can they? Don't you get to vote or something?"

"Technically. The tribal council does. But what if they vote no? Reservation land's held in trust. That's to save us from our own incompetence. Congress has what's called plenary power. When I asked Vera what that is, she said it means if there's a face-off, guess who has to blink. It would be messy to go through Congress, though. And I don't think they'd need to, if they said it was for the national defense. And classified. But it could also be something just valuable in itself."

"Or maybe both. Like platinum? That was on the list."

"Huh." He touched his pocket, then crushed out the cigarette. "It isn't platinum, though. And I don't know what the rest of the rocks on that list would look like. Rutile slag. Do you?"

She shook her head.

"How about a peanut butter sandwich?"

"Yes. I know what that looks like."

"I'm hungry. Come into my living room."

Sitting cross-legged on the blanket, she watched him smear the bread with a pocket knife. From his expression, wheels were turning, though he didn't look about to tell her why.

"Here." He held it out. "We put the sand back in sandwich. The water's a little strange up here. I think there's a Coke left." He reached back for a paper bag.

A line of sunburn showed inside the collar of his blue wool shirt, and dust along his hairline from the wind. She could feel Leni's attraction. In the way he moved. In a kind of energy that didn't consume all the available oxygen. That must be an asset for a photographer, and she thought of the picture of Leni. Something mischievous in it. They'd been making love. The light came down. He was probably feeling pleased with himself. And he hadn't been acting then.

"Why did you quit the movies?"

He laughed. "I didn't exactly resign."

"Were you in *Dances With Wolves*?"

"No. Mostly TV. The last thing I did was called *Powwow Highway*. For about three seconds, under the opening credits. Standing in a bar. Good typecasting. I liked that flick. It's about live Skins instead of dead ones for a change. It was almost the same story, too. A Cheyenne, getting framed in Santa Fe to help some mineral leasing on the rez. Like I said, there are all these stories, and they all come down to the same thing."

The sandwich was dry. She put it down. "Then in the movie, who did it?"

"Oh, a little collaboration between the mining company and the feds. You never found out who, exactly. The ending was bogus, though. It looked like the Skins got away. But if it had gone on another ten minutes, they would have run into a roadblock." He kept his eyes on the knife he was cleaning. "That kid, Taylor, said I should get you to smuggle me out in the trunk of your car."

It felt like a test, a finger-poke to see how the dough was rising. "To where?"

"That's the problem," he smiled. "Don't worry. I'm staying. At least till the ceremony's done and I can talk to a few people."

Over his shoulder, there were carvings in the rock. She got up to look at them. A corkscrew of concentric circles, with figures scattered around it. Something like a dog. A stalk of corn. The others were indecipherable.

"Those are clan signs. And the spiral's a migration symbol. They're all over the country, and they all come back to here. It's the last of the old ground that's left."

The grooves were chipped in a blackened surface that must be from cooking fires. Coal fires, from the soot, and she remembered putting out her sooty fingertip to Alan at the studio. Five days ago. Or five years.

The blanket was heavy and she let it fall. "I don't get it."

"What?"

"Why you're alone. If this is true. Why isn't your tribal government doing something about it?"

He grinned. "Vera thinks they are. She thinks they're ready to mine the whole place. It's something we like to fight about. See, all these villages used to be independent. And far apart, before cars. The language is even a little different in each one. Then along come the feds with their council idea. One voice for the tribe, etcetera. Hardly anyone voted for it. When you slap a new roof like that on top of a thousand years of something else, the furniture tends to move around a lot. There's not what you'd call an excess of trust around here and that can always be used. Like Taylor, that kid who brought you here, used to think praying brought rain. Then he went away to school and learned about storm fronts. Right now he's mad at everyone who taught him either thing. When you lose your fix on something that used to be important, you might not want anyone else to have it either."

"Like the snake dance."

"That's what Vera says." He shrugged. "Me, I think if the Hope Diamond were out there, it wouldn't be worth the grief the council would get for digging it up. In fact, if I were an evil miner, I might just back the old leaders. If they get rid of the council, you might be able to cut this place up village by village. She says I'm not really Hopi, so I can't understand. Then I tell her if she's so real, she ought to be here having babies so her clan line won't die out. Meanwhile, we've got three days to figure out where this is coming from."

"Even if I could get the satellite stuff, I couldn't do it that fast."

The fog was clearing. Walking to the ledge, she looked down. The cottonwood trees in the valley were like hazy tufts of grass. Climbing, it hadn't seemed so far, because of not looking back.

"Thanks anyway. I got a few shots last night that ought to be enough to start the ball rolling. Vera's taking the film to Flag." He came up behind her, aiming her shoulders. "Last night, a helicopter was out there with a drill. It had a small bore, and they were working a tight profile. So it's a shallow deposit, and maybe not that big. Meaning, they could do a quick hit and run. If no objections are raised."

She had a sudden image of snakes in motion, humping across the desert. "So you're going to stop them? If they don't stop you first. Someone could follow the bike tread out here. I ought to move the car. Damn it. I wanted to punch your face in."

"I thought you were going to."

"You seem almost happy about this."

"If I can get who killed Leni, I will be. I loved her. Maybe I didn't mention that."

"If you had before, I wouldn't have believed it."

The backdrop of the desert had changed again. Blue sky, with white clouds scudding along. Like a change in scenery to a cheerful motif, whether it fit or not.

He was watching her. "I liked that big pin you sent her. With the marbly stones? What were they?"

It must have been the large hoop. "Onyx and adventurine, I think."

"You have books about rocks."

"A few."

"You promised Vera you wouldn't talk about coming out here. Is that for real?"

She nodded.

From an inside pocket, he took out a folded Camel pack. "She told me not to do this. But I think if you showed up here now . . . Open your hand."

He tapped out two wedge-shaped crystals, an inch long and half as wide. "That's what they were digging last night. She can't just walk into some place in Flag and ask what it is. It could be the wrong place, and they'd know it came from here. But we need to find out. Does it say anything to you?"

She held one up. "It almost looks synthetic, it's so clear."

He smiled. "Maybe it fell off a UFO. And the aliens are coming back for it."

"And Leni got strangled by Martians?" Being killed for this seemed absurd enough. A sliver of beach glass with rounded edges. Maybe it was radioactive and lethal by itself.

She weighed it in her palm. "How about letting me try? There's a jeweler on my floor who does a lot with precious stones. If not her . . . we have a family friend who's a sort of Gyro Gearloose. Leni called him Uncle Paul? He's a meteorologist. He'll be at the funeral."

"No, thanks." He put his hand out.

"They don't know I've been here. I'll say..."

"Let's have it."

"You said you had to find out."

"Not if it comes back to here."

She closed her fingers. "What about Leni? Here isn't all that matters."

"Now, it is."

"Then you should let me."

"Why are you so helpful, all of a sudden?"

"Are you getting any better offers? What if I say I want to... work with it? But that wouldn't explain the rush."

"If you say it was hers, it's back to me."

"Unless she had it before she met you. Long before. Like, maybe ten years? I could be the only one who'd know about that. Say it was her lucky stone, and I want to know what the magic is. After the morgue, they'll expect me to be nuts."

The angle of his chin said he was close to considering it. Turning, he walked away down the ledge and stood looking out. Then he gave a hoarse laugh. "When I was drinking, I used to hang with Skins from all tribes. And even the ones who called Pueblos a bunch of bean-eating pansies cared about two things. The snake dance, and the Black Mesa strip-mine. Otherwise known as our National Sacrifice Area."

He came up to her again. "You could get killed too, you know."

It was something that had just occurred to her. Too late to matter, it seemed, at this point. "If anyone gets close enough to know I have it, they'll be way too close already."

Opening her hand, he folded one stone back in the Camel pack. "Vera's going to shoot me."

"Then don't tell her."

"No. I'll remind her that conflict's a test of the Hopi way. You'll have to use that phone number for her. It would be nice to know when there's a warrant, too."

Taking the other splinter, he polished it with a leaf of lens cleaner, then gave it to her wrapped in the tissue. "No finger prints. But I really want to know what that is. When I was a kid, my favorite thing was a little bow the kachinas gave me. They're sort of spirit-dancers. When I thought this was out of my life, I threw it away. Taylor's making his own kachinas. He puts mining hats on them. And high-tops. Like he's figuring out the pieces. It's going to take him awhile though, and there ought to still be some choices left for him to make.''

She zipped it into her hip pocket. "Is it all right with you if I stop back in the room for a shower?''

"Just be sure to check your brakes afterward.''

"Thanks a lot.''

"That's okay. I'll even climb down with you a way.''

He hooked an arm around her shoulder, so briefly she wasn't sure what if anything the gesture meant.

IN THE ROOM, the red light on the phone was flashing. Vera, of the gimlet eyes. It might be better not to risk another conversation.

She sat down on the bed and called the desk.

A quiet voice said, "You have a message from an Ed Harris.''

"Would you read it please?''

"It says, 'You have a reservation on America West from Flagstaff to Boston. At 3:30. It's the only seat in town.' Want me to call this number back?''

She glanced at her watch. "Sure.''

The phone rang half a dozen times, then he answered sounding out of breath. "Leigh. Good. That's the only flight till tomorrow night. You can make it if you leave pretty soon. Was your mission a success?''

She couldn't remember what she'd told him. "Yes. I think so. Thank you for this.''

"Don't mention it. I'll send you the Visa bill when it comes in.''

"You paid?''

"They wouldn't hold it otherwise. It's better, anyway. Less hassle. As a matter of fact, if you're done up there, why don't you come to Sedona. Crackpot capitol of the southwest. The Chamber of Commerce guarantees every tourist an authentic spirit-guide, and if you're lucky, you might get to watch the spaceships land out on Airport Mesa. It's going to happen any minute now.''

"Honest?''

"It's definitely in your karma. Seriously, I'm just a little farther than Flag, and what else are you going to do? Let me take you to lunch, and then I'll drop you at the plane and turn in your car. I wish you'd let me do at least that much.''

"How long would it take me to get there?''

"About four hours. Maybe three and a half to Flag.''

By which time it would be very nice to let someone else do the driving. If she didn't fall asleep at the wheel on the way.

"Okay. It's a deal. Where are you, exactly?"

"A place called Tlaquepaque. It's sort of a cross between a convent and a mall. It means the Best of Everything. You turn off at 179 south."

"All right. See you then."

She hung up and went to turn on the shower. The jumpsuit was floury. Stripping it off, she slapped at the dust. It didn't help a lot, but the trousers were worse, and the zipper pockets were handy.

Chapter 10

PAST THE BOTTLENECK of Flagstaff, the plunge down Oak Creek canyon kept her grip tight on the wheel. Switchbacks came one after another—dizzying glimpses of red rock spires and scattered condo villages. The motels set along the creek advertised Jacuzzis and she thought of Ben dusty and windburned in his cave.

Route 179 was a left turn past the Chamber of Commerce, which had no spirit-guides in front that she could see. The Pink Jeep Tour stand across the road offered other transport.

Tlaquepaque seemed the only old construction, a stucco maze with archways into patios lined with shops. In the parking lot, she took a quick look at the travel guide. Sedona. Center of the New Age. 'Four psychic energy vortexes (Bell Rock, Boynton Canyon, Courthouse Rock and Airport Mesa) are each said to have a different electromagnetic charge enhancing spiritual awareness. Visitors come from all over the world to explore past-life regression, ESP, automatic writing, crystal and pyramid power, telepathy, and physical healing. Many report the aura of this intense vibrational field heightens consciousness and erases the need for sleep.'

That sounded like a press release from the Chamber of Commerce. The beauty of the place would be enough alone. From the parking lot, the aura was one of money.

By a fountain in the courtyard, a man working on the iron gate pointed her around the wall to Ed's shop.

It made the one in Santa Fe look like a broom closet. Shafts of colored stone framed the windows, but jewelry filled the mirrored shelves, and carvings, fetishes, whorls of bone.

Inside, a pickled-wood ark dripping a rope of cowrie shells held masks and antique drums and bundles of dried herbs—a mingling of textures that invited touch. The mirrors reflected endless treasure, every piece obsessively arranged and spotless. Every one exquisite.

He had his back to her, talking to a customer, and she browsed along the shelves. Even the cheapest quartz had some unusual vein or tint. She thought of the chips in her pocket. But they didn't look like anything next to this.

She picked up a crystal bar embedded with a delicate spray of green, and felt a hand on her shoulder.

"You made it."

By contrast, he seemed less tall in these surroundings, but the blue shirt he was wearing brought out the color of his eyes.

Something else was different. The ponytail was gone.

"You cut your hair."

"You got some sun."

"What sun? This is the first I've seen of it."

"You don't have to see it here for it to work."

"I want everything in your shop."

"Thank you. Have you looked over there?" He pointed to a square case under a painting in the corner.

It showed the work of several jewelers, with cards giving their names. Six of the pieces were hers. Two had the celadon patina made after the trip with Leni to Ghost Ranch.

"I thought if I told you in Santa Fe, you'd think I was pulling your leg. This isn't the best display, I'll grant you. It's the only stuff I carry that isn't one-of-a-kind. But your sales rep in L.A. is good about seeing we don't get a lot of overlap here. What you do that's good is, the colors from one season kind of touch on the next, so if a piece gets held over it doesn't jar."

Meaning it was all right the celadon hadn't sold. "I'll tell my business partner you said so. That was his idea." Alan could probably use a compliment by now.

She held up the bar of quartz. "What's this?"

"Chlorite. That's called phantom crystal. I'm not surprised you picked that out. I love it, and it isn't pricy. You could use it. Or even this."

Turning, he traded it for a larger slab shot with threads of gold. "That's titanium. It's called rutilated quartz. I can get it for you wholesale."

The price tag said $50. "I thought titanium was precious."

"Not at that density."

It felt lighter than a similar chunk of Ben's stone would be, but he had mentioned rutile something. "Maybe I'll buy this. To show my partner. Retail, I mean."

"Nah. Just give me your resale number." Peeling off the tag, he went to stick it on the counter. "Daniel? We're going to lunch. And I'll need a lift from the airport later."

A grey-haired Indian stuck his head out of the office. "Okay. Give a call."

When they were out of earshot, she asked, "Is that one of your spirit-guides?"

He was steering her toward a sidewalk cafe across the plaza. "Sort of. In a way. He's Hualapai, from Grand Canyon. He's the only one I trust to buy for me, and the only one who doesn't mind the dusting."

"I'm surprised he can afford to live here."

The tables were wrought iron, with green-and-white Perrier umbrellas. He pulled back a chair for her. "Daniel does all right. He really does give tours on the side. Especially to kids. The place where he used to live is a uranium mine now."

"That seems to be the general theme out here."

But she wanted to forget it for awhile and just sit in the sun. At the center of the patio a tree grew up, fanning its branches against the velvety walls. A painted donkey peered down from a balcony covered with vines that crept up to the terra cotta roof. "What is this, the old village? Or did you really mean a convent."

"Well, I really meant a mall. But they've done a damn good job with it. The oldest part was built about twenty years ago, and a lot of it's newer than that. But, like, that gate is antique ironwork from Guadalajara. No expense was spared."

"Which no doubt helps to heighten cosmic consciousness."

"No doubt."

A waitress put two menus down. "Hi, Ed. Perrier for you?"

"And for me, please."

"And a glass of that great fumé for her too. Come on, Leigh. Relax. I'll be doing the driving."

The waitress winked. "Just watch where he goes. Airport Mesa by moonlight is a specialty."

When she moved away, he smiled. "There isn't a lot to do here at night."

"And that's where the spaceships are going to land."

"So I'm told. By the Kindred of the Brotherhood." He tipped his chair back, "They ought to know."

"What Brotherhood would that be?"

"Of the lost continent of Mu. Lemuria. The ancient civilization of the Pacific, lost twelve thousand years ago. You mean you never learned about that in history class?"

"Not that I remember. Like Atlantis?"

"Or an earlier version. Depending on which book you read."

The drinks came and she got another wink.

"Go away," he said. "I'm telling Leigh about Lemuria."

"The little red men underground? That's a good one, hon."

"Anyway," he squeezed the lime wedge precisely into his soda, "The story is, Mu lasted for two hundred thousand years. Highly evolved in the arts and government, but they had four cataclysms. So they figured they might get sunk the next time, and sent out colonists. Who had some kind of radiant crystal that repelled water, so they zoomed on over here."

"And how do we know all this?"

The wine glass looked like crystal, holding liquid gold. He slid it toward her. "Try that."

"I haven't eaten yet. I'll get drunk."

"So? We're talking about Mu here. It'll make it easier for the spirit-guides to get through."

The fumé was a soft explosion, flowery but not sweet and as penetrating as the light. "Mmm. I think I'm drunk already."

"Excellent. Cheers. How we know all this, according to the Kindred, is from some twelve-thousand-year-old tablets found in India and Mexico, and from the Sleeping Prophet, Edgar Cayce. He's the one who said they came to Arizona."

She took another sip. "Why here?" From now to Boston there was nothing else to do.

"Probably, because we're on a ley line. A sort of natural force field. Any good Druid could explain it. Theoretically, all the old megaliths are built on ley lines. And birds migrate along them. The Chinese call them dragon currents. They're from the pull of the planets. Or plate tectonics. Charging up spots on the landscape. The energy's supposed to be rejuvenating."

"I absolutely feel rejuvenated."

"Good. I recommend the Sedona salad. It's made of melon and cactus and everything good for you."

"Perfect."

He gave the order. "And how else we know about Mu is, symbols on those tablets are supposed to match ones in the petroglyphs around here. Like of Quetzalcoatl, the great serpent of the Aztecs. And the pueblos. He's in charge of death and rebirth and waiting around in between."

More serpents. Another Vivarón. "This is my snake tour of the southwest."

"Did you run into a rattler up there?"

"Almost."

He ran a finger around the rim of his glass. "We have a lunatic fringe who think the Hopis descended from the Lemurians. There's a Hopi myth about three earlier worlds, and coming on rafts from the west. And a temple at Uxmal in the Yucatan's dedicated to Mu, 'the land of the west and birthplace of the sacred mysteries.' Some of our crackpots claim all the energy here comes from a giant Lemurian crystal buried underground. Which story, I admit, doesn't hurt my business any."

The waitress set down plates that looked like a magazine ad. Glistening balls of fruit on a scroll of cactus and avocado, with red and green ribbons of sauce. Raspberry and cilantro, she said, and disappeared again.

Ben would be having more peanut butter in his haunted cave.

The patio made the mesa seem a dream. She touched the chips in her pocket. A giant buried crystal. If nothing else worked, she could tell him that. A relic of the lost world, or the last world, that was selling a lot of jewelry down here. Some of which had turned out to be hers.

Ed was eating with a tidiness she couldn't hope to match. She unfolded her napkin. "So this is really a tourist town. Don't you get bored? I mean, if you don't believe all that. Not that I'm not grateful for the market."

He shrugged. "I can always go to Santa Fe. But given the available spectrum.... The people here are nice. A little soft, maybe, some of them. But harmless. They're looking for something. If they don't find it at the vortexes, something in my shop might strike a chord. Then they have that to take home. Which keeps the artists in rent money. I grew up in Philadelphia and I don't care if I ever see the place again."

"No family?"

"Not to speak of. A cousin, who's a geologist. He got me into this. I was looking for something myself, then—like, what to do with my life. I started selling his rocks to some of the stores in Santa Fe, and after awhile he staked me so I could open a place of my own."

"A good investment." The cactus was smoky, vaguely slimy, but interesting with raspberry.

"Go west, young man." He smiled. "Leni did. You didn't have to. I must say, it's kind of amazing to me that neither of you got married."

She picked up the wine glass, then put it down. "Are you?"

"Not so far."

"So, it still could happen." But she realized she didn't believe it about herself anymore. "Our mother died at a loony bin. Did Leni tell you?"

He touched her wrist. "No. I'm sorry."

"That's all right. It happened a long time ago. But I think it had a certain . . . dampening effect."

"I lost my folks young too."

She emptied the last swallow in the glass. "Everybody's got a story, right?"

"In spite of which we've done okay. Can I talk you into another of those?"

"What the hell."

"You just reminded me of something Leni said. That it's not what you see that counts, it's what you don't see. What's in the background. That's where the push comes from." He signaled the waitress. "Like those ads of hers. Though I have to admit, I can only find the buried stuff if I've been smoking funny cigarettes. Which she said proved her point that grass is subversive and against the corporate interest. Which is why it got outlawed in the first place."

"For being subversive?" She speared a melon ball that resisted being cut in half.

"More like, against the corporate interest. It's a little-known piece of American lore. From the '30's. Want to hear?"

"Sure."

The waitress looked down at her plate. "Don't you like it?"

"I haven't given her a chance, Grace. Another fumé, please."

She took the glass away.

"Now you eat and I'll talk. I love this story. It's like a microcosm of American history. In the '30's, there were two competing ways of making paper pulp. Good old wood, and a new process using hemp hurds. Hemp is grass is cannabis. Same plant. Check out USDA Bulletin #404 sometime. It says one acre of hemp fiber gives the same paper yield as four acres of nonrenewable timber. With no sulphuric acid or dioxin needed to pulp it. Enter William Randolph Hearst, our king of the tabloids. Hearst had enormous investments in timber, and the DuPont corporation had patented the wood pulp process."

She took a sip from the new glass of wine.

"Are you with me so far?"

"Drunkenly."

He smiled. "I'll still respect you in the morning. Anyway, at that time cannabis was sort of the family friend. An analgesic, like aspirin. The extract was used for everything from depression to headache to menstrual cramps. The women's temperance unions pushed it as better than alcohol, because they said it led to less wife-beating. There was even a Jungle Wallah Hasheesh Candy you could buy through the Sears Roebuck catalogue."

"And heroin too. You could get that, then. In those home remedies."

"True. But cannabis isn't addictive. In 1988, the Drug Enforcement's own law judge called it 'one of the safest therapeutically active substances known to man.'"

"That sounds like Leni. Did she tell you this?"

"No. But we talked about it. My roommate at Penn's family grew hemp until it was outlawed. They'd been doing it since Jamestown, for rope and cloth, and they would have made a fortune from the hurd pulp process. Instead they had to switch to tobacco. He wants to switch back. He says hemp's the one renewable resource capable of meeting the world's industrial needs, while also cleaning up the environment. Literally, for cloth, paper, oil, and plastic. I've seen his research. It's incredible. You can even grow the stuff without the high now."

"So why aren't we?"

A woman at the next table looked over. He lowered his voice. "Do you think Exxon and Kimberly Clark would be in favor of going bankrupt? It's like solar, that way. You can't patent it. And those big guys are all major advertisers. Media are businesses too. That's how it worked in the '30's. Back to DuPont and Hearst. DuPont's chief backer was Andrew Mellon, who happened to be Hoover's Secretary of the Treasury. So Mellon appointed his nephew-by-marriage, Harry Anslinger, to head the new Bureau of Narcotics. Have you heard of *Reefer Madness?*"

"The movie?"

"And the news clips it's made from. It was pure Hearst yellow journalism. He had to get rid of this new hurd process, but they couldn't just go to Congress and ask it to outlaw the competition. Ben Franklin made paper from cannabis. It's how we had a free colonial press. So they cooked up this 'dangerous drug' angle, with a two-pronged strategy. And the first thing they did was give it a new name. When everyone had cannabis in their medicine chest, you couldn't make that the enemy. So they used the Spanish. Marijuana. Nice and foreign-sounding. That was the thrust of their message. There's this new drug, marijuana, coming in from the lazy Mexicans, and the 'darkies' seducing white women with their evil 'voodoo-satanic jazz music.' Hearst was ticked at the Mexicans because Pancho Villa seized his Mexican timberland. He kept running headlines about these 'demons' under the influence committing 'vicious' crimes against whites—and this was Jim Crow time, remember. It was illegal for a black to step on a white man's shadow or look at his woman twice. And Anslinger read these stories into the Congressional Record. Even the American Medical Association didn't realize till it was too late that cannabis and marijuana were the same thing. Harry Anslinger. Now there's a man who knew how to move with the times. In '37, he told Congress it was 'the most violence causing drug in the history of mankind,' and ten years later he testified it made people so pacifistic the Commies could use it to weaken our will to fight.''

The wine and sun were beginning to make her head ache. "Well, maybe he was right about that. Leni didn't fight much, apparently.''

"God, I'm an ass." He sat back. "Here I'm trying to distract you and I always seem to put my foot in it.''

"No. I'm sure she'd agree with you. This is just her kind of thing.''

"She already knew most of it. For her, the twist was my friend's hemp plantation was part of the slave economy, and blacks were blamed for drugs then and now, and yet the real white powder drug problem owes a lot to the government, from heroin from the Golden Triangle to cocaine from the Contras, and white powder keeps the underclass in place. I think that's just about true again. At least, the people I know are scared off coke now. I wouldn't try crack if you paid me.''

It was hard to picture him losing control to any degree.

She looked out across the plaza, to the windows of his shop. "That's just so easy to say here. Sitting in this beautiful place. So, you think drugs should be legalized?''

"Well, it might save the other half of Colombia from being wiped out. And the Amazon basin from being completely stripped. And kids from getting criminal records because they smoked a few leaves.''

"See, I ought to agree with that. Maybe I just can't think in global enough terms. All I have to go on is my neighborhood, but I think if some of those kids could get all the crack they wanted, and nothing else changed in their lives, it would be like that experiment where the rats kept pressing the lever to get coke until they died. No food. No water. Just coke, coke, coke. Maybe if they hadn't been in a cage it would be different. Or a housing project. I don't know."

"Leni said if she were God, she'd shut off the white powder and pump in great smoke till all the gangs chilled out."

She smiled. "Then most of the artists I know would start dressing like Crips and Bloods. They say they can't get grass anymore."

"Powder's easier to move. Less bulk, more bucks. Meanwhile, there's a ton of research showing cannabis helps glaucoma, asthma, and maybe even MS and Parkinson's, but the drug companies aren't about to lose any profits to a plant you could grow in your yard. So AIDS and chemo patients have to take synthetic pot for nausea, which doesn't work half as well as smoking a joint. Tra-la. Business and politics as usual. Maybe that's why I like it here with the dingbats who hug trees."

"No offense. I just got an earful about peyote from Vera last night."

"I forgot to ask you. What's she like?" He made a signing motion to the waitress.

Describing Vera was beyond her now. "Tough. She made me feel personally responsible for some court ruling against it."

"It should only be that simple. Thanks, Grace." He wrote on the back of the check. "I have an account here. We're all set. We better get going."

"I have to give you my resale number."

"Nah. I want you to have that rock. As a souvenir of Lemuria. Maybe someday you'll get loony enough to want to come back here too."

On the plane, she promptly fell asleep.

At the stop in Phoenix, she called home. Alan answered, and she could tell he was being overheard because he didn't ask what the hell was going on.

The funeral would be at 10 a.m., so she wouldn't miss that at least. He didn't need to add it would look peculiar that she wasn't at the wake.

When she told him not to meet her flight, he sounded hurt. Her suitcase had made it to Brookline, but he'd be glad to stop at the condo. Or the studio, if that was what she wanted, though everything was certainly under control there. She couldn't say it wasn't him but herself she didn't trust. Promising Ben not to tell was fine except when it came to Alan and his sensitive nose for fraud. Picking up the mineral books now would take some explaining.

If Sedona eased the need for sleep, its spell wore off in the air. The headache put out tentacles. On another day, the man in the next seat might have been promising company, but after two forays he took a good look at her face and went back to his folder of papers.

Each time she got to the edge of sleep, the cave opened up, but she couldn't make out the words Ben was saying. It felt like a warning, and then she came awake with a start. The details of what he'd told her were already getting fuzzy. If something happened to him, they would be important.

The stewardess came with the cart, and she ordered club soda and no meal and reached under the seat for Leni's laptop. It fit on the tray table, and on top of the screen was a dial that turned down the display. However many typos came from not seeing print, it would be safer than relying on mental notes.

The man in the aisle seat passed her club soda. "Want to leave this on my table? You don't seem to have room there."

She glanced over into shrewd brown eyes. "All right. Thank you."

"Are you giving yourself a typing test?"

"Kind of."

The stewardess said, "Are you Dr. Lee, who ordered the kosher meal?"

"That's right."

She put it down and went back up the aisle.

"Matt Lee." He made room for her glass. "I asked because I'm trying to memorize a talk, and this air isn't very conducive to accuracy."

He slid the folder into the pocket of the seat back. Printing across it said Conference of the American Psychiatric Association.

"Actually, I'm Leigh too. Leigh Haring." She nodded at the folder, "I don't suppose that means you might have a couple of aspirin."

"Or Prozac?" he smiled. "What was the movie when everyone at Bloomingdale's came up with Valium? I think I have some Buferin in my case."

It was under his seat and the contortions with the tray seemed to call for more conversation. An east coast person, she was willing to bet, which would be a relief after days of feeling as if she spoke a foreign language.

"Thanks. Is Prozac all it's cracked up to be?"

"Except for the odd patient who turns homicidal. Really, that's not my line. I do talk therapy. When people need drugs, I refer them to a pharmacologist."

"What's your speech about?"

"Depression. In adolescent girls. I conclude they have many good and specific reasons for being depressed. My sense is, it's better to sort those out than take a pill that makes you care less. In mild cases, at least." He poked his grey chicken breasts. "Doesn't this look appetizing."

She swallowed the Bufferin, remembering her old room in the Newton house. The clay table. And the silence, after Leni went to Brandeis. Working the clay had been a kind of self-hypnosis, when there was no one to talk to. Leni went out, and she had gone inward, but not to a place where reasons became clearer.

The freedom of travel, to say anything to someone you'd never see again. She thought of telling him about Leni, to find out what the psychic aftershocks would be. Knowing what symptoms to look for could bring them on, though, and the real questions she had he wouldn't be able to answer.

Except for maybe one.

"Can I ask you something?"

He'd given up on the chicken and was eating a roll between sips of black coffee. "Should I start the meter? I'm kidding. Go ahead."

"Someone I know was diagnosed as schizo-affective, borderline to manic depression. What does that mean, exactly."

"When was this?"

"Not recently."

"I know that. It's old terminology. For one thing, manic depression is called bipolar illness now."

"What about schizo-affective."

Putting down the plastic cup, he turned in the seat to face her. "When was this, again?"

"In the '50's."

"Okay. That makes more sense. It's sort of a . . . wastebasket category. Meaning, We don't know. There are some features of this, and others of that. Sort of a modern version of hysteria, or having a breakdown, put in clinical language. It's my unsupported opinion that such vague diagnoses are given to women more often than men. Anyhow, it's out of date. Schizophrenia and bipolar are more closely defined now. You'd be apt to use one or the other."

It had sounded so precise, she thought. Almost geographical. An official coordinate, that turned out to be equivalent to getting the vapors.

The stewardess took his tray, and he folded up the table. "Does that help any? I'm sorry I can't be more exact. Is this someone in your family?"

"My mother."

"Is she still living?"

"No."

"Was there a hospitalization?"

"At Mass. Mental Health Center. Only then it was called the Boston Pyschopathic Hospital."

"Well, you could try to get the records. But that's a while ago, and since there's been a change..." Pushing the seat button, he sat back. "The records might not tell much more than behavior and medication."

"It was Thorazine."

"That would have been my guess."

"Can I ask you one more thing?"

"Yup."

"In your unsupported opinion, could the symptoms for that be like if someone freaked out on LSD?"

"In the '50's?"

"They did some experiments with it there, then."

"Boy. That's news to me." He looked down at his folded hands. "Well, sure, I guess. Depending on the presenting behavior. I think, even then, if she'd been hallucinating or hearing voices you would have had a harder diagnosis. But if it were more euphoria, dissociative reasoning ... that's where the 'affective' comes in. In fact, I think it used to be called schizo-affective excitement. Is there someone who was around then you could ask?"

"That's what I'm trying to decide. My father was. But he's the one who had her committed and he feels bad about it."

"Well, so do you. At least, that's what I'm hearing. You have a need and a right to know. I wouldn't leave it too long, either."

"I think I already have. I should have asked him before."

"Didn't you? Then how did you know the diagnosis?"

"I mean, about the particulars."

He shrugged. "That's not surprising. Ripeness is all. On some level, you may have felt it could hurt you, while you were forming your own identity. Now you've done that, it isn't so frightening. The comfort should be that it is so vague. If it were schizophrenia, you might have something to worry about."

He closed his eyes, to shut her up or give her privacy. A nice man, who hadn't been looking to play shrink today. And giving her a terrific excuse, except that her identity had been formed quite a while ago.

All the other rows had reading lights on. It was getting dark, and on the computer screen she could make out a ghost of blue lettering.

She started typing what he'd said right in the middle of the notes about Ben. Later, separate files could be made. Or maybe it didn't matter. Leni had kept them together, under her rock. The monkey box and the gun.

Chapter 11

THE WAY ALAN HAD PLANNED things, there was nothing for her to do but go through the motions. When she got in Dad was too tired to ask questions. Her own would have to wait, too. He hadn't worn the dark suit since before the stroke and it hung on him like a testament to everything he had lost.

"My little soldier," he hugged her. "Finally, you're home." Under the hall light, his hair was wispy and she could feel his shoulder blades through the jacket.

Harriet said it was time for bed, and climbed the stairs behind him, her back as rod straight as ever.

Alan had ordered a buffet for after the funeral from a deli on Harvard Street, but had to leave to collect a box of pastry from the Yum Yum Tree.

He gave the knapsack a speculative look. "I unpacked your suitcase, so the wrinkles would shake out. Dress warm, for the cemetery. Your father didn't want her cremated in case there's any more need for evidence. I assume at some point you'll tell me what you've been doing."

"You mean, besides leaving the worst parts to you?"

"Just as long as you're all right. Actually, I'm more worried about your aunt than your father. I didn't know she was your mother's sister. She says this is bringing all that back. The *Globe* piece didn't help. It's up on your bed."

When he opened the door, a gust of snow blew in. Already it tipped the iron spokes of the fence around Kenwood Park. After Arizona, the square looked miniature, a red brick Christmas card scene. The evergreen trees were strung with blue lights—which could relate to Chanukah too, the Neighborhood Association had finally reasoned. Alan had taken the wreath off the door, but a scent of pine lingered when she closed it.

A bronze plaque on the park fence said the rowhouses were part of a Registered Landmark Area, but it didn't hold much family history. Leni had never lived here, and she herself had for only two years. The downstairs furniture was different from what they'd had in Newton. Teak and tan leather and a pale dhurrie rug. Lots of white space. As spare as Dad's body was now. The black pot from San Ildefonso gleamed on the mantel.

Someone had sent flowers.

She went over to read the card. Tigerlilys, from Diana. At the studio there had been a message on the machine from her, breathless and almost incoherent.

To take in the shock, she played it back twice. A forecast of tomorrow. So much had come between the first news and now, her own emotions didn't seem to fit here. One trajectory, ending at the morgue. The other, starting there, still in flight.

Carrying the pack up to her room, she found a note from Alan. 'We'll get through this too, Leigh.'

But not to how we were, she thought, and knew both would be true. He had brought her wool coat and arranged her things and she felt both lonely for and cut off from him.

Wrapping up in Leni's grey robe, she got into bed.

The *Globe* article at least was no worse than the one in the *New Mexican*.

The mineral books offered nothing beyond the remote possibility of industrial diamonds. 'In Arizona, small quantities from asteroid crust.' At the Museum School, they had been used on some tools and not unduly hoarded. Synthetic, most were now, it said.

Across the room, the window shade was up. Snow drifted in the streetlight.

BY MORNING, it had stopped. A limousine big enough for a rock band took them down Commonwealth Avenue to Waterson's funeral home. From the rows of chairs set up, quite a crowd was expected.

The director said it would be tiring to greet guests as they came in. Better to sit, and do that later.

A simple walnut coffin stood between floral arrangements so exotic only Alan could have commissioned them.

Walking toward it, a jitter of panic started. Leni couldn't breathe in that box.

She had to put her hand down on it and remember the black bruises and the steel drawer where Leni was in Albuquerque.

Sitting near the casket helped. Keeping company. A steady murmur came down the aisle. Diana slid in behind them, her blue eyes rimmed with pink, and then Alan appeared. Introducing them, she got a look at the assemblage. Some family friends, and old MIT colleagues. The Springfield cousins. Her own staff—Jean and Sarah, both wearing black and white. Uncle Paul waved his grey fedora, and sat down heavily.

Most of the other people weren't familiar.

The MIT chaplain had been pressed into service for the eulogy. He'd missed the privilege of knowing Elinor, he said, but her death had touched the whole community. Loving daughter of Richard, and sister of Leigh... A dedicated teacher, where the need for that was great.... She might ask us not to heed her death so much as the violence here at home, and consider what part we could play in love and healing.

An oblique reference to the drugs mentioned in the *Globe*.

Alan gave her arm a squeeze and went up to read from Roethke.

> *I wake to sleep and taking my waking slow.*
> *I feel my fate in what I cannot fear.*
> *I learn by going where I have to go.*

A poem he had read to her before.

> *Light takes the tree, but who can tell us how?*
> *The lowly worm climbs up a winding stair.*
> *I wake to sleep and take my waking slow.*

> *Great nature has another thing to do*
> *To you and me; so take the lively air,*
> *And, lovely, learn by going where to go.*

She heard Diana sniffle and thought one of them ought to add something personal when he finished. But she wasn't sure what might come out of her mouth in these surroundings.

As he closed the book, a young woman walked up carrying a flute. Its first clear notes called up Leni. What she played had the haunting lilt of the Zuni music in Chama.

The chaplain invited everyone to the house after the interment.

Alan said Jean and Sarah were going to hand around the wine, which was why they looked like a pair of penguins. Giggling, Diana held out her arms, "We only look like hell!"

Outside, a lone TV reporter talked into a camera. A slow news day, apparently. She couldn't read the channel number.

"Parasite," Harriet growled, bending into the limo.

The route to the Newton cemetery passed within a block of their old house. From Walnut Street, one corner showed, painted white with shiny black trim now. A memorial card to their childhood. Seeing it before, it had always made her think of silence and empty rooms. Today, watching through the window, a glimpse of something else flitted by. Two running shadows on the sidewalk, the smaller one trying to catch up and hold hands. Glee, almost, and a lot of yelling—so it must be from some time when they were left for weeks with a babysitter to torture.

A temporary solidarity, then. Secret clubs and codes. Hiding in the dusty perfume of the hall closet, or sneaking off to the woods with a canteen and squashed peanut butter sandwiches.

Annette. The one Leni really went after. A doctoral student, and maybe more, Leni seemed to think. An aspiring mother-substitute, sent in on test runs. It was only Annette she made sleep on the couch.

A potential step-child no one in her right mind would take on.

To a man still in his forties, it must have been maddening.

The cemetery had consumed the woods till there was only a border left—a tracery of branches trimmed with snow. The hearse turned at the center drive, through the old section, and she said, "Dad? Is it your plot?"

"I thought she'd like to be with your mother. You can scatter my ashes over them. I'd just as soon be compost anyway."

She helped him out. The crowd had thinned to a dozen. The Springfield cousins came toward them.

Diana was still sitting in her car, with her arms around the wheel. She went over to tap on the window.

It opened with a buzz. "Leigh, I'm sorry. I don't think I can do this. I'm getting claustrophobia already."

"Don't, then. Do you think she'd care? But please come back to the house. I have to talk to you."

Rubbing her eyes, Diana smiled. "She'd call me a coward though, huh? I always made her go first."

"You may not have had a choice. She could be obnoxious that way. She used to ride her bike up here. I wouldn't come. I didn't want to see my mother's name."

"All right. As long as there's one other chicken..." She pushed the door handle. "Let's take the lively air."

The open grave stood out against the thin white crust. Absurdly, fake green grass mats covered the shoulders of upturned earth.

The chaplain read a service comforting in its plain approach. Being "cut down like a flower" seemed relevant. Harriet said, "Richard" and turned into his shoulder as the casket was lowered.

It took a long time.

Diana's hand slid into hers. And then tears came, a surprise because she was starting to feel angry.

Leni's hands. Leni carrying her. An earliest memory. Piggyback, her red sandals hooked in the pocket's of Leni's shorts. Or sitting in her clasped arms, facing front, and suddenly Leni would fold her legs up and run forward to stop short, which always made them laugh even though or because it was forbidden behavior.

Forgotten until now.

At night, Leni swung her down the long hall, spinning her around and whispering nonsense rhymes. 'Would you like to ride a kite? Or maybe fly a satellite?'

If she was four or five then, Leni would have been eleven, twelve.

Did that only happen when they were alone?

Leni's bad behavior. Leni being 'wild' and 'irresponsible' and consistent.

It was her own behavior that changed when Dad came home. Playing quietly in her room—the good girl who didn't cause trouble. Caught between them. Blaming Leni for it, too.

But glad when he went away.

A little traitor.

She glanced up at the headstone. Ruth Fromme Haring, 1926-1957. A thirty-one-year-old near-Ph.D., who got the vapors and left the scene.

A man in a black suit lifted the mat, and awkwardly Dad threw in a spadeful of earth with his good arm. His left arm, now. The way he was, it would be cruel to make him shovel up the past.

Still, thinking of her old room there had always been a wall, invisible and numbing.

Protection. Then a prison. Leni couldn't get through. Had finally given up trying.

When he held the spade out to her, she shook her head. It felt too early yet to bury anything more.

Diana blew her nose.

Turning, she said, "Want me to drive you? Harriet's with my father."

Harriet nodded. "Go ahead, girls."

In the car, Diana took out a compact. "I look awful. I better not come in."

"Why, because you're genuinely mourning? How unseemly of you." She decided to take Beacon Street back.

"Last night, I was pounding the walls, Leigh. I scared the kids. But I can't stand it. Every day when I open the paper there's another dead woman, raped, or murdered, or both. Remember that performance piece, 'We Keep Our Victims Ready?' That's how I feel. Now Leni. No matter what you do, it just comes down to brute force and terrorism. All these slasher movies and happy psychopaths. What am I supposed to tell my girls? Be brave, or be a coward?" A curtain of dark blond hair hid her face.

"That's a good question. I don't know."

A red light came up at four corners and she touched the brake. The BMW handled like a dream. Diana had chosen safety. Like herself. What happened to Leni would make that seem the wiser course.

Turning left, she pulled up to the curb. "In case it's any comfort, Leni wasn't just a victim. It wasn't random. She was a threat to someone."

"God. Is that what the cops told you?"

Thin ice ahead. "It seems to be the consensus. Had you talked to her recently?"

"No. Not for ages. I wrote her a few weeks ago. But she never answered right away."

"I found an old letter of yours there. Hidden in her fireplace. With a *Herald* article from 1977? Look, I hate to push this now, but it could be crowded at the house. Did she think my mother was in that LSD experiment at Mass. Mental?"

Diana looked up from the Kleenex she was shredding. "Oh, yes. She got your father to admit it. But his condition was, she couldn't tell you. I only knew because I helped her get the news clip. She said if she couldn't tell you, she couldn't tell anyone. She was livid about it. She felt like he trapped her."

Leni, at the studio, the last time. Folded in the armchair, smoking that damn cigarette.

"What a way for you to find out. In the fireplace?"

The car was stuffy and she buzzed the window down. "Yes. And I don't understand why it had to be such a big secret. So, she freaked out on acid. At least that makes more sense than some nebulous nervous breakdown. I met a shrink on the plane who said her diagnosis was a crock."

"But, see, that's what they fought about. According to Leni, she didn't freak out. She had the same experience we did on our first trips, only in the '50's, no one recognized what it was. Those were mind-control experiments, Leigh. They gave them tests along with the acid. Ink blots, and draw-a-man, and tell-a-story-about-this-picture. If you happened to be merging with the cosmos at the moment, you might not be so cooperative. And then, instead of going home and keeping quiet, she went around raving about it. Leni remembered some things she said. It seems your father was the one who freaked out. He thought she was losing her mind. He told Leni, by 20/20 hindsight he could see he might have been wrong. But he had to be away a lot, and he didn't dare leave her alone with two small children."

After Sputnik. He wouldn't have had much patience then. But some doctor would have had to agree, to sign the papers.

"She wrote me about it," Diana said. "I'll give you the letter. I'm glad you know. Are you going to tell him?"

"I'm not sure." Turning the ignition key, she pulled out into the traffic. "I guess I'm surprised he thought I'd find it so incomprehensible."

"Really. I mean, they've been burning witches for at least three thousand years."

She glanced over at Diana's profile. "The problem is, I didn't know my mother. But since she did have children, maybe joining that experiment wasn't such a keen idea."

"What drugs did they find at Leni's? Her toadstool collection?"

"And some grass."

"You know, Kesey and Ginsberg were in those lab experiments too. Only later, around 1960. Kesey called his magic bus trip the revolt of the guinea pigs. Leigh. Are you upset?"

"Not really. I just feel kind of stupid, being the last to know. How did Leni find out?"

"From a book on the MK-ULTRA program the CIA ran back then. It mentioned a Dr. Max Rinkle, at the Boston Psychopathic Institute affiliated with Harvard. We'd never heard of it, but she remembered your mother talking about some Dr. Max. So I asked a reporter friend to do a library search, and sure enough. It just didn't get as much play as the wilder MK-ULTRA stuff. Psychic driving, and hookers spiking drinks with acid . . ."

"You mean, Operation Midnight Climax? I sent her a review of some play about that."

"Well, I saw the play. I thought it was great. And next day the review said, Aren't we tired of hearing about these things. Which totally floored me. So I went around asking people, Did you know about mental patients being given acid while chunks of their brains were removed, so they could describe the 'visual experience'? Or the Rand corporation studying how to use it to undermine the antiwar movement? Or the CIA trying to dose Nasser and Castro so they'd seem nuts? While at the same time holding seances to talk to dead agents. And the reaction I got was like I'd just turned into public enemy #1. It's so weird. You can talk about Viet Nam and sleeping with everyone in sight then but not this. I think some of my friends are afraid their kids will turn them in. It's like, we looked over the edge, and it was just too scary, so let's all pretend to have amnesia."

Diana had been more of a hippie than Leni, she remembered. With wispy long skirts, and hand-rolled cigarettes, and her old Triumph convertible. "Are you planning to tell your daughters Mommy used to trip out in high school?"

She smiled. "That's what Leni kept asking me. I'll cross that bridge when I come to it. In about two years."

"A friend of mine took some ayahuasca when he was in the Peace Corps in Brazil. The vision he saw floating in the night sky was a giant bar of soap."

She turned onto Kenwood. The door of the house stood open. Uncle Paul's fedora sailed by in the hall.

"Leigh, if you don't mind, I think I won't come in. I have to take the girls to the dentist, and if I see your father I'll start crying again. Just looking at the back of his head today did it. They really loved each other, underneath it all."

"I know. I guess. In an exasperated way."

The street around the park was so narrow and crowded it was hard to open the car door.

Diana shifted into the driver's seat. "I'll call you tomorrow. We'll have a booze and sob party. I want to hear more about this guy they want for questioning."

"So do I. Thanks for the info."

She waved as Diana drove away, then climbed the granite steps.

Sarah stood inside the door, her mass of red hair free of the clip she wore at work to keep it out of the color baths. "Master. There you are. I'm the coat-taker. Gimme."

"You're really letting Jean carry that tray? When she spilt that whole wash on your foot?"

The double doors were open to the buffet table in the dining room. Maneuvering around it, Alan came over holding a glass of white wine. "I was beginning to worry about you. I thought maybe you'd gone back to Arizona."

"You bloodhound. How did you know about that?"

"From the boarding pass that fell out of your jacket when I hung it up last night."

"You mean, when you frisked it. Is that for me?"

"If you want it."

"I do. I've started drinking like a fish."

"You're not alone. That . . . shall we say, portly gentleman over there just asked me where the gin was. We hadn't planned on serving anything hard."

"To him, we will. That's Uncle Paul. He's not related. We've just always called him that. I'll take care of him."

"And then you'll tell me about Arizona."

"Not here I won't." She took the glass.

"Mysterious. I like it."

Threading across the living room, she tapped Paul on the shoulder. "A martini? On the rocks? With a twist?"

"Hello, darlin'." His beard scraped her cheek and he gave her waist a squeeze. "I was just telling Harriet, my daughter saw your earrings on a TV show last week. She'd bought the same pair. It made her day. Let me come along and gently wave the vermouth."

He followed her into the small kitchen and opened the cabinet she pointed to over the refrigerator. "You moved it up here since Dad's stroke?"

"Right. If he can't have it, he doesn't want to see it, but he insists on keeping stocked for company." She thought of Michael, in his tower in Chama. The neat cart of liquor in the living room, and open pill bottles in the kitchen. Probably, he was still mad at her.

"So, how are you doing?" He held her chin to study her face through battered horn-rim glasses. "Your dad told me you went out west to do the necessaries. Good for you."

His hazel eyes looked tired. He was getting old, she saw. The first of the grad students she remembered coming to the house. Leni had a crush on him in junior high. He had a motorcycle then. And he was handsome.

Taking down the shaker, he threw in a handful of ice cubes. "What did they tell you out there? Are they going to solve this thing?"

"Did you know Leni was madly in love with you in the eighth grade?"

He looked up from the vermouth he was measuring into the bottle cap. "Well, I loved her too. Both of you."

"And I was jealous, because Dad wouldn't let me ride on your bike."

Watching him pour the gin, she wondered if he had been at MIT in 1957. Baggy Uncle Paul, who had never been appointed to the faculty but had lab privileges in spite of what Dad called his anarchistic tendencies.

Harriet must have known what happened back then. Along with half the old guard sitting in the living room.

She handed him a lemon from the bowl on the table. "Would you say Leni took after my mother?"

Pulling open the counter drawer, he stood looking down at it and she heard him exhale. "Sweet, the one time I saw your mom, she was not herself. But from her picture, there's a resemblance."

"You mean, she was crazy."

He ran a forefinger in a circle around his face. "She was all puffed up. From the medicine she was taking. And she just sat like a statue. I think she was only home for the weekend. I felt bad for both of them."

The paring knife moved in an arc and he dropped a shaving of rind in his glass. "Then today, taking Leni there . . . I've always thought I was against the death penalty, but I could personally execute the scum who killed that girl."

The phone rang in the hall. Leaning out, she saw Alan go for it. He nodded into the receiver, and then found her with his eyes and crooked a finger.

"That's for me, Unc. I'll be right back."

Alan met her half way. "You better take it upstairs. It's Big Chief Many Badges."

"Who?"

"From the Chama police department?"

"Oh, great. He would call now."

"Better now than later, if it's something you don't want Dad to hear."

When she said hello on the study phone, Alan clicked off.

"Miss Haring? It's Chief Arias calling. You have people there. If this is a bad time, you could call me back."

"No. It's all right. I'm on the extension now."

An envelope from Waterson's rested against the desk lamp.

"You came back to Chama, I hear. You should have let me know."

"Not to her house. Just the college. I wanted to see her office."

"So Mr. Zinn told me. Unfortunately, you left before we got there."

The blue Strategic Materials reports must be sitting on his desk now.

"Was that wrong? I had to catch a plane."

"Yes, I'm glad to find you there. I spoke with Dr. Ford yesterday. She said you also expressed to her your impatience with our movement on this case."

His tone said they had treated her well and she had insulted both of them.

"I'm sorry. I didn't mean to be rude. It was just upsetting."

"Yes. We know that."

He was quiet for a minute.

"At this stage, I'm not sure whether I should speak to you or to your father. We've received some preliminary test results."

"To me, please. He isn't very well. Are these the drug tests?"

"That's right. And for prostatic acid phosphatase. I'd be willing to release this information to you only if we're quite clear on two points. First, I'll need your promise to keep it in confidence for the duration of the investigation."

"Yes. I understand. I promise."

"Good. And second, Miss Haring, this has to be a two-way street. I need to know that you recognize your responsibility to inform me of anything you may come across relating to this."

His voice had the consistency of poured concrete and she wondered if he were wearing his black commando suit. Fibbing to that in person might be hard. Still, if these were rules for the future, they hadn't been broken yet. "Yes. We did call you about the break-in. But Michael Zinn knew as much about it as I did, so it didn't seem to matter if I stayed."

"I didn't only mean with regard to that."

"I know. So, what did the tests say?"

Too pushy. He let her wait again, while papers were being shuffled.

"All right. The general drug screen showed the presence of cannabinoids. Marijuana, inhaled shortly before her death. Because of the other drugs found on the scene, the lab did a further screening that showed PCP as well. Angel dust. Also inhaled."

She heard her own breath come and go. Pig tranquilizer, Leni called it. On the wildest Saturday night of the year, she wouldn't smoke angel dust. "No. That has to be a mistake."

"I'm afraid it isn't. In fact, judging by this, she may not even have been conscious when she was killed."

"Then someone must have blown it in her face."

"The autopsy report shows no indication of forcible restraint."

"You mean apart from being strangled." She remembered him sitting in Leni's armchair with the folded newspaper. The leak, that would be less awkward with PCP added to the mushrooms. "Chief, I know I'm a pain, and I realize you didn't know my sister well, but believe me, she was strictly into plants. PCP was against her religion. Could you ask them to double check that before it runs in the *Boston Globe*?"

The police radio started crackling in the background. "In effect, that's already been done. It was also present in the marijuana taken from the house. But we'll ask the FBI to match her DNA with any saliva on that evidence."

Ben's grass. He must have smoked it too. He was worried about saliva.

His PCP, then. It must be. A fact he hadn't mentioned. Once that cropped up fairly often in violent crimes in the *Globe*.

His denim jacket with the turned-up collar and sunburn on his neck. Dark and scowling. Leni's fatal type. But not if he used that.

Maybe he hadn't mentioned it to Leni before they lit up. A little extra, to turn up the heat. And then she felt it coming on, and got mad at him.

Vera had bailed him out before.

Meeting in the misty cave had been Vera's idea. The fog world. Carefully orchestrated. Because it might be 'useful later on' if she believed him. Give the girl some wampum and a sob story that she has to keep quiet about.

The Haring girls were good at keeping secrets for tricky men.

She wrapped the phone cord around her finger. "What about the other test?"

"I was just coming to that. It's positive for seminal fluid. On the basis of our affidavit, the district attorney has agreed to issue an arrest warrant for Benjamin Naya, so relevant samples can be taken. Tomorrow's Sunday, so it may not be out till Monday morning. But I spoke to the Hopi police just before I called you, and as soon as their tribal court signs off, they're ready to go. Let's hope you're right about him being on the reservation. It has very limited access."

"Me?" But the sputter of the radio brought back what she said in his office. "Am I the reason you think he's there?"

"No. We've established a pattern of travel. A Mr. Edward Harris admitted giving you that tip, though. Which he failed to give the state police in his first interview. Which makes me wonder what else we haven't been told."

Pretty soon the bus boy at La Fonda would be charged as an accessory, thanks to her.

"It was a guess, Chief. I made more of it than he did. I felt like you weren't telling me anything."

His silence said he had told her now. More than she wanted to know.

He would expect her to be glad about the warrant, after leaning on them for it. But looking at the Waterson's envelope, she wondered if Ben could be that good an actor.

"When we have news, I'll be in touch," he said. "Goodbye, Miss Haring."

She hung up.

Monday, Ben would be on the police radios. Be on the lookout for. An ink blot with an attitude. And very limited access.

She put her head down on the desk, with her ear against the blotter. The spine of the book facing her said, *The Lost Notebooks of Loren Eiseley.*

Closing her eyes, she thought, I want them to arrest you. Because one way or another you made this happen, and now I don't trust anyone. Because for all I know, it's you who wanted to use the satellite pictures. Because you turn me on and I don't even want to think about that.

A slow surge of fog came up and she was on the mesa, walking toward him along the ledge. He held the glassy stone out. It looked synthetic. Her first impression. If it was, he had lied about everything.

Getting up, she went to her room and took it out of her purse. Sunlight coming through it made a silver beam. She put it between her teeth. The surface felt as slick as glass but it was warmer and wouldn't crack.

Leni believed him. Trusted him. There might be a chance in a million she wanted to test the effects of angel dust and he wasn't about to volunteer that fact.

Given any chance, he ought to know about the warrant. From the air, with good visibility and binoculars, spotting him wouldn't be hard. If he really was camping in that cave.

She took the number for Vera to the study. Calling the fourth dimension. Three hard clicks came. Via satellite, it seemed. Then somewhere on the mesas, a phone started ringing. And kept on. In an empty house.

For now, the only answer was in the stone.

Voices converged in the stairwell. Someone was going out. Paul?

But looking over the banister, she saw the cousins saying goodbye.

A hermit like Paul might have left already.

She went around down the back stairs. He was lifting the shaker out of the freezer and gave a jump. "You scared me, girl."

"Sorry. I was afraid you'd go."

"I thought I ought to clean up my leftovers," he grinned, and poured the dregs into his glass.

"I have a major favor to ask you. But it's a secret."

"About your mom?"

He'd been waiting to finish that conversation more than the gin, she realized. "No."

"Leni, then."

"In a way. But you can't tell my father."

He peered over his glasses. "Just as long as it's mostly legal."

She held the splinter out to him. "I need to know what this is. Like, right away yesterday."

It looked tiny, sitting on his palm. "Oh? What's so special about it?"

"That's what I want to know. It was, to Leni. She thought it had some kind of power. It's probably rock salt. But I need to find out. Can you?"

"Her philsopher's stone, huh?" He rolled it between his fingers. "Sure. How fast is the question. School's out. I doubt there are any geologists lurking on campus. Or geophysicists, for that matter. What's the rush? Or shouldn't I ask."

"Rats. Can't you think of anyone?"

Taking a sip of watery gin, he made a face and set the glass in the sink. "Well, we might try my pal Al. As I affectionately call him. He's a materials guy. One of these seriously deranged types." He glanced at his watch. "The twenty-second. His wife will pry him out for Christmas Eve, but I might be able to catch him in the morning. If I get there before he's too heavy into it."

"You're a peach. Will he mind if it turns out to be quartz?"

"Hey, don't knock quartz." He put it in his pocket. "The first radios were crystal sets. I built one myself, once upon a time. Now, I think I better drive Jerry Burroughs home before he disgraces himself with one of your cute friends."

She smiled. "That could be exciting. Sarah has a black belt in karate. Go on. I'll be right out."

Moving the shaker to the sink, she put the peeled lemon in the refrigerator drawer. On the bottom shelf, a corrugated box was stamped PRODUCT OF SCOTLAND.

It took a moment to know what it was. A delicacy that wouldn't be served now. The side of smoked salmon bought as Dad's peace offering to Leni.

Chapter 12

IN THE DREAM she was on Third Mesa, trying to get to him, but the map she had was washed out by a place called Alkalai Bridge. As obvious as all her dreams. A nonexistent name. Her watch had stopped at 2 a.m., an hour after the last attempt to get through on the phone there.

The bedsheets were tangled. From the way the sun came in, it must be late morning.

Voices, in the dining room. Crossing to the study, she tried again. Maybe for the ceremony, Hopis pulled the plug on the 20th century.

The clothes packed for the trip home seemed quaintly formal now. No cave-crawling had been anticipated. A white cotton sweater that buttoned up the back, and cropped putty-colored slacks. Severe, with black tights and flats—except for the sunburn picked up in one hour at Tlaquepaque.

The shoes were almost new and pinched going down the stairs.

Dad and Harriet faced each other over the Sunday papers spread across the table. He was wearing his dark suit again, as if there were something more to do, and she bent to kiss his forehead. "I slept like a rock."

He patted the hand she rested on his arm. "You always used to, on the weekends. While the phone rang, and rang, and rang. I was glad you were so popular and sorry you'd gone deaf."

Harriet had her hair in what Leni called her Doris Lessing bun, parted down the middle and drawn back in a smooth roll flecked with grey. She took off her reading glasses. "There's fresh coffee, Leigh. With hazelnut. From your wonderful Alan. I don't know what we would have done without him."

In the kitchen, she found half a cantaloupe in the refrigerator, and was squeezing lime juice over it when Dad came in holding his cup.

He poured one for her too, with a steady hand, and carried them back to the table. "I suppose we should have a family meeting. I'd like to know what the police had to say. And the medical examiner."

"Investigator, they call it there." She kept her eyes on the melon. "There are all kinds of cops involved. The state police, and the crime lab. I only talked to the chief in Chama."

"Did he agree with what Sergeant Robbins said?"

"Now, Richard..." Not yet, Harriet meant. Not rape over Alan's pastry. But the pictures in his head could be worse than the truth, whatever that might be. In the most merciful version, Leni made love and passed out and then was efficiently killed by a hit man for some mining company.

It would be more comforting, though, to think Ben had done it and the cops were going to get him now. The target she had wanted.

The DNA match: a needle in his arm, and a thread of blood snaking away so his own genes could be used against him. A real out-of-body experience.

Her cup clattered against the saucer. "Is there anything in the paper?"

"Not today," Harriet said. "Thank heaven."

"Leigh, you haven't answered me."

"I know. It isn't clear yet, Dad. It might not have been rape. Her friends say the guy they're looking for didn't do it."

"Then why would he run off?" His grey eyes fixed her angrily. "An innocent man who cared about her would cooperate with the police."

"Not in any movie I've ever seen. Not if he's the suspect. What good is being locked up? It just makes you totally helpless."

"What does he do?" Harriet asked. "For work, I mean."

The professional element. That would matter. Is he our kind of rapist? She couldn't help smiling. "He's a photographer. Pretty good, from what little I've seen. He's had exhibits at a museum there."

"An artist? Well, I hope her friends are right. I hope he loved her. She deserved to be loved. Richard, aren't we supposed to start with a presumption of innocence in this country?"

A quiet note of triumph. They had probably spent the morning fighting over David Nyhan's column in the *Globe*.

Maybe once they had fought about Ruth. There had been some trouble between them. Harriet, taking them off on jaunts without him. Mailing Christmas presents. Reappearing on the scene when Leni was in junior high and wouldn't listen to anybody else.

In a while it might be possible to ask about that. After they had time to rest. Whatever reserve of strength had propelled him this far was visibly gone and she got up to give him a hug. "Dad, what Chief Arias and Dr. Ford said to tell you is, everything's proceeding as it should. They're both terrific and there's nothing we can do except hope they have some luck. I'm going to zoom in town and pick up some clothes and then I think we should all just try to relax until after Christmas."

"Now? But you can't, Leigh. Paul's coming over to see you. He called at ten. I thought he'd be here by now. He was very enigmatic. Were you expecting him?"

Not in person, she thought. A quiet phone call would do. "I guess I told him we could use some moral support. And some cheering up."

He didn't look convinced.

"I'll try to catch him before he leaves, Dad. It's too soon now. Is your address book upstairs?"

"Yes. But he had something on his mind. He said for you to stay here."

Not quartz, then. Or rock salt. Bad news. As if there hadn't been enough.

In the hall, a manila envelope protruded from the mail slot. The only address on it was her name. She carried it up to the study.

Paul's office number had been changed, crossed out and another carefully written in. One lab, in a hive of them. Leaning on the windowsill, she called the number and let it ring.

Down in the park, two boys were breaking icicles off the iron rail and throwing them like spears. A blue panel truck had pulled up over the curb by the fence, so close to the corner it would be served right to get a snowball through the windshield.

At MIT, no one was answering. She tried his home and waited again. He might have decided to bring along the family as a smokescreen, however unsubtle his phone message had been.

The manila envelope held a smaller one addressed to Diana from Leni's old box number in Albuquerque. A pink Post-it note on the back said:

Leigh,
   Rereading this, it's like her last will and testament, for chrissake. Hope it's not too much right now. I'll call later so we can talk.

Love,
D.

Taking it into her bedroom, she pulled the armchair up to the window to watch for Paul.

Three pages of single-spaced type from their old matching printers. Written in the trailer then, by the dusty window looking out on a ragged row of sunflowers. Which would have been stubble at the time, given the December date. In summer, when she visited, a big yellow dog lay panting in their shade.

Dear Diana,

Sorry for not calling back. I couldn't go through it on the phone, least of all from my father's.

We were right about the experiment. She signed up without telling him, using her maiden name. And probably wasn't crazy at all, but once you've been committed you sort of lose your credibility.

What's staggering is, I must have known. Overheard them fighting. It would certainly explain my erstwhile career. When I found that *Life* article on Maria Sabina, I knew I had to hide it.

I've now spent twenty years enacting that little mystery play. He said at first we were too young to tell, and later there didn't seem to be a right time—which doesn't quite jell with being whisked off to Mexico when it was about to hit the papers. Someone must have warned him MK-ULTRA was being declassified.

What a laugh. I've written papers relating the water-lily in Mayan art (the long-nosed god sipping therefrom) with the Asian lotus coming from the lips of recumbent adepts (both rhizomes have apomorphine, still used in treating mental illness); and on Gilgamesh finding a sign, a plant that could restore his wonder, and then losing it (to a serpent who promptly molts = transformation), and yet it never computed that obvious explanation for my mother could be the right one. So I must not have wanted to know, either. About him, more than her, I think.

By withholding that, it's like he ensured I'd go after it. Now, only Leigh's out of the loop—for her sake, according to him. But she's right there with him, has been all these years, and she doesn't have the memory of Mom being driven off in that car, still trying to smile even though she knew she was in their hands then. That's my ghost, and he says there's nothing to be gained by forcing it on Leigh now.

That wasn't true, she thought. When Leni wrote the letter, there was time to gain. Years to figure out how it had worked on them. A chance to renegotiate, and so a chance this might have turned out differently.

Below in the street, a police cruiser came to a stop in front of the house.

It sat blocking the corner, with the motor running and no apparent movement inside. Then just when she started thinking Paul must have sent it for her, a cop got out to stick a parking ticket on the panel truck's smoked windshield.

Her breath had fogged the windowpane. Paranoia. It was Ben the cruisers would be after.

She flattened the letter on her knee.

On the other hand, wouldn't I be censoring Leigh then? Confiscating history, like he did, with the same dubious good intentions? By which, it seems, the picture is altered dot by dot until inconvenient features disappear. Except, after a while, a pentimento comes through. Or things are overlooked. A slip of Harvard memo paper, with my mother's handwriting: 'Dr. Max—There are more things in heaven and earth than are dreamt of in your philosophy.'

She wouldn't draw-a-man for him. An affront to his scientific priesthood. Heresy. Followed by Inquisition. Calling it insanity instead of sin in 1957. The shamans may have competed with the Spanish priests and doctors, but how much threat could my mother be?

< You say you can sympathize with my father because of your own kids—and it's hard to believe we were sixteen the first time we took acid. But we had ritual: a night field on a hilltop, and Mark, a real guide. That first vibration—you started laughing and I didn't know why, and then he turned me toward the moon, and the grass came alive and the sky. Even when the devils came screaming down, that thread to him was enough to let us go with it.

It was after we gave up the ritual we got in trouble.

My mother had a bunch of suits telling her she was psycho. And I think of that worst-of-all trips in Central Square, when the cops came and Susan told me to say I was sick, but all I heard in that was that I *was* sick, and thought I'd never come down. That was the end of acid for me. The last stop before Oaxaca.

Tacitus: 'As to the acts of the gods, it seems holier and more reverent to believe than to know.' Maybe. But if you have known, it beats second-hand information. A friend in the

Native American Church says God sent us Christ, but we killed him and are left only with his book now. But Indians were given peyote because to them the world is God and they don't need words to know it. Gordon Wasson, the banker who wrote about Maria Sabina, spent his life studying mushroom cults going back ten thousand years, and says the very idea of the miraculous, the transfigurations of death and rebirth in all religion, may well have started with the fly agaric—the mushroom, incidentally, illustrated in *Alice in Wonderland.* (A subliminal you have no doubt exposed your children to already?)

Your implication seems to be that since I don't have kids I can't understand the responsibility. But I do have them, whole classrooms full, and I see them getting the same disinformation—the next to be sacrificed on the altar—because the adults around are too frightened of their own minds to be honest. Talk about 'drugs of initiation' (supposed to lead to smack, of course), but what I see is precisely the opposite. No initiation into the vastness of human nature and the symbols by which that can be read. Our puberty rites are courtesy of Coke and Pepsi, who spend $14 billion a year on them. Here is the scene you want to join: its rituals, music, chalice.

I'm hardly recommending kids drop acid now. The stuff on the street is a crapshoot, and I can't see the window we had opening for a long time. But if change begins in the imagination, and we do seem to be walking around with a million years of collective unconscious wired in our brains, it follows there might be some wisdom there more perilous to lose than find before it all gets digitally remastered.

And, as rebellion is half the fun, disclosure would puncture the aura. As a teacher, I'd favor something like: 'Kids, ten thousand ads a week to the contrary, the world is not being run for your benefit. Television programs are commercials for commercials that prey on fears and longings below your conscious mind, which direct your life. As a species, we've evolved with receptors in our brain that act as a bridge to those forces when stimulated in a number of ways. Here are the techniques and substances used throughout history to that end, and their relative potential risks and benefits. The physiological impact of each will be discussed in detail, and no false distinctions will be made: nicotine affects the same receptors as the visionary drugs. Now it is up to you to decide if, when, and how to make use of these or protect yourself from them. This is a small but crucial element of your education, and we stand ready to give our perspective on this as on any other subject.'

Instead, it's been so demonized, no real exchange is possible.

You say if you told the 50-mic. acid-poppers at the Dome they were supposed to be having mystic visions, they'd laugh in your face before skating off on their Rollerblades. That's what this country does brilliantly—dilutes anything to household strength. But you and I were first on our block to bolt, so better not be too evasive with your girls. After all, even toad venom stew is coming in for a revival.

From Palenque, 645 A.D.: a Mayan glyph of a toad with three circles around its venom gland. Bufotenine. One of the riskier trips. The frog as musician to the Chacs, the rain gods of the Yucatan. When there was no rain, a priest would call the Chacs by ingesting the holy poison of their harbinger. Then Shakespeare's witches brewed it, till the Inquisition got them. Now in Australia, neo-hippies are boiling up Giant Cane Toads, with the odd fatal result.

The return of the repressed. From English class. Coleridge, Poe, and Dickens—opium eaters all. Keats a heavy morphine user, according to a radioassay done on a lock of his hair at the U. of Iowa. "Much have I travelled in the realms of gold, / And many goodly states and kingdoms seen . . ."

Want to throw all that out too?

Maybe next time some genius will work it into the scheme of things. Just for economic reasons. Dig up the addiction and prison studies and be able to try again. There's a clinic in Holland getting people off white powder without withdrawal symptoms using African ibogaine. Only, they charge $20K plus airfare. We could do it for $200 a case here.

T. S. Eliot said that to get to where you are (from where you aren't), you must go by a way that holds no ecstasy.

Exactly the reverse of my view. Even though I'm now an almost middle-aged pillar of the community. And I don't regret what you call my caravan existence—except that I abandoned Leigh and I'm not sure in essence this isn't doing that again.

Thank you for trying to sort us out. I did get all the way back here with my yap shut. So we'll see. And in spite of the above, you'll find the right spin for your daughters when the time comes. Because if you can't, no one can.

Love,
Len

A rational explanation for why the irrational had failed. Signed with her scratchy Pelikan pen.

If Leni knew then she'd be fired for a milder version of that sermon, she might not have been surprised, though.

Brain circuitry. Four decades, broadcast simultaneously. Watching Mom's car drive away as vivid as yesterday's conversation. And for Leni, a million more years wired in, and she was welcome to them. It was tricky enough to navigate from yesterday to tomorrow.

Abandonment as family theme. It hadn't felt that way. Really, it was a relief when Leni left home, at first. It must have been after that acid trip she started staying out all night, and the fighting escalated. Once she went to Brandeis, things calmed down. Then, at the end of freshman year she disappeared to Mexico and never came back for long again.

But at twelve, it had been easier to imagine Leni's travels than to cope with her in person. Fun taking the train alone to Cambridge for dinner at the faculty club—where there always was a flurry of attention. Coming off the elevator, Dad already gesturing, reeling anyone of interest into his force field crossing the dining room, his silver hair and pearl grey suit like the flume of a speedboat towing her in its wake. Scandinavian jewelry was popular with the wives them. Beaten runic silver, against the bleeding stripes of Marimekko shirts. Rock cornish hen on Wednesday. Sole on Friday. No more babysitters. When her first cramps came, he had given her whiskey in warm water. A brief but solemn rite of passage. Then curled in a ball in bed, she had wanted Leni, and felt sorry for herself. But not abandoned. Until now, when neither of them had a choice about it.

It wasn't hard to fill in Diana's side of the conversation. Not unlike what her own would have been. And that might be the deeper reason why Leni hadn't told her. Wanting to protect Mom's ghost from any possible criticism.

As she folded the letter, Paul's old green Saab came around the square.

The only place to park was by the hydrant. He backed in without hesitation.

A younger man in a black leather coat got out from the passenger side. If that was his pal Al, he didn't look deranged at all.

Paul followed, his chin well down in his ancient Harvard muffler. They met at the end of the front walk and just as they turned in, a pulse of yellow came from the headlight of the panel truck. Just one, barely visible in the sun, but it struck an off note. The parking ticket was still under the wiper.

The doorbell got her up to look in the mirror. An anxious mouse face. Sticking her tongue out at it, she went downstairs.

Harriet was taking coats while Paul made introductions. Charlie Webber. He put out a hand and smiled into her eyes. His were golden brown, like his bristly hair and the heathery weave of his sweater. A masterpiece of fashion, next to Paul.

"Dr. Haring. You're a legend, Sir. I think I missed you by one year."

"Oh? Well, thank you," he said uneasily. "To what do we owe the honor, etcetera. You wanted to speak to Leigh?"

"To both of you." Paul gave her a sheepish glance. "Sorry, kid, but we've got to have a round table on this. Dick, I hate to bother you now. But it's about Leni and it's important."

"Leigh?" He turned. "What is all this?"

A smudgy look around his eyes told more than the annoyance in his voice. The straw that broke the camel's back. But it was too late to be sorry. "It's just . . . a rock, Dad. A pebble, really."

"Let's sit down, Dick. The dining room? We won't keep you any longer than we have to."

Harriet sat down next to Paul, who leaned his elbows on the table. "Dick, Leigh gave me a chip of crystal yesterday. She wanted to know what it was. ASAP, so I took it to the materials lab and Al Guzzi nailed me to the wall. He'd seen just one other sample like it, a few weeks ago. Charlie here is the ceramicist at Lincoln lab who brought him in on that analysis."

"Well? Are you going to tell us, or do we guess?"

"I'd tell you if I could," Charlie Webber grinned. "The trouble is we don't know yet. The structure of it doesn't exist. Not on this planet, anyway. From the iridium content, it has to be meteor crust. But not like any one that's turned up before. Often you'll see glass formed by the heat of the atmospheric impact. But this seems to be a case of what Al calls 'unanticipated chemistry.' Brand new. We don't even know what to call it."

"How interesting. Leigh? This is something of Leni's?"

She knew he wanted to hear it from her, and wasn't sure what to say. Lying to him now seemed traitorous. But Lincoln lab was spook central.

Sticking to the same lie would at least keep the story consistent. "That's right. She thought it was unusual. That's why I wanted to find out."

"Uh huh." Paul folded his hands across his stomach. "And when did she tell you that?"

She could sense the trap, but not how to avoid it. "A while ago. I think she brought it back from Mexico."

"Not likely, kid. This was cut very recently. And the other sample was sent to Lincoln from a geologist at the Living Mesa Foundation, at Chama, New Mexico. Which seems a little too close to be coincidental."

The vine pattern in the wall paper behind him reminded her of Leni's garden. Chama. Not where that stone should have been, by any story she knew. "What do you want me to say? This is the first I've heard of that."

"Leigh . . ." Charlie Webber looked tenderly at her. "My lab's funded by your father's old shop. DARPA, the Defense Advanced Research Projects Agency. After Sputnik, Eisenhower set it up in the DOD, and then NASA split off. Now it's mostly into research in communications technology. This . . . discovery, because that's what it is, could be awesome. Wonderful. So great, there's a chance your sister was killed to keep her from passing on what she knew about it. The geologist, Jonathan Addison, who sent the other sample, died in a car accident two weeks ago. A fact I only found out when I tried to call him back on Thursday. The police out there say it looked like a straight skid. It had been snowing. But there weren't any witnesses. And no one else at the foundation will admit to knowing anything about this."

Michael Zinn had mentioned something about a car crash. And the "cops out there" could only mean Chief Arias, who would be making connections of his own. Threads crossing over in a web, a net, coming down too fast.

"Leigh's just told you she doesn't either," Harriet said. "She has no reason to lie. What's so awesome? I didn't think the defense department used such adjectives."

"Rarely, Ma'am. In this case, it's warranted. I've been cleared to tell you that what this compound seems to be is your basic all-temperature superconductor. Right up there with cold fusion on every wish list in science. But in the one talk I had with Dr. Addison, he said getting the rest of it out of the ground would take the persuasive power of a choir of angels. He wouldn't say where it was. It's critical that we find out. Dr. Haring, did Elinor say anything to you about this?"

"Unbelievable. And you think she was involved somehow with this Addison?" He pressed the tips of his fingers into his temples. "I'm just remembering. You know, there was one thing. On the phone, when she told me she was coming home. She asked how much I knew about the U.S. Geological Survey. An optical system of mine was used in it, but that's about all I could tell her."

"Then she must have known something." Charlie Webber sat back. "Which means, Leigh, I'm afraid you're not being honest with us. I don't think your sister could have had her sample much longer than we've had ours. So from what Paul tells me you couldn't have seen it while she was alive." His voice expressed infinite regret. Sorry. Disappointment in her.

She smiled at him. It felt like an unattractive smile. Give him only what he could get from Arias anyway. "She left some reports at a friend's house. On strategic minerals. Which seemed odd, but Cather's a mining school. Then I found that stone, wrapped up in six different envelopes. I asked Paul about it so I wouldn't seem like a total fool if it turned out to be some New Age thing."

He smiled back evenly. "Who's the friend?"

"He doesn't know anything about it. He didn't even know she'd left the reports."

"Is he Indian, perchance? Doctor Haring, please tell her how serious this is."

"Dammit, man. Give us a chance! I buried one daughter yesterday. I won't have the other harassed in this house. You seem to have formed some opinion. Let's have it. Why Indian?"

"Because of what Dr. Addison said about access, partly. And where he was situated. Right on the edge of the Navajo and Jicarilla Apache reservations. This strike is worth so much, it shouldn't be a problem to get a mineral lease. Unless it's in the middle of a burial ground. Or some other place with taboos attached. I made a few calls, and both those tribes have signed leases in the past. The Jicarillas made a bundle on natural gas, and the Navajos with coal and uranium. But they're superstitious people. Money doesn't always talk. I spent three years at Los Alamos cooking up superconductive crystals, and the pueblos around there can get pretty strange at times."

He couldn't be much older than thirty-five, she thought. An aging prodigy. The bushy-tailed ex-boy of ceramics, who'd love to take credit for this. So far, no one here knew Ben was Hopi. Once they did, they'd get out the thumbscrews. Along with satellite cameras.

"But…" Harriet shook her head. "If you've already made these crystals…what's so wonderful about Leni's?"

"The temperature, I think, Aunt Harriet." The *Globe* had a story on it every other week. "The ones they have now only work very cold. Like, way below zero. Which isn't practical. Otherwise they'd be in everything from electric cars to Star Wars. What I don't see is, if this is just one meteor, why it should be so valuable. Unless it's huge. In which case you'd think it would have shown up before now."

"Good girl." Paul smiled. "You wouldn't want to design a system around an irreplaceable element. True. But with even a few hundred pounds of this, there's one machine that's a special case. That has what you might call a generational effect? Come on, Leigh."

"You mean, as in a computer?"

"Bingo. As in a supercomputer. Like the Cray, or one of the parallel processors. With the Cray, the limitation's been the speed of the signal. But the closer the engineering's packed, the more heat, the more the electrons slide around. Unless you use some of Charlie's crystals, chilled to -200 below. With the Addison sample, it's like water in stream. A pure channel. No resistance, no heat, no waste. And incredible speed. Maybe a thousand times faster. Maybe ten thousand. With just a few like that, you could solve things that could take years otherwise. Like, how to synthesize that material, for one thing," he laughed. "They could even design their own successor, like a genetic transfer, and we might not even know how they'd done it. Which wouldn't matter, as long as it put us in front of the Japanese."

"Leigh…" Charlie Webber gave her his 'significant' look again. "You mentioned strategic materials? We have a parallel with that. Twenty technologies now are deemed critical to national security, and the Japs are ahead of us in a lot of them. I'm not talking VCRs here. With the right computer, they could crack any banking, business, or defense system in this country. And suck the data out so fast we wouldn't even know we'd been hit."

"Something we'd never do ourselves, of course," Harriet said dryly.

He ignored her. "So we have two absolute criticalities here. Our need to have it, and a more urgent need to keep it away from the competition. If this really is on Indian land, that could be a problem. With their so-called 'sovereign nation' status, there are openings for direct trade with, say, Germany or Japan. The rising sun is an Indian symbol too. I'm not sure it's safe to rely on the loyalty of people who accuse us of genocide. The Addison Crust ought to top the list of critical materials. We sent half of it on to Washington. Once it gets through channels, I think we'll see a declaration of national security interest. And at the moment, you're the only link we've got."

Ben might be a new Hopi prophet, she thought. He even had the terminology right. Except that he'd also been dumb enough to put the sample in her hand.

This could clear him, though. It fit beautifully with his mining-company scenario. All he needed was reasonable doubt. Dr. Addison dead. A bogey hit man. Charlie Webber could testify... that Ben's motive could have been to stop Leni from bringing it home to Dad, whom she had asked about a geologic survey.

Unless Ben and Taylor were willing to talk about what they'd seen in the desert. Which might happen shortly after hell froze over. If Vera had to pick which one to save, the snake ground would have to win.

But it could be too late even for that now.

Charlie Webber's whiskers seemed to have grown in the time he'd been at the house. Called up early to come to the lab and hash this out with Paul. A front-man techie, as different as the time was from Paul's scruffy generation. Semi-classic nerds back then, with leather pen cases clipped into the pockets of their white shirts. Guys who went running before it got trendy and did noisy yoga breathing sitting cross-legged on their desks. Working in the eye of the storm could make some kind of zen sense. Microscopic measurements, with no political charge. The plasma of the universe. The source. The tiny pixels in all Leni's visions of heaven and hell.

Paul was looking at her now from under half-closed eyelids. His glasses down a little. Mild reproach. Sure that she would come around, and wrong this time. Paul, whose phone number had been changed while she wasn't paying attention. When classified research was banished from the campus in the '60's, featureless buildings grew up around its rim—discreet plaques announcing company names with one or more of the syllables: syn, bio, gen.

Maybe his phone rang in one of those now, where Charlie Webber came from.

Last Sunday morning, Leni was alive. No. Dead in Chama. But thought to be alive. If Charlie had come with this announcement then, he might have found a better audience.

She met his gaze. "I'm not a link, though. I don't attach to anything. You could go through her house yourself. But the police have taken a lot away."

"Then why make up that story for Paul? About it being her lucky piece."

"Just embroidery. It was stupid but I was asking him for a favor. I had to give some reason."

"I don't believe that. Why not simply the facts? Dr. Haring," the deferential tone was gone. "With your clearance, you see the implications of this. Would you ask Leigh to tell us the truth, please?"

"All right, that's enough!" He bolted up out of his chair and his left hand came down to grip her shoulder. "Both of you can leave. Right now. I mean it. We've heard what you had to say. Leigh's answered your questions. Now, get out."

"Dick." Paul stood up. "Are you all right? It's a bad time, sure, but for Leni's sake, the police ought to know..."

"Tell them then. I'll just bet he will. With his security clearance. Don't tell me what's good for my family."

Looking up at his darkening face, she wondered where this was coming from. Ice was his weapon of choice. As Paul knew very well.

Charlie Webber got up and pushed his chair back to the table. "I'm sorry if we upset you. Of course we'll go. But you can expect other visitors. As I said, it's in the pipeline now."

"Fine."

"Let me show you out," said Harriet, going for the closet.

"Dick?" Paul was smiling with pained surprise.

"No." Charlie Webber took his elbow. "Come on. They need time to talk. Goodbye for now, Leigh. Dr. Haring."

He kept her clamped to the chair until the front door shut. "That bastard. What a suck-up little worm he is. I'm a legend. Sure. Well, the legend wants a drink. Come on, before Harriet stops me."

Following him into the kitchen, she watched him fish for the bottle of Glenmorangie in the cabinet, cursing under his breath. "You found this rock at Leni's house?"

"Uh huh." She handed him a glass.

"How big is it?"

She measured an inch with her thumb and forefinger. "Like something out of a crackerjack box."

"It probably is."

"But if it's a meteor, wouldn't it have shown up before? On whatever that satellite survey was?"

"Maybe." He set the glass down on the calendar on the counter. "If you look through that, what do you see?"

"The date."

"And not the glass. So, maybe not. The southwest's littered with meteor crust. If some have this X compound, it might just read as the layer underneath. Especially if that were iron. There could be a faint . . . chiaroscuro around the edges, but insignificant numerically unless you knew what you were looking for."

"There can be diamonds in meteor crust. Maybe this is a crock."

"I don't think so. Gemstone diamonds are volcanic. General Electric can synthesize any other grade. Do you think her Indian boyfriend is in on this?"

She smiled. "How did you know he was Indian?"

"Alan told us. And good luck to him. Once they pick him up, he'll have the FBI and the Army Corps of Engineers for roommates. Along with DARPA and the Office of Surface Mining. It'll give the boys a treasure hunt for New Years." He took a swallow of scotch. "What tribe is he?"

"I'm not sure. He lives in Santa Fe, not on a reservation." Then she wondered why she was lying now. "What if it does come from a burial ground?"

"Then, my guess would be, they'd get it out fast and apologize afterward. Outrage being easier to deal with than organized obstruction. If he was cleared to tell us about it, that will likely be the strategy. Say how thrilling it is, and how too bad . . . but look at it this way. Etcetera. The Indians might stay outraged, but they aren't statistically significant either." He shrugged. "At least Leni can't blame me for this. My system didn't pick it up." He took another sip from the glass. "Unbelievable. I spend my life trying to keep you girls safe, and then she walks into this. Incredible. I hope there's nothing else you haven't told me?"

She shook her head. "How could you have kept her safe, Dad. She was hardly ever here."

"That's right. It was better that way. Till this."

"Better how?"

"For her. To be away from here." Glancing toward the hall door, he emptied his glass. "Where's Harriet got to?"

"She's in the powder room. What do you mean, it was better for her?"

"With her interests? Don't be naive, Leigh. You just met a perfect case-in-point."

"Charlie Webber?"

"And his clones."

"You mean, because of Mom."

He cocked his head as if he heard a sound he couldn't quite identify. "What?"

"I found an article at Leni's about the CIA experiments. Diana told me Mom was in them."

"Oh." He put the glass down. "Diana. I see. How good of her."

"Richard, we can't let this happen again."

Turning, she saw Harriet leaning in the doorway, and realized she had been crying.

"We can't let them take Leigh, too. What are we going to do?"

"Nobody's taking me anywhere, Auntie." She went to put an arm around her. "Did they scare you?"

"You bet. They scare me plenty. And that Webber said he'd be back."

"So? I told him what I could. Let him sue me if he doesn't like it."

"But . . . dear . . . weren't you just talking about Ruth?"

"Yes. Finally. A little."

Harriet seemed to float out of her grasp and bob toward the sliding glass door overlooking the garden. She stood with her back turned. "They took Ruth. I couldn't stop it. Then she came home in a coffin. Like Leni."

"For Godssake!" He slammed a hand down on the counter. "Leni was murdered. There's no comparison. Ruth was a victim of plain incompetence. Talk about lawsuits. I should have sued that hospital. At the time, I just wanted it to be over with."

"But who put her there?" Harriet's voice was reedy.

"That was for her protection."

"So you've told me. But it didn't work. Leigh, you tell them. Whatever they want to hear. Maybe you'll have a better chance like that."

"Dammit, woman, no one's touching Leigh!"

"You thought you could control it all with Ruth, though, didn't you? Wasn't that the idea?" Turning, she smiled bitterly. "'Just a temporary thing,' you said. Well, it didn't turn out that way."

He reached for the scotch. "Ruth was over her head. She didn't understand what was in play. Any more than Leni did. You can have all the great ideals in the world, and they can do more harm than good."

A slur was creeping into his speech. A warning. But the door was open now, and might not be again.

"Dad, what Diana said was... maybe Mom had some kind of mystical experience from the acid, and that wasn't understood then?"

"Oh? Did she? I'll tell you what wasn't understood. Want to know where those experiments came from? Right out of Dachau concentration camp. The Nazis were looking for a drug that would break down human will. After the war, the U.S. Technical Mission brought out their mescaline studies, along with the doctor responsible for them. Hubertus Strughold. Who, it may interest you to know, NASA later called the 'father of space medicine.' It's hand-in-glove, you see? Just like Rinkel's work at Harvard. He was using LSD for its 'psychotomimetic' properties. Meaning, to mimic psychosis. Which it did. Very effectively."

"And she didn't come down from it?"

"That depends on what you mean," Harriet said. "She wouldn't back off, is more like it. She wanted to write about it the way Aldous Huxley did."

"She was raving. You were worried about her yourself."

"Yes." Harriet turned away. "I was young and she embarrassed me. I blame myself too."

"How about blaming her, while you're at it? Signing up under her maiden name. As if that would fool anyone." He was shaking. "Leigh, when those MK-ULTRA boys wanted to cover their mistakes, they'd simply destroy the subject's brain to get rid of the evidence."

"At Harvard, Richard?"

"If elsewhere, why not there? I had to be away then. There was a witch hunt starting about Soviet moles in the CIA and Rinkel was spooked. I didn't know what they'd do."

"Dad, it's all right." His expression frightened her. "You could have told me this."

"God, I wanted to keep you out of it. I knew I couldn't stop Leni."

"But it's better than thinking Mom went crazy."

"Is it?" Harriet said brightly. "Was it crazy for her to say atomic bombs are monstrous? Or to want to make a birthday cake for Leigh?"

He took a step toward her. "Stop it. Leave Leigh out of it, I said."

"But she isn't out of it, Richard. Can't she know her mother loved her?"

"You want to make Ruth a martyr. Even if Leigh has to suffer for it?"

"Dad, will you please take it easy? I won't suffer. For a birthday cake? That's what you wouldn't tell me?"

"Go ahead, Harriet." His face was stony. "You win. Give your speech."

For a moment, she looked at a loss. Afraid to make him angrier. Then she folded her arms. "From what Leigh just said, I should have a long time ago. You've always made Ruth sound like some escaped lunatic. But I talked to her the night before . . . two days before your birthday, Leigh. She said they were making her take so much Thorazine she could hardly function, and she wanted to get off it enough to go home and have a party for you. She wasn't running away. She wasn't crazy. She just wouldn't give in to them."

"You mean, she got run over coming . . . because of me."

"Oh, good, Harriet. Wonderful," he said. "I hope you're very proud."

"No, dear. Not because of you. Because she was trying to fight what they did to her. Richard, all these years you've told me it would hurt Leigh if she knew. That's your version. Leigh, what I'm saying is, she loved you. She was a good mother. And they took her away from you."

Leaning back against the stove, she felt its knobs dig into her waist. It seemed important to get this straight. But it was like a broken mirror, each piece showing a different scene. Dangerous. In danger. Nazis in the woodwork. Ruth slipping out into heavy traffic, inadvisedly. A string of errors in judgment. A birthday cake she would only have remembered as a picture in an album anyway.

Instead there was no picture. But he was standing hunched, a damaged bird, and she had to rescue him. Leni had blamed him enough for both of them.

"If Mom wanted to be with me so much, why would she risk doing that experiment?"

"Because she'd been reading too damn much Huxley," he said. "About the 'door' to the other world, passed through 'on wings of mescaline.' And Havelock Ellis and his peyote 'paradise.' The Jungian mytho-poetic mind. She was ready to throw out her thesis and start over again on that."

The slur was gone, and yet she felt she hadn't heard him right. Or rather, had heard something out of order. "You mean, she read Huxley before she took it? That's why she wanted to try it herself?"

He nodded. "And, afterward, poof. Three years of thesis out the window, because God had been delivered courtesy of the CIA."

"But..." she tried to catch it and it felt just out of reach. "If you knew...about Huxley, then why did she seem so crazy? It sounds like he was saying the same thing."

The glass of whiskey stopped half way to his mouth.

"Yes," Harriet said. "I'd like to hear your answer to that."

He set the glass down. "You're looking through the wrong end of the telescope. Both of you. Huxley's book had only just been published. Hardly anyone knew what he was saying."

"But you did, Richard. And you forbade her to try it. And when she disobeyed, you punished her for it."

He gave a groan of frustration. "Will you listen to me? In 1957, in the United States, LSD was a weapon, not a sacrament. Yes, she had the misfortune to be married to me, and the research I was doing then was as classified as it gets. After Sputnik, everyone was spooked. For my wife to start writing about how the Russians are our brothers and we should beat our swords into plowshares...that was not going to wash. Not coming out of anything connected with the CIA, when they were on their mole kick. It was a dangerous situation. If my clearance had been compromised, it would have cost us years of work."

"You mean, the Pentagon," Harriet said. "It would have cost the government. So Ruth had to be sacrificed instead."

He closed his eyes. Meaning yes. Meaning, you'll never understand. Meaning, are you happy now?

He had been ten years older than Ruth was. Faculty, to her student. She could probably be as irritating as Leni, and on the same subjects. But who would pay attention to them, really?

"Dad, are you saying you had her committed to keep her from writing articles? Or joining the ban-the-bombers, or something?"

"No. To prevent what might follow from that. Just for while I had to be gone, Leigh. It was supposed to be temporary."

A line from Leni's letter came back, about losing credibility. That would have been permanent, though. And handing Ruth to that doctor to protect her from him didn't make a lot of sense.

A smear that couldn't be erased. Like what the papers were doing to Leni. A silencing. What he had done, even when Leni found out. Presented now as a gift to her. One she must have wanted. Sibling perversity. Choose up sides and go blindly on from there.

"Leigh, can you understand this?" Tears shone in his eyes, and she wasn't sure who they were for. "You were so young. There was no way to explain it to you."

"Sure I can. I'm a chip off the old block, Dad. When I read about the drugs at Leni's, all I could think of was what it would do to me. Your name is certainly more important than mine."

She could sense Harriet about to close in, and put up her palms to stop it. "I just need some time to digest this now."

"Leni told me it started here," he said. "The Germans synthesized mescaline from peyote Parke-Davis sent from the Kiowa and Apaches. Then Huxley read the German studies, in the '30's. The CIA used mescaline before LSD. In Project Chatter. It was supposed to release repressed material. Which I guess we're doing now."

He looked so relieved she wanted to punch him. And Harriet too.

"I have to call Alan," she said. "To thank him. Then I'm going for a walk."

They couldn't object. And when she left, they could go on arguing about which points they'd each won.

Walking down the hall, she saw the blue panel truck with the orange parking ticket under its wiper. So it hadn't disappeared with Charlie Webber after all.

A long walk to the cemetery might be in order. To visit the other half of the family. If only Vera or someone would answer that damn phone.

From the study window, the truck looked more of a sore thumb, and half way through calling the number, she put the receiver down. A hundred bad TV shows with listening vans—snoops plugged into tape recorders. It seemed too tacky to be true. By now, there must be some micro-bug that could transmit for a mile.

They hadn't had much lead time, though. A flash of headlights
telling him: we're ready for you, Charlie. He had been too willing
to go away at the end.

Now they would have picked up the area code. Unless that came
off as a mistake. She called Alan's number quickly. His machine
kicked in, but he interrupted it.

"Hello?"

His voice was so guarded it made her smile.

"It's me. Just calling to thank you. For yesterday, and everything else."

"You're welcome. How's everyone holding up?"

"Not so great, at the moment. We had a sort of fight. Look, this
might sound off the wall, but I want to do some Christmas shopping. I have to get my mind off this. Is there any chance you could
come with me?"

"Where do you want to go?"

"Just down Beacon Street." On foot it would be obvious if the
van were following.

"Okay. I can come now, if you want. I was going out to get an
easel for my nephew anyway."

"Hurry, will you? I really need some air."

"Fifteen minutes."

He hung up.

Opening the laptop on her bed, she typed in Charlie Webber's
story, through to the actions of the panel truck. It was harder to
know how much to tell Alan of what Ben had said. She settled for,

< Don't answer out loud. Just help me get out of this. >

Her fingers stumbled over the keys. A jet of adrenaline. An in-
direct way of letting herself know it wasn't safe here now.

That truck couldn't sit on the park for long. And there was
nothing clumsy about Charlie Webber.

Using Leni's knapsack would be another giveaway, though.

In the back of the closet, she found a black canvas bag, circa
Museum School era. The laptop and her purse left no extra room
in it, but taking even a toothbrush could set off bells and whistles
too.

As she sat to pull her boots on, Alan turned up the front steps.

Harriet answered his ring, and her relief carried up the stair-well.

"I thought I'd take the girl out for some exercise," he said.

"Good. Here she comes. Leigh, dear, it's Alan."

When she got into her jacket, Harriet gave her a hug, and there was something different in it. The melting snows of a life of hold-ing on to secrets.

She couldn't return the feeling and stood awkwardly till Harriet let her go.

On the sidewalk, Alan said, "I thought you'd called off Christ-mas for this year."

"We did. But I want to get a book for my father. Some nature writing. Loren Eiseley, maybe. It seems to have a calming effect."

"What did you fight about?"

"Old stuff. About Leni and my mother." Stopping to adjust the bag, she came around on his other side where she could scan the car mirrors. If the blue truck didn't show up by the time they got to the Booksmith it would mean she had a Grade B imagination.

"Well, this is when sleeping dogs do tend to raise their hoary heads," he said. "It's always fun at the hospice when parents find out their kid is gay and dying at the same time."

The rear window of the car ahead showed the intersection be-hind them, and the hood of the blue truck coming into it.

A tingle shot up from her fingertips. Confirmation and sudden panic. Half a block more to the Booksmith, which must have some blind corner where Alan could read the computer screen unob-served.

The studio might not be a safe place, either, to break the news to Vera that she'd handed the sample to the feds, and they'd find out about Ben and put Hopi together with the area code. Except for the call to Alan, pressing Last Number Redial would have given all the digits. Leni was right about things being overlooked.

Steering him into the Booksmith, she picked out the poetry sec-tion on the far wall. "Let's try over there first. I should get some-thing for Harriet, too."

Out of sight of the window, she put a finger across her lips, and opened the laptop on a shelf. Typing, at the head of her notes,

< SOS. Don't say anything. Just read this. We're being followed. I'm going to make myself conspicuous till you're done >

He raised an eyebrow, but she jabbed a finger at the screen. "That's nonfiction, by the way."

Drifting down the center aisle, she kept her eyes off the window. No Loren Eiseley under Science. Mostly picture books, under Nature. The van could track down Beacon Street, but not into the subway. If they didn't know where she got off, any pay phone would suffice.

Unless no one answered again.

Going out to the Hopi reservation from Chama was a deliberate act. And handing the chip to Paul. If she'd told Ben: I'll ask the guys at MIT, he wouldn't have given it to her.

Now he'd have to bolt, and there might be just enough time to beat the warrant. Going back out could be more efficient than trying to get a message through. Vera couldn't call back here, and there was no way of knowing who might be answering that phone now.

The trick would be not to leave a trail. And for Ben not to leave one, bolting.

A problem best šolved by people who knew the area.

Dallas airport seemed as safe a place to spend the night as any.

Wandering up beside Alan, she typed,

< I think I've got a plan. >

She was stopped by the stricken look in his eyes. But why should he believe it.

< I don't blame you. >

she put in,

< But I'm not crazy. Honest. If we get on the train we can talk. >

She said, "They don't have that Eiseley book here, but I saw it at the Lauriat's near Quincy Market. On the tube, it wouldn't take long. Would you mind? It'd be nuts to try to drive down there to-day."

"All right," he said tightly. "Let's go."

She typed,

< Pretend you're having fun. >

Outside, the trolley came rattling along so fast she almost missed a glimpse of the blue van pulling into Beacon.

Alan sat facing her, trying to decide, she guessed, whether she'd come unglued. When the train plunged into the tunnel, she said, "Listen, now. I've only got two more stops. I'm getting off at Copley Square. Is your full name on your Visa card?"

"Wait a minute." He slapped her knee with the gloves he was holding. "I've had just about enough of this. I want to know what's going on. Get you out of what? And why? Do you think they're going to arrest you? I don't understand what it is you don't want to tell them."

"It's more like, what I need to tell the person that chip belongs to. It wasn't mine to give. But yes, I'd also rather not be 'inter-viewed' again. Let them do their own damn work, all right?"

He bent closer, and she could smell his sandalwood aftershave as the car swayed. "Leigh, are you sure you've thought this through? Couldn't we use a great scientific breakthrough about now? What if this computer could help with the AIDS vaccine? Or some of the treatment research?"

Trust Alan to come up with an angle she hadn't considered. But it was hard to picture Charlie Webber dedicating his new toy to anything so far beyond his field of interest. "With what the feds have spent so far? You're the one who always says if they really wanted a cure, we'd have one now. Anyway, it isn't my decision."

"Then at least let me come with you this time."

"No. It wouldn't help, and staying here could. As long as your car's at the house, they'll expect me back. If you can stand it, I wish you'd call there at six or so and say I'm feeling dizzy and we're going to get a sandwich. Or tell them I'm staying over. He'll think I'm still mad at him. That's all right."

"For how long? When he finds out, he'll be wild. Is that okay too?"

They were coming into Copley station and she waited for the crowd to shift. "Maybe. If he thinks I've taken off because of our fight, he might keep quiet about it for a day or so. And by then, I'll be back. Tell him I probably went to Provincetown, to walk it off on the beach. That will sound familiar. I have to get off here. What about your Visa card?"

He took it out and handed it to her. It said only "A. Markson." "And you won't tell me where you're going?"

"If I tell, so could you."

"Great. They're going to torture me."

"Not if you say I'm an idiot, prone to run away from things."

Slipping off the quilted jacket, she turned it inside out to the plum side and put it on over the black canvas bag.

"Take this, too." He pushed some folded bills into her hand. "You can't call me either, I suppose."

"Not right away. I'll be back soon. Go on to Park Street." The car stopped and she kissed him and got off to climb the stairs.

From a street vendor, she bought a knit charcoal scarf and soft beret that came down to her eyebrows.

A cart outside Back Bay station offered Guatemalan satchels. Even a purple and grey one with both a drawstring and a snap.

An exercise in melodrama, given the small chance of turning up as a missing-person photo in tomorrow's *Globe*. But at the airport she added sunglasses, and the mirror in the restroom told her even Charlie Webber would have trouble spotting her now.

Standing in one line after another, she began seeing Charlies in every man who gave her a second glance. The Sunday before a Christmas Eve Monday, and every flight was booked, until finally a seat came up on American to Washington, D.C. The lion's den. But better than waiting any longer.

Charlie didn't meet the plane, and when it landed, a few standby seats to Denver were being called by United. She got through the gate with another ticket issued to Anne Markson.

At Denver, West Wind airline had room on a 9 a.m. flight to Flagstaff, but no company in the book could rent her a car there. The possibility of one in Phoenix turned up and then vanished before the clerk finished making the reservation.

Drinking tea from a Styrofoam cup, she wondered how Alan had made out and how angry he would be. High-handed tactics, in return for his generosity. Always before they had each had a vote on decisions affecting both of them, and a coin to flip when they strongly disagreed.

A blond ponytail passed by on someone of indeterminate sex. A skinnier person than Ed. Who would be lashed to his store today, on Christmas Eve, trying to make up for a slow year. If he could spare his Jeep, the money from Alan ought to be enough for a taxi to Sedona.

Going back to the pay phone, she counted out change.

On the third ring, a sleepy woman answered, "What."

"I'm sorry to call so late. Is Ed Harris there?"

"It's four in the morning!"

Then she heard his voice. "Tell him it's Leigh Haring."

He came on. "Leigh? What's up?"

She apologized again. "I'm sort of in a jam. I'm flying into Flagstaff, just for the day, and I need a car, but there aren't any. Is there any chance I could rent your Jeep, if I get down there on my own?"

"Today? You're coming back here? Why?"

The woman in the background was talking to him too. The waitress from Tlaquepaque, or some other lucky girl who had shared a glass of that great fumé blanc.

"Don't ask. It's as screwed up as last time. Is there any hope? I'm already in Denver."

"I think Daniel needs the Jeep today. It's got a tough clutch, too, if you're going back to the mesas. Let me think."

The line went mute, long enough for her to smile at her own silliness. An hour in the sun with Ed, and so taken aback to find a woman sleeping next to the beside table with his phone.

The background hum came back. "When's your flight?"

"At nine. On West Wind."

"I know that one. You come along. I'll figure something out by then. Call me when you get to Flag."

"I mean it about paying. Anyone, for any vehicle. Thanks for trying."

"De nada."

The connection broke too quickly for him to have hung up. A finger on the button because the woman with him had said: Not my car on Christmas Eve.

When she got off the plane, he was standing just inside the gate and gave the beret a tug. "You can get rid of the woolies here. Back to hug a tree, huh?"

"Has this really messed up your day?"

"Nah." Taking her elbow, he pointed to the parking lot. "Daniel's going to run me back. He had to come up anyway."

"Then who's minding the store?"

"A cast of thousands. Got any baggage?"

"Nope."

"You're a twenty-four-hour turnaround. Next time let me know and I'll be ready."

"I'm not sure your roommate would like that." It came out sounding arch.

He pushed open the glass door. "Jill? That's nothing serious."

"You're brave, then." But she thought of Sven and his turpentine-scented studio.

"No. That's what I mean. It's strictly auld lang syne. The car's down here."

Even through sunglasses, the white lines seemed to leap out of the tarmac. He wasn't wearing any, and she knew that for roughly three seconds they had been thinking the same thing.

He let go of her arm. "It's the burgundy Audi. A freebie, too. Can you drive a stick?"

"I used to, all the time."

The Jeep was parked behind it. When she got behind the wheel of the Audi, he bent to the open window. "There's a map in the visor but you'll see the route signs. It's 89 to 160, and hang a right at Tuba City."

"Got it. How late will your shop be open?"

"Till nine or ten. Depending on the traffic. Can you make it back by then?"

"I think so." She adjusted the rearview mirror.

"Then why not stay in town? I can get you a room. You don't want to spend Christmas morning on a plane. I'll even make you breakfast."

"And show me Airport Mesa by moonlight?"

"Only if you really want to see it." He checked his watch. "I have to pick up Daniel now."

She wanted him to leave first so he wouldn't hear it if she stripped the gears. But he was too much of a gentleman for that.

"I'll call you when I know. Thanks, Ed."

"No problem."

He stepped back and she pulled out carefully.

KEEPING THE SNOWY mountain ridge on her left, she followed the postings to Route 89. A fancy car he had found her, with tan leather upholstery. His bedroom must be quite a place too. A crystal palace, the better to channel all that vortex energy. No wonder he never got bored.

Still, after a session with Vera, the invitation might be tempting.

North of the city, the driving got dicey as trucks and semi-rigs sped up to pass each other in the narrow lanes. Makeshift stands along the highway displayed Indian jewelry, and then arrows for different rims of Grand Canyon started to appear.

The car radio pulled in "KTNN, all-hit country Navajo, 660 on your AM dial"—a lone English sentence, followed by a language with a rhythm that reminded her of rap music.

By a sign for dinosaur tracks she had noticed on the trip down, she stopped to buy a Coke from the sinewy man collecting admission.

At Tuba City, 264 turned right, into the full glare of the sun, red rock giving way to the pale reflecting earth of Hopi land. The color of Ben's cave. Taylor's bike had better still be in that drainpipe.

She pulled the visor lower on the windshield. The map stayed tucked in its pocket, but a tissue credit card receipt fluttered to the floor on the passenger side.

Glancing down to make a grab for it, she swerved nearly onto the shoulder.

A signature, darker than the imprint, of a name heard only yesterday. Written in clear, precise strokes. Jonathan Addison.

Chapter 13

WATCHING VERA thread the needle to sew his torn shirt, Ben thought how clear her face looked, more than he'd ever seen it. Last year, when she decided to save his life, a little ice had melted. A slight thaw in international relations.

Now that she was his only ally, the cold war seemed to be winding down. An occasional flare arced in the distance, but she let him look at her face without closing it in a mask. And the bundle she carried up to the cave held gifts from the ending of Soyál, "for the children," she said in the deadpan voice she used to tease him now.

Somiviki, sweet blue cornmeal wrapped in husk. Piñon nuts. The sun had turned, and it was time to go.

The way out she described ran through the Navajo reservation along an old Hopi pilgrimage trail, then west across the Coconino plateau on red land most of the way to Nevada. A cousin he'd never met who 'knew everyone' agreed to take him just for the change of scene.

Since the Huey hadn't come back, two days had already been wasted. But seeing her like this was worth the loss. Getting into a truck with a stranger tonight sounded like much more fun than trying to hitchhike past the state police.

He spit a bad piñon nut over the ledge. "There's nothing about a warrant yet?"

"Not on Taylor's radio. But it doesn't get much beyond Flag."

"Did his uncle say if that rock is like his little CAT-scan thing?"

"He's my uncle, too," she smiled. "It isn't the crystal that lets him see. That's just sort of a lens. Anyway, he said this is lighter and it feels hot to him. My grandmother says it's burning water, from the World before, becoming precious the Hopi way, with a lot of time and effort. And it might be why the snakes live there, so we better leave it alone."

He could picture the tiny old woman fingering the stone—her clouded eyes and single glowing strand of turquoise heishi. Made by Huruing Wuhti, she had told him once. Hard Substances Old

Woman, who made every rock and shell, and for a moment he thought she was naming herself.

"Randall's friend will be able to help when he gets back from vacation." She took quick stitches and he looked for the resemblance in her fingers. Rounded knuckles and square nails. A feature they had both inherited. "I wish I could think of someone else. I hate waiting that long."

He caught another nut in his hand. Each time he started to tell about giving Leigh the stone, he lost the nerve. If Leigh found out, Vera would hear it first and that would be soon enough. "If it belongs to the snakes...." He tossed the nut. "I told Taylor we should get them an agent."

"A lawyer, is more like it. Stop throwing those away." She snapped the knotted thread. "The other thing she said was, we've been running away from ourselves since the beginning of the First World, and it's about time for something to make that stop."

"And then all the pahanas will disappear? And no more reggae music rotting Taylor's brain. Or, in his case, heavy metal?"

"You might be surprised by him." She held the shirt out. "Come back in ten years."

"If I'm lucky." Adding it to the pile, he reached for another knob of husk. "Did you make these?"

She nodded.

"They're good. Maybe once the pahanas go up in smoke, you can move back here yourself."

"I'm here, Ben. I just work somewhere else." She stretched her legs out. "You think it's all kind of cute, don't you. Our stories about other worlds. But these disasters happened. We're finding out more about it all the time. Not just how we describe them, but in the Old Testament and the Enuma Elish of the Babylonians. In our first two worlds, the sun rose in the west, and then the Hoya twins left the poles and the axis spun around the wrong way and everything froze. Maybe a giant comet changed the rotation. You could read the book of Exodus that way. There was no mention of the planet Venus before 1500 B.C., even though there were great astronomers then. What if a comet came into our orbit, and pulled the Red Sea back, and made the cloud of smoke and the pillar of fire the Israelites followed?"

"Right. And Noah's ark was like the flood at the end of the Third World. My mother told me."

"Well, it's worth considering. There was a supernova in 1054 that's recorded in rock art all around here. The pahanas just discovered that, even though Vine Deloria wrote about it twenty years ago. But he's Indian, so what could he know. I'm just saying, these aren't only parables. They're observations and memories too. The pahanas think we're all too dim to have recorded history, and everything started when they showed up. Or wrote it down."

"Is that why you wanted your degree? To be put-down proof?" He meant to tease her, but it didn't go over.

"No. To do what I need to."

"You mean, out there. Like wanting to put the toothpaste back in the tube, without getting put back in yourself."

Picking up the knife, she sawed off a thin slice of apple. "No. It's about being careful. I was reading a poem yesterday that reminded me of you. It's by a Chickasaw writer, Linda Hogan. I only remember a few lines and I'll mangle them, but it goes, like, 'I say, it is dangerous to be of two countries. You've got your hands in the dark of two empty pockets. Even though you walk and whistle like you aren't afraid, you know which pocket the enemy lives in…and you remember who loved who and who killed who. For this you want amnesty.'"

"Hey, pretty good. You're right. I do."

Now that they'd traded jabs a sudden frost could be expected. But she leaned back on her elbows, smiling. "Look, in Hopi time, the pahanas showed up about three minutes ago. For eons before that, we had our own way of doing things and it wasn't devoid of a vote. The Kikmongwis made the decisions, but only after everyone else had talked it to death. Beat it to death. It drives me crazy when they always have to go back to the beginning of every story. But it serves a purpose too."

The good old ways. In which he had no place here. "Now let me tell you a story I've always remembered. When my mother died, I was 18 and I gave the social worker shit about taking so long with the burial voucher. She said, 'I understand your feelings, Mr. Naya, but frankly I'm in favor of more bureaucracy rather than less. Otherwise, we all surrender to the businessmen.' Isn't it better to have extra layers for them to get through?"

"It might be. If that's how it worked." Abruptly, she turned her head to look out over the desert. Patchy sun had given up trying to break through the cloud cover. Four o'clock. It would be dark in an hour.

Fighting now would leave things in the wrong way.

He grabbed her sneakered foot and shook it. "Hey, I'm a heathen, but I'm trying. I told you. I want to move in and learn dry-farming. One of my best lines used to be, 'Let's go out and talk to the wind.' Now I've really been doing it. I don't want to leave.''

Last year, drying out up here, it felt like his skin was peeling off and the sky made a screen for a horror show that drove him back into the darkest corner. Shaking there, fingers hardly able to unwrap the groceries left up at the wash. But if the last hope didn't work, the last stop would be a Dumpster down in Gallup, and the faces that came howling by from that trip helped as much as not knowing where to buy bootleg on the mesas.

For these days the ghosts brought other pictures he must have been part of once, judging by their angle. A screen door, framing a dusty plaza where a girl in a black jumper stood, an uneven smudging of cornmeal on her cheeks. Not Vera, but with eyes as beautiful, never quite meeting his but seeming to see him and everything around him.

Then he started hearing the *ssshh* of bending leaves of corn, wagging on their scrubby stalks in the breeze. Tickling his ribs as he climbed the patch on a scrap of mesa, warm sand gritty in between his toes.

Ears of corn, stacked in a crib in a room with painted kachinas peering down, beaked and feathered and ready to come to life any minute, he knew. The small bow, taut. Hands lifting him, high overhead in the hot sun.

The houses were built of this sandstone, and today when the light woke him up, it touched the spiral carving and he thought the cave would be a kind of home even in jail.

Vera smiled grudgingly. "Tell Taylor how much you love it. I'm not sure you would for long, though. The women own the houses, remember? If your wife gets mad, she can just put your things outside and all you can do is . . . go home to mother!''

He laughed. "That could be a problem.''

"Even if you had one here. It might be crowded. I don't know. I have a feeling you're going to get out of this. Tomorrow night I'm meeting with the Kikmongwis. The pictures you took will be back on Thursday, so we'll have proof. We'll make a plan. It won't end when you leave, Ben.''

"Is Robert taking both of us? It's almost time.''

She looked at her watch. "You're right, it's late. No, you're going for a nice long walk. Up the wash. He'll drop me at my car and then come back for you.'' Shading her eyes, she pointed down the slope, "What on earth is that?''

"Where?''

"Right...there. That purple dot? Someone's coming up here."

"Taylor?"

"I hope not."

Unzipping his camera case, he took out the zoom lens. The dot had disappeared. Then it came out from behind a boulder, and twisting the barrel, he brought Leigh into focus.

"Holy crow." Her face was flushed, and dust clung to her clothes. A striped bag hung from one shoulder that she had to keep hitching up behind her as she climbed.

"It's Leni's sister." He couldn't say her name.

"What?" She took the camera, squinting through the viewfinder. "I thought she went home."

"She did."

"Then why..." Looking up, she saw his face. "You told her? What?"

"Worse. I gave her one of the samples. She said a jeweler friend of hers is some kind of expert. I thought you didn't want to wait."

"For someone we could trust? Her?"

"She's not so bad."

Pushing the camera at him, Vera crouched to look down. "After half an hour you know this." Her dark eyes flickered angrily. "If Leni couldn't tell her, why should you?"

"That was before."

"Before it affected you. And that's what counts."

"Right. And I thought she was cute, so what the hell. Is that what you want me to say?"

A gust of wind blew her hair up in a cloud. "This can't be good."

"I'm going to give her a leg up."

Climbing down to the next ledge, he dropped to the flat rock below it. She was thirty feet away, and stopped. "I hurt my frigging knee!"

When he got to her she was leaning with her right foot propped on a rock. Fresh and dried blood matted the torn wool over a swollen cut. "Nice, huh? What happened to the bike?"

"It's in use. Vera's here."

"Great." Her breath came in gasps. "She's going to kill me. I don't blame her." In the set of her eyes, he saw not fear but something growing out of it. "Maybe we can do a prisoner exchange. I think I know who killed Leni."

The words had an edge of disbelief that sounded like a lie.

He looked down but no one was following her. "Who?"

"Ed Harris. Rare Earth? As in, really rare?"

"Ed . . . How the hell do you know Ed?"

"I met him in Santa Fe. The first night. At La Fonda. He was the one who told me about you. About your being here. What a mean drunk you are. Quite a picture. For the cops, too. He told them he gave you that piece of tiger eye they found at Leni's. Although I don't see how he could be sure you'd leave it. I've been thinking about this all the way up here, and I think he made a lot of lucky moves."

"Why didn't you tell me that?"

"You never asked. It didn't come up. I saw him for half an hour that night and he looked like Mr. Santa Fe, not some goon for a mining company. God, I'm such an idiot. But he said everything right. He even had some of my jewelry, that I bet he got as a rush order from my L.A. sales rep last week." Shivering, she hugged her hurt knee. "He killed her. And I sat there drinking wine with him."

He bent to push her shoulders back. "But why would he kill her? Tell me."

"Because . . . what you said. He or his cousin found that stone. And found out it's worth a bloody fortune. It is. Maybe he killed his cousin, too." Dropping her head, she closed her eyes and he thought she could be passing out.

"Come on. We have to go up so Vera can hear this. Hold my arm." He caught her elbow with his and slung the bag over his shoulder.

"There's a warrant out on you."

"Since when?"

"This morning. At least we know it's him now."

"Even if you're right, we can't prove it."

"All you need is reasonable doubt."

"Maybe where you come from." He put a hand down from the ledge. Behind her, the cloud bank was moving, boiling out from the center. The San Francisco peaks floated in a shimmer on the horizon.

Vera was looking past him at Leigh, her face a mask again.

He said, "You know Ed Harris, in Santa Fe?"

"Blond Ed? Who wears the bolos?"

"Right." Leigh put a hand back to ease down on an outcrop. "That's another lie, then. He said he didn't know who you were. Ben, did you smoke PCP with Leni?"

"No. Just grass. Not even that. I left the joint there, though."

"It was in the joint."

"Jesus. Ed gave me that. At the gallery." From the little silver case he always carried, with three or four neat rolls. Pushed across the counter. Take your pick. Smoke too good to pass up.

But not with PCP before.

"What's this?" Vera looked back to Leigh. "What about him?"

"He's the one who killed her. He has a cousin who's a geologist at the Living Mesa Foundation. Or was. A Jonathan Addison?"

"I know him," she said quietly. "So did Leni."

"He made a discovery."

"He's dead."

"I know."

Vera was so still he could feel her vibrate. "Go on."

Listening to it, he kept seeing a reel of Ed spool by—a bland face, Philadelphia cream cheese. His colored rocks, like toys next to the strip-mine at Black Mesa. He was strong, though. Even without PCP, he wouldn't have had much trouble with Leni.

That day, Ed was leaning on the counter at the gallery. With the tiger eye in his pocket. Ed and his off-hand questions. Yawning. Offering the silver case. 'Are you on your way up to Chama?'

Earlier, it must have been, 'Do you know when Bird's coming by?' Everyone was getting paid early for Christmas.

Remembering his blank blue eyes, it wasn't so hard to believe.

Vera was hearing a different story, and looking at her brought him back to it. She was trying not to show a reaction, to draw out all the details, but her eyes were burning. She'd trusted him, knowing it was dangerous, and his hand had been in the wrong pocket.

". . . I thought you came back to Leni's that night, but it must have been Ed. And then I called him up and asked him how to get here. He didn't need to follow me. I told him where I was going."

"And how about now? With the people in Boston? How long do you think it will take them?"

She shook her head. "Charlie Webber said, 'when it gets through channels.' I don't know if that means a day or a month. But my father said that to find the crust, you'd almost have to know where it is. Ed won't tell them. It would cut him out. Could he get a lease on his own?"

"Maybe. If he had the right people lined up. But he's cut out already, from what you've said. They've got our number, right?" Folding her arms, Vera walked to the rim to look out. "So it's all for a computer. What a joke. Slavery, smallpox, most of our land and water stolen, and finally it seemed this much was safe for us to screw up on our own. Stupid. As long as there's anything they want, they'll try to take it."

"I'm sorry," it was almost a whisper. "If only I hadn't . . ."

"Don't bother with that. Ifs can't change anything. If I hadn't been at Leni's when you got there.... So? The question is, what to do now."

Ben took out his last hoarded cigarette. "You said we should get a lawyer. Maybe that's not a bad idea."

"To file what injunction? Against an Executive Order that hasn't been written yet? Which would be classified, and not subject to subpoena, probably. This would have to be a decision on the whole question of sovereignty. Which is one vast legal swamp."

"Charlie Webber mentioned that. 'Sovereign nation status.' Meaning what?"

Vera smiled. "That you can't interfere with us. That we really can be self-determining. There's starting to be a body of law, from precedents here and there. On things like gambling and licensing. But when the Kiowa fought land allotment, the supreme court ruled they had no title to their land at all, just occupancy rights. Ben, do you have any more of those?"

He'd never seen her smoke before, and handed it over. She didn't inhale, just took a pop and let it float up like an incense burner.

"What about calling the newspapers?" Leigh said. "Wouldn't this make a good story? Spooks coming after sacred land? I'll bet the *Globe* would print it."

"Why?" Smoke curled up from Vera's mouth. "Because you tell them something might happen? I don't think so. There isn't any story yet. Every Thanksgiving, a piece comes out on the Lakota and the rape of the Black Hills, and who even reads them anymore? Except people who are dying for an excuse to pull the plug on the reservations. This could be it. The Japanese already have joint ventures with tribes for uranium mining. So, why not this too? Against the national interest. Is the American public going to think our snakes are more important than having the fastest computer in the world?"

Including you, she seemed to mean, and it registered in Leigh's eyes. "It doesn't sound like all of you might agree about that, either."

"When it comes to minerals, what most of us believe hasn't mattered here for a long time."

"See, it's like a bad marriage." He took a sideways look at Vera. "You can fight about what happened, but at this point it's almost irrelevant. You just hope something will keep it together for the sake of the children.''

"I know, Ben. You believe in accommodation, because that's how you've survived." Vera crushed out the cigarette on a rock. "But we aren't going to stop this just by playing their game. By their rules. That's what I've been trying to tell you. On Pine Ridge, the tribal council gave a huge chunk of land to the Park Service—self-preservation being the first law of nature. It was hardly a scenic area. Uranium, is the best guess. And no one's even building reactors in this country anymore."

As if she had just noticed Leigh's cut leg, she unzipped her parka and took out a folded man's white handkerchief.

"Thanks." Leigh pressed it to her knee. "Well, if they try to force it here, at least you know what the rock is worth."

"That's for our religious leaders to decide. Tie that on. We need to get moving. Ben, take whatever you want to bring."

"How about telling the chairman first? Since there may not be much time. He's the one who could cut off access quickly."

"No." She put the cigarette butt in her pocket. "Not first. That's not our order of priority. But second, maybe so. We're responsible to Massau for this land. All of us, together. Maybe it's time." Turning to the bike, she wheeled it out onto the ledge. "I'm going to take this and ask Robert to make a meeting. I'll meet you at the overlook."

"Let me." He hooked the handlebar and hoisted it down after her. Then, on impulse, jumped down himself and followed her along the broken jaw of rock leading to the wash.

"It's going to rain," she said. "You better get started."

"Say it, first. Go on. I want to hear it."

"What?"

"That I blew it with her."

"I'm not sure you did. I gave her my number. I sent her to you. That makes it my fault. This isn't about us, though. It's about them. She's just the latest installment."

"She came back. Isn't it better to know?"

"She's having an adventure, Ben. It happens all the time. I know how she made Leni feel. So she must know that too. This is to put a Band-aid on that. Help the Indians. It's how most of the damage around here's been done."

Taking the handgrips, she swung the bike out. "On the other hand, maybe something else is happening. Being played out. Like what sovereignty's going to mean when it comes to a real crunch.

We still have the core of our old land. If we can't stop this, what about the tribes who aren't so lucky? Now, go get our little missionary. And make sure she has her car keys."

Pushing the bike ahead of her, she gave a sharp glance back and he turned and started climbing toward the cave.

Leigh had knotted the handkerchief around her knee. Her face was pale under what he saw now as a sunburn. "She hates me, right?"

"No." But the question seemed to ask him to make a choice. "It's nothing personal. Her clan's supposed to give protection. Right now, that could be a high-stress job." Stuffing the mended shirt into the camera bag, he rolled up the blanket with everything on it.

"Who's Master?"

"What?" He threw the blanket against the wall.

"Didn't she say, you're responsible to Master for the land?"

"Massau," he smiled. "He told the people they could live here, when they came up from the Third World. He's the death spirit. With the power of fire. You wouldn't want to tick him off too badly."

She stood up. "That sounds like a hard god to have."

"Yah. Well, they take everything into account here. The good, the bad, and the scary." Twisting the straps of the bags together, he pulled them on. "Got your car keys?"

She tapped her jacket pocket and they jangled. "Am I going to this meeting?"

"I don't know. We might need to borrow your wheels."

"Ed's cousin's you mean. According to the registration."

"He must have wanted you to find that."

"I wouldn't have, though. If the receipt hadn't fallen out."

"You said it was in the visor. Wasn't it sunny in Flag?"

A buffeting came up the mesa, whipping her hair back. "Yes. And now it's almost dark."

"Come on." He put out a hand and she took it. "You go first."

Maneuvering down to the trail, he could feel her quick pulse against his arm. A lighter bird than she looked in Vogue. Her name written on the back of all the jewelry she sent Leni. The opposite of Vera, that way, but he thought they had more in common than he did with either of them. A certainty about where to belong that left bruises on Leni too.

Deliberate bruises, from Ed's hands. Cutting the brakes on the truck. Spiking the joint. Not caring much which one he caught that night.

Leigh's haircut left her neck bare. A hollow at the nape. Ed wouldn't have been high himself, after all that planning. Taking off his boots first. A tight little smile when he got back out on the road.

He said, "I'm going to kill that bastard."

"Tell me about it." She glanced back, "I'm glad I'm not the only jerk. I thought I must have fallen for his bimbo sex appeal."

Above the mesa, the sky had turned a weird, almost neon blue. He saw her hand come up just as a drop hit his own face and a branch of lightning shot from east to west.

"Terrific. Are your snakes doing this?"

"Shh. You don't knock rain. It's always good. Anyway, I think you brought it with you. It's been straight sun till today. Where are you supposed to be now?"

"Provincetown. If anyone's looking. I think I'll tell my father I took the train to New York instead and wandered around Times Square. He might have me committed, though. I'll say I just want some Prozac. It even makes you lose weight."

Threads of rain came drizzling down. She stumbled and he caught her arm. "Watch out."

"I can do it on my own from here."

It was uphill to the overlook where he could make out Vera standing and a black pick-up pulling away. Going west.

He gave Leigh a boost to the stone wall. Rain had soaked through her padded jacket. Vera's hair was plastered down and Leigh took out her car keys. "I should have given these to you."

"Give them to me now. I'll drive. Robert said our police were looking for you in the village, Ben." She twisted the key to flip the doorlocks. "We don't want to be stopped. You better lie down in the back."

Taking her striped bag, Leigh got in the passenger side. "That's the defrost. I can't believe it got this cold so fast."

A blast of air came from under the seat as Vera pulled out. "It's the desert." She turned the wipers on high.

He could feel the twisting of the road up Second Mesa, but fog blanketed the windows, showing up Leigh's profile turned uncertainly toward Vera. Trying to think of something to say, and nervous it would be wrong. A feeling he remembered.

A set of headlights came through the windshield, turning down to low beam. Leigh looked back at him. "We can't see anything

The heater was starting to work and he flexed his cold hands. "These are nice wheels. Maybe after I kill Ed, I'll give this baby a paint job."

"You're the one who needs a paint job, Ben." He saw Vera smile in the mirror.

"I've been thinking. Maybe I should get arrested. And make a stink, while we've got a chance. If you'll get me a good lawyer."

She shook her head. "It's too soon. It's the same problem. They'll deny it. And wait for this to blow over. And then one day we'll wake up and find out reservations have been abolished because it's long past time to stop humoring these Indians. And if you don't think they can do it, you don't know your history. Every ten years, there's some new theory and it's always about us giving up rights we got in return for giving over a few billion acres of land. Relocation, Termination, New Federalism. Now there's a national organization trying to break treaties. Next it will be something catchy, like a giant Pepsi commercial, with a thousand Taylors singing 'We Are the World.'"

Light shone through the back window now, high beams, making her squint in the mirror. "Damn." She flicked her own lights. "They better not tailgate on us here."

"Is it the cops?"

"I can't see. It could be ours. It's a Jeep."

The lights faded, cresting the mesa, then came down even faster. No Hopi cop would drive like that without a siren.

He sat up and saw the beige hood just before the bumper hit. Mud plastered over the license plate. White knuckles on the wheel. A visor hid the driver's face.

"He's trying to run us off!" Vera worked the gear. "This car won't downshift."

"Ed must have screwed it while it was parked back there. He beat us out like rabbits. Is there anywhere to pull off?"

"Here? Are you serious?"

"It was here." Leigh's eyes were unfocused, looking past him up into the light. "The rabbit came out. And then a Jeep."

"Ben, I know what he's trying for. The cutout. We have to do something by then." She gave Leigh a hard poke, "Don't watch him. Listen to what we're saying."

The cutout had a sheer drop of a hundred feet. Not great for the complexion. "Could you swerve first and crack him up someplace?"

"Not without crashing us too."

Light ran in rivers on the windshield. The Jeep accelerated and the Audi's left rear fender gave with a crunch, jolting him against her seat.

"So that's what we'll do." She hit a button that put down the windows. "We'll crash it. I know where, too. The wall's out on the next curve, and it's not much of a drop at first. If I go over carefully, you should be able to roll out there." A rush of wind came back with her voice. "At least these brakes are good."

Her eyes met his in the mirror, asking him to buy it, because they had about thirty seconds now. Then she smiled, as if they were going to a party.

"What about on your side?"

"I'll wait till we're just over, and catch the shoulder. He won't have time to react. Leigh? You can do it."

"Sure she can." He clapped her shoulders. "She'll fly. I'll even give her a push."

"Over the headrest? No. You both have to go at once."

It was almost a kind of music the wipers were making with the weather and the streaming light. "Come on, Leigh." The Jeep had the momentum. "It beats going over at the cutout."

"But where?" She wound her hand around the strap of her bag. "I don't see where you mean!"

"That gap," Vera pointed. "Just pull your head in and push off. I can open all the doors at once. That ought to make him jump."

A tongue of fog licked through the opening and she said, "Ready? Go."

He saw their own lights aim up and then down at the chasm, and ahead of him Leigh hurtled out of the car. Because he knew, taking the blow of the slope against his back, in that second Vera had thrown the weight of her body to push Leigh out, and he didn't hear the Jeep go by before the Audi crashed.

Chapter 14

A SOFT BUBBLING, sounding like a scuba tank and the moving shadows were murky enough to be underwater. Then, opening her eyes, she saw the coiled green caterpillar sitting on her chest, big as a house cat, slimy, grinning as he sucked on the mouthpiece of the hookah, and with the inhalation, a sword of pain, a black tide, drowning in it.

Bubbling, again, and he was tearing off chunks of the mushroom, the flesh of her body, and the warp of the room shrank as he grew into a balloon floating over the bed. Tethered to the hookah, his sticky antlers waving, the mouthpiece of a knife he drove into the left side of her chest.

The smallest dot imaginable. A black speck, with no edges. Holding still. In the quiet, she could see the small man living in the wall. Covered in bark, and he never spoke, but once in a while stepped into the room and it felt better then.

The tide came roaring back. Cascading yellow rock. A teepee at the bottom, with the tapestry design of the cushions at the Hopi Cultural Center. The man who climbed up out of it had the same design, and that was wrong. There were no teepees on the mesas.

His yellow face hovered over her. Yellow eyes. "You were so easy, Leigh. Like your sister. Such a straight little girl. When you came into my shop I was just waiting to see which rock you'd pick up first."

She started to open her mouth but the pain was stronger even than fear.

"See?" He ran a fingertip along her cheek. "You don't want to make a fuss. Be a good girl."

Rocking on the swell of nausea, she couldn't tell how he was touching her face and holding her wrists at the same time. Then opping her head, she saw one stuck to the railing of the bed.

"See?" His teeth were yellow too. "You're helpless. I could kill you now. So let's be sensible." Slowly, he moved the hand down to her breast. "Pretty. I'm almost glad you're alive. Why don't we get married so we can't testify against each other."

The blade of the hookah cut harder with each breath and sh
shut her eyes.

"You told me everything, one way or another. You ought to b
more careful. The Hopis wouldn't want you to tell anymore. S
why don't you shut up now. Say you have amnesia. Unless yo
want someone else to get hurt."

A wet towel pressed against her forehead. Cool as fog. "A Hop
found that crystal. Taking a leak near the Leupp road. He sold
to me for ten bucks, so there's enough blame to go around. Let
just call it a Mexican standoff."

Wet cold blanketed her face and then a fire blossomed in th
foggy night. A red glow, burning along the mesa with a stink o
rubber and gasoline. Even at a distance, she knew from how Ver
lay that she was broken.

Dark billowed up, taking her, and she gripped the railings, aim
ing the boat out to sea with the wind, out of reach, out of sight.

BUBBLING. An aquarium. The man made of bark took her hand
"It's all right. You fell out of a car. You're in the hospital. I
Flagstaff. Can you tell me what your name is?"

It might be a trick, she thought. To see what she would tell. Th
badge on his pocket said: Dr. Merlin. Next to the name, a cro
with two snakes coiling up around it. But his hand was warm, an
she knew him from the wall, the feeling of safety he brought in
the room.

She touched her tongue to her dry lips. "Leigh. Haring."

He smiled through the bark that was a curly greying beard
"Good. I know you're in a lot of pain, Leigh. We had to take yo
off the morphine. You had what's called a paradoxical reaction
Instead of sedating you, it made you a little crazy. That's partly o
fault. You have a punctured lung and that can be unbearab
painful. So when you started thrashing, we turned up your drip
little. Now, how many fingers am I holding up?"

"Three."

He moved them across her line of vision.

"Two, now."

"Excellent. I think it's mostly out of your system."

The lines around him came into focus. A monitor with red dig
ital numbers counting, 86, 92. The pumping of her heart. Awak
all of a sudden, in a room with avocado walls. Empty beds on ei
ther side.

Going to the sink, he brought back a wet towel and touched it along her mouth. "Fortunately, your father told me he'd had that reaction to morphine once. It tends to run in families."

"He's here?"

"No. We spoke on the phone. I told him you'd be fine. Your friend Alan's down the hall. From what he said, I thought your father might be unduly upset by all this hardware. But you can't see what I'm talking about."

He moved his arm, to show the plastic tube running into the left side of her rib cage. "The tip of that rib collapsed your lung. So this goes down to a pleur-evac machine at the foot of your bed. That's the gurgling sound. It sucks out the blood and air and heals the lung back to your chest wall. And you're doing great. When you came in, you were in shock from loss of blood. And knocked out. You've had a couple of transfusions. But the CAT scan says you're fine." He pointed to the IV tube bandaged to her arm. "That's your Ultra SlimFast. Or, more like the opposite. You were pulling at the tubes, so we had to use restraints. I can take them off now."

Opening the Velcro, he rubbed one wrist, then the other. Helpless. Ed had been here, with a tapestry design?

A spiderweb, being blown away.

"I thought you lived in the wall."

He smiled. "Sometimes it feels that way. You were lucky, really. You couldn't have been wearing anything better than a nice fat padded jacket."

Vera had a parka on. A black one.

"What about my friends?"

She saw it was a question he didn't want to answer.

"Are they here? Ben and Vera. Naya?"

He rested a hand on hers again. "Ben's in tough shape right now. He fractured a vertebra, and it was a tricky one. We had to operate again this morning. And he broke a leg. But I think he'll be getting around all right in a month or two. His room's right under yours." Looking down at her hand, he blinked, and she knew what the rest would be.

"Vera's dead?"

"I'm sorry. Yes. She was gone by the time the paramedics got to you. She hit her head. If someone had found you earlier.... But I shouldn't say that. I don't know. The car burned, but it was raining so hard.... Apparently, you weren't visible from the road till it got light. They called a Medivac to bring you two here. But her cousin told me her people took her body home."

"Was that . . . a guy about eighteen?" She didn't know Taylor's last name.

"Yes. He's down with Ben right now."

Closing her eyes, she let her head fall back. The dark swelled and opened out again. Vera, at the cave. Watching her there, it seemed impossible ever to know her. Leni's friend. Who hadn't trusted her even before they met at Leni's house. Knowing what she'd fail to see. And that must have come from Leni. Eyes front, and don't look back at the wreckage left behind.

The doctor took his hand away. "I'm going to get your friend Alan. And we'll bring up a portable X-ray machine and have a look at your chest. If it's healed as well as I think, we can take the tube out."

"How long will I have to stay?"

"We'll have to see how you do on your feet. All things being equal, I should think, till morning. If you lived in Flagstaff, I could send you home tonight. Once this is out, you'll have a small incision that will scab right over. And you'll have pain. But you'll be ambulatory. Oh, here he is."

Alan stood in the doorway.

"You can come in now."

Alan bent over her, and his eyes were tired and bloodshot and relieved. "How are you feeling?"

"Wonderful. How about you?"

"Worried sick. But you've got a good doctor, and he said you'd be all right so I've been trying to believe him."

"Did he tell you Vera's dead?"

"Yes. I didn't know her. But I'm sorry."

The hesitation in his voice said she had kept all this from him and he still didn't know why.

"It's my fault. I told him."

He clasped her arm awkwardly above the tube. "Leigh, it was an accident. They say that isn't so unusual on those curves."

"Accident?" It was hard to put the words together. "What? He ran us off."

"You mean, Ed Harris?"

"Yes."

"Listen to me, Leigh. You were saying that, when you were hallucinating. He was here. He heard you. It just isn't true. Dr. Merlin says it's common not to remember, or be confused about a traumatic accident.''

"You're telling *me?*"

"We checked it out. I went up there and looked with the state police."

"I *was* there. So was Ben. What did he say?"

"He hasn't been conscious since then. But the Hopi police and the paramedics went over every angle with us. They wrote detailed reports. Before you started in on Ed, you were talking about snakes crawling over you, or something. I think I was as scared as you were."

An echo of the morgue in Albuquerque. An official version, versus an unreliable source.

"Alan. Listen to me." She tried to sit up. "It wasn't an accident. He killed Leni too."

"Wait. Calm down. You'll pull out your thing again. Let me tell you first. There's a low stone wall along that road. A section of it was out. At night it looks like the road goes straight through there. Let alone in fog. I saw it myself. There weren't any skid marks."

"It was raining then."

"I mean, no rubber. That wouldn't have washed away."

"But Vera meant to go off there. So he couldn't force us off further on."

Pushing his hands into his pockets, he walked over to the window.

Beyond it, snowy mountains rose up. Their delicate lines were familiar. The same peaks she had seen from the cave. Had passed while driving up to it from here.

He turned with an unhappy shrug. "Then I don't know what to say. The police checked Ed out too. An Indian gentleman who works for him said they were together all evening in his office, doing credit card checks. It was Christmas Eve. And the night Leni died, his girlfriend was staying with him in Santa Fe."

"Is her name Jill?"

"That's right. She answered the phone when you called to ask to borrow his car. They were both here. The accident was on the radio. He was afraid the transmission seized up—which happened before, but it was supposed to be fixed. I let him see you for a minute, but I stood right there in the hall. He felt terrible. He must have told you it was his fault, because it was after that you started shouting about how he tried to kill you."

"No. That isn't what he told me."

She looked over to the doorway. Ed had kept his back to it. From the hall, he must have looked the picture of concern. Alan wouldn't have heard what he said. Or seen the touch that made her shudder.

Daniel. His other alibi. The nice old Indian who taught little children about respecting mother earth.

Her lips felt numb. "You don't believe me."

"I didn't say that. We'll talk about it. I'm just trying to give you a reading on your mental state at the time."

"I wasn't on morphine before the accident."

That seemed to register, at least.

"No. You weren't."

"But the doctor said I wouldn't remember? I do."

The fender, crashed in from behind. "What happened to the car?"

"It's probably the size of a suitcase by now. A wrecker towed it."

"Ed told you that?"

He nodded.

"You've all been very busy."

He gave an odd, surprised smile. "Maybe that all depends."

"On what?"

"The date you think it is. You've been out for four days. Didn't Doctor Merlin tell you?"

He held out his watch, with the number window. December 28.

So there would be nothing left. No car. No marks. No witnesses. Except for Ben, and the warrant that gave him a good reason to lie.

And for the history stored in the computer.

A woman in a white jacket came in, pushing a machine on a cart. Alan said, "I'll wait outside."

"Wait. Do you know if the paramedics brought in my bag? A purple and grey one? Can you find out while I'm doing this?"

"Sure." He stepped around the cart, then went out to the hall. And stood listening while the technician gave instructions for the X-ray.

Keeping her eyes on Alan, she answered in the soft tone Ed had used with her.

WHEN THE CART ROLLED AWAY, she closed her eyes to listen to the bubble machine. The tube going down through the floor to the bed where Ben was lying now. Helpless, as he would be for a long time, and the tapestry of Ed came back. It was Ben he had been threatening.

Better, maybe, not to be believed. To have amnesia.

Until there was some kind of proof. If Ed's friends were so willing to lie, they probably wouldn't stop there. Couldn't stop, now. It was too late to change direction.

Better for Ben to have amnesia too.

A CLATTER OF METAL woke her up. The doctor and a nurse were standing with another cart.

He smiled. "We've got some good news and some bad news. The good news is, you've healed up and we can take the tube out. The bad news is, it's going to hurt like hell. Unless you want to risk going back to bug land. The amount of codeine or any other painkiller that would help is likely to give you the same reaction the morphine did."

The monitor said: 88, 92, 90.

"No, thanks. How long will it take?"

"Just a minute. But a bad one."

"So let's get it over with."

The nurse bent to the machine and the bubbling faded. The hookah. The friendly aquarium.

He peeled back the twist of gauze. She closed her hands on the railing. "Alan said I was pretty wild for a while."

"That won't happen again. Don't worry about it." He picked up a narrow scissors. "There are just a few stitches here."

Four sharp tugs got them out.

The nurse said, "I'm going to hold your shoulders, so the tube won't wiggle."

He gave her hand a squeeze. "Try to relax. Keep breathing. And in a minute, I'll tell you how brave you are. Ready?"

"Sure." Looking up at the white ceiling, she thought, now it's my turn. The last of the hallucinating Harings. I have to make this work for me.

From his hands, a bolt of pain shot up against the hands holding her down—white, hot, a sword drawn out with exquisite concentration, everything reduced to and radiating from that. Even lying rigid, it kept on, and a sound came from her throat and sweat broke her grip on the railing.

"Done," he said. "Good for you."

"It still . . ." A stab came with each breath.

"I know. And it's going to hurt. You won't sleep well for a month."

He taped a gauze pad over the incision. "I'll give you some of these to take with you. And some betadine ointment. You'll change this once a day. Now, I want you to rest, and in an hour or so, we'll go for a walk."

"Tell me, first. The hallucinations. You say they weren't real. But I got you half right."

"Maybe more. I liked what you said about living in the wall." Taking the scissors, he cut through the IV bandage on her arm. "They're some concoction of drug/brain chemistry, the effect of that on optical structures—which is often a geometric pattern— together with whatever animals happen to be in your head." The needle stung coming out, and he stuck on a dot of adhesive. "There. You're free."

"Thanks." The bruise around it was an ugly mustard yellow.

"Thank your body. You could have died of exposure. Or Ben. When it hurts, remember that. I'll see you later."

He dropped the bandage into a basin on the cart and they rolled it out.

Without bubbles, the room felt colder.

She looked down at her arms and legs. Sticks under a blanket.

A wheezing pain began defining the place where the tube had been. A knife bullet in the ribcage. Wanting special consideration.

Pushing on her toes, she measured the pain's reach. Walking wasn't going to be a pleasure.

Alan stuck his head around the door. "Okay?"

He came in with a young brunette in a red business suit. The clear plastic bag she carried held the Guatemalan sack.

"Miss Haring? You have to sign for this. It's been sealed since you were admitted."

The flap of the sack was open and the drawstring loose. She lifted her hand to take the pen. The right arm worked, at least. But her signature didn't look the same.

Alan closed the door after her. "Do you think it survived? The talking computer? Isn't that what you want?"

He ripped the tape off the Ziploc. "It's in here. And your wallet. Good lord."

"What?"

"There's broken glass." He slid the computer out, and wiped it with the towel the doctor had left. "No rattling, that I can hear."

"Let me try it."

"I'm taking the rest into the bathroom."

Lifting the lid, she touched the power button. Harder. Nothing showed on the screen. "It's dead." Even that mechanical memory.

"When did you use it last?"

She counted back. "With you."

"So, it could be the batteries."

There had been a cord to plug it in. At Leni's. Where it still must be.

Through the open door, she could see him shaking the bag out over the wastebasket. "Is there a lot of glass?"

"Apparently, just that one piece."

Vera had put down the car windows. "Let's see."

He held up a shard of mirror, about three inches long.

Testimony, of a sort. The rearview mirror had seen it all. "I want to keep that."

"For a souvenir? Are you crazy?"

"So you tell me. You know, you could be right about Ed. I asked the doctor. He said it was all in my eyeball."

Putting down the sack, Alan wrapped the glass in a paper towel and put it in the plastic bag. "There's your keepsake. Are you sure, Leigh? You had me pretty convinced before."

"You should have seen the green caterpillar. Stabbing me with his hookah."

"I believe you mentioned that." But something in her voice had hit wrong. "Which is it? Tell me the truth, for a change."

"All right. He was covered with upholstery. I don't know anymore, okay? This hurts." It was shameless. However true.

"Well, I hope it was just an hallucination. Otherwise, I'd hate to think I let him anywhere near you. He was here for quite a while, too."

She thought of Ben. "Have you seen the guy who was in the car with us?"

"The brother? I took a peek in. They've got his head in what looks like a giant pair of ice tongs."

"Is there a guard on his room?"

"Hon, he isn't going anywhere. Officially, he's under arrest, though."

The door creaked, and Dr. Merlin said, "Ah, good. It's time to rise and shine."

SHE TEETERED between them down the hall. The stabbing waxed and waned. A peculiar grouping, like the Manet painting of a picnic with a female nude and three buttoned-up men—except that she was wearing an enormous terrycloth robe, and foam slippers like the ones Michael had in Chama.

The Red Shoes. Or the mermaid, who couldn't walk on land and had to conceal the hot arrows in each step.

The Alien.

She said, "I want to see Ben. Is there any reason I can't?"

The doctor gave her a canny look, as if he knew her limits better than she did. "Now? You want to go downstairs?"

"There must be an elevator."

"Yah. It's all the way back again, to the right. If you can make it, I'll take you. But he won't be awake."

"Lucky him."

As they passed her room, the bed beckoned. Even the scratchy sheets.

On the elevator she felt decrepit, shuffling in the slippers.

The door to room 312 was closed. The doctor looked in, "There's someone who'd like to see him."

She didn't hear an answer. "Can I go in alone, please?"

"Just for a minute."

To find out if she could do it, she pulled back the hooked door handle, and tried not to show the hot arrows. "I'll be right out."

The door closed with a hiss.

A curtain ran most of the way around the bed.

Ben lay precisely angled between the hoop of the metal head vise and the pulley holding up his leg. A shattered statue, under repair. A landscape of plaster casting.

In the chair beside the bed, an old woman sat, her feet not quite touching the floor.

Taylor leaned in the window bay. "He's not going to be around for a while."

"I know. Do you remember me?"

He didn't dignify it with an answer.

She took another step to look at Ben's face. His left eye had a bandage. And left hand. And his arm, for the IV.

"The doctor told me he'll be all right."

Taylor shrugged. "Our grandmother knew it. Before she saw him. That's he's healing on the inside."

The woman turned her head from the bed and her eyes were milky. She spoke to Taylor in a language that seemed to have few breaks but the word pahana figured prominently.

"I'm sorry about Vera. Will you tell her that?"

It was only then she remembered the shove that got her out of the car. "I think she saved my life."

Vera, who hadn't trusted her even to jump.

He translated, and listened carefully before giving the answer in English. "She said, Vera died in the right place. And then she said, The dead are not powerless."

"It was my fault. I was stupid . . ."

He stopped her. "Robert told us what happened. We all know now."

Again his grandmother spoke Hopi, and he seemed unsure how to interpret it. "Umm. . . . She says, If a thief is coming, it's good to think about what he wants to steal." Taylor shook his head. "Then, something like, We're made of stars. All the beings in this World are from a star, once, that blew up and came here."

Poetic, if not immediately relevant. "Taylor, I have to tell you something. About the accident."

"What accident?"

"You know?" She took another glance at Ben, immobile between the pincers. "How?"

"My cousin Randall looked at everything. Before the Medivac came. He said the windows wouldn't have been wide open in the rain, and Vera couldn't have hit just her head in so many places, and not her body too. He found a rock with blood, down over the rim."

Pressing his lips together, he folded his arms.

The last part of it had some new element she couldn't get a hold of. "What about her head? A rock?"

He held a fist up.

"You think Ed killed her with it? But . . . then why not us? We were breathing. I couldn't have looked so bad."

Three matching head wounds might seem a bit strange, though.

There was the warrant, to take care of Ben.

If Vera had been conscious, he wouldn't have left her able to flag down a car. In the burning halo of the Audi. Not when he needed time to get back to Sedona.

Picturing it, she had to hold the bed rail to keep steady.

A rock. A fist.

The tapestry of Ed saying 'I'm glad you're still around.'

To play with. Because he could tell from her joking at the airport no one had a clue about him. So it could be safest to play it out in the open, and turn all the signals crooked. Lucky again. The police had cleared him.

When she called to borrow the Jeep, he must have guessed she knew about the stone. And didn't want the information to go further on the mesas. Where a pahana from Boston wouldn't count for much.

She said, "Why didn't you tell the police? Give the rock to them? They could do some tests." Then she thought of the damage the DNA test would do, and wondered if they'd drawn blood for it yet.

His grandmother started talking again, and from Taylor's face she realized the woman understood English very well.

"I'll tell you," he said. "When there's a murder on the rez, the FBI can come in. Randall says, don't give them an excuse now. Second is, they'd have taken her away from us. And cut her. Just to cover up what they really want. Today her spirit went free. In the right place."

"And the dead aren't powerless?"

He wouldn't look at her.

The old woman stood up. She wore a plain blue dress, darker than the turquoise beads around her neck. Her eyes seemed to be blind, and yet she took Ben's hand as though she could see it.

Taylor said, "She told me he'll be all right here. By these mountains."

"Good. I'm glad." It sounded lame. "Tell him to be quiet, until he's better. Tell him, I will too. It would be so easy to get to him here."

"Not while I'm around."

There wasn't much to gain by pointing out that wouldn't always be the case.

More Hopi. A private conversation. Then raising a forefinger, the woman aimed it at her, at the center of her chest.

He said, "Good. Keep quiet. And she says, It's all right for you to go now."

Dismissal. Unmistakable, unsurprising, but still hard to take. Going out would be going nowhere, now. An alien, abroad.

The monitor over Ben's head was reading in the fifties.

Screws into his skull, holding the tongs in place. His face looked creased and clammy. Turning, she wondered how long it would be until she saw it again.

IN THE CORRIDOR, the lights were blinding. The doctor stood with a wheelchair. "I thought you might be ready for this now."

AT NIGHT, her door was open—so the monitors would show, the nurse explained. At Christmas, they were short-staffed and she couldn't be pinned down to the screens at the desk.

The red digits had come down a bit. Alan said if she watched them and tried to relax, it would help, like biofeedback. But in the dark, under the blanket, she couldn't stop pulling at her flesh, squeezing and rubbing to make sure it was there and would still react. The way cats licked themselves madly after a trip to the vet, she thought. From the violation, more than anything.

After Ben's room, she wanted to be alone. Not blood tests, and broth, and too much attention from Alan, whose protective instincts were starting to get in the way—although of what, she wasn't sure yet.

Go away and shut up, the old woman said. Orders, to be obeyed. But there still was Leni to think of.

And Ed. Being so charming at La Fonda after he killed her.

A procession of scenes.

The knife hurt too much to cry. Or scream. That would have to wait. Easier said than done, when she thought of Ben and the bruises on Leni's neck.

Cold-blooded.

Vera, at Leni's house. The wild bouquet on the bed.

Going back to Boston and the hive of the studio would be like leaving crucial body parts strewn around out here. A bloody apparition. Alien. With Charlie Webber parked outside.

Better to stay in the alien place.

Cold-blooded. It was something to aspire to.

Lie down again on Leni's bed and see what it had to suggest.

She touched the dressing on her left side. Driving, it would be possible to prop that elbow out the window. Leaving Alan at the airport. Which he wouldn't forgive. But it was too late to change direction, and the trajectory didn't seem to allow for another passenger.

Chapter 15

AT A GROCERY STORE near Tierra Amarilla she stopped to buy bread and cans of soup, and a bottle of scotch that caught her eyes as she stood at the register.

Painkiller.

A blur of tears kept coming up, like the cloudbursts on the last trip, and swallowing them for so long left her choking.

Frightened by her face in the mirror. A crazy person. Not fit to be seen by the Chama chief of police. Who might refuse to give her Leni's key, and call the men in the white coats.

Alan would agree with that. He was fed up. At the airport.

Los Brazos. The turnoff for Leni's house. Break a window. Board it up. Quickly, before the dark came down from the black ridge up ahead.

And then call Alan. Or else he'd call the police, he promised at the airport.

Alan would have landed in Boston now. Gone home to call Brookline and say she was all right, all better, just not ready quite yet to talk to anyone.

Driving past where she parked last time, she could see the rutted tracks filled with slush. The log house, boarded up, a few extra planks scattered in the yard. Stopping short, she collected them and threw them in the car.

Leni's old Blazer in the driveway. Shifting to first, she made it up. The house and the Jeep looked abandoned. Soon the utilities would be shut off, and then the adobe would start to crumble and the rugs rot and slowly things would go back to the way they were before. As long as the mortgage was paid, no one could stop that happening. Or her from sitting in the middle, watching it.

She got out to look at the garden, and the twine running up to the wind chime. Not for rabbits, after all. The dead vines. An alarm. But he hadn't come through the bedroom window.

He had a key.

A surge of wind cut through the jersey slacks Alan brought, making her teeth chatter. Soft clothes, Dr. Merlin told him, for the invalid's trip home. Apart from the jacket, only the white sweater had survived the accident and it had a bloody handprint on the back.

Walking around to choose a window to break, she found just one low enough to climb through, by the kitchen door.

She used a plank to smash it, blindly, with the jacket pulled to cover her eyes. The sound and feel of glass giving way brought up some hidden welcome strength and she kept on battering till there was nothing left and she stood shaking, looking in at the darkening room.

The bowl she had left sat in the drainer. The computer cord on the table. Stepping over the sill, she tried the light switch and the green hanging lamp came on.

Unlocking the door, she went back for the other things in the car.

IT TOOK AN HOUR to get the boards up, with nails from a tin can under the sink. The window frame barely held them. She had to use both arms and each blow of the hammer drove the knife deeper. The shout of it came back from the empty rooms.

A Flintstones jelly glass in the cupboard had to be a yard sale relic. Fred and Barney. She poured in an inch of Dewars, feeling vaguely sacrilegious. Took a swallow and gagged on it. Then swallowed hard again. One kick would knock the boards in, but they looked secure enough. The third mouthful sent heat in all directions.

She carried the glass to the bedroom and turned on the lamp.

The armful of reeds and bittersweet still lay across the blanket. Pleated where she had slept on it. Ten days ago. Nothing had changed here. Only a sense that the house was waiting now and knew what would happen next. A necessary symmetry. The steps already traced. Silence, and a full moon at the window.

Opening the closet, she pulled the ribbon to the bulb.

Dust motes rose in the light beam, and the closet in the hall in Newton came back. Leni's bony shins wrapped around hers. Whispering in the dark.

Setting down the glass, she pushed her arms in around the clothes and hugged them, burying her face in wool that smelled of Leni and felt like the living body of an older woman. Comforting, but also waiting. Watching. And not powerless.

The pain was good, she thought. It would keep her awake.

Taking down a red sweater, she pulled it over the black jersey and went back to empty the satchel.

Stuffed in on top, the bloody white sweater. Saying she wanted it had brought on fish-eyes from Alan and the doctor. Crazy woman. Which worried her then, while they still could stop her. On the road she started thinking it might be true and could be useful.

A handprint, where someone lifted her, but the blood couldn't be hers. Rusty now. She folded it over the armchair.

The computer slid out, and after it something else that wasn't hers. A black metal flashlight the length of her hand with the word Brinkmann around the lens. She twisted the barrel and it came on bright. From Ben's camera case, probably. Another mememto.

Reaching in, she pulled out the wadded papers. Leni's envelopes. The broken mirror, in plastic. The blue wallet of snapshots. No tissue credit card receipt signed by Jonathan Addison.

Vera was last to look at it. Had slipped it into her pocket.

The computer cord needed a 3-prong outlet, which meant using the kitchen table. When she hit the power button, the aqua cursor came up. Then the logo. She opened the file, and it all was there. 'Today I cursed for half an hour following the UPS truck, and it turned out to be bringing me this and Adelina's chili noodles.'

Leni's diary. Written sitting here. Her voice for company. Noodles.

She got up to open a can of soup, to add some food to the whiskey.

Campbell's vegetable. Quite a nursery setup, with the Flintstones glass.

As she turned the burner off, she felt a sudden absence of sound. A barely perceptible drone that had stopped, down below on the trail. Last time she hadn't heard the second Jeep when it came up.

Even with the kitchen window boarded, it was the most exposed part of the house.

Yanking the computer free, she pushed it into the sack. Threw that in the closet. Someone was walking up the drive and not being quiet about it. Her heart beat in red monitor digits, 98, 99, 100. The light. The fireplace. The gun. If it was still there. Too late to try now. Any move would be visible through the gap in the curtains.

A two-way street. She took a breath and went to look outside.

Chief Arias. Not in uniform. And not happy. In that shaggy sweater, a ticked-off bear who nodded and used a key to open the lock.

"Miss Haring." He stepped in. "Did I miss you today? Your father called me." His eyes were taking in the boards. The open bottle of scotch.

"No. I was afraid if I went into Chama, it would get too dark. I broke in. It's our house now."

"Is someone with you?"

She closed the door. "No. I meant, the family's. Would you like a drink?"

He started to shake his head. "All right. Maybe a small one."

Pouring it, she knew he thought it might help. To find out if she was crazy. Observations of tone and gesture. She handed the glass to him. "Cheers. I was just having supper. Did my father interrupt yours?"

"As a matter of fact . . ." he took a sip. "I'm glad to see you're on your feet."

"I'm fine, Chief. Please tell him that."

"Uh huh. May I sit down for a minute?" He pulled the other chair out from the table. "Go on. Have your soup while it's hot. You must be hungry, after coming all this way."

She sat opposite him. "It was that or six hours on the plane. I want to be on my own for a while."

The set of his mouth said he wished she'd do that anywhere else but here.

"I thought someone might be with you because Mr. Harris came back up to Santa Fe today. You made some allegations about him. Is that why you're here?"

It seemed funny not to have thought of the chief. That he'd know all about what happened.

"I was crazy, didn't they tell you? I didn't know he was coming back. I don't care." Because he can't kill me too, she thought. Not without Ben to blame it on.

But hearing Ed was that close raised a prickle at her hairline.

"How about a cup of soup yourself. Since you've come all this way."

Behind the pale grey glasses, his eyes were disapproving. "Miss Haring, I want you to know I took your allegations seriously. For one thing, it's the only way I can account for the number of lies you've told me."

"I haven't, though." She stood up to pour some soup. A safer prop than the whiskey.

"Then, for your dishonesty. And I want you to know there's some physical evidence from this house we can't account for yet."

She kept her back to him. "Such as what?"

"Some wool fibers, from the bed. Black and grey. And fibers of dark blue Thinsulate. We have a shoe size, from a watermark on the rug. From an unshod foot, and a size 10. Mr. Naya is size 9."

Alphabet letters floated up in the soup. A. O. T. "So all you have to do is find the clothes the fibers came from. Which are long gone, don't you think? Have they done the DNA test yet?"

"The samples were just sent to Washington. That's what you wanted, last week."

"So I did."

"So jumping to conclusions can be dangerous."

"I'm not. I was hallucinating then." She brought the mug to the table. "Anyway, Ed has an alibi. For both nights."

"That's been known to change pretty quickly under interrogation." He took another sip, with the measured tilt of someone who rarely allowed himself a vice. "Lately, we've had a number of phone calls from Boston. I have a feeling you may know more about them than I do."

An interesting face he had, she thought. Strong, regretful of the human stupidity he could only clean after. Over and over. No one learning, except for him.

On the phone, Charlie Webber would have been polite and slippery. "You mean about Jonathan Addison?"

He nodded.

"Ed's his cousin."

"Yes." His large hands cupped the glass.

"Tell me something, Chief. If the DNA matches, and you can't find what those fibers came from, will Ben be charged with murder?"

"That's up to the district attorney. Unless we can dig up some new information, I'd say it's a good bet."

If not for what Charlie Webber would do with it, he could have everything. "Do you think he did it?"

"I don't know. Can you enlighten me?"

"I don't think so."

He let the ambiguity stand. "And it's only a coincidence you both came up today."

She raised her right hand. "I swear. I didn't know about Ed."

"Well, now that you do, is there anything you'd like to reconsider?"

Such as staying here alone, he meant. Such as whether you're as smart as you like to think.

She shook her head.

Pushing the glass away, he rested his hands on his knees. "Let me leave you with this, then. I know Boston's a big town, compared to Chama. You may find us a little old fashioned here. I'm a Christian man, and I've learned one practical lesson. Which is, if I have a problem with someone, the best thing I can do is ask the Lord to take care of it for me. Because sooner or later, that seems to pay off. When I try to settle it myself, I always get in trouble."

His voice was heavy. Unhopeful. But not resigned.

"Is praying how you catch criminals?"

"Maybe. Sometimes. Along with hard work. That's my job, not yours. I meant a personal problem, not a professional one."

It didn't really feel personal anymore, she realized. More like the way the house was, in its waiting.

She thought of repeating the words that finally worked with Alan. Empty. Sorry. Temporarily inconsolable. But for the chief, she was a professional problem, not a personal one.

For Alan, a bit of both.

She said, "Would you do me a favor? When you call my father back, would you ask him to tell my friend Alan I'm okay? I'll call them in a day or two."

He glanced at the phone sitting by the armchair. "You could tell them yourself."

"Not tonight. It's selfish, but I can't take care of anyone else right now."

He stood up. "All right. Alan? I'll say that. And I'll tell him I'm going to keep an eye on you, Miss Haring."

"He'll be glad to hear it. Thanks for coming."

"You be careful."

She watched him walk down the driveway. Hands in his pockets, elbows out. A shake of the head to say, I need this?

If he would have picked her up in his big hands, like a doll, it would be so easy. If he had touched her. But he'd never be that unprofessional.

He didn't look back. He had dinner waiting at home.

Even with the door locked again, the balance of the room felt different. His energy dissipating the weather pushing north from Flagstaff. A kind of fog in which things came up out of nowhere, isolate against the grey so the essential outline showed.

Confusion was what showed here in the odds and ends strewn around. Telling too much, like Michael Zinn's open pill bottles.

The complicity of the house seemed to require a certain order.

The break-in was permitted. The chief had been expected. Now attention had to be paid to the details.

Being careful.

Drinking soup from the mug, she walked over to the fireplace. The ashes hadn't been disturbed and this time she knew how to lever the rock slab to get out the metal box.

Still heavy. The three monkeys grinning and posing. A thumbprint of soot where she opened it.

The gun fit her hand and she felt a bit less like a piece of cheese in a trap.

Waiting for the house to tell her what to do, she found herself moving supplies into the closet. The flashlight and the Dewars last. Putting away the groceries.

In the bathroom, she ran sooty fingers over her face. A raccoon muzzle, for camouflage. Without the red sweater, she would be invisible in the dark.

Knowing what to do about the bed was harder. Vera's arrangement, but for a different time.

Scooping up the branches, she piled them under the blanket. Then carefully built a person around them with Leni's clothes and slippers. Knees bent, generous hip curve, a stuffed brown sweater for the head.

Covering up the scarecrow, she shone the flashlight around the house, and moved into the closet, satisfied.

A compost of old coats and bedspreads made a nest behind the rack. Propped on the side that didn't hurt, she took a final sip. With the door cracked, moonlight came across the floor.

Drawn into the dark of the house. A dinghy, tipping on an ocean black as oil.

Passing in and out of consciousness with all the animals in their lairs. The long-eared squirrel. Waking, frozen, until the shape of the night defined itself again. Then going back under fur and bone to sleep.

IN THE MORNING, washing off the soot, she noticed a change in her skin. Transparent, around the eyes that seemed to belong to another person surveying the terrain for future use.

Making instant coffee, she took Leni's binoculars from the peg and went out the kitchen door and up the slope.

From above the house, the whole length of the trail could be seen. With the glasses, even the ruts made by the Jeep. At night, not much would be concealed in any of the rooms.

Circling the house, she began tying up the string where it was trampled down. Pulled on it and heard the brass chime ring against the window.

The bulletin board on the kitchen door stopped her, going back in—the photo of Ben, pushing his Harley in a blur of forward motion. Behind the goggles, she could almost see his cultivated squint. Paralyzed, now, in Flagstaff. His thin defenses gone.

Ed had painted a picture of him she wanted to believe. Had read her, from the beginning, very well.

Looking down at the snapshot Leni took at the Cafe Florian, she could remember what she was feeling that day too. Smug, and faintly superior. Leni was in VISTA, making bricks out of mud, and on Newbury Street she stuck out like a goatherd.

That she had come for the graduation when she couldn't afford good shoes somehow made it more pathetic.

A massive, idiotic failure of love.

Keeping that distance, to keep from knowing, and only post-poning the moment, until nothing could be salvaged but whatever shreds of history still existed to be read.

Taking down the pictures, she brought them in to open the blue wallet of family shots.

Leni on a tricycle. The two of them with a jack-o-lantern, too artistically carved to be a child's effort. A baby with one tuft of black hair in a wading pool. And then a sepia photo she hadn't been expecting. Ruth and Richard on their wedding day.

Once before she had seen it, and it looked prehistoric then. Ruth's off-white '40's suit and pancake hat with the little veil, measured to the shiny black hair curving along her jaw. A hand on the knife to cut the cake, and Richard's guiding hers. At twenty, with dark sparkling eyes, she rested, an exotic orchid, against his white dress military uniform.

A picture taken two years after the war.

It must have been quite a coup for Ruth, and all those styles were back now. In the next one, she held up Leni like a trophy.

Dealing out the pictures. A hand of solitaire. Ruth's hair grow-ing, Leni taller, a second baby. Richard burping it on a diaper over his shoulder.

The last three snaps, with scalloped edges, were from Leni's old Brownie camera. Faded, badly angled, of what looked like a mid-dle-aged woman whom she hadn't recognized before. But Ruth again. Ruth on Thorazine, with the moon face Paul's finger had drawn. Ruth holding a toddler with tufty black hair whose mouth was open, howling, because it didn't recognize her either.

The change had come so quickly. She put down the picture and backed away from the table.

Not being good, this was what could happen. Be prescribed. For a diagnosis meaning 'We don't know.'

What they had understood was, she could throw a monkey wrench into their works.

The same thing Ed had figured.

And Charlie Webber.

Leni might have stripped the albums not to keep the pictures from her but to keep them from being edited out of the record.

It wasn't clear who was to blame for Ruth. At the very least, she wouldn't have expected Richard to sign commitment papers.

The same way Leni had left the gun out of reach in the fire-place.

Three monkeys, on the metal box. Third time and you're out.

Keep good records and your powder dry.

Collecting the pictures, she put them back in the wallet except for one Richard might have taken. Ruth and her girls, on a narrow flight of steps outdoors in summer. Stacked up, herself by Ruth's knee, and Leni, below, reaching back. The line of their arms made a diagonal across the horizontal risers.

A tree toad sat on Leni's other palm and nobody was smiling.

Setting the shot on the ledge carved in the beehive fireplace, she put the one of Ben there too.

The honorable jury.

Adding to the record in the computer came next, but not teth-ered to the outlet. A Radio Shack in Española, for batteries. Maybe sixty miles. A long fast drive to get the current going.

The gun would have to come along. Smothered in a towel.

From the satchel, she unwrapped the fragment of mirror. Evi-dence, for the jury. Its dagger of light arced between the photos like a waterfall.

There were television tricks about telling if anyone had come in. On both doors she used daubs of mud to glue a hair over the frame, down at the bottom, where it wouldn't be noticed.

An earlier warning would be to know if someone had driven up.

Stopping the car by the pull-off, she tried to memorize the pat-tern of tire treads, but the slush was melting them in the sun. Af-ter a minute, she got out and tore down sprigs of pine, sprinkling the needles around so any new tracks would mark them.

FOLLOWING THE ASPENS down along the Rio Chama, she thought whatever the Hopis decided about their rock, or Vera, Leni was separate. A personal ghost. Deserving of an accounting. And Ed deserved that too.

Cottonwood trees, in Española. Their bare branches shivering, dwarfing the single-story buildings.

The Radio Shack in Boston showed identical displays. Com-puters at the front. Then audio. Little TVs behind the counter. And probably the same after-Christmas sale filling the store today.

The dark man behind the counter wore peculiar side curls of mustache. Quotation marks around his mouth. His badge said Juan Martinez.

She held out the computer. "I need batteries for this."

"What does it take?"

"I don't know. It isn't mine." She smiled. "Can you tell me?"

"Sure. Let's see." He broke off the battery pack. "We've got 'em."

"Could you put them in for me? I know you're busy, but I don't want to blow it out." The helpless female. True enough, when it came to electricity.

"I'll show you," he said patiently. "It's easy. They point that way."

But she was looking down through the glass counter at a row of tiny tape recorders.

The silver one on sale, big as a cigarette pack, had a voice-actuate button.

"What's the range on these? That the microphone will pick up?"

Shrugging, he packed in the batteries to give her a better view. "Depends on the acoustics. And what else is going on. And what you're recording. Could be two feet. Could be ten."

She thought of Leni's house. This could make a separate record. Hidden. One Chief Arias would find if anything happened there.

"I'll take three of the thirty-dollar one."

He grinned. "Bugging the place, huh?"

"Just like on TV."

"Then you'll need some batteries for those too. And cassettes."

When she signed the Visa receipt, he gave her a card with checkboxes across the bottom. "You can get a free battery every month. Not always the same kind, though."

She was about to say she wouldn't be around that long. But it was starting to seem nothing could be predicted.

Thanking him, she carried the bag outside.

A low, chilly golden light came from the south. The winter afternoon, settling.

Driving north, she felt a hand of pain reach around her chest, and thought of the Dewars on the closet floor.

AT THE PULL-OFF, no tread marks scored the veiling of pine needles. The hairs were still in place on both the doors.

Going in the back, she switched on the laptop and filled the kettle for tea. Killing pain created more problems than it solved. This morning, changing the dressing, the incision had looked like a small mouth cut into her chest—another witness, adding its shriek to the uproar. But not as bad as a whiskey headache.

Loading the tape recorders, she tried one on voice-actuate from different points in the house. "This is for Chief Arias, in case I'm not around." For anything above a whisper, three would do the job, and the bed and the armchair by the fireplace had easy hiding places. Only the kitchen table would be a trick. That, and knowing when to turn them on.

The cupboard was stocked with herbal tea, and she brought a cup of orange spice to the window to watch the sun go down. Crimson, with a haze of purple melting into the mountains. Again, the eerie feeling came that on many nights Leni had stood this way. Steam coming up. Sometimes Vera with her. Plotting their lesson plans.

In pushing her out of the car, Vera had acted as Leni's proxy. The reflex of someone used to taking responsibility.

Down the ledge, a flicker of movement showed and she drew back. But it was only a deer, stepping out between the cedar trees. Maybe the same doe as last week, looking hopefully toward the house.

If it came to be fed, Leni might have said what somewhere in the computer.

Drawing the curtain, she went back to the table.

The <SEARCH> function. Used at the studio for inventory, and not often by her. As she punched in one bad command after another, the menu lit up in panic. Then she hit it, hardly knowing how.

<SEARCH:> She typed in: <DEER>

A directory came up: <NO REFERENCE IN THIS DOCUMENT>

She sat back, smiling at it. Alan would be so proud.

Repeat, a more pointed question, <SEARCH: ED>

No reference again, and <HARRIS> got the same reply.

That was about to change, though.

She took a last swallow of tea and on impulse typed in her own name.

Seven listings for Leigh. She was almost afraid to look.

But cruising through the pages numbered, she found only one item not come across before, buried in the class notes. A painful scarcity, until she remembered the journal was started after Leni's promise not to tell her anything.

<September 10>
<Today Leigh sent me a new incarnation of my favorite dirty ad. For Southern Comfort. It must be a gold mine, since they've used this same art-work for five years—on the back

cover of the *Globe Mag,* before, at Christmas, but this is from last week's *Time.*

< It's the one I always use with people who don't believe the stuff's there, because it's so obvious: First, ice is always artwork because real cubes would melt under the lights. Then let your gaze slowly enter the world of the old-fashioned glass, filled to the brim, a lacy, peekaboo harbor scene sketched over it in white. From the lower right, a lumbering phallus swims near an orifice gaping under the scene, while below it another pair of lips is waiting to be ravished. The cock is hard, and yet the glass has a seminal frosting of droplets—Key's classic orgy scenario. And all around the edges, enough death masks, skulls and symbolic animals to keep a Jungian busy for a month.

< Poor old Wilson Bryan Key. Everybody bashes him—and then proceeds to use his analyses anyway. As in the *Spy* article on Newport cigarette ads, with 'doctored' scenes of 'misogyny...rape...forced fellatio.' 14 color glossies, in national magazines, and not a single detail left to chance. *Spy:* 'And how does Lorillard get away with retailing sexual animosity? Anyone who claims to see cryptic messages in the ads is apt to be relegated to the lunacy fringe.'

< All right. I'll go—but not quietly.

< Now it seems only advertisers are paying close attention to what can be done with these images. Conjuring the dreamlife beneath the cosmetic manufactured surface of things. At UNM, students would get mad at me when they saw it—a scary departure from the script they wanted to believe in.

< Huxley: When technology can provide the ultimate in bread and circuses, the term coercion becomes meaningless.

< Imaging: hallucination vs. dreaming up your life. De Rios says tribes in the Amazon take ayahuasca to re-create in visions the most intricate behavior of the animals they hunt, to learn in a conscious way what they saw at a subliminal level. A ritual for becoming one with and honoring their prey. A strengthening of the mystical bond between them.

< Our own traits are studied with less affection, but equally potent results.

< And yet other possibilities keep on seeping through. The kindly mycologist on Letterman explaining how a mushroom common to New York State will release a 'light show' in the eye without causing any damage.

< Sex and death are the biggies though. Together forever, especially now. Along with 'Mommy and I are one.' >

Looking back up to the part about Indians studying their prey, she thought of a class at the Museum School. An instructor who loved thrill tactics, tacking up a poster of a bull painted in the Lescaux caves. 'Behold, the greatest artist who ever lived. Fourteen thousand years ago.'

She still thought he was right about that bull. The grave nobility of it. Black and stylized, the momentum of the body blurred along the spine, like Ben with his bike. The eye alone a study in will and sorrowful knowledge. Tentative, probing horns.

He had used almost the same language, too. An exploration of reverence. Rendering the soul of the beast to comprehend and merge with it. The hunter and the hunted.

Till now, Ed had been the artist here. The architect. The hunter. And without any classes for it. He had talent.

Choosing the Museum School in the first place had been a mistake. Cowardice. Scared of the raunchy plebes at Mass. College of Art.

Instead, it was all as civilized as the faculty club. No harpies like Leni or Vera. No blood on the floor.

She could picture Ed making drawings of them. Tacking on stolen strands of hair and toenail clippings. A savored ritual. Which costume to wear at La Fonda that would appeal to her fashion sense—first impressions being what counted most.

When he dropped that mask at the hospital, he wanted her to see exactly what it had concealed.

Groping her, with her hands tied. It brought up streaming fear again. The rain on the windshield right before the crash.

What came next had to be worthy of Ed and all his stratagems. Painted surfaces. She had a gift for that, too.

Under the sink, she found masking tape to stick on the tape recorders, thinking of another way to use them. Not just 'in case something happens.' For an intended, improvised event.

The only chance would be if Ed admitted it, and her role as his hand-puppet entailed that much responsibility. And with it, the need to make him say it, to win some dignity back.

The table corners had an overhang. With the recorder taped in tight, it didn't show from any angle she tried.

The second disappeared under the arm of the rattan armchair.

The next, for by the bed.

The doll on it caught her breath at the door. How Ed must have left Leni crumpled there.

Sitting in front of the computer again, she turned to her notes at the end and typed:

< Characteristics of Ed. Vain, above all. Sure of his ability to finesse any situation. If I use the right words, I can get him here. Flattery, and a lure. He doesn't know about the gun, and probably won't bring one.

< Since the cops and Dr. Merlin didn't believe me about him, maybe by now I'm not so sure myself. >

She got up to make soup and toast. Whole wheat bread, for fiber, which seemed hilarious now.

In the chicken noodle soup, specks of grease floated up instead of alphabet letters.

He had to be made to talk, but not too much. Not about where the rock came from. So there would need to be deflecting tactics. Questions. And maybe some shock tactics, too.

She typed,

< Tell me, when did you decide to kill her? That day, or before? >

Then a few others. Groping for them.

Finishing the toast, at ten o'clock, she thought unless he slept at the store a machine ought to be on the phone there.

She said, "This is only a test."

The bare room amplified a tremor in her voice. He'd play the message over, listening for anything like that.

A belt of Dewars smoothed it out. It was all right to sound a little woozy.

Braced for the chance he might answer, she smiled at the recording. Rare Earth. Santa Fe and Sedona, with fax numbers for both. At the tone she said, "Ed, it's Leigh Haring." A pause. "I guess maybe I owe you an apology. They say I was seeing white rabbits, and all." Full stop. "I'm up at Leni's again, and I've found something I'd like you to see before I turn it in. Give me a call."

She hung up. It sounded okay. And couldn't be undone.

Turning the recorders on voice-actuate, she moved the computer into the closet along with the wallet of snapshots. But tonight the clothing looked like shrouds hanging in a row. For her, there wasn't going to be any mystical intervention. Only her wits, in whatever state. A performance piece. Needing all her powers.

Closing her eyes, she folded her arms around the satchel. A mascot, in the dark.

THE CRACK OF A BRANCH outside and she sat up with a gasp at the pain the sudden movement brought. A jingle of brass. She could see a shadow in the moonlight on the floor. Someone peering in at the scarecrow. She fumbled for the flashlight and the gun.

Waiting for a scrape at the door, she could hear only the rush of blood in her ears. Immobilizing fear. To have drawn it down on purpose, suicidal.

When she got hold of her breathing, and could listen, the man had gone around to the front. A few steps on the gravel driveway, fainter, and a moment later the sound of an engine starting.

Drenched with sweat, she waited for the sound to fade, then got up to check the chain lock.

It wasn't going to work, being so frightened.

Leave, then.

No, she exhaled. I can do this.

Pretending not to be scared wouldn't help. You had to let it come and go. Someone had said that. Let it come and move through you like a wave through water.

A dress rehearsal. To pick out the areas needing readjustment.

She built a fire out of piñon scraps and sat watching it in the dark, counting the steps that had led here until it seemed right to stay, and to sleep.

AT DAWN, she walked down to look at the tread marks, wading in a groundcover of mist. The quiet and the aroma of pine gave the air a velvet finish and she could picture going into the woods as deep as they went on.

A pleasant walk, a pleasant talk, along the briny beach . . .

The zigzag looked like Chief Arias' Bronco, unless that was wishful thinking. A pitting of drizzle, over all. A stipling.

Making coffee, she noticed the calendar by the sink. New Year's Eve. The chief would be busy tonight. But if Ed had plans with Jill, he'd break them. Or else she'd wait for him in the Jeep, as she might have done before. On the lookout.

If the chief came too early, he'd spoil it. So the scene had to move along quickly.

The big chief. Irresistibly tempting to rely on him, the safer way, a hero, justice for the innocent. Trusting Paul had put an end to that, though. Confusing what he seemed to be with what he'd do in the world.

Asking for protection meant buying all the rest. One helix of the Haring gene. The other, disobedience.

The jury nodded. Solemnly. The shard of mirror winked.

Picking the soup cans out of the trash, she took them with the gun up the slope to a spur of rock and set them side by side.

Rehearsal, with live ammunition.

After a few tries, she got the clip out. Six shots. No more than two could be wasted. But accuracy from a distance wouldn't matter. Just the nerve to pull the trigger, in the moment.

Walking sideways down the ledge, she aimed at the can of vegetable.

The muzzle wavered as her grip tightened. Relax, and think of the target. One with it. A bond.

The target came, jerking her arm up. A blow to the eardrums echoing back and forth down the ravine. The shot had missed, though not by much. The can lay on its side.

Her hand and the gun. In unity. Warm and infinitely expressive. Walk into a liquor store, 'give me all your money.' Bang. Obliterating fear. A drug. A revelation.

Raising it again, she was sighting to the target when the telephone rang.

On the third ring, she squeezed the trigger. Bang. The chicken noodle jumped.

Lowering her arm, she picked up the cans and went down to the house.

The receiver felt clumsy by contrast. "Hello?"

"Leigh. Ed Harris. I got your message."

For the first time, she heard a wary note. Be careful, or he'd spook.

"Thanks for calling back. You must be mad at me."

One inhalation came and went.

"I wouldn't say that. So, what did you find?"

No foreplay. She swallowed a glitch in her throat. "Well, it's just . . . some writing of Leni's about mineral reports. And a map. I can't tell of what."

"The cops didn't take them?"

"They were hidden. In the fireplace."

Three beats, and then he chuckled softly, "So the circus is back in town. All right. Where are you?"

"At the end of the Los Brazos road."

"See you later."

The line broke and she hung up.

Later. A hundred miles to come. Later could mean anything.

It wouldn't be too soon, though, at a guess. He'd need time to sit, and think, and hope the waiting would have an effect.

Time enough for the stage to be set. Her eyes moved around the room. Where to put the gun. What to do about the bed. Leaving the dummy there would scare him off.

She went in, turning the blanket back, and hung up Leni's clothes. The bouquet fanned out nicely in a gallon jar from under the sink. Set next to the fireplace, an autumnal accent.

Yellow caps of bittersweet led back to the bed, Lying down across it, a bosky smell of dry leaves came. Jumping into piles of them, in the fall, back when burning leaves was still legal in Newton. Signal fires all over the neighborhood.

Now the only middle ground, this house. Shared objects. Ben.

No instructions came from the bed. It was more a clarity. What had been. What had been done. What was left to do.

Taking the bloody sweater into the bathroom, she turned on the shower and hung it in the steam to get the wrinkles out.

The fireplace should be disarranged. A cue. Pulling the flagstone crooked, she looked down at her hand, and in a spin the picture from the studio came back. Soot from the open window on the finger she lifted to Alan. Black pearl. 'Too fragile,' he said, 'We'd get too many returns.' And then the phone had rung.

Death patina. That was two weeks ago. Many returns of the day. Her hand was shaking and it had to stop.

The best teacher at the Museum School was a woman who looked like a sad bag of laundry, until she lifted her charcoal. Line-drawings, one after another, each a single intention. No second thoughts. At once control and spontaneous.

Looking for something to draw on, she found a package of brown paper bags in a drawer.

The flagstone made a pallette. Rubbing a finger in the soot, she tried the dome of the fireplace. Exhibit A. But part of it was missing. She went to get the gun.

And the flashlight. The computer. Pieces of the mosaic. Ben with his bike, the mirror arching. The monkey box. First separately, each itself. Then together. Related by consequence.

Ask the gun where it should go.

Not back in the box.

Where Leni should have kept it. Underneath the pillow.

The police had taken that, but extra bedding was piled on the closet shelf. Clean sheets, to make the bed up.

Then stripping off her clothes, she took the sweater out of the shower and stepped under the needles of hot water. The fog world, billowing up again, reassuring this time.

From the front, the sweater looked all right. With a shawl, the handprint wouldn't show. Ben or Vera's blood, for courage. She tried on jewelry from Leni's box—her own, and some silverwork, but it only emphasized how gaunt her face was now. Not a yuppie anymore. Leni's joke. A nopey.

At nine o'clock, she poured a shot of scotch and realized what was nagging—her call to Ed, picked up by the recorder at the armchair. She rewound to erase it and was sticking it back when she heard an engine coming uphill quickly.

Ed, in a blue car, not the Jeep. Pulling behind the rented Toyota. Note, one exit blocked.

No Jill in evidence. He got out, tucking in his shirt. A soft white number, for tonight. Then he bent for some things on the passenger seat.

A sweater and a bottle of champagne.

Pushing aside the curtain, she motioned him around to the back of the house.

When she opened the kitchen door he seemed twice her height.

"Leigh." He held the bottle out. "Happy New Year. Boy, this really is out of town."

Möet Chandon. She took it to put on the table. "That's right. You said you hadn't been here before."

He kept his weight pitched on the balls of his feet. "No. Mind if I look around?" He didn't cross into the bedroom, just gave the closet door a push. "It doesn't bother you? Sleeping here?"

"At first. Not now, so much."

He pulled the grey sweater over his head. "I had the heat on in the car. You must be cold."

Going to the fireplace, he ran a hand under the flagstone. "How did you ever think to dig that up?"

"I didn't really. I was looking for the flue, and I saw it didn't quite fit."

"Last night? But you've had a fire."

"I moved that again afterward. I thought you'd like to see it."

"I'd rather have a look at what you found."

"Have a drink first." She pointed to her glass. "I'm on whiskey. I better not mix." His champagne would be too much to stomach.

He smiled. "In Sedona, you'd hardly drink wine."

"That was before I cracked my ribs. I can't take morphine, remember? Why don't you save the Möet for whoever you stood up tonight. Jill? Alan said she was at the hospital."

"Yah. She felt bad about not lending you her car. All right, whiskey it is."

"Anything with it?"

"Neat."

She chose a wide glass, to minimize the volume poured. A reversal of Sedona. His face had put on mileage too since then, and with the haircut, creases showed around his neck. Not so many more years when he could be the stud of Tlaquepaque. Or would want to, probably. That crust must have seemed like a one-way ticket to the moon, from Airport Mesa.

He took the glass. "A toast?"

"Not to the new year. How about, to the end of this."

"All right." He didn't sound enthusiastic, but took a healthy swig. "I think we could do with a fire now."

"There isn't very much wood." Hardly more than kindling in the box, and the crackling could screw up the recording. Still, if he felt comfortable playing boy scout, it might be easier. "Let's use it, though. You're right, it's getting nippy in here."

She pushed the flagstone back. It left a bar of soot on her fingers.

Shaking the wood box, he built a steeple out of the twisted scraps. "Got something to light this with?"

She held up her blackened hand. "Look. I think it's going to be my new patina."

"Messy."

"You'd be surprised. I was using it to sketch today." Sliding the pile of bags out from under the chair, she crumpled up the top sketch, of the fireplace. "We can burn these too."

The next drawing was less successful, because of not getting the reflection right. "It's that bit of mirror. I found it in my purse after the accident. So, really, I guess it's yours." Rolling up the bag, she got the matches down and lit it.

He looked from the mirror to Ben's picture. "What's this? A shrine?"

Balling up the sketch of the computer, she wedged it in and the kindling caught. "More like an easel. Or, a storyboard. To help me put it together. I really lost my marbles on that morphine."

Picking up her drink, she sat in the left armchair, leaving him the one with the recorder. "That's not a bad fire after all."

He sat down, flipping through the sketches. "A flashlight?"

"Yup. That was in my bag, and it isn't mine, either. Look at the next one."

A receipt, with columns and numbers and the signature Jonathan Addison.

After a minute, he nodded, and fed it to the fire. "So, you do remember."

"Not everything. He's the cousin you told me about? Who set you up in business?"

Another nod. "Cousin Jon. He always was a lousy driver."

"And you gave him the rock and he sent it to Boston. They've named it for him, did you know? Officially, it's the Addison Crust. That's immortality of a kind."

"Too bad he doesn't know." He touched the glass to his chin. "Then there really isn't anything you want me to see."

She swallowed the last of her whiskey. "To tell you the truth, I just wanted to talk to you, and I was afraid you wouldn't come. Why should you? You're safe now. I took your point about a Mexican standoff. Only, I have to go back to Boston, and I'd like to finish things here." But she saw from his eyes it had been a mistake to take away the bait. "At the hospital, you said I told you everything. That isn't true. There are things you don't know."

"Such as?"

"What the stone is good for."

"Jon told me he thought it was a superconductive."

"That's not all. And maybe you can still get the lease."

"With the feds in on it now?"

"My father said it could be impossible to find if you didn't know where to look."

"So you want to make a deal."

An angle she hadn't considered. But perfect. His reading of her character.

She tried an offhand shrug. "You said we ought to collaborate. My business didn't do so well either this year. Getting my jewelry was a nice touch, by the way. That celadon was ahead of its time."

The side of his face to the fire was red. "What would you have to offer me? Besides keeping your mouth shut?"

Charlie Webber came to mind. "A line to what the guys at MIT are doing. Maybe I can point them in the wrong direction."

So close. It was in his breathing, in the way he lifted the glass. "How come now, all of a sudden."

"Till I found that receipt, I didn't know you'd be interested."

"And you want what?"

"If you can get the lease, say 20 percent? That's not so much. You said we shouldn't testify against each other."

He stood up to get the bottle, and she held out her glass. "Let's drink to it."

"Boy. You're cool."

"I'll take that as a compliment."

"You don't care about Leni?"

"I care. But the truth is, she drove me nuts, so why be a total hypocrite about it."

"That's almost funny. I liked your sister."

"So you said. You've got an odd way of showing it."

A gust of a sigh came from his throat. "See, I didn't have a choice. You were crazy after that accident? So was I, after Jon's. When he crashed, everything else went. He's the one who had the connections. Till I could pick them up, I had to stop anything else from happening. On the ground. Or from Leni. Either way."

"I thought maybe you gave him a nudge too. Because you didn't want a partner."

"You got that wrong. We were close." He threw back the drink and she was struck by the self-pity in the gesture. Lonely, behind his string-pulling. No one to talk to anymore. Hurt, even, that she'd think him capable of such a thing.

A note of sympathy seemed to be in order. "Then I guess we both had a shock. But stop her from doing what?"

He gave a thin smile. "Just what you did. Asking Daddy questions. Putting together Jon's sample with the survey team we hired to take the reading out there."

Too close. "Wait. What I don't see is, how you could tell what she'd do. Or that Ben would leave that night. Just a good guess?"

"Not exactly." He rocked back in the chair. The rattan creaked and an edge of masking tape stuck out under the arm. "This is a little strange. But I almost felt like I was being programmed. For a while, I thought I was hearing voices. I had a fix on what Ben was doing, and about your old man, and all of a sudden Leni's going home, and I just knew. When I went to see Ben at the gallery, he said he was heading back to the rez from here and that tiger eye floated out of my pocket. . . ." He shook his head. "It felt like Jon was doing it, I swear. I loaded the grass and Ben took it and practically gave me a blueprint, for chrissake."

She shivered, and to cover it reached for another bag to burn. A spirit-guide of another stripe. "But you had to make a key."

"Uh-uh. Daniel has a locksmith's gizmo. That worked too. Everything did."

"So you thought it was meant to happen." Almost to the bedroom now. The threshold. Hands around her neck. "Did Leni know it was you?"

He lowered his eyes. Modestly. "I don't think so. She was pretty out of it. I thought they'd split that joint, but it sounds like she smoked most of it. I don't think she really knew what hit her."

"Lucky. For both of you."

"Yah. Maybe even for you." Hooking his elbows around the arms of the chair, he tipped it back again and the curl of tape lengthened. Not now, she thought. It's almost finished. The chief can come anytime. Please.

She picked up the bottle. "One for the road?"

"Not unless you want me to crash too. You're something, you know that? No wonder you're in *Vogue*. I figured you had to be tough, but you're way up on me. I didn't want to kill anyone. But there's a law foundations can't do business for profit, so Jon had to set up a straw with the company. Then he died, and I wasn't about to lose it. That's our only find in ten years of digging up dirt."

He hunched forward. "20 percent. All right. If you deliver. I'll give you that. If you do what I tell you."

The head of the tape recorder dangled, slipped, then spun down to the rug and she saw it in her eyes before the thud came.

"What the hell . . ." He picked it up. "What are you playing?"

A vacuum was sucking her into the chair, an undertow, pulling her blood away with it. "Just . . . insurance. Just in case. You try to cheat me."

"Yah, or for blackmail? I'm not stupid." He popped the tape out. "You little bitch."

"But . . . I couldn't. You don't have the stone yet."

"I mean about Leni. I'm not broke. Your sales rep. in L.A. could tell you that." Edging a fingernail under the tape, he reeled it out and threw it on the fire. "Is that it?" He was up, wrenching her out of the chair. "Got any more tricks?"

Paralyzed, in his hands. The same hands. "It's not blackmail. Just . . . protection."

"No." He let go of her. "No, no. Something's going on here." Rubbing a hand over his jaw, he walked around the room in a circle. "You're setting me up. But what's the con? Taping me. Maybe there's another tape." In one thrust at the mantel, he cleared it and splinters of broken glass jumped in the firelight.

The crash and flames of the accident, spewing up out of nowhere.

The rush of air. Other hands at her back.

"You killed two people. Almost four. Don't tell me you're sorry. And that stone isn't yours. It never was."

"What do you care about it?" He came at her again, "Are you going to get holy now? Where do the rocks in your jewelry come from? Heaven? Try the Amazon jungle. God, you self-righteous little bitch. Both of you. If you'd kept out of it, we could scoop that up at night and no one would know."

Stumbling back, she came up against the wall and he grabbed her jaw, "So, are there any more? Partner? Let's have a look."

Twisting her arm behind her back, he pushed her in front of him toward the kitchen. "Not too many places. Here?" He groped along under the cupboards, and she thought, if I can get free, I can make the door.

Pain filled her eyes. His salty smell reached around her to the counter. His heat.

The door or the bedroom. The gun. Or else it's for nothing.

Hooking a foot around his right ankle, she kicked out hard and broke away, grabbing the table, going forward, over the threshold, and with a roll across the bed, had it in her hand.

He hung in the doorway.

"Get out. Now."

The bellows of his breathing filled the room. "Or what."

"I'm giving you a chance to leave."

"That's a toy."

As he moved, she got to the other side of the bed. Aimed past him and pulled the trigger. Bang. Louder, indoors. He recoiled. "So."

"So we can stand here forever. But the chief will be here soon. He's come every night. So you should go."

"How generous of you."

"It's more chance than you gave Leni. Or Vera."

"Vera was your fault. Clever girl."

Circling around the foot of the bed, he held her eyes. "Tell me where the other tape is. Then I'll go. You aren't even holding that right."

The muzzle wagged. A gun in a hand not belonging to her body. "You can't kill me too, Ed. There's no one left to blame it on."

Stepping back, she could feel the cold draft coming from the window.

He took another step. "How about on you? A tragic suicide. While of unsound mind. Or, we can stop this nonsense."

It had to stop somewhere, she thought. Here, for instance.

When his hands came at her she fired, looking right into his face, his slow, disbelieving smile, ragged, open, then both their eyes were fixed on the red jet spurting from his chest, straight out, so much red life and death it was just amazing. Dropping the gun, she put her arms up as he fell against her.

Pinned to the frame of the window, she felt it shake with another crash.

Chief Arias stood in the doorway.

He stood with his gun drawn. "No."

A river of blood ran. He dropped his arm. "Dios."

V

CHAMA

Chapter 16

DO, A DEER, A FEMALE DEER...

It came almost every day now to stand in the clearing across from the house, no matter how far away the bowls of Wheat Chex and lettuce were left.

Re, a drop of golden sun. The obvious reason. The warmest spot. Watching the house in a guarded way. Not leaving, when she carried her tea out, but tilting its head for a sharper look. The effect being of a question.

Mi. A name I call myself. The only name, for now.

Putting down the cup, she sat on the top step and opened her hands to the sun.

In three weeks, many rituals had been established.

Opening the laptop on her knees, she typed:

< January 24.

< This morning I gave the printout to the guy Ben said would come—a kid hardly older than Taylor. He didn't knock, just stood in the driveway, and it was only after he left I found the wood piled in the yard.

< It now seems the district attorney may not press charges against either of us. A waste of public money. The other two recorders picked up enough of Ed that with the tapes merged, it amounts to a confession. Did I plan to kill him, too? I called him. The message is on his machine. And all I found to show him, as far as they know, is the gun.

< Motive, means, and opportunity.

< Ben's affidavit says he bought the gun in November, and brought it to the house.

< The chief described a scene of self-defence. Cornered. The first shot, and my warning, on tape.

<His eyes refuse to absolve me, though. A sin, if not strictly a crime. Free will and devious purpose being inseparable from the act.

<Chaos. In the life of any system, an instant of irreversible slippage. Seen only in retrospect. In this case, the sound of Ed's engine interrupting the masking tape job on the chair.

<That Charlie Webber wouldn't want a trial is the most hopeful note. Michael sent his lawyer, and her fingers play subtly upon the keys. Given the press so far, Ben's testimony would get attention, and there really isn't much chance of a conviction.

<A bluff. Ben won't tell even her most of what was going on. But she's good at sounding ominous about attorney/client privilege.

<There remains, however, the risk of a deal, engineered from Boston, to get me committed for observation. In Dr. Merlin's view, I'm suffering post-traumatic stress. Charlie must be afraid I'll spill his beans in the wrong place. Or maybe that I'm coming after him next.

<Ben thought of the printout, as a hedge. An insurance policy.

<Another bluff, by lunatics lacking credibility. But at least a record will be kept. Written down somewhere else.

<It turns out this machine has an automatic backup—a silicone subconscious, with Leni's deletions intact. Many will need erasing. A new set of commands to be learned. This isn't a safe place for record keeping.

<Ben is standing, now. Or rather, 'being dangled.' He says he found out making a migration can be a prayer.

<He's still on a lot of morphine.

<I see Vera's face, and want to say if it took Leni thirty years to find out about Ruth, carrying around that *Life* article like some undeciphered Rosetta Stone, how much more obscure these other omitted histories.

<Still, I can almost believe if that rock is taken, the world could end. Not necessarily cause and effect, but as with the crash of the tape recorder, a marker on the continuum just beyond the point of no return.

<According to the guidebook, the reservation is 1.5 million acres. The size of a window of time.

<Alan doesn't ask anymore if he should come out. Doesn't want to. Doesn't know what to say. He's trying to find a way back for me. Maybe, to face down the gossip, an Annie Oakley outfit, with white boots and a holster. When I'm feeling

less shattered. But that sounded not a bad thing to be. When he said it, the pieces got up and danced around like bones.

< I never got to tell Leni I'm proud of my little sweatshop and all the many groceries it buys. Only, I think Alan knows I won't be doing that again. Patina washes, and the buffing wheel. He and Jean have already finished the Spring II collection, and their pistachio is a hit.

< I've been thinking about the blowtorch. Welding. Bone and blade of wind chime. So far, just one piece done, inspired by the deer, when I began to see her belly is growing.

< Another art school memory. The serpent circle. Oroboros, in Greek. Tail held in the mouth, with no end or beginning. Slithering out of its own dead skin like a dream. From the fragment of mirror, smashed to smaller bits on the hearth, a mosaic of oroboros is now glued to the wall by the beehive fireplace. Glittering.

< Every day the bowls are placed farther out. But the deer keeps coming back to that clearing. If another animal gets the food, she could be starving.

< Balanced at the risk of becoming too tame.

< Leni must have worried about this problem too.

< The deer comes, and stands, and I have to remind myself this is not the way it seems.

< Not a fawn, yet, cute as Bambi. The impulse folded inside her.

< Now, a possibility, and only to be thought of as the dark and struggling thing it is. >

A RECONSTRUCTED CORPSE

SIMON BRETT

A Charles Paris Mystery

First Time in Paperback

A STIFF ACT TO FOLLOW...

If playing a dead man could be called a role, Charles Paris
has sunk to new lows when he agrees to play missing
Martin Earnshaw on the true crime TV series "Public Enemies."

The show has all the hallmarks of a hit: a vulnerable, tearful
wife, a sexy female detective and, best of all, dismembered
limbs probably belonging to Earnshaw turning up each week
just before airtime.

As viewers shudder gleefully and ratings soar, Paris discovers
there's more to the whole production than meets the eye...and the
climax is a killer.

"A perfect vacation read."   ***—People***

Available in March at your favorite retail stores.

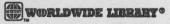

BACKFIRE

First Time in Paperback

JANICE LAW

An Anna Peters Mystery

TORCHED

A high-profile, arson-murder case is not in her usual pro bono line, but Anna Peters is intrigued by the anonymous caller soliciting her aid in clearing Maria Rivas in the death of Helena Skane. Mrs. Skane, invalid wife of wealthy restaurateur Joe Skane, was killed when his showcase home burned to the ground.

Maria, Mrs. Skane's nurse, has been rendered mute since the tragedy by what Anna believes is fear. She also believes that everyone—from Joe Skane to his handsome son to the servants—know more than they're telling.

And soon Anna's following a trail from Washington, D.C., to Tucson that's littered with dirty money, desperation and death....

"Terrific plot twists..."   *—Mystery News*

Available in May at your favorite retail stores.

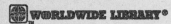

WORLDWIDE LIBRARY®

BACKFIRE